DIAMONDHEAD

Books by

PATRICK ROBINSON:

NOVELS

Ghost Force

Hunter Killer

Scimitar SL2

Barracuda 945

Slider

The Shark Mutiny

U.S.S. Seawolf

H.M.S. Unseen

Kilo Class

Nimitz Class

NONFICTION

Lone Survivor (written with Marcus Luttrell)

Horsetrader: Robert Sangster and the Rise and Fall of the Sport of Kings (written with Nick Robinson)

One Hundred Days: The Memoirs of the Falklands Battle Group Commander (written with Admiral Sir John Woodward)

True Blue (written with Daniel Topolski)

Born to Win (written with John Bertrand)

The Golden Post (written with Richard S. Reeves)

Decade of Champions: The Greatest Years in the History of Thoroughbred Racing, 1970–1980 (written with Richard S. Reeves)

Classic Lines: A Gallery of the Great Thoroughbreds (written with Richard S. Reeves)

DIAMONDHEAD

PATRICK ROBINSON

Vanguard Press
A Member of the Perseus Books Group

Published by Vanguard Press,
A Member of the Perseus Books Group

Books published by Vanguard Press are available at special discounts for bulk purchases in the United States by corporations, institutions, and other organizations. For more information, please contact the Special Markets Department at the Perseus Books Group, 2300 Chestnut Street, Suite 200, Philadelphia, PA 19103, or call (800) 810-4145, extension 5000, or e-mail special.markets@perseusbooks.com.

Designed by Trish Wilkinson
Set in 11.5 point Minion

Library of Congress Cataloging-in-Publication Data

Robinson, Patrick.
    Diamondhead / a new novel by Patrick Robinson.
        p.   cm.
    ISBN 978-1-59315-509-4 (alk. paper)
    1. Assassination—Fiction. 2. Iraq War, 2003—Fiction. 3. Weapons industry—Fiction. 4. Arms transfer—Fiction. 5. Political fiction. I. Title.
PR6068.O1959D53 2009
823'.914—dc22   2008041520

10 9 8 7 6 5 4 3 2 1

PROLOGUE

The boardroom of Montpellier Munitions was constructed inside concrete and lead walls sufficiently thick to suffocate a nuclear reactor. Each night it was swept for electronic listening devices, and each day the business of international arms dealing was planned and executed within its confines.

This was the smooth business end of the industry, the trading room occupied by sleek, distant men, way above and beyond the screaming factory floor below, where high-explosive material was moved around on hydraulic loaders, and reinforced metal was cut and molded into the twenty-first century's most refined state-of-the-art guided missiles.

Montpellier was one of the least-known, most secretive arms manufacturing plants in France, set deep in the 150-square-mile Forest of Orléans on the north bank of the River Loire, east of the city.

Rumors suggested the Montpellier chairman, Henri Foche, had parted with upwards of five million euros, bribing officials to permit the construction of the arms factory in the middle of one of the great protected national forests of France—a place where herds of deer still roamed, and wild, nesting ospreys were vigilantly guarded.

In the normal way, anyone presenting such an outrageous proposal would have been shown the front door of the Planning Department. But Henri Foche was no ordinary applicant. In fact, it was highly likely that Henri Foche, at forty-eight, would become the next president of France.

This morning, his three principal executives, the men who arranged Montpellier's enormous sales to the Middle Eastern sheikhs, tyrants, and assorted African despots, were waiting somewhat impatiently for his arrival. There was, in fact, trouble in the air. Very big trouble.

At 10:35, the great man arrived. He was dressed as always in a dark pinstriped suit, white shirt, dark-blue necktie, with a scarlet handkerchief in the breast pocket. He was a man of medium height, heavyset, with jet-black hair combed neatly on either side of a shiny bald dome. His complexion was sallow, and he had a jutting Roman nose, as hooked and predatory as the beaks of the osprey sea eagles that circled the nearby banks of the Loire.

He entered the room accompanied by his two personal bodyguards, Marcel and Raymond, who closed the door behind him and then stood guard on either side. Both men were dressed in faded blue jeans with black T-shirts; Marcel wore a dark-brown suede jacket, Raymond a short, black leather zip-up that plainly shielded a holstered revolver.

Foche entered the room in silence and without a smile. He took his seat at the head of the polished mahogany table, and then greeted each of his three right-hand men in turn . . . "Yves—Olivier—Michel, *bonjour*."

Each of them murmured a respectful acknowledgment, and Foche moved directly into the serious business of the day. Speaking in swift French, he ordered, "Okay, let's see it."

Michel, sitting to his right, picked up a remote control and activated a big flat-screen television set on the wall, same side as the door, about four feet off the ground. He scrolled back to "Items Recorded" and hit the button to replay the 0800 news bulletin on CII, France's international CNN-style twenty-four-hour news service, broadcast in French, English, and Arabic.

Monsieur Foche normally had a certain amount of catching up to accomplish, after spending the night with one of several exotic nightclub dancers he patronized in Paris, eighty miles to the north. But not often on a day as critical for Montpellier as this most certainly was.

The broadcaster was quickly into his stride: *The United Nations Security Council in New York last night formally outlawed the lethal French-built guided missile known as the Diamondhead. The UN banned the "tank buster" in all countries on humanitarian grounds. The American-backed edict was supported unanimously by UN delegates from the European Union, India, Russia, and China.*

He explained how the searing hot flame from the Diamondhead missile sticks to and then burns its victims alive, much like napalm did in Vietnam. The broadcaster confirmed the view of the UN Security Council that the Diamondhead was unacceptable in the twenty-first century. It was the cruelest weapon of war currently in operation.

He added that the UN had specifically warned the Islamic Republic of Iran that the Diamondhead represented nothing less than an international crime against humanity. The world community would not tolerate its use against any enemy under any circumstances whatsoever.

Henri Foche frowned, a facial expression that came more naturally to him than smiling. It replaced his regular countenance of dark, brooding menace with one of ill-expressed anguish.

"Merde!" muttered Foche, but he shook his head and attempted to lighten both the mood and his facial expression with a thin smile, which succeeded only in casting a pale poisonous light on the assembled chiefs of Montpellier Munitions.

No one spoke. No one usually does after a bombshell of the magnitude just unleashed by the CII newscaster. Here, in the heart of the forest, these four executives, sitting on a potential fortune as grandiose as a Loire chateau, were obliged to accept that all was now in ruins.

The Diamondhead missile, with its years of costly research and development, its packed order books and clamorous lines of potential clients, was, apparently, history. The missile, which could rip through the heavily armored hulls of the finest battlefield tanks in the world, must be confined to the garbage bin of military history, destroyed by those who feared it most.

The Americans had already felt its searing sting on the hot, dusty highways around Baghdad and Kabul. And in the UN Security Council they found almost unanimous support for the Diamondhead ban.

The Russians feared the Chechens would lay hands on it, the Chinese were unnerved that Taiwan might order it, and the Europeans, who lived in fear of the next terror attack on their streets, could only imagine the horror of a handheld tank-busting missile in the hands of Islamic extremists. The prospect of the Islamic Republic of Iran distributing the damn thing to every wired-up al-Qaeda cell in the Middle East was too much for every significant UN delegate to contemplate.

Henri Foche's mind raced. He had not the slightest intention of scrapping the Diamondhead. He might have it moderated, he might change its name, or he might rework the explosive content in its warhead. But scrap it? Never. He'd come too far, worked too hard, risked too much. All he wanted now was unity: unity in this concrete-clad room; unity among his closest and most trusted colleagues.

"Gentlemen," he said evenly, "we are currently awaiting an order for the Diamondhead from Iran which will represent the most important income from a missile this factory has ever had. And that's only the beginning. Because the weapon works. We know that in Baghdad it has slashed through the reinforced fuselage of the biggest American tank as if it was made of plywood.

"We also know that if we do not manufacture it, and reap the rewards, someone else will copy it, rename it, and make a fortune from our research. There's no way we will abandon it, whatever rules those damn lightweights concoct in the UN."

Olivier Marchant, an older man, midfifties with an enviable background as a sales chief for the French aerospace giant Aerospatiale, looked uneasy. "Making money is one thing, Henri," he murmured. "Twenty years in a civilian jail is something else."

"Olivier, my old friend," replied the chairman, "two months from now, no one will dare to investigate Montpellier Munitions."

"That may be so, Henri," he replied. "But the Americans would be absolutely furious if the ban was defied. After all, it's their troops who end up getting burned alive. And that would reflect very badly on France. No one would care who made the missile, only that it was French, and the wrath of the world would be turned against our own country."

Foche's expression changed into one of callow arrogance. "Then it's time the U.S. military started vacating their bases in the Middle East and stopped pissing everyone off," he snapped. "It's taken us three years to perfect the compressed-carbon missile head into a substance which is effectively a black diamond. We're not giving it up."

"I understand, of course," replied Olivier Marchant. "But I cannot condone a flagrant breach of this UN resolution. It's too dangerous for me . . . and, in the end, it will prove lethal for you . . . as president, I mean."

Foche flashed a look at his longtime colleague that suggested he was dealing with a small-time Judas. "Then you may, Olivier, find yourself with no alternative but to resign from my board of directors, which would be a pity."

And once more Foche's expression changed. A somewhat sneering cast swept over his face, the whore's scorn for virtue. "What we are doing," he said, "is beyond the law, not against it, Olivier. And please remember it would be particularly damaging if you ever decided to go public with your reasons for resignation."

In that split second, Olivier Marchant realized the danger of his position. Only Foche himself had an equal knowledge of the Diamondhead, its development, its secrets, and the subtleties of its firing and homing mechanisms. Only Foche knew its export routes—especially the one out of the Forest of Orléans and onto the jetties of Saint-Nazaire, the ocean voyage to Chah Bahar, the Iranian Navy's submarine base, way down east on the northern shore of the Gulf of Oman, close to the Pakistani border. This is a top-secret place, four hundred miles short of the Hormuz entrance to the Persian Gulf. Chah Bahar is the port for unloading illicit cargo, for ultimate distribution of high-tech weaponry to the outstretched hands of the relentless killers of Hamas, Hezbollah, al-Qaeda, and the Taliban.

Nonetheless, Olivier Marchant stood up and said quietly, "Henri, I will always have the highest regard for you. But I cannot—will not—be associated with flagrant defiance of international law. It cannot be worth it, and my conscience cannot allow it. Good-bye, Henri."

And with that, he walked resolutely to the doorway, and without a backward look stepped out of the room, right between Marcel and Raymond. But before the door was closed, Henri Foche had the final word: "Good-bye, my old friend. This may be a day you will deeply regret."

Olivier Marchant knew the stakes were high. And certainly he was aware that Foche's presidential campaign, conducted from his home region of Brittany, was almost certain to succeed. Foche was correct to state that no one would dare to investigate Montpellier's missile division, not if Henri himself was president of France.

But Olivier not only had a righteous streak, he also had a timid one, coupled with a highly developed imagination. He suddenly saw himself in an international courtroom, charged with fellow directors of Montpellier with crimes against humanity, in flagrant defiance of a unanimous UN resolution.

He had long recognized Foche as a ruthless chancer, with the morals of an alley cat. But he would not go to the wall for him. Olivier was a wealthy man, with a much younger wife and a nine-year-old daughter. There was no way he was going to jeopardize his way of life, his family and reputation. He would not end up ruined, sharing a cell with a known megalomaniac, as Foche very definitely was.

He walked slowly back to his office, stuffed some personal files into a large briefcase, and called home to his grand residence on the outskirts of the riverside village of Ouzouer. His wife, Janine, was thrilled he would be home for lunch, and even more thrilled to learn he had no plans to return to the rather sinister arms factory in the great Forest of Orléans.

Olivier pulled on his overcoat and vacated his office. He walked along the executive corridor and took the elevator down two floors to the front lobby. Without looking left or right, he stepped out of the building, into bright sunshine, and headed toward the directors' small parking area.

He had no need to use his remote-control car key because his Mercedes-Benz was never locked. Montpellier was surrounded by a high chain-link fence, and there was only one entrance, patrolled by two armed guards 24/7. Olivier opened the driver's door and shoved his briefcase onto the passenger seat. Then he climbed in, started the engine, and clipped on his seat belt.

He scarcely saw the garrote that would throttle the life out of him before the thick, cold plastic line was tightening around his throat. In the rearview mirror he caught a glimpse of the expressionless mask of the face of Marcel, and he struggled to grasp the ever-tightening grip of the plastic noose, to try to prize it free from his windpipe.

But Marcel had the jump on him. Olivier tried to scream. And he twisted sideways, lashed out with his foot, and felt his own eyes almost bursting out of their sockets. And now the noose was choking him, and with one final superhuman effort he reared back, and booted out the front windshield, which shattered with just a dull modern popping sound.

It was the last movement Olivier Marchant ever made, before the silent blackness of death was upon him.

CHAPTER 1

The American military base, colloquially known as Camp Hitmen in central Iraq, shimmered under the anvil of the desert sun. No one needed a thermometer to check the temperature, which had hit 104 degrees long before lunch. And no one felt much like moving out of the shade of the bee-huts or the tents.

Camp Hitmen derived its name from its proximity to the ancient Iraqi town of Hit, which sits on the west bank of the Euphrates River, 130 miles from Baghdad. This was essentially an overflow military base, constructed by the U.S. Army for Special Forces, the Navy SEALs, Rangers, and Green Berets, the heavy muscle of the U.S. frontline military.

And even as the pitiless sun tried its southern-fried best to drain the energy out of the residents, Camp Hitmen stayed always on permanent high alert. It was a place of hair-trigger readiness, a dust bowl populated by watchful, vigilant U.S. troops, whose training had turned them into coiled springs of aggression and, understandably, vengeance.

The tools of their trade were lined up under canvas shelters wherever possible, anything to reduce the temperature of the metal. The Humvees, armored vehicles, tanks, and desert jeeps were constantly under the attention of mechanics and engineers. Gas tanks were full, oil gauges checked, shells and rockets in place. Every component of the military transportation system was battle ready. Just in case.

The Camp Hitmen complex was surrounded by heavy concrete walls, high, with a walkway just below the ramparts for guards to patrol. Beyond its outer rim was a three-hundred-yard "no-man's-land" that was glaringly lit at night by sweeping arc lights. In the day it was just a burning flatland of sand and dust, a wide exposed area upon which any intruder would be shot down instantly.

Nothing's impregnable. But Camp Hitmen was just about as secure as any outpost could ever be in a polarized land, where the population cannot make up its mind whether to hate or welcome those of a different branch of their Muslim faith—never mind a foreign army trying to keep a semblance of order on a lawless Middle Eastern frontier.

And there were still Islamic extremists whose hatred of the Americans was so severe they would willingly sacrifice their own lives just for the chance to murder or maim members of the U.S. and British militaries, serving personnel who were essentially trying to help the country rejoin the international community. Every night they came, trying to fire rocket-propelled grenades, or RPGs, into the complex, trying to rig cars and trucks with explosives, trying to send in their suicide bomb squads to breach the complex before the American guards gunned them down.

It was a deadly environment, and everything was a struggle. The air conditioners struggled, the generators permanently had their backs to the wall, and the electricity supply was under constant surveillance. Men were always on edge. No one walked between the tents. Instead, all personnel wore hard combat hats, and raced over the sunbaked sand, crouched low, ready to hit the deck, at the distant scream of a rocket-propelled grenade. Or indeed the sight of the telltale white smoke that signaled the grenades of the Holy Warriors were coming in from across the far side of no-man's-land.

No one went anywhere unarmed; every day there were missions, and every day there were armored convoys growling out onto the hot, dusty roads, dealing with trouble spots in the treacherous nearby towns of Fallujah, the notorious enclave of the insurgents, or, more likely, ar-Ramadi, often said to be the most dangerous place on earth.

Sorties into Habbaniya, which lies between the two, were less frequent but just as dangerous.

There was a large reinforced concrete bunker inside the complex. This housed the main Command Center and the Military Intelligence Center. Like all U.S. military outposts where the main objective is to locate terrorists and insurgents, the entire operation at Camp Hitmen ran on information, gathered either electronically or firsthand. In the latter case, the information was either voluntarily offered or obtained by force.

Either way, it made no difference to the sun-bronzed warriors of the Camp Hitmen garrison. Their task on a daily basis was to round up the diabolical forces of al-Qaeda or the Taliban, and either capture or kill them, wiping out or imprisoning their commanders. Any damn thing necessary to stop the crazy pricks from taking another shot at a big American skyscraper.

We need to take 'em out, or pin 'em down, either right here or in Afghanistan. That way those suckers aren't going anywhere else. That's the plan. And it's a plan that works.

The creed of the United States Special Forces was that simple. And every man understood it. They knew the risks, and were trained to take those risks. Which did not, however, make it any less dangerous or scary. It just made everyone better prepared, and angrier when things occasionally went wrong.

And during the past six months, there had been a new trend among the car bombers, booby-trap operators, and suicide killers that was causing the utmost concern among U.S. commanders—all of them, SEALs, Rangers, and Green Berets. The insurgents in Iraq seemed to have laid hands on a missile, fired from a handheld launcher, that could actually penetrate a tank or a heavily armed vehicle. And that was something to which no one was accustomed.

Powerful roadside bombs and various RPGs could certainly inflict heavy damage on a Humvee or a jeep, and some damage on an armored vehicle. But those brawny U.S. battlefield tanks could always take a hit and keep coming.

In the past six months the game had changed, though. Suddenly, there were instances of a tank-buster missile being launched by terrorists—a high-speed weapon that could rip through the fuselage of a tank, and decimate any other vehicle it hit. Americans were dying. They were being burned alive by this new enemy: not in large numbers, but sufficient to cause stern protests by Western nations about a missile that threatened to turn modern warfare into a horror scene from the Dark Ages.

One month ago the Security Council of the United Nations had categorically banned it, in a unanimous motion that declared the use of the missile "a crime against humanity." With the support of Russia, China, India, and the European Union, this seemed a solid-enough UN edict to calm everyone's fears about a new modern napalm outrage. The pictures of U.S. tank commanders burning alive from a chemical that could not be extinguished had shaken historians, politicians, and even journalists worldwide. And happily the ban was now in place.

However, as always, things looked very different out on the burning, sand-strewn highways of Iraq. Because someone had what seemed like an endless supply of this confounded missile. The Arab television station al-Jazeera referred to it as "the Diamondhead." And the goddamned Diamondhead kept smacking into American armored vehicles and burning U.S. servicemen alive.

They did not, of course, all hit their targets. But two days ago, one of them, fired from the eastern side of the Euphrates, had slammed into a U.S. tank that was transporting an elite Navy SEAL team to a classified mission. None of the four Americans survived. Neither did the tank's crew. No one could put out the fires that swiftly engulfed them.

The SEALs were seething with fury, and not just at the insurgents who had fired it. They were enraged by the Iranians who had supplied the now-illegal missile. That much was known, and never denied. But the SEALs were especially enraged at the arms corporation that manufactured the Diamondhead. The U.S. high command believed it was French, but could not pinpoint the factory. Unsurprisingly.

The Pentagon decreed the missile had been developed in its early stages by the vast European arms-producing network MBDA, a conglomerate made up of the top guided-missile corporations in Britain,

France, Germany, Spain, and Italy. MBDA has ten thousand employees, and many subsidiaries. It is without question the world's number-one maker of guided weapons systems. Its major shareholders are the European Aeronautic and Space Company, which in turn includes Aerospatiale-Matra Missiles of France.

So far as the head honchos in the Pentagon were concerned, the part that mattered was MBDA's Euromissile, based in Fontenay-aux-Roses in France, home of the MILAN medium-range antitank weapon, godfather of the Diamondhead.

The latest MILAN packs one hell of a wallop. Within a two-mile range it can penetrate a thousand millimeters of Explosive Reactive Armor, or more than three meters of reinforced concrete. It has fantastic antijamming systems, weighs only forty-five kilograms, and can be handled by a two-man crew, the gunner to carry the firing post and the loader to carry the two missiles.

Whoever was responsible for the seriously improved Diamondhead was a missile genius. Step forward the shadowy scientist/salesman, known only as Yves. His pride and joy, the Diamondhead, was probably eight years ahead of anything Euromissile had on the drawing board for the MILAN. And it contained a barbaric burning ingredient that the big public European conglomerate would never dream of including.

However, the new United Nations edict had rendered the missile an outlaw even in the most vicious, amoral trade on earth. If anyone ever found out where the Diamondhead was being manufactured, that plant would become instant history.

The trouble was that no one had the slightest idea where this new "SuperMILAN" came from, not even the hard-eyed members of the widespread security system at MBDA. The Diamondhead was an international pariah, and it was currently protected by one of the most powerful men in France, a man who might shortly become impregnable.

Generally speaking, this was extremely bad news for the U.S. servicemen operating in Iraq. Like all national armies in pursuit of terrorists, the Americans operate under the most colossal disadvantage, because they cannot see their enemy, and neither can they see their enemy's strongholds. Without effective military intelligence, they cannot locate the tribesmen who wish them dead; there is no recognized garrison at which to aim their fire. Their enemy wears no uniform, and often has no regard for his own life. Mostly, he strikes and retires. Other times, he surrenders immediately, seeking the ludicrous protection of the sixty-year-old Geneva Convention, the signatories of which did not have the murdering modern-day jihadist in mind.

In general terms, insurgents and terrorists are at a powerful disadvantage in terms of weaponry, using old, inaccurate Kalashnikovs and unreliable homemade bombs. Give them, however, a state-of-the-art Diamondhead guided missile, newly delivered from Iran, and the game swings dramatically away from the status quo, in favor of the jihadists.

Navy SEAL Lt. Cdr. Mackenzie Bedford was reflecting on this precise new danger as he wrote home to his wife, Anne, in Dartford, Maine. Sprawled back on big olive-drab desert cushions in the corner of his tent nearest the air conditioner, Mack had just written:

> I guess by now you've read about the new tank-busting missile these maniacs are using against us. There's no need to worry, the UN ban has kicked in now, and there's only been one incident involving us during the past two weeks. We all watched that CBS report on television last week. Wildly exaggerated. As usual. . . .

Mack Bedford was thirty-three, a six-foot-three, bearded, 220-pound SEAL team leader of the highest caliber. When he shaved off his desert combat beard he looked like a youthful Clint Eastwood, same open, hard-eyed frankness, same rough-hewn edge to his face, same shock of dark hair except cut shorter. Mack had long been considered to be destined for top command in SPECWARCOM—ever since he'd passed out number one in his BUDs Class, Honor Man, ten years ago.

A native of coastal Maine, son of a shipyard engineer, Mac was a sensational swimmer, once having made the U.S. Nationals. Underwater he could make a porpoise look clumsy, and on land he was a tireless runner, with tree-trunk legs and lungs like a pair of Scottish bagpipes. He carried not one ounce of fat, and was just about unstoppable in unarmed combat. Mack, like almost every SEAL, was a high-intelligence killing machine.

Five local thugs, in a lonely bar in the Allegheny Mountains, had once made the truly astounding decision to pick a fight with him while he and Anne were enjoying a quiet drink just before they were married . . . *Hey! This guy's a Navy SEAL. Let's find out how tough he really is* . . .

Three of them ended up in the hospital, with two broken arms and a fractured skull. The other two ran for their lives, with Mack's parting words ringing in their ears: "You're lucky little sonsabitches. I might've killed you all by mistake."

That was reputed to be the only civilian fight Mack Bedford had ever indulged in. But he'd seen close-quarter combat in most of the world's hot spots, especially Afghanistan and Iraq. He was a brilliant sniper/marksman, and had himself been shot twice, both times in the upper arm while taking control of a Pashtun/Taliban village in the Afghan mountains. Jungle or desert, mountain or deep sea, Lieutenant Commander Bedford was a SEAL's SEAL—trusted, relied upon, and the consummate American patriot. Honor Man indeed.

He ended his letter to Anne with the subject they were almost afraid to mention—their seven-year-old son, Tommy, and the terrible disease that doctors suspected may be destroying his nervous system. *"I've checked the insurance out over and over, Anne,"* he wrote,

and the Navy has been fantastic. We're covered and Tommy's covered. But we have to find a place in the USA where they can carry out an operation on a kid this young. Let's just hope the disease is not confirmed, and we'll get a breakthrough in the next few months. I have to go now, but I'm always thinking of you. AND DON'T WORRY ABOUT ME. WE'RE FINE. RIGHT HERE IN CAMP HITMEN. WEATHER SUNNY! CHARLIE'S FRYING EGGS ON THE HOOD OF THE JEEP!

ALL MY LOVE, MACK

The big SEAL folded the paper and tucked it into an envelope. He had a lot on his mind, what with the missile and Tommy. For a few moments he just sat there on his king-sized cushion, contemplating the tough hand life had apparently dealt him, and hoping to God the friggin' Iranians had at last exhausted their supplies of the Diamondhead.

Just then the tent flap was pulled back, and four of his buddies, Chief Petty Officer Frank Brooks, Petty Officer Billy-Ray Jackson, Gunner's Mate Charlie O'Brien, and Chief Gunner Saul Meiers, came wandering in, all wearing desert "cammies" and their favored olive-drab-and-brown bandannas, or, in SEAL parlance, their "drive-on rags." All four of them were sweating like dogs, armed and bearded, like most Special Forces operating in Muslim countries, where it may be necessary to work undercover among the tribesmen.

But the beard disguise was strictly double-edged, because every al-Qaeda leader understood that a bearded American serviceman was, without question, a lethal combat-trained member of the SEALs, Rangers, or Green Berets: a soldier to be either given a very wide berth or, if possible, captured, interrogated, tortured, and then beheaded. The half-trained tribesman did not usually have much luck in achieving any of the latter four options.

"Hey, Mack, how's it looking?" asked Billy-Ray in that informal way SEALs have of speaking to each other, the serious business of rank being almost entirely cast aside among the front line of the U.S. combat elite. The practice of ignoring officer status among the SEALs was well known but often frowned upon by other service personnel. But other service personnel had not been through the murderous training of the SEALs, that relentless ordeal that hurls officers and men into an unbreakable brotherhood. Like a secret society, one that will bind them together for all of their days.

Mack looked up. "Jesus, you guys look awful. What's up?"

"Training run, and a lot of people noticed you weren't on it," replied Billy-Ray, his good-natured black face beaming with humor.

"Tell 'em to go fuck themselves, would you?"

"Roger that, SIR."

Laughing, all four of the visitors flopped down on the big cushions.

"We going out this afternoon, Mack?" asked Charlie O'Brien.

"Fifteen hundred hours, down to Abu Hallah if the guys aren't back."

"They'll be back," chuckled Billy-Ray in that deep Alabama voice of his. "Because we're getting roast ham and black beans for lunch, and there ain't *no* way Bobby and his guys gonna miss that."

"Bobby and his guys might be under a bit of pressure this morning," interjected Frank Brooks. "That truckload of marines those bastards blew up in North Baghdad last Friday got hit by a missile that caused a very big fire. Intel reckons the main insurgent force retreated way up-river to Abu Hallah. Bobby's supposed to roust 'em out."

"Better be careful they don't have any of those goddamned Diamondheads left," grunted Mack. "We'll have to send Frank in to find 'em—his beard's longer than Bin Laden's."

"Hey," said Charlie. "Did I ever tell you what happened to Frank one time in some bar out in the eastern Rockies?"

"Jesus Christ," said Chief Brooks, suspecting he was about to become a figure of fun.

"Well," continued Charlie, "that beard of his was about as long as it is now. You know, can't see his face, 'cept for his eyes. And sitting right there in that bar was an old Indian guy, kept on staring right at Frank.

"Finally, Chief Brooks looks up at him and says, 'Who the hell are you lookin' at?'—in that deep bassoon voice of his."

And the SEALs predictably started laughing, even Frank.

"Well," says Charlie, "the ole Indian took his pipe out of his mouth and said, 'Sir, I ain't staring. Nossir. But I ain't been in this town for twenty-nine years, and last time I was here they put me in jail for fucking a buffalo . . . and I just thought you might be my son!'"

Charlie should, of course, have been a professional comic, and the SEALs rolled around on their cushions, laughing helplessly, as they usually did at his endless supply of jokes. Even big Frank Brooks was guffawing amiably.

Mack Bedford was more accustomed to the high standard of Charlie's jokes because they had served together many times in SEAL Team 10's Foxtrot Platoon. But the lieutenant commander had not heard this one before, and he fought off the all-encompassing sadness of Tommy's illness, and yelled with laughter with the rest of his guys.

Charlie O'Brien was a top-class SEAL team gunner, a bull of a man in unarmed combat, who often acted as personal bodyguard to his CO. But he was younger than the others, and there were still those who considered his greatest asset to be his uncanny ability to make the boss laugh. Lieutenant Commander Bedford thought the world of Charlie. Like many another Special Force commander, he also understood that the ability to find a touch of humor in even the most diabolical situation was an important military asset.

A lot of Foxtrot Platoon guys still remembered Charlie O'Brien after they blew apart a Taliban stronghold in southern Afghanistan. He had leaped to his feet, flung both arms diagonally skyward, yelling, "*TOUCHDOWN!*" At which point one last dying tribesman clambered out of the rubble and shot a hole in Charlie's helmet. "*FLAG ON THE PLAY!*" bellowed Charlie. "*NUMBER NINETEEN DEE-FENSE.*" Then he picked up his rifle and blew the tribesman away. "Rude fucker," he muttered.

Right now, in the tent, the laughter subsided, and Billy-Ray Jackson suggested they get out and find some of that roast ham and beans. But as they raised themselves up from the cushions, a SEAL lieutenant came running in shouting urgently, "Mack, Mack! We got a big problem. The guys have been hit badly in Abu Hallah. Tanks on fire, and Christ knows what else. Bobby's dead. The guys are pinned down under heavy attack. We gotta go. This is battle stations—*NO SHIT!*"

All five SEALs leaped to their feet, and, without a word, headed to the ammunition cupboards, grabbing extra magazines, grenades, and a heavy machine gun. They tightened on their harnesses, slammed on their helmets, and literally stampeded out into the heat of the Iraqi desert, Charlie and Mack holding the machine-gun straps between them. They raced across the hot sand toward the line of armored vehicles. In the background the Klaxon sound of the camp alarm drowned out the thunder of the massive engines as the tank crews revved them up. The ground crews were shouting above the racket. Drivers and commanders were checking the controls, gunners were loading shells, armored vehicles were backing up to make room for the four lead tanks to rumble forward.

Billy-Ray and Charlie clambered aboard the first one; Frank Brooks and Saul Meiers were up and into the hatch of the second. Mack Bedford loaded the machine gun and jumped into the passenger seat of the front armored car, which was driven by his regular combat driver, Jack Thomas, from Nashville, Tennessee.

Bedford's vehicle automatically moved to the forefront of the convoy, waiting, revving impatiently for the tanks to form some kind of a mobile line of battle before they headed for the exit, composed of massive, thick wooden gates, reinforced by steel. They were gates that had withstood the impact of shells and bullets, and once had stood up under the onslaught of a half-crazed suicide bomber, who managed to blow up himself and his car but nothing else.

Within four more minutes, the five-vehicle convoy was under way. At the last moment the guards heaved back the gates, and high above, on either side of the entrance, Ranger machine gunners opened fire, raking the boundary wire three hundred feet away, across no-man's-land, just in case an insurgent group was feeling ambitious.

Mack Bedford stuck his right arm out of the window and gave a thumbs-up to the lead tank, which contained Billy-Ray Jackson, Charlie O'Brien, the crew, and enough ammunition to start Desert Storm all over again. They rumbled through to the outer rim, where the automatic reinforced-steel barrier rose to allow them through. When all five vehicles were out, the gate clicked electronically shut and automatically activated four land mines inside the entrance, strategically placed to obliterate any transgressor.

They turned right, heading southeast down the sandy highway that follows the Euphrates River, through the burning-hot, silt-covered alluvial floodplain where temperatures can reach 120 degrees. This flat, arid area, which receives only eight inches of rain per year, was once the cradle of Mesopotamian civilization. Today it is a glowering region of rabid hatreds and violent reprisals.

The mighty seventeen-hundred-mile-long river at this point had flowed through eastern Turkey's Taurus Mountains and right across Syria before narrowing through the limestone cliffs of western Iraq. It ran softer, wider, and browner now, south of the desert town of Hit, and clusters of date palms occasionally dotted the left side of the SEALs' route. The riverside palms looked almost biblical, but there was nothing biblical about the aged Russian machine guns that frequently spat fire at passing American vehicles, straight between the trees, though mostly from the far side.

Mack Bedford's men were on high alert all the way along their five-mile race to Abu Hallah, the heavy guns of the tanks often swiveling to face areas of rough ground cover or copses of palm trees, where unseen Muslim fanatics might be lying in wait.

The men of Foxtrot Platoon had been in Iraq for five months now, and were well versed in the requirement for acute vigilance in all of their sorties beyond the great walls of Camp Hitmen. And this week was turning into an extremely dangerous time, given the continued existence of the Diamondhead, and the Iranians' apparent willingness to keep supplying it, United Nations or not.

Lieutenant Commander Bedford spotted the black plumes of smoke rising from the western bank of the Euphrates two miles out. He signaled a halt to the convoy and stood up, fixing a pair of powerful binoculars on the uproar up ahead. From what he could see, there were two tanks still ablaze. He thought he could see U.S. Army ambulances, but the smoke, dust, and fire obscured the view.

He signaled for the convoy to continue, *flank speed*, the SEALs being a branch of the navy rather than the army. "Step on it, Jack, for Chrissakes," he muttered. "This looks like a real shit-fight."

All five armored vehicles accelerated, their already hot engines screaming in the grim silence of the Syro-Arabian desert. In front of a billowing dust cloud they surged onward. Inside the tanks, Mack Bedford's men slammed magazine clips into their rifles, the gun crews staring through the sights of the big swiveling barrels that would almost certainly be turned onto their distant enemy across the river.

As they approached Abu Hallah they could see the gray outlines of buildings on the far bank beyond the bridge. Almost immediately opposite those buildings were the remnants of the morning task force. Two tanks had been hit and destroyed. The only surviving armored vehicle was positioned behind them, away from the river, with its gun pointing directly across at the buildings. The smoke, however, was still so intense that there was scarcely any hope of taking a decent shot at anything.

The closer they came, the more obvious it was that this had been a major disaster. Mack's warriors could see the ambulances now, and the fire trucks, not to mention the pure hopelessness of trying to carry the dead away from the searing heat and melting metal.

The rescue services were from the U.S. ar-Ramadi base, some fifty miles to the south. They had been on another rescue mission, a roadside bomb farther north, but had turned back immediately when news came in of the attack on the SEALs at Abu Hallah.

Mack Bedford exercised a hard-earned caution about getting too close to burning vehicles when there was still a lot of gasoline in the immediate area. He signaled his convoy to halt, well short of the fires, around fifty feet beyond the bridge. He alone jumped out onto the road and walked toward the disaster area. A young SEAL lieutenant, dressed in battle cammies and carrying a rifle, walked toward him. The two knew each other well, and Lt. Barry Mason said simply, "Thanks for coming, Mack. Afraid there's not much we can do right now, except wait. We got 'em pinned down in that building over there. But they got us pinned down right here, and I'm not anxious to break cover until we've cleared 'em out.

"Jesus Christ. You shoulda seen the missiles they hit us with. Both of 'em went straight through the fuselage of the tanks. Holy shit. Like a goddamned hot knife through butter."

Mack Bedford could already feel the heat in more ways than one. "These fires start when the explosive reached the fuel tanks?"

"Hell, no. They seemed like part of the missile. Everything ignited right away. The guys never had a chance. They were burned alive. I could see two of 'em trying to get out, but the flames were kinda blue and burned like chemicals. We couldn't get near them. Christ, it was hot. No survivors."

"Obviously the Diamondhead," said Mack.

"No doubt," replied Lieutenant Mason. "Couldn't have been anything else. Fucking thing. Never seen anything more horrible than that. And this is my third time in Iraq."

Mack nodded. For the first time he could see tears streaming down the young SEAL's face, a certain sign of the shattering cruelty he had witnessed along the south road down the Euphrates.

For a few moments, neither man spoke. They just stood back and stared at the misshapen, seared, and twisted metal of the tank, each of them trying to fight away the terrible thought of their brothers who had been incinerated inside the cockpit. For Barry Mason it was all about sadness, remorse, and, inevitably, self-pity, as the brand-new memories of his lost friends stood starkly before him. For Mack, it was something altogether different. Deep in the soul of the SEAL commander there was a constantly burning flame of vengeance. Mostly, it just flickered and could be ignored. Mackenzie Bedford knew full well that all military leaders need to be free of cascading emotion, because anger and resentment are the first cousins of recklessness. But all of them carry this unseen burden, and they constantly grapple to avoid being forced into hasty decisions.

Mack Bedford often found it more difficult than most to hold back the demons that urged him to lash out at his enemy with all the uncontrolled violence he could summon. He even had a name for the surge of fury that welled within him. He called it the "hours of the wolf," a phrase he recalled from some morbid Ingmar Bergman movie. It was a phrase that perfectly described his feelings, mostly in the hours before dawn, when he could not sleep and yearned only to smash his enemy into oblivion.

Right now, standing on this burning desert road, watching the molten iron tombs of his fellow SEALs and three Rangers, Mack entered the hours of the wolf. And deep inside he could sense that familiar burgeoning rage, currently aimed at everything about this godfor-saken hellhole in which he must serve.

He turned his head sideways to the hot wind and stared across the river, at the ancient stone dwellings, built mostly on just two floors, all of them pockmarked with bullet and shell holes. Mack could see them clearly through his binoculars. Abu Hallah was an insurgent strong-hold, no doubt—a place where Islamist fanatics came and launched at-tacks on U.S. troops before vanishing once more back into the desert.

"Did you see where the missiles came from?" he asked Lieutenant Mason.

"Nossir. But they came straight across the river, from one of those houses, and they did not swerve. Just came straight at us."

"Two only?"

"Yessir. One hit the lead tank, clean as a whistle. The second one came in right behind it, smashed into the next tank, just as if they had been individually aimed from two firing posts."

"Were you stationary at the time?"

"Nossir. We were making about thirty miles per hour. By the time my vehicle had stopped and I hit the ground, both tanks were blazing like a couple of goddamned bonfires. Except with that blue flame I mentioned. Never saw anything catch fire that quick."

"Jesus Christ," said Mack. "And we don't dare flatten those fucking houses across the river, because they're probably full of unarmed civil-ians and someone will put us all in jail."

"And it's hard to know if the missile men are still in there," said Lieutenant Mason.

"Tell you what, Barry. I can see a small group of vehicles just beyond the houses. I'm gonna drive back down this road and take a look. I'll take my guys with me and turn around. If I see one sign of a hostile enemy on that side of the river, I'm taking them out."

"Probably make us both feel a whole lot better, right?"

"Guess so," said Mack, who was now conscious of the ever tighten-ing knot of pure anger in his stomach, the old familiar one that her-alded the hours of the wolf.

He signaled for his driver to come forward and for the four tanks to follow. He climbed aboard the armored car and led the way down the road for four hundred yards, stopped, and instructed the tanks to turn around, back toward the fires, and to aim their main artillery at the buildings across the river.

"Don't fire. Just be ready."

Positioned now at the rear of the convoy, Mack trained his binoculars on the small gathering of Arabs and trucks on the other side of the water. There was a stone wall, however, between the SEAL commander and the insurgents, and Mack's car backed up another fifty feet to improve the angle. Now he could see clearly.

There were two unmistakable tripods placed in the ground midway along the wall. He could not identify the equipment mounted on top of the tripods, but since he was most certainly not looking at a highway surveyors' unit preparing for a new freeway, Mack assumed the worst. He was looking at a missile sighting system and a guidance assembly, almost certainly identical to the ones that fired the new and improved French-made MILAN 3.

Mack knew enough about the MILAN to understand it fires in two stages, the first burn being for one and a half seconds, just to eject the missile out of the launcher. The second stage burns for eleven seconds, accelerating the missile to two hundred meters per second. The guys in the U.S. tanks never had a chance.

He had every reason to believe the secret Diamondhead may have been a shade faster, with perhaps a tougher cone protecting the warhead. As he stared at the small group across the river he suddenly observed the arrival of a new vehicle. And this was not a rough 4x4 desert truck; this was the sleekest of Mercedes-Benz limousines.

He watched the chauffeur hold open the door for the man who occupied the rear seat. Out into the desert stepped an immaculately dressed Western man wearing a dark pinstriped suit, with a blue tie and a scarlet handkerchief stuffed into the breast pocket of his jacket. He was essentially bald, with slicked-back dark hair on either side. Even from this side of the river Mack Bedford could see the jutting Roman nose.

The Arabs clustered around the new arrival, shaking his hand and smiling. He walked to the first tripod and spoke briefly. He examined a long tube that had been in the back of one of the trucks. Then he returned to the tripod and stared through the sights. For five more minutes he spoke to the men, all of whom were wearing Arab dress. Then he placed his arm around the shoulders of one of them and steered him to the limousine, which immediately accelerated away.

Mack walked back north, along the line of his tanks, instructing them to move on up toward the fires and to prepare to shell the wall that shielded the missile launchers. All four began to rumble forward, and the commander jumped into his own vehicle for the short ride.

As they came to a halt Mack climbed down from the right-hand side of the vehicle. As he did so there was a roar from the lead driver, whose head was above the hatch.

"INCOMING! . . . HIT THE. . . . " But it was too late. The missile from the other side of the Euphrates lanced across the water, belching flame, and slammed straight through the starboard-side fuselage of the lead tank, the one that contained Billy-Ray Jackson and Charlie O'Brien.

Mack Bedford watched aghast as the entire thing burst into a bright-blue chemical flame, the inferno in the interior now blasting through the hatch like a blowtorch gone berserk. A blowtorch from hell. Someone was trying to get out, but his entire head was on fire. He never even had time to scream before he died. It looked like Billy-Ray.

The roar of the fire drowned out the next missile that streaked across the river, leaving a fiery tail, and smashed into Mack's second tank, the one that contained Chief Frank Brooks and the master gunner, Saul Meiers. No one had a prayer. Once more the missile ripped through the steel of the tank and detonated into a sensational fireball, incinerating everything in its path.

Lieutenant Commander Bedford just stood there, as did Lieutenant Mason, both of them in shock at the sudden and terrifying impact of the hit from the insurgents. Again they watched as someone, this time the tank commander, battled to get out, but it was a grotesque charade. Everyone in the tank was plainly on fire, burning alive, caught in the roaring chemical flame that extinguished life instantly. The SEALs, on their rescue mission, were gossamer moths trapped in the devil's inferno.

Men were leaping from the other two tanks, anything to get clear before the next Diamondheads came in. Mack Bedford stood there, staring, in some kind of a dreamlike trance. He could not quite work out who was dead and who was alive. Was this hell, and had he died with his men?

The roar of the flames drowned out everything. The billowing smoke was rising a hundred feet in the air. No one could even see the far bank of the river. SEAL team leaders were hustling everyone into positions beyond the shattered convoy. Someone rushed up to Mack shouting, *"THIS WAY, SIR—WE GOTTA REGROUP—WE GOTTA GET CLEAR OF THIS FIRE!"*

Mack joined the rest, running over the rough ground, keeping the burning convoy between his men and the death-trap missile launchers across the river. Like everyone, he was scared to climb back into the tanks to open fire on the enemy. It seemed nothing could stop the Diamondhead on its chosen course, and its deadly mission.

He assumed a loose command, instructing that no one move until he was certain the insurgents had made an escape. SEALs had already phoned for help from every available quarter. Within fifteen minutes, rescue helicopters would arrive, but there was no one to rescue. It was impossible to live within the periphery of the Diamondhead missile. They waited in silence as the flames crackled beneath the desert sun. And then slowly they rose up from the sands and began to walk toward the pile of tortured metal, which contained the tortured, charred remains of their friends and colleagues.

It was still too hot to get close, but they walked around the outside until, one by one, they saw a strange sight on the far side of the river. There were a dozen robed Arabs, their hands held high, walking toward the bridge. The Americans watched, amazed. One of them yelled, "Don't do anything, guys! This is the oldest trick in the book. They've unloaded their weapons. They're surrendering as unarmed civilians. They know we're not allowed to touch them!"

And this assessment was accurate. The jihadists knew the rules well. Rather than retreat into the desert and face an aerial bombardment from U.S. aircraft, they chose to deny what they had done and pose as a group of local Bedouins, going about their peaceful, lawful business, innocent of any form of attack on the forces of the United States of America.

Mack Bedford looked back at the dying flames of the tanks, and tried to hold back his tears for Charlie O'Brien and the rest. He stared again at the bridge, and the anger welled up inside him—*But these fucking towelheads crossing the river. . . . Jesus Christ! . . . They've just murdered my guys!*

The silence seemed to cast a mantle of unreality over this tiny corner of Iraq, a land of such unaccountable hatreds. There was no movement among the stone-faced SEALs as they watched the little group of wraithlike figures still walking toward the center of the bridge. Still with their hands held high.

From here their sandals made no scuffing sound on the sand-swept flagstones of the bridge. It was as if the Americans were watching through a long-range slow-motion camera lens, watching the advance of this murderous little cabal that had caused lifelong heartbreak for these serving U.S. troops.

But the Arabs kept coming, kept walking. Only the Foxtrot Platoon commander recognized them as the missile men he had watched through his binoculars across the river. And once more he raised the glasses and stared at the oncoming killers, unarmed now, but still with that unmistakable loathing etched on their faces.

There was no doubt in anyone's mind that these were the perpetrators of this shocking crime, committed in cold blood with four of the internationally banned Diamondhead missiles. And now there was a murmur of restlessness among the Special Forces as they watched the bizarre scene on the Euphrates Bridge.

Team leaders, fearful of the rule-book consequences of attacking men who carried no weapons, were muttering softly. *Steady, guys. . . . Take it easy. . . . Let 'em keep coming. . . .*

Now, as the twelve Arabs reached the center of the bridge, their footfalls could be heard in the hot, shimmering air. It was a flat, subdued, yet poisonous sound, and still they held their hands high. On the far bank, women and children were gathering to watch as the twelve men walked quietly toward the infidels of the U.S. Special Forces, their sworn enemy.

Everyone on the western side of the river would remember the quiet. And every one of the Americans standing there would recall the sudden sharp metallic snap, as Lt. Cdr. Mackenzie Bedford rammed a new magazine into the breech of his M4 automatic rifle and began to run hard, straight at the bridge. These were not the "hours of the wolf." Mack Bedford *was* the wolf, an all-American wolf, snarling, bloodthirsty, right out of the deep forests of the great state of Maine.

Lt. Barry Mason reacted first. He swiveled around and set off in pursuit of the SEAL team commander. *NOSSIR . . . NOSSIR . . . FOR CHRIST'S SAKE, STOP . . . DON'T SHOOT!*

Mack reached the bridge first, a full twenty yards in front of the lieutenant. There was a desperation in Barry's voice as he yelled, "DON'T DO IT, SIR . . . FOR CHRISSAKES, DON'T DO IT!"

He was racing across the ground now. But not fast enough. Mack Bedford's gun spat fire, cutting down the four leaders in a hail of well-aimed bullets. The big SEAL stood facing them, his rifle leveled straight at his enemy. Lieutenant Mason was almost on him, arms outstretched, but Mack rammed his finger on the trigger and sprayed bullets into the oncoming group. No one had time to run. No one had time to plead. The SEAL commander just kept firing. And one by one the Arab missile men fell dead into the dust, until they formed a ghostly white shallow hill, their robes fluttering in the hot, dusty southwest wind.

Lieutenant Mason hit his boss with a full-blooded block about one hundredth of a second too late. They both crashed to the ground, and as they did so the Americans stampeded forward, shouting and cheering. From across the river there was a sound of weeping and wailing, as the women ran toward their fallen loved ones.

Lieutenant Mason helped the boss to his feet, and the Americans engulfed the two officers. One young SEAL, with tears rolling down his smoke-blackened cheeks, kept repeating, over and over, "Thank you, sir. Thank you. My brother was in that tank."

There was no voice of dissent among the thirty Americans who had cheated death that morning. Several of them came up and offered a handshake to the SEAL commander. Others said loudly, "Those bastards had it coming!" or "'Bout time, too!" or even, "We ought to do that a whole lot more often!"

For a couple of minutes, Mack Bedford seemed unreachable, as if the bloodlust of the wolf had subsided. He stood there at the bridge, and merely continued to say, "They killed my guys. They murdered my fucking guys. And I owe them that."

Across the river, residents of the village were walking forward to claim their dead, carrying the bodies back to the east bank of the river. Three SEALs stood in a line facing them, rifles leveled, but there were no recriminations, no shouts of anger from the Iraqis. Not on this day, when the death toll on both sides was comparable—twelve insurgents, twelve SEALs, and eight Rangers.

In the background the burned remains of the tanks still sent black smoke into the sky. And every soul on either side of the river, mourning their dead, understood what had been done, and why the outcome was as it was. Here in this ancient biblical land of Mesopotamia, an ancient pact from one of the most celebrated books of the Old Testament, Exodus, had been enacted—*life for life, eye for eye, tooth for tooth.*

High above, two U.S. Army Chinooks were making their approach, clattering down toward the rough ground beyond the burned-out hulks of the tanks. Each of them contained medical supplies, nursing staff, military investigators, and combat-ready Special Forces. But at this point none of it was necessary. There were no wounded. Anyone in proximity to the missile was not only dead but cremated. For most of them, there were no remains. In time there would be white crosses, erected in scattered communities back in the USA, bearing simply name and rank in commemoration. A fallen soldier, known to God.

The dust storm created by the mighty rotors of the Chinooks obscured the horror scene on the road. And through it walked the SEAL officers who must ascertain precisely what took place. Only one of them, the Camp Hitmen CO, Cdr. Butch Ghutzman, outranked Mack Bedford.

They met at the cornerstone of the bridge and talked briefly. The tanks were still too hot for examination and would be for several hours. Commander Ghutzman looked across at the Iraqis still carrying away their dead and asked Mack, "What the hell's going on over there?"

"I guess they're looking after their casualties, sir."

"They get shot or shelled or something?"

"Shot, sir."

"In the middle of the bridge? Were they making some kind of a charge on our guys?"

"Nossir. They were pretending to give themselves up. I shot them."

"Jesus. Were they armed?"

"How the hell do I know whether they were armed?"

"You understand why I ask the question?"

"Affirmative, sir."

———•◆•———

It was only a rough garret set high in the roof of a squalid gray stone house three streets back from the riverfront, directly across from the area the Americans were now evacuating. Huddled in the corner murmuring into a cell phone, in Arabic, was an elderly Iraqi, a veteran of the ill-fated Desert Storm and now a trusted "stringer" for the al-Jazeera television network based in gleaming modern offices in Doha, the capital city of Qatar. That phone call represented the vital link al-Jazeera holds to the battlefields of Iraq, the embodiment of its determination to make the United States look bad, really bad, at every available opportunity.

The al-Jazeera network is the most controversial Arabic news channel in the Middle East. It was founded in 1996, and since then it has burgeoned from a small localized station broadcasting only in Arabic to a vast international network, broadcasting twenty-four hours a day in English. It has forty foreign bureaus worldwide with dozens of correspondents. Its staff has been recruited from all the big Western television newsrooms—the BBC, CBS, CNN, and CNBC. Al-Jazeera may be counted on, implicitly, to report any form of negligent or ill-disciplined U.S. military action anywhere in the Middle East.

On this day the newsroom was busy. Bill Simons, a former BBC editor, tired of its childlike left-wing bias, had elected to pack up and join the Arabs, moving his life from South London to downtown Doha, on the east coast of the Qatar Peninsula. Bill knew a good news story as well as anyone, and the urgent tones of Abdul calling from faraway Abu Hallah on the banks of the Euphrates set his journalist's antennae alight.

How many did you say were dead? Twelve, shot down in cold blood by an American officer? Right there in the middle of the Euphrates Bridge? Jesus.

Had there been a battle of any kind? What's that? A couple of U.S. tanks slightly damaged after they opened fire on the village? Nothing serious, right? And then this American went berserk? Wow! And where are the bodies of the twelve villagers? Oh, you have them? Completely unarmed farmers just walking to their fields . . . Gimme your number, Abdul, and stand by.

Forty minutes later, al-Jazeera went to work in its customary mode. Its familiar chimes, which always sounded as if they emanated from the heart of a mosque, signaled for the 4:00 P.M. news headlines. A dark-eyed beauty from Riyadh began the broadcast:

Reports are coming in of a terrifying atrocity committed by U.S. Special Forces on a bridge over the Euphrates River near the Iraqi desert town of Hit. Twelve unarmed local farmers were apparently shot down in cold blood by an American officer. All of them died.

Our correspondent was unable to provide the names of the dead, but Iraqi police are expected to supply details later this evening. So far, U.S. military chiefs in Iraq have declined to comment until more of the facts are known. The Pentagon denies all knowledge of the incident and instructed our reporters to speak to the U.S. authorities in Baghdad. We will bring you more on this breaking story as the evening progresses.

For years it has been impossible for Western news networks to ignore al-Jazeera, which has been labeled the mouthpiece of both Osama Bin

Laden and al-Qaeda. Any time there is an unusual military problem in the Middle East, the chances are the story hits first on al-Jazeera. And boy, was this ever unusual.

Inside all newsrooms, both print and broadcast, in London, Washington, and New York, there is a near-permanent watch on the Qatar station, which is tuned in, always, to the eyes and ears of the Arab world. And when the possibility of a U.S. atrocity on the Euphrates came bounding onto the screen like a Labrador puppy on steroids, the left-inclined media of both countries could hardly wait to savage the military that guards their freedoms and keeps their nations safe.

One "enterprising" journalist made a phone call to the U.S. military in Iraq and was told, "Yes, we do have a report of an armed clash along the Euphrates, and yes, there is a Navy SEAL commander assisting right now with an internal investigation. We have reports of some casualties on the U.S. side, no knowledge of Iraqi casualties."

By the time various editors and rewrite men had finished with this and added it to the "report" from Abdul in the attic, it was on for young and old.

MASSACRE ON THE EUPHRATES— ### SEAL COMMANDER FACES COURT-MARTIAL

There was, of course, an absence of real facts, like what caused the battle? Which side opened fire first, and with what? Did Americans die, which compelled their colleagues to retaliate? Did they come under attack, unprovoked, from roadside weapons? Was there any complaint from official Iraqi authorities?

Never mind all that. What mattered was the chance to demonstrate murderous bullying by U.S. troops, shooting and killing innocent Iraqi farmers, slamming the iron fist of Uncle Sam into the guts of unarmed Bedouins.

There had plainly been glaring failures by U.S. commanders to control their unruly troops. And how did this make the USA appear in the eyes of the world? (See editorial on page 21.)

Not since the disgusting behavior by U.S. troops in Abu Ghraib prison in the spring of 2006 has the ethos of the United States military been called into such question . . . etc., etc.

This bombardment of journalistic half-truths, misapprehensions, and exaggerations almost caused the roof to fall in at the Pentagon, especially on Corridor 7 on the fourth floor, in the head offices of the United States Navy. SEAL activities have been known to raise the blood pressure of navy chiefs, but mostly at the HQ of SPECWARCOM in San Diego. Only when an incident looks likely to spiral out of control does general disquiet start rippling along E Ring and into the office of the chief of naval operations.

Adm. Mark Bradfield, a former U.S. Navy carrier battle-group commander, occupied the CNO's chair in the Pentagon. Right now he was staring at the front page of the *Washington Post,* and uttering the time-worn phrase of those in high command but not on the battlefield— "What in the name of Christ is going on over there?"

His personal assistant, Lt. Cdr. Jay Renton, was staring at the front page of the *New York Times,* and grappled for the most calming phrase he could think of. Jay's kid brother was a SEAL, serving in Afghanistan, and he knew firsthand about the low cunning of the Taliban and al-Qaeda, the way they had open lines to al-Jazeera and reported the most lurid and unlikely scenarios to the Qatar station, the way they knew how swiftly the left-wing press of the United States would jump all over American troops. "Looks like a pretty nasty battle along the Euphrates, sir," said Jay. "And, like always, the insurgents get to al-Jazeera television a long time before we're on the case."

"Doesn't say anything about al-Jazeera here," replied the CNO, somewhat gloomily.

"It does here in the *Times,*" answered Jay. "Quotes the source of the story as *al-Jazeera, the authoritative Arab-based television station.*"

"Hmmmmm," replied the CNO, an element of suspicion entering his voice.

"Sir, Garrison Hitmen is probably eight hundred miles from Qatar. Now how do you think the television station found out? Because some al-Qaeda killer hopped into a chicken shed and phoned 'em—with the information that a dozen of his guys had been shot. Never mind why, never mind the circumstances."

"And how did al-Jazeera find out about the SEAL platoon?"

"They did not find out about it. The U.S. media phoned through to Iraq and discovered the SEALs had been in action on that day along that part of the Euphrates. They took it from there."

At that point a call came from Jay Renton's office. "Sir, we got something coming through right here from San Diego. Shall I download it or send it through on the link?"

"Hold it right there. . . . "

"Excuse me, sir—be right back."

The lieutenant commander left the office and walked through to the bank of computers that was relaying reports from every theater of war in which the United States was involved. Especially Iraq.

The signal from SPECWARCOM was from Rear Adm. Andy Carlow, commander of the Navy SEALs. Its message was stark but, in this instance, extremely helpful: *Two SEAL platoons came under separate attacks south of the Hitmen Garrison yesterday. Four U.S. tanks hit and destroyed by insurgent missiles. Twenty dead: twelve SEALs, eight Rangers. The attacks were unprovoked. SEALs returned fire. Iraqi casualties sustained. No final count.*

"Guess that wraps up this newspaper crap about cold blood," growled Admiral Bradfield. "In the worst possible way, of course."

"Sure does," agreed Jay Renton. "Do we make any public statement?"

"Not yet. First of all, the bereaved families have to be informed, and then we need to get a full report from the senior SEAL commander on the mission."

"And what do we tell the media, which is going to bombard us with questions about a possible court-martial and God knows what else?"

"Instruct the press office that the United States Navy does not make statements until the facts are known and diagnosed."

———— • ◆ • ————

There was an undercurrent of pure disquiet running all through Camp Hitmen. Reeling from the deaths of so many of their officers and buddies, the men of the SEAL, Ranger, and Green Beret platoons were stunned by the version of events that was currently appearing in U.S. newspapers and, in particular, on television.

The accusations that a SEAL commander had shot down twelve insurgents on the bridge were being presented as if he had just met them on the street and then turned his rifle on them for no reason whatsoever. As one-sided accounts go, this one was right up there.

It seemed that no one at al-Jazeera had bothered to check the validity of the secret Arab correspondent, who had slunk away from the battlefield and telephoned a truly outrageous account to the television station, without even mentioning the horrifying, and flagrantly illegal, damage the Americans had sustained before they retaliated.

And the tone of certain U.S. media editorials was directed accusingly at the troops on the ground, the guys who put their lives on the line every day, on behalf of the government of the United States of America.

"Why am I doing this?" The question was not often asked by Special Forces, whose training provided them with a cast-iron wall of self-righteousness. How else would it be possible to turn men into an unstoppable professional fighting unit, contemptuous of the enemy, and ever aware of one shining part of their creed: "Professionalism is about the total elimination of mistakes. It has nothing to do with money"?

But this was different. The U.S. media were chipping away at their very reason for existing, suggesting they were ruthless killers, devoid of any sense of decency or justice. They watched the television; they could read the newspapers on their computers. They knew what was being said.

This new sense of bitter unfairness pervaded their actions. No one wanted to go out on missions where they could come under heavy fire yet, somehow, be reluctant to shoot back.

For two days, Lt. Cdr. Mackenzie Bedford was ensconced with the senior officers of the garrison. There had still been no official complaint from the Iraqis, which suggested the missiles had been fired from an illegal insurgent unit. As for Commander Bedford's actions, he admitted he had opened fire on the Arabs on the bridge and that he did not know if any of his men had also retaliated. He did not know how many had died, and, quite frankly, he did not care.

In the opinion of the senior command at Camp Hitmen, the real atrocity of the conflict had been the firing of an almost certainly illegal missile that had killed twenty U.S. military personnel in unprovoked attacks.

There was great disquiet in the garrison. And enormous sympathy for Mack Bedford. Behind it all, though, was the unspoken fear that the veteran SEAL commander had simply gone berserk after witnessing the shocking death of his closest friends, Frank Brooks and Charlie O'Brien. Both burned alive.

There was not one single resident of Camp Hitmen, serving officer or other rank, who would ever be persuaded to utter one word against the lieutenant commander. In fact, there was genuine worry among senior staff that men would lie, say anything, in defense of the commander.

Lies have never been tolerated in the navy. Instructors at the U.S. Naval Academy, in Annapolis, will tolerate all manner of transgressions, except for lying. For that, a midshipman will be thrown out. Not might be, will be. Young men being prepared to take command of very expensive warships cannot veer from the truth. Ever. Every man on the ship is dependent on the straightforwardness of the captain and his commanders.

The navy's SEALs, the combat elite, though normally far removed from life at sea, were nonetheless bound by the same dark-blue code of conduct. And here was an entire garrison of men preparing to close ranks in support of a hugely admired officer, who had essentially carried out what all of them would have wished but didn't dare. Even Lt. Barry Mason.

There is a natural inclination in circumstances such as these just to shut up and say nothing. And it has doubtless been achieved many times when personnel were under constant attack. But this scenario had the added complication of a hysterical media, demanding justice, demanding punishment for the guilty, demanding the USA does not operate under the same lawless regimes as the terrorists. Which is all very well, unless you happen to have been Charlie O'Brien, Frank Brooks, or Billy-Ray Jackson. Or their many highly regarded, trusted friends.

As Admiral Bradfield had so succinctly put it—*Hmmmmm.* Very tricky.

In the end, the opinion that would count was that of the navy's serving judge advocate general, the JAG, so often a reasonable and charming naval officer, but the one man whose shadow looms large over every single Special Forces operation.

A Navy SEAL, armed to the teeth, trained to the minute, with strength closer to that of a mountain lion than a regular human being, is a very dangerous character. Each one of them is conditioned mentally and physically to destroy his enemy. Which can be very awkward when he doesn't know who the hell his enemy is.

In theaters of operation like Iraq and Afghanistan, the insurgent wears no uniform, may or may not be armed, may or may not be a spy, or a lookout, for a lurking al-Qaeda hit squad, may or may not be concealing a deadly cargo of explosive somewhere in his local streets. The Navy SEAL has a lot of thinking to do, which is why the vast majority of them have college degrees.

But SEALs are often placed behind enemy lines. Behind the lines of an *unseen* enemy. Way, way behind the lines of that unseen enemy. Which is where the game is likely to change—among young American servicemen who are far from home, far from help, and will not admit they are scared. These are guys who are operating under terrific tension, and who might blow some tribesman's head off merely because of the massive twin pressures of fear and past experience. For such young men, the shadow of the JAG looms extralarge.

He is there to carry out the most impossible task—to decide the truth, to weigh the circumstances, to try to place himself in the SEAL's combat boots for a while. And then to try to get al-Jazeera, the U.S. media, and all the appalling fabrications of the Islamist militants off the back of the Pentagon. The JAG, for a thousand reasons, must always be seen by all parties to be scrupulously fair on behalf of the U.S. military.

The JAG currently on duty in Camp Hitmen had his back to the wall. His current inquiry involved a very special man, Mackenzie Bedford, Honor Man in his BUDs Class, a decorated SEAL commander, beloved by almost every man who had ever served under his command. And worse yet, a man currently trying to cope with the most awful personal problem involving his only son, Tommy.

The JAG, Cdr. Greg Farrell, was not loving it. Not one bit. He had known Mack Bedford for many years. No matter how hard he struggled, though, he could never take away the atmosphere of prosecutor and prosecuted in their interviews together.

Even more unsettling was the reaction he was receiving from the other SEALs who had witnessed the murder of their colleagues. He could see it in their eyes: *You bastard—you're trying to court-martial our commander, and just for openers, don't look for any help from me.*

Greg Farrell understood the ramifications. He had worked in the navy's legal department for several years. He had graduated from law school, passed the bar, and gone into private practice with a big Boston firm. But after a very messy divorce at a very young age, he had effectively elected to run away to sea, and joined the navy.

He blasted his way into officer training school almost immediately after he completed boot camp. He was a highly intelligent student and passed all tests the first time he took them. But at heart he was still a lawyer, a man who strove to see both sides of the equation. He always imagined first what he would plead if he were defending, and then what he would allege if he were prosecuting. Like many lawyers, this iron-clad training left him somewhat light on common sense.

In this particular case he understood one thing clearly: in terms of a popularity contest, he would earn the gratitude of the entire camp if he decided that the SEAL commander on the Euphrates Bridge that day had no case to answer.

However, *on the other hand*—the words that are engraved on every lawyer's heart—the political climate was immensely problematic.

There were new Middle Eastern peace talks coming up. Pakistan, which, up on the Northwest Frontier, had become the cradle of rabid Islamic fervor, was trying to enter a nuclear nonproliferation pact with India and China.

And right here, in his, Greg Farrell's, backyard, there were a dozen dead Iraqi tribesmen, the supporters of whom were prepared to swear to Allah they had meant no harm to anyone and had never owned a firearm between them. Even the new Iraqi president had begun to refer to the incident on the bridge as the Massacre.

The JAG was nonplussed. The legal issue was in danger of being shunted aside between the two warring factions, the men on the ground and the powers that be. It was nothing short of a no-win situation, hereinafter to be known as "a sonofabitch."

Commander Farrell decided that whatever the case against the SEAL commander was, it could not be shelved. The profile was too high; there was too much at stake. The Pentagon was insisting the case be put to rest, in a way that presented the United States in the best possible light. And that could not be done by sweeping it under the carpet.

Everyone involved in the Foxtrot Platoon disaster was leaving for San Diego in three weeks. And at 0800 hours, on a clear desert morning, Lt. Cdr. Mackenzie Bedford was formally told the case would be going to the U.S. Navy Board of Inquiry at SPECWARCOM. The recommendation was that he be court-martialed on charges of reckless conduct in the face of the enemy and, very possibly, with the murder of twelve Iraqi tribesmen.

CHAPTER 2

The vast military Boeing C-17 came in low over the seaward suburbs of the city of San Diego. Still at only five hundred feet, it came screaming across the bay and touched down on the southwest runway of the U.S. Naval Air Station, North Island, Coronado, world headquarters of the SEALs. The aircraft, bringing home from Iraq the men of SEAL Team 10, finally taxied to its turning point out near Zuniga. And from there the SEALs could see the sprawling military cemetery high on Point Loma, a couple of miles across the water. Frank Brooks and Charlie O'Brien both had memorial gravestones there.

It was not much of a homecoming. The shadow of Mack Bedford's probable court-martial hung over the entire team. Where normally there was laughter and joking around among men who have returned safely after a deployment in some Middle Eastern hellhole, this evening there was a grimness that pervaded the entire base.

Every man in the compound knew there were outside forces, political overtones, present in Lieutenant Commander Bedford's case. The SEALs, by the very nature of their calling, were an insular group, men apart, and the intrusion of outsiders into their hard-edged world would always raise hackles.

The highly detailed report from the judge advocate general in Iraq had made the task of the Coronado Board of Inquiry relatively simple because the facts were not in dispute. The Iraqis had crossed the bridge with their arms held high, but that did not mean they were unarmed. It only meant they appeared to be unarmed, which is different. Shrewd observers of the Iraqi theater might conclude that such a surrender is an old trick, designed purely to prevent the U.S. troops from retaliating and killing them all. Against this, there were more than a dozen SEALs who had been present in the disaster zone, and who all gave the same reply to the question, "Were the Iraqis armed or unarmed?"

"No idea, sir. They might have been. They might not."

Members of the Inquiry Board wished to speak to the men again before reaching a decision. And for that, they obviously had to wait for Foxtrot Platoon to land in San Diego. There would now be a three-day delay while they completed their work. Three days of hell for Lieutenant Commander Bedford, while his fate hung in the balance. He was a lifelong naval officer perhaps on the verge of being shown the door.

In the end, pressured by the Pentagon, which was in turn being pressured by the White House, the board decided there was a case to answer. They referred the matter to SPECWARCOM's force judge advocate general, Capt. Paul Birmingham, who studied it and passed it on to the navy's Trial Service Office.

From there, the wheels of military justice turned slowly. The burning question was, were the twelve Iraqis ruthlessly shot down in cold blood when they had plainly surrendered and were plainly unarmed? Some thought, probably; others thought, who the hell knows? But the SEALs, to a man, believed Lieutenant Commander Bedford had been amply justified in gunning them down, because no one could possibly have known what the crazy fuckers might have done next, having already murdered twenty of their buddies with a goddamned illegal missile.

Three days later the Trial Office made its final decision. Lieutenant Commander Bedford would be court-martialed for the murder of twelve Iraqi tribesmen, reckless conduct in the face of the enemy, and numerous offenses against the Geneva Conventions. These latter charges were not yet finalized but would involve Article 13, concerning the treatment of prisoners of war and the issues surrounding troops *pretending* to surrender.

As far as the SEALs were concerned, this was outrageous "grand-standing" for political purposes only, because the USA wishes to be seen by the world as fair to everyone at all times. Politicians and members of the administration were aware of this, and several prominent advisers to the president were warning against upsetting too badly the Special Forces of the United States.

The truth was that no one knew what, in the name of God, was the safest course of action. The only definite issue was that the USA could not be seen to turn its back on the problem. And with twelve Iraqi tribesmen shot dead on the bridge outside their home village (possibly) by a top SEAL commander, there was a very obvious problem.

The U.S. Navy Trial Office named the military lawyers who would take the lead in the case. Cdr. Harrison Parr, a forty-eight-year-old former frigate executive officer from Maryland, had given up the chance of full command ten years ago in order to concentrate on completing his law studies. He would handle the case for the prosecution, which was seriously moderate news for Mack Bedford.

Harrison Parr had already been offered partnerships in three San Diego law firms if he would retire from the navy. But little Harrison, who stood only five-foot-six and was built like a jockey, was passionate about the U.S. Navy and its role in the world. Nothing would coax him out of dark blue and into a pinstriped civilian suit. Harrison had no taste for legal tricks and the shenanigans of a civilian courtroom. He believed in the truth—the plain, unvarnished truth. And he had earned a towering reputation for locating that truth. He also believed the Iraqi tribesmen were not armed and that Mack Bedford had essentially gone berserk. The issue was, for him, did his masters want the big navy SEAL found guilty of murder or not?

Harrison would do his utmost to prosecute successfully, but he was also an astute politician, and he would rely on his officer's antennae to alert him to the wishes of his superiors. If they wanted "guilty," he was confident he could deliver. If, however, they tipped him the wink that this must *look* harsh, and resonant, but the lieutenant commander must, in the end, walk free, he'd make quite certain that happened.

Harrison was a loyal servant of his commander in chief, the president of the United States. An idealistic zealot, he was not.

Against him, the Trial Office appointed Cdr. Al Surprenant to defend Mack Bedford. Al, at the age of fifty, was much more of a zealot, and he had a quiver full of absolute core beliefs, the principal one of which was an unshakable confidence in the U.S. Navy's officer class. Al Surprenant did not believe that any U.S. combat troops should ever be hauled before a court-martial and accused of mistreating the enemy. As far as Al was concerned, the enemy was the enemy, and the first moment any of them raised a hand against the United States, then that enemy had no rights whatsoever. This did not apply to a formal war where one sovereign nation was in combat against another, with correct uniforms, codes of conduct, and observations of the Geneva Conventions. But it most certainly did apply to terrorist operations, insurgents, jihadists, al-Qaeda, Taliban, or any other armed group who opened fire, in any form whatsoever, on the armed forces of the USA.

Commander Surprenant had stringent views on all U.S. Special Forces operating "behind enemy lines," where he believed they had every right to do anything necessary to protect themselves and their mission. Al's creed was simplified: *If they are not permitted to hit back at the enemy any way they see fit, then they ought not to have been sent there.* He considered the unwritten law of natural justice quite sufficient to protect U.S. servicemen, but if it wasn't, then he, Commander Surprenant, would give that universal "law" all the teeth and legal correctness it required.

Mack Bedford could scarcely have been in safer hands. Counsel for the defense would carry the courtroom fight to the prosecution and demand to know under which rule the Navy SEALs were suddenly forbidden to smash back at the men who had just murdered twenty of their teammates.

Surprenant was born with a silver spoon in his mouth. His wealthy father had sent him to Choate School, and then to Harvard Law School, but the young Al did not relish the mountainous paperwork, written judicial opinions, and overall bureaucracy of a big law firm. So one day, despite his excellent law degree and ensured future, he just left and joined the United States Navy. He swiftly earned his commission, and rose rapidly to the rank of lieutenant commander and found himself serving as missile director on a U.S. destroyer in the Gulf War. The following year he became a navy lawyer on the base in Norfolk, Virginia, and then moved out to San Diego after he married a Hollywood actress.

Everyone on the SPECWARCOM base understood that senior command was not anxious to destroy Mack Bedford, and the appointment of Commander Surprenant was a probable sign that he was not going down for murder. Nonetheless, opinion persisted among the men that political forces were making the accused SEAL commander a sacrificial lamb on the altar of appeasement in the Middle East.

The court-martial would be heard in the courtroom of the Navy Trial Service in the middle of the San Diego base, far from the inquisitive eyes of the media, which had not, as yet, cottoned on to the judicial proceedings surrounding the incident on the bridge.

The Trial Service appointed a five-man panel to sit in judgment on Lt. Cdr. Mack Bedford. As usual, they assigned one young lieutenant and three lieutenant commanders whose experience covered a wide range of naval activities both in war and in peace.

The court-martial's president, Capt. Cale "Boomer" Dunning, former commanding officer of a nuclear submarine, was only a few months short of promotion to rear admiral. This was another sign of sympathy toward Mack Bedford. Captain Dunning was a hard-eyed combat veteran destined for extremely high rank. In the opinion of the SEALs, his natural allegiance and loyalty would rest with the accused officer. He was also a known friend of Cdr. Al Surprenant, both of them having family homes back east on Cape Cod. On the face of it, the trial was somewhat stacked against the prosecution assembled by Harrison Parr, because the issue was political, and no one knew which way it would swing.

And therein rested the disquieting aspect of the case. It was as if the final decision had been taken out of the navy's hands, that somehow the verdict had been agreed before the trial started, won and lost before it was heard. Was Mack Bedford the officer whose fate was already decided? No one liked the sound of that.

The days passed slowly in the two weeks leading up to the trial. Bedford himself became very withdrawn. The navy had arranged for him to spend this time in private officers' quarters and make his own decisions about attending work and training with Foxtrot Platoon. Almost surreptitiously, new men had been brought in to replace those who had died.

No one mentioned the tragedy, and the leading petty officers supervised the brutal fitness regime being played out on the long beaches, out in front of the world-famous Hotel del Coronado. Every day, damn near all day, they pounded along that tidemark in their boots and shorts, searching for the firmest wet sand, trying to beat the clock. Some days Mack Bedford joined them, running easily alongside the new kids, demonstrating a naval lifetime of supreme physical fitness, strength that bordered on that of a wild animal, determination, and discipline ingrained in him since he had first pounded this same stretch of beach as a BUDs student.

In the evenings, he saw very few people, not simply because his close buddies had all died in the tanks but because he sensed he was now isolated until the court-martial was over. He spent long hours with Al Surprenant, endlessly poring over maps of that western side of the Euphrates where the SEALs had been hit by the missiles.

Every night Mack wrote to Anne at their home in Maine, trying to explain that the forthcoming court-martial was only a formality and that he would not be found guilty. But he also needed her to understand that he was the unnamed commanding officer in the newspaper reports describing the "massacre" on the bridge. He did not go into any detail, and neither did he point out that he was the only American to have opened fire on the tribesmen. Mostly, his carefully written lines concerned Tommy and the fact that there was no improvement in his condition.

Anne's news from the health insurance company was not encouraging. Despite that blanket coverage the navy had provided for him and his immediate family, none of the underwriters had come forward to volunteer payment to the Swiss clinic, which increasingly seemed to be the Bedfords' only hope.

It was difficult for Mack to find anything much to feel cheerful about. On every front there was trouble—career, money, and family. Sometimes, in a darker mood, he felt the shadow of death formed an unfair canopy over him alone. Every day the court-martial loomed closer, that moment of truth when his peers would sit in judgment. After all these years, was he still a right and proper person to lead the front line of U.S. military muscle?

Five days after the return from Iraq, the story leaked out to the *San Diego Telegraph*. They did not name the commanding officer at the bridge, but someone had briefed them well. The story ran over four columns on the front page of the newspaper beneath the headline:

U.S. NAVY COURT-MARTIALS SEAL COMMANDER CHARGED WITH MURDER OF SURRENDERING IRAQIS

The United States Navy confirmed last night that the SEAL commander whose men shot dead twelve surrendering Iraqi tribesmen has been court-martialed. He will be tried this month in the navy courtroom at the SPECWARCOM base on Coronado Island, San Diego. The officer stands accused of murder, shooting unarmed men in cold blood.

The incident took place three weeks ago on the western bank of the Euphrates River south of the ancient Mesopotamian town of Hit. According to the navy, armored vehicles transporting the SEAL team had come under rocket attack from insurgents on the other side of the river. The SEALs had prepared to return fire, but, according to the Arab television network al-Jazeera, the tribesmen had surrendered and started to walk across the bridge with their hands held high.

At this point, the Arab network states, the SEALs opened fire, gunning down the unarmed tribesmen until not one of them was left alive. Several witnesses from the Bedouin village of Abu Hallah have come forward to confirm this account. A spokesman for the Iraqi parliament says the prime minister is "shocked beyond belief" at the conduct of the Americans.

No details have ever been made public regarding losses sustained by the SEAL convoy. And the navy has resolutely refused to reveal the names of any SEAL combatants who took part in the action. They have also refused to reveal the identity of the officer who will stand trial in San Diego this month.

Last night there were rumors in the SEAL compound that the SEAL team had come under sustained attack across the Euphrates and suffered many casualties. A military source, who cannot be named, confirmed that at least four U.S. tanks were damaged in the battle. He stated that the account from al-Jazeera was dangerously one-sided and was unlikely to stand up to searching cross-examination at the court-martial. A spokesman for the SEALs' public information department, Lt. Dan Rowe, explained to our legal staff that, pending the court-martial, nothing further could be confirmed.

Would the identity of the commander eventually be revealed? "Unlikely," he said. "Unless the SEAL officer is convicted of murder. And no U.S. serviceman has ever been found guilty on such a charge. Not if it was based on a confrontation with the enemy."

The story was masterminded by the *Telegraph*'s formidable news editor, Geoff Levy, a former military staff reporter in the San Diego navy yards. Geoff knew his way around both the service and the law. He also knew what he called a "rattling good yarn" when he heard one. And the fact that the Silent Service had apparently turned on one of its own had a special, private journalistic glory all its own.

It is a remarkable achievement for the navy to keep anything quiet, considering it owns dozens of warships chock-full of knowledgeable, and extremely talkative, sailors. For Levy to be handed a leak as significant as Mack Bedford's court-martial was a fantastic coup. Geoff knew what he had, and he knew he was about twenty-four hours, plus several light-years, ahead of the opposition.

When the *Telegraph* came out, every major news organization in the United States found itself playing catch-up—which was extremely difficult since the navy would neither confirm nor deny the story. And this put the nation's newshounds in a quandary, since their only options were, effectively, to believe the truth of the San Diego paper, steal the information and proceed accordingly, or to ignore the story altogether. The latter option was out of the question. But the former was fraught with peril. What if the story was untrue? What if Geoff Levy was wrong? What if no court-martial was planned?

All of the above were troublesome issues, but not nearly as troublesome as missing out on the story altogether. The Fox twenty-four-hour television news channel was quickest into its stride and decided to round up Geoff Levy for an interview, ASAP. Exclusive, please. But the news editor for the *Telegraph* was too shrewd for that. No exclusives, and a fee of five thousand dollars, or you can all stop bothering me. Fox paid and put Geoff Levy on a telephone link in the very next slot, with a camera in a private telegraph office.

What he said confirmed, albeit unknowingly, the master journalist's craft—bearing in mind he had already scooped the world. "I have been either gathering or preparing stories about the United States Navy in San Diego for a dozen years now. And this story about this court-martial was entrusted to me by a very senior commander. He revealed it to me not because he wished for extra publicity for the navy, because that's the last thing they want with an issue like this. The officer gave it to me because of the outrage, the feeling of pure indignation felt by fighting men who put their lives on the line and then are told they are, somehow, murderers because they attacked and killed their enemy. In all my years, I have never sensed such outrage in the U.S. Navy, right here in San Diego. That applies especially to the SEALs, who give everything, and say almost nothing."

The interviewer was a dazzling blonde in her late twenties who was a lot more likely to become Miss California than News Reporter of the Year. "But, Geoff," she said, "surely the man had to face a court-martial if he just shot innocent civilians. I mean, that is murder, right?"

Levy sighed the sigh of the truly exasperated. "Ma'am," he said, "picture the scene, if you will. We're in hostile desert country; the temperature is 110 degrees. We're nine thousand miles from home. We got maybe four tanks on fire, we got men, American men, husbands, sons, and lifelong friends, either dead or burning to death. We got the screams and whispers of the dying. We got fear, terror, outrage, and shock. We got young troops in tears. We got a goddamned horror story right there in front of our eyes. And suddenly an American officer races out of the pack and opens fire on the tribesmen who committed these acts of war. He guns them down, perhaps in rage, perhaps in grief and sadness for his lost brothers. But he hits back, as he's been trained to do, amidst all the blood and carnage. In the middle of a gruesome and terrible specter the likes of which most of us will never see . . . he hits back."

Levy paused and let his words hit home. And then he said quietly, "And you, ma'am, and others like you, want to charge him with murder? I hope I've made myself clear about why there's outrage on the San Diego Naval Base."

Jessica Savold, the blonde interviewer, had not often been lectured like that. And she was almost overwhelmed at the lesson in journalism she had just been handed. Jessica did not live in the real world; she lived in the quasi-fantasy realm of media reporters, guys who knew a few facts, some of which might be true, but had no time or patience for the true depths of the events they related to the public. Jessica understood at that moment why her employers had paid five thousand dollars to hear the words of a big newspaper editor, a man of vast experience who would be a cut way above the rest. "Thank you, Mr. Levy," she said, reluctant for another exchange of thoughts, even more reluctant to be made to look more like a child.

Geoff stood up and nodded. But as he reached the door, he turned once more to Jessica, and he patted the left-hand side of his chest. "Heart," he said. "Until you learn heart, you'll never be worth a damn as a reporter or an interviewer." Luckily for the luckless Jessica, that part was off-camera. And with that he left the room and headed back to the news desk to urge his boys to (a) identify the SEAL officer he believed to be a towering hero and (b) provide him with backup evidence of the inferno of death, hard by the bridge over the Euphrates River. At least that's how he phrased it. Geoff, after all, was a master of his craft.

A round of applause from the newsroom greeted him when he returned, delivered by colleagues who had watched the Fox telecast. His deputy said, "Tell you one thing, Geoff. Right now we got e-mails flooding in, and half of them are saying this SEAL commander should be given the Congressional Medal of Honor, never mind a court-martial."

"Trouble is," replied the boss, "I don't really know what the hell's going on, except that they are about to court-martial him on murder charges and that a lot of guys at the SEAL base are very seriously pissed off. And that's got to be the thrust of our story tonight—the outrage. Because we're on the side of the guys who do the fighting, because we're a very pro-navy operation, not like those comedians in Washington and their lightweight puppet reporters." Geoff ended his little pep talk with the words, "C'mon, guys, let's round up some real hard quotes from named sources, people railing against charging our combat troops with serious civilian-type charges. Let's round 'em up, and then stick it to these assholes, right here in the *Telegraph*. Right now, while we got national attention."

Three thousand miles away, in the White House, the president of the United States was in a major quandary. Yes, he had approved the court-martial of Lt. Cdr. Mack Bedford, mainly because of the upcoming Middle East peace talks, and also to head off accusations from Iraq that U.S. troops could do anything they damn well pleased in the land between the Tigris and Euphrates rivers. In his own mind, as commander in chief, the president had approved the court-martial "for the greater good." Greater good, that is, unless you happened to be Mack Bedford.

However, this story in the *San Diego Telegraph*, and this interview with the goddamned news editor, had painted the entire issue a very different color. The Middle East peace talks could go to hell in the face of a domestic uproar, currently being ignited and fanned and publicly blazing on California's coast.

There are only a few true copper-bottomed taboos that all presidents must observe, and one of them is, Don't Pick Fights with Your Frontline Troops. There are several billion reasons for this, the main one being you will receive zero sympathy from the public, who do not trust any politicians but are apt to worship the ground upon which America's Special Forces walk.

The president was, inadvertently, on the dark side of this one, and in his deep, and somewhat cunning, soul, he knew he was not in control. He and his advisers had a tiger by the tail, and it was just a matter of time before that tiger not only roared but started showing very snarly teeth.

As C-in-C, he could, of course, step in and cancel the court-martial. But if that news ever leaked, the liberal press would tear him up. Right now the president found himself working out how to placate the liberals, appease the towelheads, and save the peace talks—all of which involved a wide and varied group of politicians and media execs. Unlike him, however, none of *them* was about to be bitten hard in the ass by the U.S. Navy SEAL tiger.

Rarely had a navy court-martial, to be heard behind locked doors on a secure naval base, aroused such consternation in the corridors of power. Whichever way it went, there would be big trouble for many people, aside from Mack Bedford and his family.

"Jesus Christ," said the president. He understood precisely how the *San Diego Telegraph* had brought the matter right into the public eye with the seemingly simple story that the unnamed officer, who had lurked behind so many headlines, was now to be formally court-martialed. That much was plain. What he did not fully comprehend was why the pendulum had swung the wrong way. For the past month, ever since al-Jazeera revealed the uproar at the bridge, the liberal media had held sway. As far as he and his advisers could tell, the mood in the United States had been one of anger and disappointment at the behavior of the SEAL. But right now things were completely different. The liberal media were, as ever, still angry and disappointed, but the public, and members of the armed forces, were in the opposite corner, angry that a brave and patriotic officer was somehow to face trial, right here in the USA, like a common criminal.

And now the entire matter was threatening to dominate the domestic news. The Department of the Navy in Washington was under siege from the media. The switchboard at the San Diego base was logjammed by phone calls from newspapers and television networks. Outside lines to the command bases at both Coronado and Virginia

Beach were entirely occupied by journalists. Reporters, photographers, and cameramen camped variously at the gates of SPECWARCOM, on the West Coast and the East. And they were growing more and more irritated at the total lack of cooperation they were receiving from the United States Navy. Up on the fourth floor of the Pentagon, Adm. Mark Bradfield had issued clear instructions that no one in the press office was to utter one word about the forthcoming court-martial.

Within hours, the massed ranks of the U.S. press corps would switch its attack to the White House, specifically requesting whether there was approval from the commander in chief to court-martial the SEAL officer. Magnanimously, they informed the White House Press Office they did not much care whether they received an answer from the president, the national security adviser, the secretary of defense, or the chief of naval operations. Any one of them would be fine. But there had to be an answer from someone.

As it happened, there was no answer from anyone. The days passed acrimoniously until, on a bright California Tuesday morning in late June, the court-martial was convened in the sunlit, heavily air-conditioned headquarters of the Navy Trial Service in the heart of the Coronado base.

Capt. Cale "Boomer" Dunning gathered his panel in an anteroom at the back of the courtroom before the proceedings began. The force judge advocate general, Capt. Paul Birmingham, had a private observation desk to the left of the great curved mahogany table at which the five officers would sit in judgment. Behind the central chair that would be occupied by Captain Dunning were large twin flags of the United States of America, hung at an angle. Between them was placed the imposing emblem of the United States Navy. Four captain's chairs, carved from mahogany, were set next to Boomer Dunning, two on either side.

Two navy guards were already on duty at the entrance to the courtroom. Two more were stationed inside, on either side of the door. Before the panel there were two large tables. The one on the left was, appropriately perhaps, for the prosecutor and his assistant. The one on the right was for Cdr. Al Surprenant and Lt. Cdr. Mack Bedford.

Also sitting in on the trial was the SEAL commander Rear Adm. Andy Carlow, plus the commander in chief of the Pacific Fleet, Adm. Bob

Gilchrist. The two regular court stenographers would take down the official record, and witnesses would not be permitted to confer. They would be accompanied into the courtroom, sworn in, and then accompanied out without further contact.

The trial began at 0900. The courtroom was relatively full, for a navy court-martial, and four members of the panel were already seated. Commander Surprenant and the accused officer were the last to arrive, before Captain Dunning himself took his place and said immediately, "Please proceed with the case against Lt. Cdr. Mackenzie Bedford."

Capt. Paul Birmingham, who stood six-foot-five, climbed to his feet and stated, "Lt. Cdr. Mackenzie Bedford, of Foxtrot Platoon, SEAL Team 10, is charged that on the twenty-ninth day of May this year, in the Republic of Iraq, he did willfully murder twelve unarmed tribesmen, residents of the town of Abu Hallah . . . "

Al Surprenant shoved back his chair, stood up, and snapped, "OBJECTION!"—which was just about unprecedented in the history of United States Naval justice, since the full charges had not yet been read, the prosecution had not uttered one word, and the defense counselor was somewhat rudely interrupting the force judge advocate general, one of the senior legal minds in the entire United States Navy.

Paul Birmingham swiveled around to face Al Surprenant, and Captain Dunning looked quizzical, turning toward Captain Birmingham as if to seek advice. No one knew quite how to treat this sudden violent swerve from the orthodox. But no one needed to. Al Surprenant made himself clear, extremely quickly.

"Captain Dunning, sir," he said. "The word 'unarmed' cannot be permitted in this charge because no one has the slightest idea whether they were armed or not. No member of the United States armed forces, nor indeed of the diplomatic services, has even seen the bodies. Thus, the word 'unarmed' is, at best, hearsay, or, at worst, untrue. Neither are acceptable. I ask the word 'unarmed' be deleted from the charge."

Captain Dunning turned once more to Paul Birmingham and said, "Advice, please."

The force JAG, boxed into a legal trap, replied, "Sir, the matter was referred to the Naval Trial Services, who considered it appropriate for the word 'unarmed' to be included, since that is the essence of the accusation by the Iraqis against the U.S. It is not my place to step in and alter the charge, though I do see there is cause for some anxiety."

"Captain Birmingham," said Boomer Dunning. "Am I required to pass judgment on this? And have the charges altered?"

"You are not required, sir. But it is within your power to rule on it. Alternatively, you could just adjourn and have the matter referred to the legal department in the Pentagon."

"I think Lieutenant Commander Bedford has suffered quite sufficient anguish without me prolonging it," replied the trial president. "We will proceed. Commander Surprenant's objection is sustained. I rule the word 'unarmed' will be struck from the record, on the basis we most certainly do not know whether they were armed or not.

"Paul, perhaps you will make the changes. Admirals Carlow and Gilchrist should initial their approval. Any problems?"

Everyone indicated agreement. And three minutes later Captain Birmingham began again: " . . . did willfully murder twelve tribesmen, residents of the town of Abu Hallah . . . "

"OBJECTION!" Al Surprenant was again on his feet. "Sir, no one has any idea whether they were residents of the town of Abu Hallah or not. We don't even know their correct names. They might have come in by bus or camel or whatever to join the fight against the SEAL platoon. I object most stringently to the word 'residents,' which has connotations of stability and responsibility. For all we know, these were just wandering insurgents, troublemakers, residents of nowhere. Gunmen. And I ask the word be stricken from the charge."

"Objection sustained," said Captain Dunning. "Same procedures. Remove the words 'residents of the town,' and substitute 'near the town.' Then try again, Paul." Captain Dunning added, somewhat archly, "If, of course, Mr. Surprenant has no further objections."

Resignedly, Captain Birmingham again read out the murder charge. Al Surprenant nodded his assent. The force judge advocate general continued: "Lieutenant Commander Bedford is further charged with reckless conduct in the face of the enemy, and offenses against the Third Geneva Conventions signed in 1949."

"OBJECTION!" called Al Surprenant. "The Geneva Conventions were originally drawn up and signed by sixteen nations, and they are designed to specify the conduct of nations at war, particularly in the realm of prisoners and the wounded. Nations have national uniformed armies, and, subsequently, codes of behavior, one to another. The conventions do not include the protection of lawless outcast gangs of tribal killers firing probably illegal missiles."

Commander Surprenant hesitated, turning toward the president, who looked thoughtful and then said, "Please continue. I'm interested in this."

"Sir, how can the defendant possibly have offended those codes if they do not apply to this terrorist conflict? You may as well call upon the Geneva Conventions to protect bank robbers or street hooligans. Plainly, the rules are designed to protect only national forces, fighting, formally, on behalf of a nation-state. And I ask that this charge be withdrawn because it does not, and cannot, apply."

Captain Dunning said nothing. But he wrote notes on a legal pad. And then he ruled, "Counselor, I understand the prosecutor intends to challenge your opinion on this, on the grounds of human decency, the original objective of Geneva. For the moment I overrule your objection, but only for the moment."

"Thank you, sir," replied Al Surprenant.

"Very well," continued the president. "Perhaps Commander Parr would outline, for the benefit of the court, the case for the prosecution?"

The Marylander, Harrison Parr, rose to his feet and instantly slipped into political mode. "Sir," he said, "it gives me no pleasure to prosecute a United States Navy SEAL, a man of exemplary character, surely destined for the very pinnacle of our profession. It is especially difficult for any navy legal counselor to stand right here and attempt to destroy the career of such a man, particularly when his offenses, if offenses they are proved to be, were committed in the very obvious heat of battle. But the judicial traditions of the United States Navy demand such actions, the compulsory process of arriving at the truth. And it was ever thus. Gentlemen, the United States stands accused by a friendly foreign power of gunning down its citizens, citizens they claim were not armed, civilians who were in the process of surrendering.

"The basic facts are not in dispute. No one denies the Iraqis had their hands held high, and no one denies Lieutenant Commander Bedford ran forward and shot each one of the twelve men dead. We have already heard that the tribesmen may or may not have been armed. But the Iraqi government says they were unarmed. Every television report in the Middle East says they were unarmed. Every newspaper report in the Middle East, and many in our own country, submit that the twelve Iraqis were indeed unarmed. And it would be the duty of any Western democracy to examine those allegations thoroughly and, if found to be true, to take action accordingly and punish the miscreant.

"It is my sad duty to stand before you to test the validity of these accusations. And I call the principal eyewitness for the prosecution, Lt. Barry Mason of the SEAL team's Foxtrot Platoon to offer his account."

Lieutenant Mason, immaculate in his uniform, swore to tell the truth, the whole truth, and nothing but the truth. He confirmed his name, rank, and date of birth; stood rigidly to attention; and succinctly answered the questions of Harrison Parr.

I believe you were on combat duty on the west bank of the Euphrates River on May 29th this year?

"I was, sir."

And were you under the command of Lt. Cdr. Mack Bedford?

"Not at first. I came with the first convoy on a rescue mission under the command of Lieutenant Harcourt. But we were hit with an anti-tank missile, and everyone in the lead tanks was killed."

Lieutenant Harcourt?

"Dead, sir. I tried to save him because he got out of the tank, but he was burned alive. I was lucky."

And what happened then, Lieutenant?

"We tried to put out the fires and radioed for help. Lieutenant Commander Bedford's convoy reached us within about forty minutes. And we came under his command."

And then?

"Two more tanks were hit, sir, by the same type of missile. Fired from across the river, from the edge of the town."

How do you know they were fired from across the river?

"I saw the last two come in, sir. We never had a chance."

Would you say Lieutenant Commander Bedford was enraged by all this?

"He was very, very angry, sir. Some of his close friends were burning to death, and no one could do anything to save them. The heat was melting the fuselage of the tanks. Our other lieutenant was in tears."

Were you in tears?

"Yessir."

Were other SEALs in tears?

"Yessir."

And were you not ashamed, as a SEAL officer, to be in tears?

"Nossir. We all were."

Perhaps not the reaction one would expect from trained combat troops?

"You didn't see it, sir. Our guys burning to death. If you had, you would not have made that remark."

As you wish. Now perhaps you'll tell the court what happened next.

But Lieutenant Mason was too upset to continue. Boomer Dunning immediately stepped in to save the young officer from embarrassment. He called a ten-minute adjournment and told the guards to bring a glass of water for the lieutenant.

When the court resumed, Lieutenant Mason was once more prepared for his ordeal, to relive the memory of that day in Iraq, and the recurring horror of what he had seen—the horror that haunted his dreams every night of his life.

And when the Iraqis began crossing the bridge, was there any doubt in your mind that these were indeed the same people who had opened fire on the U.S. tank?

"None at all, sir. They were the same people. We could see them on the other side of the river. There was no one else there."

Is there anyone who can corroborate this?

"Certainly Lieutenant Commander Bedford, sir. He was sighting them through binoculars for about ten minutes before they tried to cross the bridge."

Have you been told that? Or did you actually see him?

"I saw him, sir. He was standing right next to me. He was constantly checking out the enemy through the glasses."

But how could either of you have known that the men crossing the bridge were the men who fired the missiles?

"OBJECTION! The question's been asked and answered." Al Surprenant looked extremely irritated, and was unable to prevent himself from adding, "Of course the lieutenant and his commander understood precisely who the men on the bridge were."

"The objection is sustained," interjected Captain Dunning. "But perhaps, Commander Surprenant, you would restrict yourself to a plain format of objecting, rather than providing us with personal elaborations."

"I apologize, sir," replied the counsel for the defense, somehow humbled but nonetheless looking absolutely delighted with himself.

Harrison Parr continued, but he was shuffling papers, playing for time, slightly concerned at the intensity of his legal opponent's attack.

And was it at this time you first saw Lieutenant Commander Bedford make a run for the bridge with his rifle raised?

"OBJECTION! Counselor is blatantly leading the witness," snapped Al Surprenant.

"Sustained. Please rephrase the question." Boomer Dunning's face, too, was concerned, worried at the level of bitterness this case was already revealing.

Lieutenant Mason, what did you see next?

"Sir, we were all staring at about a dozen men crossing the bridge."

Were their arms raised in surrender?

"Their arms were raised. Whether or not they were raised in surrender I have no idea, since they were not military, just killers, and I am unfamiliar with their codes of conduct."

Well, if you had seen American soldiers walking forward like that, would you assume they were surrendering?

"They were not American, and they were not soldiers. They were brutal tribal murderers who had just launched a sneak attack on us, and wiped out some of the nicest, most loyal guys you could ever meet. Don't compare those bastards to Americans, sir. At least not to me."

Boomer Dunning again stepped in, as the young lieutenant was becoming visibly upset. "Lieutenant," he said, "I know this is very difficult for you. I don't suppose many people could understand just how difficult. But the question was simple: if Americans had walked like that, would you have assumed surrender? You are at liberty to reply yes, no, or I don't know.

Lieutenant Mason nodded and said, "Yes. I would think Americans were surrendering."

Then why would you doubt the motives of the Iraqis walking toward you with their hands held high?

"Because that's what they do, sir. They pretend to surrender, and they might be carrying suicide bombs, strapped to their bodies under their robes."

Do you really believe that, Lieutenant?

"Believe it? I know it. An Iraqi surrender is just about the most dangerous maneuver in the book. To us, that is. They wait till they are near us, and then either detonate a bomb or open fire."

Did Mackenzie Bedford believe that?

"OBJECTION! How could Lieutenant Mason possibly know the deepest innermost beliefs and suspicions of his commander?"

"Sustained. Rephrase, please."

Was this a common belief among Special Forces serving in Iraq?

"Very definitely, sir."

Well, Lieutenant, perhaps you would now tell the court what happened next?

"Yessir. We could now see the Iraqis moving forward. And Lieutenant Commander Bedford ran toward our side of the bridge and confronted them."

Was his rifle raised in battle mode?

·"Yessir. And I did think he was about to open fire on them."

And what did you do, Lieutenant?

"I ran forward to try to stop him, sir."

And you were obviously not successful?

"Nossir. I was too late. Lieutenant Commander Bedford opened fire on them."

Did anyone else in the platoon join him in this exercise?

"I cannot say, sir."

I mean, was there one other single person in Foxtrot Platoon who felt inclined to join in these cold-blooded murders?

"OBJECTION! Again the question has been asked and answered." Al Surprenant was visibly furious. "Counsel is not only leading the witness, he is bullying the witness," he added. "He is asking the same question in a way that demands the lieutenant state how other men felt. And how could he possibly know how other men felt?"

"Objection sustained. And would defense counsel kindly restrict questions to military facts? I am aware this case has already taken a curious turn, perhaps because Lieutenant Mason would far rather be standing here in defense of the accused rather than against him. Proceed."

Harrison Parr smiled good-naturedly and said to Barry Mason, "The court understands this is very difficult and that you have been ordered to appear here and assist in the prosecution of Lieutenant Commander Bedford. You have been an excellent witness so far, and I am sure my learned friend, Commander Surprenant, will provide you with ample opportunity to express your personal opinions as we continue."

"Thank you, sir." That was not "Yessir"; that was "Thank you, sir." And everyone understood the significance.

Lieutenant, do you remember what you said when you reached Mack Bedford?

"I said, 'Don't fire, sir.'"

I believe you also said, "For Christ's sake, don't fire."

"I believe I did."

And may I ask why you said those things?

"Mostly because I thought we might all end up standing right here if he did."

Did you believe it was necessary to shoot them?

"I thought we might get away with not shooting them."

And did you realize the Geneva Conventions expressly forbid the shooting of surrendering personnel?

"*OBJECTION!*" Al Surprenant was on his feet now. "The revised Geneva accord also forbids the practice of troops *pretending* to surrender. I consider it utterly unreasonable to quote from Geneva so opportunistically."

"Sustained. For the time being we will leave Geneva out of this."

Very well. Lieutenant, may I presume you thought it categorically wrong to shoot down these men?

"Nossir. You may not. I just thought it was a goddamned bad idea. But not wrong."

Not wrong, perhaps, because you are not fully acquainted with the rules of war?

Al Surprenant's chair almost cannoned into the row behind so sharply did he leap to his feet. "*OBJECTION!*" He knew there was no need to elaborate.

"Sustained. And Commander Parr, try to remember that such tactics, frequently heard in civilian courts, are neither applicable nor fair in a navy court-martial. Particularly when you are questioning an upstanding and extremely brave young officer who's been through the fires of hell on behalf of our country."

"No further questions," replied Harrison Parr.

Commander Surprenant remained on his feet.

Lieutenant, have you ever witnessed Iraqi insurgents pretending to surrender?

"Yessir. I have, once in Baghdad, once in Fallujah."

Could you tell the court what happened?

"In Baghdad, sir, we had a group of them trapped in a house where we knew there was a major cache of arms and explosives. About a dozen of us were out front, maybe thirty feet back from the front door, when they suddenly came out with their hands held high."

Were you given orders not to shoot?

"Nossir. Just to hold fire."

How many of them came out?

"Six, sir."

And then what happened?

"When the last one stepped onto the sidewalk, sir, he just detonated like a bomb and right behind him the whole house blew up."

Did the six die?

"Yessir. Still with their hands up."

And your platoon?

"The two young SEALs in the front line were both killed, five more of us were hurt, three quite badly. One of them died later."

And you?

"A hunk of flying stone hit my helmet and split it. Seven stitches."

And who commanded that platoon that day?

"Lieutenant Commander Bedford, sir."

And Fallujah?

"Oh, there were only two insurgents. They just walked toward us with their hands high. From about fifteen feet they suddenly produced their AKs and opened fire on us."

Was anyone hit?

"Yessir. Two of our guys. But we returned fire quickly and took 'em both out."

Was Lieutenant Commander Bedford there?

"Not with us, sir. He was right across the street, and he was the first one over to help us with the wounded."

Were those thoughts running through your mind at the bridge?

"Sure were. I was just deciding what scared me most—a courtroom like this or the enemy pulling some trick on us."

And in your case it was the courtroom?

"Guess so. I really thought there might be big trouble if the boss shot 'em."

But did you think they might pull a bomb or a rifle on you?

"I sure did. And there were several guys with their weapons drawn in readiness."

Lieutenant, were you surprised to see Lieutenant Commander Bedford run for the bridge and confront the Iraqis?

"Nossir."

Why not?

"Mack Bedford leads from the front, sir. Always has."

In your view, was Lieutenant Commander Bedford making sure he did not lose his own life?

"Hell, no, sir. He was just looking after his guys, the SEALs standing right in front of the bridge, who would have taken the impact head-on— I mean a burst of gunfire, or a bomb."

How would you describe Lieutenant Commander Bedford's actions?

"Courageous. Like we would expect from him. He was the best officer I ever served with."

Thank you, Lieutenant. No more questions.

Commander Parr called two more SEAL witnesses, who quickly confirmed almost word for word the significant sections of Lieutenant Mason's testimony. When this was completed, Commander Surprenant declined to cross-examine, preferring instead to allow the devastating impact of Barry Mason's words to remain with the panel.

Commander Parr then called Mackenzie Bedford, the accused, who, in a military court-martial, is required to stand and explain his actions before the defense is invited to question him.

Lieutenant Commander Bedford stood rigidly to attention, in full uniform, glancing neither to left nor to right. He carried no notes, no reference, and he faced the prosecutor with an expression that might reasonably be described as fearless. His attorney, Al Surprenant, looked as much like a coiled spring as any 225-pounder can. Mack swore to tell the truth, and identified his rank and date of birth.

Commander Parr immediately began the process that had preoccupied the powerfully built SEAL officer for so long.

Was there any doubt whatsoever, in your mind, that the men walking across the bridge were the precise same protagonists who had fired the missiles at the SEAL convoys?

"None."

How can you be so certain?

"I'd been looking at them through very powerful glasses for a long time. I'd observed them even before they fired the second set of missiles. I would have recognized them anywhere."

You did not need glasses to see they were apparently unarmed, did you?

"What do you mean 'apparently'? What the hell's that supposed to mean? These men survive on sheer cunning. They're tribesmen, not American salesmen. They're trackers, killers, gunmen. And if you're interested, they'd fired at us from behind a stone wall, well hidden."

Lieutenant Commander, there remains no proof before this court that these men, now dead, were guilty of anything. And even you would admit they were now surrendering.

"If they weren't guilty of anything, how come they were surrendering? Sir. People who haven't done anything don't usually go around surrendering, do they? Sir."

"Steady, Mack." Captain Dunning, who was very close to the SEAL officer, could not help this involuntary word of caution. Everyone could see the suppressed outrage in his demeanor.

But it appears only you, Lieutenant Commander, were so certain of their guilt, you found it necessary to take action.

"OBJECTION!" Al Surprenant flew to his feet. "Mack Bedford has no idea whether the others had reached the same conclusion, and he ought not to be asked questions that are plainly beyond his knowledge. He merely reacted faster. That's all."

"Sustained."

Your quick reaction is, in its way, commendable, Lieutenant Commander, but I submit it was also unnecessary. These Iraqis were harmlessly submitting to American interrogation.

"These 'harmless Iraqis' had just murdered twenty of my guys! Burned them to death right in front of our eyes. How dare you suggest I shot the wrong men? I am a SEAL commander, constantly in harm's way, right on the front line. You are a lawyer with a big desk. You might do well to remember that."

"Strike that last remark from the record," said Captain Dunning. "Lieutenant Commander Bedford, I am obliged to say that the sympathy of this court is almost entirely in your favor. Please try to contain your understandable anger. No one is enjoying this, believe me. Certainly not Commander Parr."

Mack Bedford nodded his assent, and Harrison Parr continued his uphill struggle.

I am almost through, Lieutenant Commander. And I have to say the position of the prosecution remains unchanged—you shot down these unarmed men in a fury . . .

"OBJECTION!" Al Surprenant was again on his feet. "The question of whether they were armed or not is a matter of opinion. Not fact. The word has been stricken from the charge. Counselor has no right to reinsert it. I ask the word be removed from the record."

"Objection sustained. Request granted. Strike the word."

No more questions.

Once more counsel for the defense rose to his feet. "Lieutenant Commander Bedford," said Commander Surprenant, "I believe you have been a Navy SEAL for more than ten years and during that time have been decorated for valor twice."

"Yessir."

I also believe there is another decoration awaiting ratification, awarded to you for gallantry under fire in a very serious action in Fallujah?

"I believe that is correct, sir."

Your character record as a Navy SEAL is unblemished. You are regarded among your superiors as an officer destined for the highest rank?

"I hope so, sir."

And now you have been dragged before this court to explain why you happened to mow down an enemy that had just murdered, burned to death, twenty of your men, and may have been planning even more mayhem on that bridge, on that infamous day?

"Yessir."

You believed they might still have been armed. You have dramatic experience in Iraq of false surrenders, which I have no doubt you realize is completely illegal under international rules of war?

"I certainly do, sir."

And so, you attacked your enemy ruthlessly, in order to prevent further casualties to your own men? You were prepared to take no more risks with these people?

"Correct, sir. No more chances. They'd done enough goddamned damage for one day."

Before we close this part of the proceedings, I would like to touch on just one more aspect of the attack, and that was the missile used against the SEAL convoys.

"Yessir. A highly dangerous missile."

It's what's known as a tank buster, I understand?

"Yessir. But this was a kind of supersonic tank buster. Just rips through the fuselage like it was made of cardboard."

You were familiar with it before May 29th?

"Yessir. They get it from Iran, and they've hit American vehicles quite a few times. One time they fired it at the Hitmen compound. Didn't penetrate, but it made a darn big hole in the concrete."

Is its penetration force the only thing that sets it apart?

"Nossir. What really sets it apart is that it burns everyone to death— anyone anywhere near the hit area."

Lieutenant Commander, were these the banned Diamondhead missiles, the ones that burned alive the SEALs and Rangers on your mission?

"Yessir. No doubt in my mind."

Thank you, Lieutenant Commander. No more questions.

Captain Dunning now addressed the defense. "Counselor," he said, "is there anyone further you wish to call? This hearing is restricted to material witnesses only."

"Just one more, sir. I call Gunner's Mate Second Class Jack Thomas, who serves as Mack Bedford's combat driver, armored vehicle."

Jack Thomas stood and swore to tell the truth. In reply to Al Surprenant's first question he said, in his rich Tennessee accent, "Sir, I served with Mack Bedford on three tours, one in Afghanistan, two in Iraq. If there's a better officer in the United States armed forces, well I ain't met him yet."

Al smiled. "And what qualities have you seen in him that allows you to offer such high praise?"

"Sir, on that day at the bridge, it was all I could do to stop him rushing into that fire to save Charlie and Billy-Ray and Frank. They was burnin' up, on fire in that real blue flame."

Did you think this was unusual behavior?

"Nossir. Mack Bedford would do anything for his men. They're his prime concern, at all times."

Was he a good combat officer?

"The best. Fantastic marksman, stealthy, and as strong as a lion. The best swimmer on the base. Folks say Mack Bedford was more dangerous unarmed than most guys holding machine guns."

You ever seen him in action?

"Yessir. In the mountains fighting al-Qaeda. Boy! He's somethin'. And we all look up to him. Because when you fight with Mack, no matter who the enemy is, or how many of 'em, you've always got a real shot at comin' home."

Thank you, Jack. No more questions.

Captain Dunning addressed the courtroom and asked, formally, if either the prosecution or the defense wished to make any further statement. This would not be a full summary of the evidence, just a short summation of the case for both sides.

Harrison Parr declined, on the basis that he was quite certain the court had already made up its mind about the murder charges. Al Surprenant said he would like to make a short statement to the panel. Captain Dunning nodded his assent.

Mack Bedford's attorney faced the five officers. "Gentlemen," he said, "we have heard two incontrovertible pieces of evidence. First, the men who crossed the bridge were the same men who fired the missile. The defendant saw them before and after, and no one has dared to suggest he was incorrect. Second, an illegal Iraqi missile had destroyed four U.S. tanks and murdered twenty serving SEALs and Rangers, all burned to death. And all of this, beyond question.

"The subsequent measure of doubt against the surrender was so strong, the SEAL commander opened fire on them because they may well have been pulling one of their regular tricks, pretending to surrender. In his opinion, and in mine, they had done quite sufficient damage for one day.

"I therefore ask the court to find Lt. Cdr. Mackenzie Bedford not guilty on all charges. Thank you for listening to me."

Captain Dunning stood up and called for a two-hour recess during which time everyone could have lunch. The court would reconvene at 1400 hours, when the verdicts would be announced.

The captain led the way out, followed by his four-man panel. Mack Bedford walked across to Commander Surprenant and offered his hand, stating quite simply, "Thank you, sir. No one could have done more."

"We're golden on the murder," replied Al. "And I've crushed the Geneva Conventions. Our only problem is they may have been told to find you guilty of something. Just to placate the media and to protect the Middle East peace talks. I don't think the navy is that corrupt, but the president is our C-in-C, and if he has nudged Defense, informing them his advisers do not want you exonerated completely, there may be trouble ahead."

"Well, what have I done wrong?"

"Nothing. But I have to warn you—we are dealing with politicians, right here in the near background. They might just want some small, vague offense to be proven, and that way they can pension you off."

"Pension me! You mean end my career?"

"Possibly. Honorable discharge with full pensions and rights. But nonetheless dismissed from the navy, perhaps for reckless conduct in the face of the enemy."

"Jesus Christ—you mean they can throw me out just like that, with no appeal?"

"They can. But I also think no one wants to do that. Everything depends on the pressure that's been put on the navy by the goddamned politicians. Because to those guys, the life and career of one single naval officer are nothing. They'll go on about such a small sacrifice, perhaps to help bring peace to the entire Middle East."

"Guess it's only a small sacrifice if you're one of them," said Mack.

"Yeah. But not if you happen to be Lt. Cdr. Mackenzie Bedford, right?"

———•◆•———

Captain Dunning and the other four panel members gathered in the anteroom behind the court. Sandwiches and mineral water were brought in, and two armed naval guards were on duty outside in the corridor. The atmosphere was very formal, and unaccountably tense. Not a smile passed between them as they silently weighed the evidence that could destroy the career and life of one of the most outstanding SEAL officers on the base.

"Gentlemen," said Boomer, "I would like to deal first with the critical issue that dominates the murder charges. And that is the question of the surrender. Because plainly if it had just been a missile and gun battle across the river, then Mack would never have been charged."

Everyone nodded agreement.

"However, we do have a very different set of circumstances here, and we are all well aware of them." The captain read from his notes, and then from a file of papers in front of him. "The Geneva Conventions," he said, "permit using deceptions, or ruses, to mislead the enemy. That much is definite whether or not we agree with Commander Surprenant about their relevance to this particular case. I, by the way, do agree with him. Nonetheless, Geneva specifically prohibits some deceptions. And, I quote, 'Feigning surrender in order to lure the enemy into a trap' is one of them. Maybe the most important. The gist of this convention is obvious. The ruse is strictly forbidden because it causes soldiers to suspect all surrendering combatants of using this subterfuge. And this can lead to horrifying results, the principal one being that soldiers, as a matter of course, may become unwilling to accept any prisoner, and much prefer to kill him right away."

Boomer Dunning paused and looked around. Everyone was stern, thoughtful, and willing to be led by the former nuclear submarine commander.

"There are ample examples of Iraqi terrorists feigning surrender. Mack Bedford was correct to be cautious, to take no chances. I find him not guilty on all charges relating to murder. . . . Any dissent?"

Each man said no, as Captain Dunning knew they would. It was impossible not to understand this trial was being run under some kind of code. No navy court-martial was going to convict the lieutenant commander of any kind of homicide. Not unless they wanted to risk outright riot conditions in the U.S. armed forces.

As to the issue of the Geneva Conventions, Boomer Dunning said flatly, "Surprenant is plainly right. The accords cannot apply to these murderous mobs with the illegal missiles. And, with your support, I'm going to order any and all charges involving the rules of war to be dismissed. Agreed?"

"Agreed."

"Which brings us to the final, somewhat minor, issue of reckless conduct in the face of the enemy." Captain Dunning seemed saddened yet resigned to the wearisome issue of finding the SEAL battle commander guilty of *something*. The orders had been passed down from the highest authority in the nation. Not to cooperate would be, in effect, to defy the commander in chief, the president of the United States. Boomer Dunning was privately sickened by the entire process. Reckless conduct! Jesus Christ, these fucking madmen had just murdered twenty members of the Special Forces. And he, Boomer, had been charged with the task of finding Lieutenant Commander Bedford guilty of being reckless.

Now he spoke confidentially to his panel. "Look," he said, "none of us much likes this, being more or less told to find Mack guilty of recklessness, and I would like to ask the views of each one of you."

All three lieutenant commanders were reluctant to convict but were not sufficiently rebellious to go against the wishes of the president of the panel. The fourth and youngest member, the lieutenant, Jonjo Adams from Alabama, was a SEAL. And he was very concerned. He looked at Boomer and said quietly, "Sir, like all of us, I'd be proud to fight under Mack Bedford's command. And we can sit here for a thousand years, and I ain't never going to find him guilty of anything. He did what was right. I was in Baghdad when that bomb went off strapped to one of the surrender guys. A buddy of mine had his head blown off. If I'd been at the bridge with Mack, I'd have shot 'em myself."

"I understand," replied Boomer. "And since I feel much the same, I'm going to find him not guilty of reckless conduct. That's the best I can do. But I will have to issue some kind of a reprimand. That's the absolute minimum I can do"—he paused for almost ten seconds before blurting out—"in this whole fucking lousy, rotten business." All four members of the panel saw Boomer Dunning brush his coat sleeve across his eyes and walk to the other side of the room because he could not bear anyone to see him this upset.

They ate their sandwiches almost in silence. The clock ticked away the minutes until 1400 hours, at which time all five of them walked back into the courtroom and took their places. Everyone else was awaiting their arrival.

Captain Dunning made no preamble. He said simply, "Lt. Cdr. Mackenzie Bedford, you have been charged with the murder of twelve Iraqi citizens. The court finds you not guilty. You were charged with several offenses against the Geneva Conventions, and these the court has dismissed out of hand, thanks to the wise counsel of Commander Surprenant. You were further charged with reckless conduct in the face of the enemy. The court finds you not guilty."

Mack Bedford turned to shake the hand of his attorney. But Captain Dunning was not through.

"The court, however, finds that this was not a textbook military operation. Several SEALs were ready to open fire if a fake surrender was being enacted. And the court detected an element of panic. With this in mind, I have issued against Lieutenant Commander Bedford, a GOMOR, a General Officer Memorandum of Reprimand. The court is now closed."

Mack Bedford was appalled. He turned to Al Surprenant and almost cried out, "Sir, this ends my career as a SEAL team leader. I'm banned from command, out of the promotion ladder."

"As I feared," replied his attorney. "Very much as I feared."

CHAPTER 3

My dearest Anne,

Right now the whole world seems to be falling apart. Only the thought of seeing you and Tommy is keeping me going. The Navy has been very decent about my payoffs, my pensions, and the extent of our health insurance. Commander Surprenant says it's "conscience money."

By the way, one of the guys on the panel which heard the court-martial has resigned from the Navy "in disgust." He's Brian Antrim, a surface ship missile director and a lt. commander. There's a lot of unrest over what happened to me, but at least they never released my name.

I guess I mentioned I could have stayed and taken some kind of office job, maybe INTEL or Mission Planning. But I would never have advanced, not with a GOMOR hanging over me. Anyway, I only know combat command, and that's now denied me.

There's no place here for an out-of-work Team Leader. So it's gotta be sayanara SEALs. God knows what will happen to us now. I've had a lot of offers of help from some highly placed guys. But I guess right now we need to concentrate on Tommy and getting him fixed up. Tell him to get ready for a lot of fishing with his dad.

All my love and I'll see you next week,
Mack

He walked over to the mailbox and posted his letter. After all these years, it was the last letter he would ever send from this old, familiar place. Mack was scheduled to leave on Tuesday from the North Air Station on a navy flight to Norfolk, Virginia, then take another navy flight up to the New Brunswick Navy Station in Maine. From there he would take a bus home to Dartford.

Walking back from the mailbox, he passed a couple of young SEALs he had helped to train. Each one saluted him sharply, but it wasn't the same anymore. There was something in their eyes, something wary, cautious, as if they were offering the ultimate military sign of respect to the wrong man, to some kind of an outcast who really should not be here.

Everyone knew Mack Bedford was finished, though very few knew why. Those who did were inclined to keep their distance in these final days of the brilliant SEAL commander. They were keeping their distance from a man whose heart was surely broken. A man whose private grief and regret really had no place on a naval station where young tigers were being revved up to face the enemy.

Mack Bedford understood. His friends were dead. His acquaintances were reluctant. There was no longer much to say right here in this cauldron of military training. This is a place where joy is measured in battlefield triumph, and where defeat has not a friend in the world. Lieutenant Commander Bedford had become the embodiment of that defeat.

He took his meals alone in his room, mostly because it was too awkward for him to engage in conversation. How many times could he hear other SEALs tell him how sorry they were that this had happened and how much he would be missed?

What was there to say? Certainly not the gut-wrenching truth that in the blackness of his own despair he had given very serious consideration to blowing his brains out. And that if he had not been married to the spectacularly beautiful Anne, with a little boy who needed him so badly, he probably would have done so. SEALs don't bare their souls like that. Self-examination does not sit comfortably in their profession. They are trained to ignore personal feelings and needs, and to complete the mission. They are taught to train physically until they are close to the breaking point. And then to kill. Always to capture or kill the enemy on behalf of the United States. Men like that don't usually spend a lot of time on self-pity.

"Oh, hell, I'll be all right." "Don't worry about me. I got plenty of options." "Maybe a security business, or a partnership in a fishing boat back in Maine. I got all kinds of stuff." "Anyway, I've probably been in the navy for long enough."

Long enough? How could it ever be long enough? What would "long enough" be? Maybe a thousand years? Because it would surely be a thousand years before the ethos of the SEALs could ever be driven into the backwaters of his mind.

Mack Bedford could scarcely remember any other life. He knew only the discipline, the unquestioning code of conduct, what was expected of him, and, as he grew into a field commander, what he expected of those young men who fought alongside him.

He had once read, and never forgotten, a book written by John Bertrand, Australia's victorious America's Cup helmsman in 1983. The Aussie wrote of racing yacht crews, men fighting against the odds to defeat the Americans in front of a world audience. "You can get them to go a long way for you by frightening them," he wrote. "But if you want them to go all the way, they've got to love you."

Mack's men had always loved him. And they were surely going to miss his steadfast words of command, sometimes cautious, sometimes daring, but always sound. They were going to miss the hell out of him. And most of them did not yet realize how much. All they sensed was an inner anxiety. *What the hell's it gonna be like out there, without the boss?*

The last three days passed slowly. Mack spent most of them alone. He packed and shipped to Maine some books and memorabilia, his uniforms, permanent SEAL equipment, personal mask and flippers, bearing the number he had been given at BUDs. He would travel home in civilian clothes, carrying just his big battle-scarred leather suitcase, the one he'd carried to hell and back, from the Afghan mountains to Baghdad, ar-Ramadi, Qatar, and Kuwait.

First thing tomorrow morning Jack Thomas would drive him to the North Air Station in the middle of San Diego Bay. Meanwhile, with less than twenty-four hours before his departure, Mack would attack the four-mile course along the beach, just one more training run along the edge of the water, straight down memory lane, one more attempt to drive his body to the limit.

He was, of course, no longer doing this in a manic last-ditch effort to hit a peak of fitness before combat duty on some foreign field, as he so often did. This run was not for any reason really. He was doing it, just . . . well . . . for the good times. The only difference was, now Mack would run all alone.

He jogged down to the ocean, and far down the beach he could see a BUDs Class pounding back toward him, strung out, in a long, irregular line, splashing, gasping, striving, driving on, keeping up, dropping out, instructors shouting, demanding to know whose heart wasn't in it, who wanted to quit, who had nothing more to give. Nothing much changed here on the SEAL training beach at Coronado, where, every week, hearts were broken, reputations forged, and men became such men as they had never dreamed possible.

Mack could see a group of guests at the Hotel del Coronado standing out on the terrace watching the guys running. It looked like the opening scene from *Chariots of Fire*, but these runners were not the carefree young bucks of Cambridge University Athletic Club in 1920s England. These runners, right here in Coronado, wore khaki, the color of violent men.

This strip of tidal sand represented some kind of Greek tragedy where Navy SEALs prepared to go to war. It was a place of broken dreams, a place where ambitions were ruined, limitations ruthlessly exposed. Where only the best of the best could possibly survive.

My country expects me to be physically and mentally stronger than my enemy. . . . If I am knocked down, I will get up, every time. . . . I am never out of the fight. . . . I am a United States Navy SEAL.

The words of the SEAL creed whispered through the mind of Mack Bedford as he settled into his stride, every pace a stretch, every ten yards of wet sand covered with maximum effort. That was the way to complete the run, the only way, to make every yard of the journey the hardest yard you ever ran—just to be the best, the best, always the best.

Mack passed the BUDs Class a mile up the beach, and then drove himself on to the two-mile mark, where he turned back, running with all of his strength toward his start point. Only a very few of the BUDs students would ever attain fitness like that, because Mack Bedford's long years of brutal daily training—running, lifting, swimming—had granted him animal strength. He was not like other men. Nothing like other men.

He smiled as he looked across at the BUDs Class, sweating and straining, lifting logs the size of telephone poles, nearly killing themselves hoisting the huge weight above their heads, the bigger guys taking the biggest strain. Mack watched them finally drop the logs down onto the sand, heard the familiar thud that shook the beach, and then the old SEAL ritual.

Class leader: *Instructor Mills!*

Followed instantly by the class roar: *HOO-YAH, INSTRUCTOR MILLS!*

No one really remembers precisely how it happened, but U.S. Navy SEALs have this private word: "HOO-YAH." The BUDs students use it for greeting an instructor, and they use it instead of "Understand and will comply." They use it instead of "Yes" or "Right away, sir."

Standing there on the sand, catching his breath, Mack Bedford remembered his own stint as a SEAL instructor, pretending to be Gengis Khan, right here on this very spot. Frightening the living daylights out of the guys, pushing them, humiliating them, testing them, to find how much unfairness each of them could take without cracking. And how moved he was that, in the end, the survivors understood he wanted only the best for them.

HOO-YAH, INSTRUCTOR BEDFORD!

And now it was over. He walked back up the beach, and past the Grinder, the square of blacktop where generations of BUDs trainees had given their all, trying to become full-fledged SEALs. This was the square where they handed out the golden Tridents. The square where

Mack Bedford, Honor Man, had received his from a SEAL admiral. That remained the proudest moment of his life.

That night he dined alone in his room. The last supper. He couldn't face company, understanding, questions, support, and sympathy. Not tonight. He sat in solitude, still trying to accept that in five weeks he had somehow gone from highly regarded SEAL lieutenant commander to civilian, with an official officer's reprimand forever hanging over his head.

Captain Dunning had mentioned the word "panic." What a truly shocking allegation. If anyone had asked, Mack would have settled for "blind rage." But not "panic." He reached for a pocket dictionary he always kept in his room. And the definition made him feel, if anything, worse: *Panic—a feeling of fear and anxiety.* If anyone had panicked at the bridge, it sure as hell was not him. He could have been accused, probably fairly, of seeking revenge for his dead buddies, or even of using unreasonable force. Those moments had, after all, occurred during his own "hours of the wolf." But not fear and anxiety. The hell with that.

Mack slept not a wink through his last long night within the confines of his personal alma mater, SPECWARCOM. It was a night he had never dreamed would come. If he slept, he would wake up a civilian. Which was probably why he lay awake, staring at the ceiling, torturing himself over the events that had all proved to be beyond his control. He couldn't face company, and understanding.

At first light he climbed out of bed, showered, and stepped into his civilian clothes. He put on a clean white shirt, dark-gray slacks, loafers, and a blue blazer. He wore no tie but still looked every inch an officer. He picked up the morning newspaper and had a cup of coffee, black with sugar, and then sat quietly to wait for 0730 when Lt. Barry Mason would arrive to collect him and walk with him to Jack Thomas's armored vehicle for the drive over to the air base. He felt like a man awaiting the arrival of the executioner.

Barry Mason arrived on time and picked up the leather bag. Neither of them felt like speaking. The young lieutenant just nodded and said, "Mack," before adding, "This is probably the most God-awful fucking day of my life."

"Mine too," said the boss.

They stepped out into the morning light and began the three-hundred-yard walk toward the main gate, and as they did so, both men became conscious of throngs of people crowding around the entrance, beyond which was parked the armored vehicle. It quickly became apparent that it was some kind of formation. It also became apparent that every single member of the SPECWARCOM campus, officers and other ranks, were, on this morning, at the gate.

They stood in silence. It was an unmistakable silent protest at the "justice" that had been handed out to the retiring SEAL officer. As Mack and Barry walked between the two four-deep lines of stone-faced men, a chief petty officer suddenly roared at the top of his lungs, *LT. CDR. MACKENZIE BEDFORD!* That deep-voiced SEAL response split the morning air, echoing up into the clear skies, rehearsed yet at once spontaneous. Every last man from admiral to BUDs student shouted the response—*HOO-YAH, MACK BEDFORD!* It was a cry from the uneasy soul of this stern and dedicated garrison of Special Forces. The last HOO-YAH.

Mack Bedford looked to neither his left nor his right. But as he reached the gate and the barrier was lifted, he turned one final time and formally saluted them all. Then he turned away, toward the waiting car. And no one saw him fighting to control his tears as he left them.

They rode in silence out along the familiar road to North Island. When they reached the air station's administrative building they pulled up and stepped out onto the holding area. The U.S. Navy Lockheed Aries jet was already running, and Lieutenant Mason carried Mack's bag to the steps that led up into the cabin. He handed it over while Jack Thomas stood to one side, visibly more upset than the other two.

Mack put down the bag and threw his arms around him. "Thanks, Jack," he said. "Thanks for everything."

Jack managed to mutter, "Good-bye, sir."

The lieutenant commander picked up his bag in his left hand and walked toward Barry Mason. "Good-bye, kid," he said. "It's been a privilege to serve with you."

Lieutenant Mason shook Mack's hand and said softly, "You'll always be a hero to me, sir."

And with that, Mackenzie Bedford left them, moving swiftly up the steps and taking his seat on the right side of the aircraft. The door slammed shut, and it immediately taxied to the end of the runway.

Both SEALs stood and watched it race down the blacktop, gathering speed to 200 miles per hour before lifting off to the southwest, leaving the great military cemetery on Point Loma to starboard. Mack stared out at the lines and lines of white and gray headstones, and he thought again of Frank and Charlie and Billy-Ray and the rest, and the aura of sadness rested crushingly on his mind.

Within him once more, he sensed the rising "hours of the wolf," the anger, the resentment, the desire for brutal vengeance. But it was too late for that. Much too late.

Back on the edge of the runway Barry and Jack stood to attention. As the aircraft left the ground they both snapped one last formal, solemn salute to the departing SEAL commander. Unrehearsed. Then Barry Mason shook his head, and said, "HOO-YAH, Mack. You were some kind of an officer."

The Aries banked hard left over the western reaches of San Diego Bay and turned onto its course over the southern part of the city and out over the northern peaks of the Sierre Madre. From there the aircraft headed east, straight across Arizona, New Mexico, North Texas, and Oklahoma. They flew at around 500 miles per hour to Tennessee, running north of both Memphis and Nashville. They crossed the Appalachian Mountains and dropped down to 20,000 feet over North Carolina before landing in Norfolk, the great U.S. Navy base that lies hard by the southern coastal border of the state of Virginia.

It was 1700 hours, and they were right on time. Mack's onward flight, another Aries, was waiting, engines running, as if a slightly embarrassed navy did not wish to spend one extra second saying goodbye to Mackenzie Bedford.

Mack grabbed his bag and walked down one set of aircraft steps and straight to another 50 yards away. No one met him, no one spoke to him, no one made contact. The second flight was empty save for the flight crew, and they took off immediately on this 650-mile journey to America's most northeastern state.

It took almost two hours, and by the time the aircraft arrived it was dark, around 2100, long after the last coastal bus from Brunswick had left for the picturesque ride down Route 127 to Georgetown and Bay Point. Mack was given an officer's room in which to spend the night, and the following morning, shortly after 0700, he walked out of the base and down to the bus stop.

The summer morning was already warm, and there were seagulls overhead wheeling above the bays, swooping down toward the mighty Kennebec River, the longest in Maine, and the great waterway that for four centuries has floated Maine-built ships of all types down to the sea on its high, rough tides.

Mack's bus was on time. It was an elderly single-deck wagon that would take him down a little-used route to his home on the outskirts of the little town of Dartford on the east bank of the river. Dartford lies 10 miles downstream from the great shipbuilding town of Bath, home of the century-old Bath Iron Works (BIW), whose motto is "Ahead of schedule and under budget."

Here great yachts, cruisers, and warships have rolled out of the workshops and down the ways to the Gulf of Maine in an unstoppable convoy of excellence. J. P. Morgan's gigantic black-and-gold yacht *Corsair,* all 343 feet of her, was built at BIW. As was Mike Vanderbilt's sensational America's Cup J-Boat, *Ranger,* winner in 1937, and never beaten in any race she ever entered.

In World War II there were more destroyers built at BIW than were constructed in the entire empire of Japan—eighty-two of them. Today, BIW still concentrates on guided-missile destroyers, frigates, and cruisers, principally for the U.S. Navy.

Bath stands on a fabulous deepwater harbor with a mean range of tide of 6.5 feet. All the facilities at BIW are on the west bank of the Kennebec, and above it all, like a spare part from Jurassic Park, looms the tallest lifting crane in the Western world—old Number Eleven, which can hoist a 220-ton modular ship's part straight off the jetty and into place on the hull, accurate to about a billionth of an inch, depending on who's driving.

The Kennebec River itself is 150 miles long, rising way north out of Moosehead Lake, which stretches for more than 30 miles among the high peaks of the Longfellow Mountains. The upper reaches are scarcely navigable until the hard-flowing stream out of the mountains reaches Maine's capital city of Augusta, 45 miles from the ocean.

At this point the Kennebec widens, and by the time it reaches Bath it becomes saltwater and tidal, so powerful are the ebb and flow from the gulf. The lower reaches are truly majestic, as the great river surges by wooded islands and jutting promontories, coves, back channels, and marshes.

Dartford itself lies on the north bank of a deepwater bay that cuts northwest out of the main stream. It started off as a boatyard at the beginning of the nineteenth century but slowly grew into a major shipyard surrounded by a small town almost entirely dependent on the shipbuilding industry for its existence.

In the boom years, when Bath Iron Works was swamped with work, the yard at Dartford was used as a runoff to construct warships. As the years passed, many a skilled shipwright, engineer, or welder made the southern journey from the ironworks to set up home in the picturesque seaward community of Dartford. Though dominated, like Bath, by the industry, this was a more bucolic spot, with a small fishing fleet and a way of life that was more relaxed. At least it was as relaxed as may be expected on the spectacular, but often viciously cold, windswept coast of Maine, where the summers are short, the snows long, and the seas powerful.

Mack Bedford's family members were true Down-Easters. His forefathers hewed granite and sent massive tree logs down the Kennebec River to help build some of America's greatest cities. His great-grandfather built yachts at BIW, but his grandfather came to live in Dartford around the same time old Sam Remson took over the shipyard and started to build warships.

The Bedfords had been a fixture at both Remsons and Dartford for almost a century, ships' engineers, and in the case of Mack's father, a guided-missile specialist, one of Harry Remson's most valuable men. Mack himself was the first male member of his family for six generations to seek a life beyond the rugged coastlines, rough waters, and awesome beauty of the Pine Tree State.

Remsons had built frigates for the U.S. Navy, and the yard had provided many specialist parts not only for Bath Iron Works but also for the huge naval shipyards at Newport News, Virginia, Todd's in Seattle, and General Dynamic's Electric Boat Division in Connecticut.

But the complex patterns of modern warfare had caused an undeniable shrinkage in the numbers of ships being ordered by the U.S. Navy, principally because no one dares to sink them—at least not very often, save for the occasional bunch of turbaned maniacs happy to detonate and destroy themselves and the warship together. Strike rate since 9/11: zero.

Remsons' survival now depended not on the U.S. government handing them a $500 million frigate contract every three years. It depended on Marine Nationale, the French Navy, and its regular order for Remsons to build them a guided-missile frigate. It came every three years, the only orders placed by Marine Nationale outside of France since the 1980s.

The French have, by any standards, a powerful navy, larger than Great Britain's, with a twelve-strong submarine fleet, fifteen guided-missile destroyers, twenty frigates, a forty-thousand-ton *Charles de Gaulle* aircraft carrier, and more than forty-five thousand personnel with sixty-five hundred active reservists.

The old tradition of purchasing one frigate from Remsons every thirty-six months was continued partly out of loyalty to a shipyard where the craftsmanship was legendary. And partly because the French Navy enjoyed owning state-of-the-art U.S. technology. However, almost every other warship in the French fleet was built at the naval yards in either Brest, Brittany, the main Atlantic base of Marine Nationale; Cherbourg on the English Channel; Saint-Nazaire on the Loire estuary; or Lorient on the north coast of the Bay of Biscay.

Remsons was unique in the French military's pantheon of operations. As the years passed, and every order for U.S. frigates and destroyers seemed to go automatically to Bath Iron Works, the position of France in the lives of Dartford's citizens grew in importance. The fact was, without the Marine Nationale, Dartford would almost certainly perish.

And there were rumors, always rumors. But during the past six months, with the French elections looming, there were worse rumors than usual: that a new Gaullist potential president was on the rise and had made it clear that there would be *no foreign orders* for the French military. None, that is. *Rien.* That included guns, missiles, tanks, aircraft, and ships. In the future, everything would be made in France. France for the French. *Viva la France!* And the proud little shipyard on the coast of Maine was facing the Valley of Death. More than 87 percent of Dartford residents owed their living to Remsons.

It was to this rather gloomy prospect that Mack Bedford was now headed. Because of the overriding problem of Tommy's illness, Anne had spared her husband from the worst of the rumors. He now sat quietly on the bus as it rolled down Route 127, all along the east bank of the Kennebec River, upon which an unusual gusting summer squall was blowing off the gulf, against the ebb and causing a very rough surface.

He still felt a sense of unreality, as if his cell phone would somehow ring any moment now, and a voice would snap, "Lieutenant Commander Bedford? That's it, sir, we're going. Prepare platoons for packdown. Depart 0500 hours Thursday. Bagram Air Base, Afghanistan. Classified rules apply as from now."

Even the thought of his old life brought an ineffable sense of utter sadness upon him. He stared through the bus window at the typical Maine waterfront view, with dense dark-green pine woods growing so close to the ocean they would feel the lash of the spray. The granite ledges that stretched far out into the coastal waters formed a minefield for all but the most careful and skillful of mariners.

The bus drew to a halt at the head of a long, straight road that led down to the wide estuary of the Kennebec. The doors opened, and he stepped down carrying just his leather bag. There was no one at the bus stop and no one walking along the long, narrow road home.

Mack and Anne owned a classic white clapboard Maine farmhouse with a barn and a view across marshland to the water. The shipyard was located way behind the backyard, more than a half mile away, but it was omnipotent, a backdrop to the little town, with rising cranes, tall, but not as tall as old Number Eleven up the road at Bath.

From the bus stop it was a one-thousand-yard walk, and Mack set off, marching down the middle of the road, staring at the waterfront beyond the house, longing to see Anne, longing to see Tommy, but dreading the latest news from the doctors.

No traffic passed him, and the wind dropped, giving way to a warm morning in what ought to be paradise, but on this day was not even close. Fifty yards from the front gate Mack saw someone come hurtling out of the front door and across the driveway to the road. For a split second he held Anne's gaze, and then she ran toward him, and hurled herself into his arms, saying over and over, "Thank God, my darling, thank God you're here—I saw you from the upstairs window."

For almost a full minute he held his powerful arms around her, saying nothing, marveling as always at the beauty of her body and the dark luster of her hair, which cascaded over her shoulders and his eyes. Finally, he released her and stared into her deep blue eyes, and said softly, "As homecomings go, this one's sure got a lot of promise."

Anne laughed at him. She always laughed at him. In fact, it was his gift of real humor, coupled with a vibrant physical presence, that had first attracted her. She once told him it was like being married to a cross between Johnny Carson and Rocky Marciano.

"You don't even remember Rocky Marciano," he'd chuckled. "He died about twenty years before you were born."

"Yes, but my grandpa knew him—he was a police chief in Brockton, Massachusetts, where Rocky lived. I've seen pictures."

"Well, he was nothing like me. He was a fighter. I don't know how to fight. I only know how to kill."

"Oh, that's a relief," she said. "At last I'm safe."

They walked slowly up to the house, and just before they opened the front door, Mack stopped and said, "Annie, how is he?"

"Not good. Just starting to show all the early signs of the disease."

"What are they?" asked Mack, frowning.

"Oh, signs of aggression, unreasonable, and of course the memory loss. Long-term, that is. He can remember anything for about five minutes. But the next day he can't seem to grasp that he ever learned it. The school's really worried about him."

"Jesus," replied Mack. "Where is he? Poor little guy."

"He's still in bed right now," she said. "This is another sign—unusual tiredness. And the doctors say it will get worse and worse."

"Is it leukemia, like they first thought?"

"Not really. It's similar, but it involves a complete breakdown of the nervous system. And he needs a complete bone marrow transplant to give him any chance of long-term recovery. The hospital says he's just too young for them to attempt it. Trouble is, if we wait, it may be too late."

"And no one knows how the hell he caught it?"

"Not really."

"Christ!" said Mack. "It's not as if he's from weak bloodlines, right? He's from generations of stonecutters, lumberjacks, shipwrights, Navy SEALs, and goddamned police chiefs. He ought to be as strong as a fighting bull!"

"Guess it doesn't work like that," said Anne. "I just find it all so sad."

Mack closed the door and put down his bag. Once more he took his very beautiful wife in his arms, and kissed her longingly. Then he told her, "We'll get him fixed up. Somehow, by Christ, we'll come up with something."

"Look, he may come down any moment now. Is there anything you'd like to do beyond the obvious? Let me fix you some breakfast?"

"That would be great," he said. "But you look wonderful, and fried eggs with sausage and hash browns comes a very distant fourth to the obvious."

"Shhh," she said, staring into his gray-blue eyes. "Or you'll persuade me to cast care to the winds. And we have to be at the hospital at noon. Tommy's test results are ready. They may even want to keep him there overnight."

"Does he mind that?"

"Not really. I put him to bed and stay in the room with him. But he gets very tired, very quickly, and then I drive back here by myself, and worry about him for the rest of the night."

Mack kissed her again, and said, "Can I have my breakfast out on the front stoop? And do we have a newspaper yet?"

"I'll just check Tommy, and then I'll bring it. Go and sit down. I'll get you some coffee."

Mack's father had long ago turned the front stoop of the house into a screened porch, and Anne had set a milk-white cloth on the table, with a small vase of pink beach roses in the center. The wicker furniture was wide and comfortable with broad blue-and-white-striped cushions. Mack sank gratefully into the rocker and stared out, down to the ever-widening estuary of the Kennebec. The great tidal flow, which had started far to the north in Moosehead, would soon be spilling out into the ocean. Within two miles it would surge past its lonely guardian island of Sequin, a place for which President George Washington personally signed the deeds more than two hundred years ago.

Above the island stands one of the most famous, and indeed the second oldest, lighthouse on this vast and rugged coastline. The Sequin light towers 180 feet above the ocean, just two miles offshore. Mack Bedford, despite his wonderful seaward view, could not quite see it, even on the clearest day. But when the autumn fog banks rolled in and a dank, hollow white blanket spread over the inshore waters, Mack could hear the powerful lighthouse foghorn boom out its warning, as stark and as lonely as a Basin Street trombone.

He loved this place. He passionately loved Anne. And he loved his little boy. What a cruel trick of the Almighty to deliver two such hammer blows to his life—charged with murder and effectively sacked from the SEALs and the monstrous threat of Tommy dying from an untreatable disease.

Still, there had to be hope, and when Anne came sashaying onto the porch bearing hot coffee and that morning's copy of the *Portland Express,* the clouds lifted from him, and he smiled at her and pulled her down onto his lap and kissed her yet again. "I love you, Mrs. Bedford," he told her. "And I'm always thinking of you, no matter where I am."

"Even at that firefight on the Euphrates?" she said.

"Even then. Especially then. Because I thought for one awful moment our marriage might end the only way it ever could—until I reloaded, that is."

Anne, as ever, laughed at him. "You want burned sausage and hard-boiled eggs?"

"Not really."

"Then you'd better let me get up."

Mack released her and reached for the coffeepot, poured a mugful, and hit it with a couple of lumps of brown sugar. He stirred it thoughtfully and then picked up the newspaper and scanned the front page.

FIVE MORE U.S. DEATHS IN IRAQ—
ILLEGAL MISSILE BLAMED

Baghdad. Tuesday. The French-built tank-buster missile known as the Diamondhead hit and destroyed one tank and one armored vehicle on the desert road west of Baghdad yesterday. Five American combat troops were killed in the attack, which was launched from a derelict house in the northern suburbs.

It was not conducted in battle conditions. The Americans were returning to base after a mission against an insurgent cell operating in the bombed-out regions near the Tigris River. The attack was sudden, without warning. There were no survivors in either of the two armored vehicles, and reports again confirm the victims were burned alive.

The U.S. military has protested in the strongest possible terms to the UN Security Council, which has unanimously banned the missile throughout the world as "a crime against humanity." The UN secretary-general confirmed that the attack had all the hallmarks of the banned missile, and that a formal warning was being issued to the government of Iran against supplying the Diamondhead to Iraqis or any other Muslim terror group currently operating in the Middle East.

A spokesman for the U.S. armed forces in Iraq stated last night that the insurgents seemed to have a constant supply of this missile. "Either that," he said, "or they still have a large stockpile—probably hidden in the desert with Saddam's goddamned uranium 235, which was also difficult as hell to find."

The spokesman, a U.S. Army lieutenant colonel, was clearly very angry at this latest attack. "We're all angry," he said. "You'd be angry if you saw how these guys died. The worst part is we have twice been close to intercepting the supply.

"Both times we were just a fraction too late. We believe the missiles come through the foothills of the Zagros Mountains and then cross the frontier into Iraq, somehow getting across the river to the north of Abadan. But that's a huge area to patrol, and we have limited resources."

A White House spokesman said last night, "The president has sent a signal to the government of Iran pointing out that the Diamondhead is officially banned in all countries. And that the world community will not tolerate any Middle Eastern regime continuously ignoring the UN edict." The president had warned the Iranian prime minister that if there was one more American death from the missile, the Security Council would meet in emergency session to consider the possible launch of military action against Iran.

The names of the American dead will not be released until after the families have been informed. But it is believed that at least two of them were U.S. Navy SEALs, one of them a lieutenant junior grade.

Mack Bedford shook his head and muttered, "Those murdering bastards." Then he turned inside the newspaper to an Associated Press feature, which concentrated on the source of the missile, France. The writer, a retired U.S. Army colonel, claimed the Diamondhead was still being shipped to Iran. He also believed the French government had a duty to find the arms factory and bring the owners to justice. He stated that the current scandal was bringing no glory to the French Republic and indeed reflected very badly on the nation as a whole. "The mere image of anyone growing rich off the lives of U.S. military personnel

being burned alive would, in the end, sicken all right-thinking nations." However, his contact in the Elysée Palace gave something of a
Gallic shrug and told him, "France has always been the world leader in
the manufacture of heat-seeking guided missiles, and the industry has
many branches in many departments throughout the country. Sometimes things happen which are beyond our control." He added, unhelpfully, that France was a very big place, and they had no idea where
the Diamondhead was made. "There is a shady side to the arms industry, *monsieur*, as I am sure you realize. Mostly, both buyers and sellers
cover their tracks very well."

Mack put down the newspaper and sipped his coffee. In his mind
was a vision of the Phantom of the Opera in a black cloak hoisting the
killer missile onto a horse-drawn farm wagon driven by cackling Arabs
wearing robes and turbans. "Murdering bastards," he said for the second time in as many minutes.

Midnight
Montpellier Munitions
Forest of Orléans, France

It was impossible to see precisely what was being loaded onto the
sixteen-wheel freight truck that was backed up to the concrete dock on
the deserted south side of the arms factory. A huge tarp was draped
over the entrance and right over the back end of the truck. Only someone standing inside the cargo area could possibly have seen the five-
foot-long wooden crates, three feet high and three feet wide, being
transported on forklift loaders and then stacked inside the heavy-duty
vehicle. They piled them three wide, and three high, and there were
four stacks, thirty-six crates, each one containing six guided missiles.
The crates were unmarked.

Beyond the loading dock, six armed guards patrolled. There were
four more constantly walking around the chain-link perimeter fence.
The gates that led out to the private road that cut through the forest
between Montpellier and the highway were locked. Two armed guards

manned the concrete security office outside the gates, where a steel barrier formed another line of Montpellier defense. Until that barrier was raised, no one was going anywhere.

Inside the canopy the first shipment was loaded and secure, attended personally by Montpellier's chairman and owner, Henri Foche himself, attired as usual in his immaculate dark suit, shiny black shoes, white shirt, and dark-blue tie. No overcoat. Just his trademark scarlet handkerchief placed jauntily in his breast pocket. Satisfied that almost eleven million dollars worth of military hardware was safely in place, he ordered the rear door of the truck to be slammed shut and locked. Not even the driver would be told the combination that would open it. The chairman would take care of that personally. Only his trusted number two, rocket scientist Yves Vincent, was privy to that information, and he was waiting in the black Mercedes with Marcel and Raymond, ready to accompany the convoy on its journey.

There were three more trucks waiting to be loaded, which would bring the total number of missiles to 864, with a street value, as they say in the drug trade, of one hundred million dollars. Wholesale value to Henri Foche was a little over forty-three million, paid before shipment from the coffers of the Iranian government, which had been, literally, awash with cash since oil prices went straight through the roof of the mosque.

Not all the missiles were going to the Iraqi insurgents. There would be a shipment of 200 for the army of Hezbollah, currently hunkered down in Beirut, awaiting their next chance to strike out at Israel. There would be 200 for the embattled warriors of Hamas, in their grim but hopeless fight against the iron-souled regulars of the Israeli defense force. Around 200 were earmarked for the Afghan tribesmen of the Taliban in their war against the United States and Great Britain. And there would be 162 for the insurgents fighting in Iraq, to be distributed by terrorist commanders. The rest would remain in Iran.

The remaining three security trucks were loaded within an hour, and at one thirty the convoy pulled out, running through the blackness of the forest toward the city of Orléans, which was, essentially, deserted. They drove past several thousand statues of Joan of Arc, the Maid of Orléans, who, right here in 1429, persuaded King Charles VII to attack the besieging forces of England and liberate the city. Joan thus provided the turning point in the Hundred Years' War, and the city fathers, ever since, have been determined that no one should ever forget *La Pucelle,* the French peasant girl–warrior from Lorraine. There was thus something gruesomely poetic about Henri Foche's convoy of death, speeding through the historic cradle of French military defiance in order to provide hardware for several different wars.

Also, it was raining like hell. With wipers slashing the downpour off the windshields, they rumbled over the bridge that spans the Loire River and headed south through the Forest of Sologne, forever the refuge of the French aristocracy, a flat, damp, and dismal area. Here French kings for centuries hunted wild boar and deer across the empty heathlands. The area is redolent with marshes, lakes, and wetlands. It also boasts some of the most beautiful châteaus of the Loire, including the mighty Chateau Chambord, the largest and grandest on the entire river. This is a gigantic palace of 440 rooms and 85 staircases, built by King François I in 1519 in a bold attempt to outshine the pope.

François was schizophrenic, since he claimed his chateau would establish him as "one of the greatest builders in the universe." Yet to the end of his days he referred to it only as his "little hunting lodge."

Henri Foche, who nursed similar grandiose ambitions as a national leader, charged straight past this monument to sixteenth-century French architecture, leading the way at the head of his convoy, speeding down Route A71, a few miles east of Chambord. They ran on for another twenty miles before turning west off the highway onto a truly desolate landscape, flat, featureless, and very, very wet. The rain continued to lash down, and the headlights from the trucks cast the only light as far as the eye could see.

Eventually, they turned off and ran through a wide path cut though a small woodland area. When they emerged from the trees on the far side, there before them was a one-mile-long blacktop surface, with small bright lights on either side running into the far distance. They

were switched on only when Foche's four trucks growled their way out
of the woods.

Up ahead was a small cement building, with one single light. Outside was an air-traffic man holding two illuminated sticks to steer
them to the correct spot. To the controller's left stood the four-engine
wide-bodied cargo aircraft, the Ilyushin 11-76, workhorse of the Russian Air Force, Iranian owned but built in the enormous Khimki aviation plant, northwest of Moscow, near Sheremet'yevo Airport.

The Ilyushin is essentially a military freighter, a specialist in heavy
tonnage, requiring ramp loading through its huge rear doors under
the distinctive T tail. Its designers, the Tashkent Aviation Production
Association in Uzbekistan, gave it a high-mounted "shoulder" wing,
with a span measuring more than fifty yards. Its four Russian engines
generate more power than the U.S.-built Lockheed C-141 Starlifter.

The Ilyushin was specifically designed for short-field takeoff, with a
special capacity to handle rough fields, both incoming and leaving. A
total of twenty low-pressure tires on the landing wheels are designed
to bear the weight. This evening the Ilyushin had not even attempted to
land until the Montpellier convoy was within two miles of the runway.

And right now, the air traffic controllers at Tours Airport were wondering where the heck the big Russian military freighter had gone.
Their efforts to locate it, however, were pretty halfhearted, since it was
after all almost two o'clock and no one had suggested an emergency.
They resolved to keep a close lookout for its reappearance, but meanwhile decided to pretend it had not been sighted.

Right now, the entire loading process was being conducted mechan-
ically from hoists and lifts inside the cavernous aircraft. The aircrew
was Iranian, Henri Foche was pacing like a caged jackal, and time was
short.

With every one of Iran's new missiles now loaded, Henri Foche
signed the airway bill and watched the Russian freighter move swiftly
to the head of the runway. The missiles weighed only around forty
thousand pounds, half-capacity, and the aircraft would be gone as rapidly as it had arrived.

Foche and Yves Vincent stood in the rain and watched it screaming forward, climbing steeply away from this rain-swept private runway, accelerating toward its cruising speed of 460 miles per hour. Immediately, the lights went out down the whole length of the blacktop. And spontaneously the two Frenchmen turned and solemnly shook hands before stepping back into the Mercedes for Marcel to deliver them home. It had been an excellent night's work.

Back in air traffic control at Tours Airport, they picked up the radar of the Russian freighter once more, but it was headed due east, directly toward the Swiss Alps, passing only over rich French farmland. They sent a short signal to the airport at Dijon, advising that the freighter had not identified itself, but was not transmitting military radar and anyway was headed for Switzerland. Like the night shift at Tours, the Dijon crew decided to pretend it had never been sighted. Let the Swiss deal with it.

And so the shipment of 864 Diamondhead guided missiles sailed serenely over the high peaks of the Alps and headed for the Balkans, then Bulgaria and the Black Sea. From there they would swerve right along the ridge of the Caucasus Mountains, and on down over Iran to the airport at Ahvaz, which lies a little more than fifty miles from Abadan, down on the Iraqi border.

The journey was less than twenty-five hundred miles and could be accomplished without refueling. By the time the Ilyushin landed, it would be eight o'clock in France, and a brand-new production line of the deadly tank buster would be coming online. Henri Foche did not anticipate business with Iran drying up. Not at all. And for the next few months he resolved to concentrate on his political career and leave the high-tech end of the missile manufacture to the heroically greedy Yves Vincent.

———◆———

Mack Bedford could hear Anne making her way toward the porch, telling Tommy she had a great surprise for him. When he came bursting through the screen door, no one could possibly have dreamed there was anything wrong with him.

Tommy was a very cute kid, tall for his seven years and well built. He had a shock of dark hair and his mother's eyes. When he saw Mack he just stood and yelled, "Daddy! Daddy! Where've you been? I needed you right here."

Mack laughed and grabbed him, holding the little boy high above his head, and then lowering him and wrapping his huge arms around him. "I'm home, Tommy," he said. "Really home, and I'm not going away again. Jesus, you've grown since I saw you. Soon you'll be bigger than me."

"No one's bigger than you, Daddy. Not even a giant."

At this point Anne returned with Mack's breakfast and placed it on the table. For herself she just brought fruit salad and toast.

"What does he get?" asked Mack, and Tommy laughed. "I get cereal," he said. "But not here with you guys. Mom says I can eat it in the kitchen and watch *Invasion of the Deadheads* on television. I see it every week."

"Invasion of the what?" asked Mack, slightly incredulously.

"The Deadheads," said Tommy. "They're so cool. And they do a whole lot of killing if anyone attacks them. Gotta go."

"This is unbelievable," chuckled Mack. "I get back here after fighting a war, my guys are massacred, I'm court-martialed, and my own son rejects me for the goddamned Deadheads."

Anne laughed and said, "I always let him watch it before the hospital. He gets very excited, and he's always in a good mood after seeing it. I have to tell you, in the past month or two he's had a couple of uncontrollable fits of rage. Completely out of character. The doctors say it's part of it."

Mack nodded and chewed luxuriously on a SEAL-sized chunk of sausage. "Are they absolutely sure he's got this ALD?" he asked.

"Not quite. But Dr. Ryan says he keeps displaying more and more of the symptoms."

"And that uncontrollable rage is one of 'em, right?"

"Yes. I guess we have to accept it's a disease of the brain. And it involves the central and peripheral nervous systems. Something about being unable to conduct an impulse. It's a kid's disease, boys only, and from somewhere, somehow, Tommy seems to have it."

"He won't die, will he?"

"I don't know. We might find out more today."

"Anyway, what the hell does ALD stand for?"

"The actual word is kind of in three parts. It's adreno-leuko-dystrophy. Very rare, and apparently incurable. At least it is in this country."

"Does that 'leuko' bit in the middle means it's something like leukemia?"

"I suppose so. But we'll have to wait to speak to the doctor."

"Can they arrest the disease? I mean, stop it from getting worse?"

"I don't think so. I guess that's why everyone is so downbeat about it."

Mack finished his breakfast. "Think he's done with the Deadheads yet?"

"Just about."

"I'll get the gloves, play a little catch with him."

Anne smiled. "I'll get him. But don't wear him out. I don't think he should be asleep when the doctor sees him. He never used to get this tired."

Mack pulled two baseball gloves out of the basket in the corner of the porch. He picked up a couple of baseballs and walked out onto the front lawn. Tommy came running out and joined him, pulled on his glove, and walked out to his regular spot, fifteen yards from his dad.

"Okay, big guy," said Mack. "Lemme see what you got."

Tommy leaned back and threw the ball straight at his father's right shoulder. Mack whipped his left arm across his chest and snagged it neatly. He threw the ball back to Tommy, nice and easy, on his left side. Tommy caught it in the middle of the glove, and then threw a high one straight at his dad. Mack raised his glove high and snapped the catch.

"Thought you'd catch me by surprise, eh?" Mack spoke and threw at the same time, sending the baseball low toward Tommy's left thigh.

The kid snagged it, looked up, and said, "I'll get you, Daddy." And he leaned back and hurled one with all of his strength high and wide. Anne, standing on the porch, heard the ball whack into Mack's glove.

"Hey, that's a pretty good arm you got there," said Mack. "And you've been practicing, waiting to get me."

Tommy laughed again. "I'm gonna get you, Daddy," he said, crouching down, ready to receive. Mack threw one to the right this time, medium height but needing a stretch. Tommy brought his glove over and reached. He caught the ball but fell backward, clumsily, landing on the grass with more of a thump than necessary.

Anne looked concerned and immediately walked over to him. Tommy climbed to his feet, looked at his father, and said, "I don't want to play anymore."

"I thought you were gonna get me," said Mack. "C'mon, big guy, you're tougher than that."

For a moment father and son stood and stared at each other, Mack with a quizzical expression on his face. The ball had not been thrown hard, and it was not *that* wide. He'd seen Tommy catch a baseball a yard farther, with his quick feet and fast glove. But that was six months ago, and this was different.

"Okay, Daddy," said Tommy. "I'll play. Sometimes I'm not as good as I was. Can't get the wide ones."

"You'll get 'em," said Mack. "We can get some big practice in, now I'm home."

Anne watched them throw the ball back and forth another ten minutes and noticed that Mack never threw the ball wide, always at the glove, and Tommy always caught it.

Just before they came in, Mack missed the ball altogether, and the little boy jumped in the air. "Told you I'd get you!" he yelled. "I can always get you, Daddy!"

Mack picked him up. "You're my rookie, kid. You'll always be my rookie."

He carried Tommy inside while Anne fetched the car from the garage, ready for the drive to the Maine Coastal Hospital on the outskirts of

Bath. Anne said she'd drive and turned the Buick station wagon north toward the shipbuilding city. Tommy fell instantly asleep in the rear passenger seat.

They reached the hospital at five minutes before noon. The receptionist said Dr. Ryan was waiting and would see them right away in his consulting room down the corridor. When they walked in, there was a nurse waiting with the doctor. She took the little boy's hand and said, "C'mon, Tommy, I've got some things to show you in the playroom." She led him outside, and Dr. Ryan turned to face Anne and her husband. He offered his hand to Mack, whom he had never met, and said immediately, "I am afraid I have no good news whatsoever. The test results are back, and it is as I had always feared."

"ALD?" whispered Anne, her hand flying to her mouth.

"Almost unmistakable," he replied. "I'm seeing some visual impairment, and there is some weakness, and numbness, in the limbs, especially on his right side."

He turned to Mack and said flatly, "Lieutenant Commander, this is a disease invented in hell. We can't cure it, and we mostly can't even slow it down. The whole thing is involved with Tommy's inability to process long-chain fatty acids in the brain. It nearly always shows up in males between the ages of five and ten."

"Is it rare?" asked Mack.

"Very. It all comes down to some stuff in our bodies called myelin. It's a complex fatty material that somehow insulates a lot of nerves in the central and peripheral nervous systems. Without myelin the nerves cannot conduct an impulse. Tommy's myelin is being destroyed, and we can't do anything about it. We're trying—God knows we're trying. The National Institute of Neurological Disorders and Stroke is dedicated to finding a cure. But so far, there has not been a breakthrough."

"Will Tommy die?" asked Mack.

"Yes, he will. As things stand at present he is unlikely to reach his tenth birthday."

"You can tell us, Doc. How long has he really got?"

"At his present rate of degeneration . . . six months."

Anne Bedford finally broke down and wept uncontrollably in her husband's arms.

"I'm so sorry," said Dr. Ryan. "But don't lose hope just yet. We are on the case, and there is a chance of prolonging Tommy's life with dietary adjustments. Though the real hope may be in Switzerland, where they are claiming a complete bone marrow transplant may yet be the answer, just as it often is with leukemia."

"Can it be done here?" asked Mack.

"Not yet. There are complications in performing such an operation on someone this young. And we're not yet ready to undertake that high a risk of mortality. But the Swiss claim to have solved some of the problems."

"How much would it cost?"

"One million dollars. They won't conduct life-or-death surgery on a child for less. Tommy would be there for at least a month, maybe six weeks."

"Does that operation bring back the myelin?" asked Mack.

"They claim it will stop the destruction of the myelin—if the patient survives."

"What kind of a place is it?"

"It's a highly specialized children's clinic, somewhere near Geneva, overlooking the lake. These places normally have a flat rate to include room and board for one parent, and an open-ended treatment center, post-op. Even if they have to reoperate, the price remains all-inclusive."

"But the American insurance companies don't provide coverage for foreign treatment?"

"Not on that scale. And I've only had one patient where the parents were prepared to risk everything to send their son to the clinic. They even sold their house."

"What happened?"

"The kid made it. He was in Switzerland for six months. But he made it."

"We couldn't raise even half the money."

"Lieutenant Commander, most people can't," replied Dr. Ryan. "But don't lose heart. We could get a breakthrough at any time. And if we do, I'll make sure we move very fast. Tommy's a great kid, and you're well covered by the navy insurance."

Tommy came back into the room, and they said their good-byes and left. Before they did, Dr. Ryan took Anne aside and said, "I'd like to see him in a week, and I want you to watch for memory loss. That's very important. And let me know if you see any signs."

They drove home almost in silence, unknowingly moving into a very dangerous zone, common to many families that face the onset of a major tragedy. Mack, the breadwinner, was conscious that he was not able to provide the means to take Tommy to Switzerland. He was at once fearful of Anne's ultimate resentment and assailed by a thousand terrors that she would in the end blame him.

Anne drove faster than usual. Her normally quiet, logical mind was in turmoil. She had suffered a mortal blow, the pain of which only a mother could possibly understand. Her little boy was dying, and would go on dying because no one could help. And there was no refuge in her family, not even in the arms of her husband. Not even he, the great SEAL commander, everyone's hero, could save Tommy. Anne Bedford was on the brink.

Right now, their personal troubles unspoken, one to another, the little family was on the verge of tearing itself apart. Tommy again fell asleep, and Mack could think of no words to comfort his wife. There were no words. If Tommy died, he was not sure his beautiful wife would ever recover.

They reached home, and while Anne put the car into the garage, Mack carried his son into the house and rested him on a sofa in the living room. When she returned, she quietly awakened him and took him into the kitchen for some lunch, just a grilled hamburger, which he loved, and some chocolate milk, and then she steered him upstairs to take a nap. Tommy never minded being led up to bed in the middle of the afternoon. Not these days. Every step to the second floor almost broke Anne's heart.

"I invited your dad around for a cup of coffee later," she said. "I don't think we'd better bother him too much about his grandson."

"How much does he know?" asked Mack.

"He knows Tommy has an illness that may be complicated, but no more. I don't really want to worry him, unless you feel he has to be told everything."

"I think we'll leave it for a bit. The old man's only just retired, and he and Mom are doing a few things together. Let's not spoil it all, because you know they are going to take it very badly."

And so they waited. Shortly after four o'clock George Bedford turned up, resplendent in a violent blue-and-silver Hawaiian shirt and a white Panama hat. He came straight into the house with the confidence of a man who had put down the initial deposit on the place for a wedding present. George kissed Anne and shook hands with his son. "Welcome back, kid," he said. "Hear you've had kind of a rough time."

"Wasn't too good, Pop. One of those quasi-political things. They never found me guilty of anything, but I wasn't going anywhere in the navy. Not after a trial like that."

"You got a plan, son? New career and all?"

"Not yet. I've only been home for about eight hours."

"That's okay, but you need a plan. Normally I'd say go and see Harry. He'll fix you up. But I'm hearing some weird things about the shipyard, and ain't none of 'em good."

"Oh?" said Mack. "What's up?"

Anne came in and announced she had made iced coffee. She asked if Mack and his dad would like to sit outside on the porch. George said that would be just fine, and they sat on the big wicker chairs, relaxed on the blue-and-white cushions, sipped their coffee, and pondered the fate of Remsons Shipbuilding.

"It's only rumors, mind you," said George. "Nothing but rumors. But when you hear 'em often enough, you start to wonder. The fact is, everyone's saying the French frigate order is going to be pulled."

"Jesus Christ, Dad. After all these years? How come?"

"I hear it's all political. There's a new man running for French president, for the Gaullist Party."

"Is that good or bad?"

"That's bad, son, real bad. Because the Gaullists are basically isolationist in terms of the French military. They do not wish to have one item of military hardware made anywhere outside of France. Especially fighter aircraft, tanks, and warships. They believe these compulsory military machines should provide jobs for French people, not Americans or anyone else."

"Who's the guy?"

"I don't know his name. But he's supposed to be in the arms business, which in France is massive—multinational outfits all somehow tied up with Aerospatiale. But a lot of people think if he gets elected, the game will be up at Remsons."

"Won't affect your pension, will it?"

"No. Harry's been real careful protecting that money. But it will affect the rest of the town, because if there is no further order for those guided-missile frigates, Remsons cannot survive."

"What happens if the guy doesn't get elected? Are we still dead?"

"Oh, I don't think so. It's this one guy, but apparently he can't lose, because the French have had it up to their eyeballs with left-wing semicommunist governments. Brought 'em nothing but problems and a virtual static standard of living."

"So he'll win and steer France to glory?"

"That's what he says. I just wish I could recall his goddamned name . . . But I can remember something he said a month ago: 'A rich nation can survive anything, except for civil war and socialism.'"

"Sounds like the kind of guy who will get elected. Is everyone sure he'll freeze Remsons out?"

"Oh, he's been in the French parliament for a while, and he gets up and starts ranting about any major commercial orders going overseas, like coal and steel from eastern Europe. He's never going to stand for a five-hundred-million-dollar warship being made in the USA."

"GRANDPA!" Tommy was making a comeback. He came charging onto the porch and climbed all over George Bedford.

"And how's my little tough guy today?" said the patriarch of all the Bedfords.

"Good. I'm very good now that Daddy's home."

"He's staying home, too, eh? And that's even better."

"Yup. That's a whole lot better. We'll probably go fishing tonight, 'cept I didn't ask him yet!"

"You want me to ask him for ya?"

"Sure. That'd be good."

"Okay, Mack, what about taking this boy fishing tonight? I'll come too for a while."

"Okay, let's all go. Meantime, Pop, I'll show you something real good. Because right here we got a baseball player, a kid with a great arm and an eye like a hawk. Wanna see him?"

"Sure I do. And if I like what I see, I'm gonna fix a tire on a rope from that old maple tree out there. That's the way to get some real training."

"Okay, Tommy, let's go. You fetch the gloves and baseballs, and we'll show Grandpa what you've got."

Tommy looked a bit doubtful. And then he said, "Hey, baseball. That's a real good idea. We haven't done that for a long time. Which hand was the glove?"

None of them saw the blood drain from Anne Bedford's face as she turned around and retreated into the house, tears streaming down her cheeks.

CHAPTER 4

Tommy seemed better on the weekend, as if the arrival of his father from the battlefields of the Middle East had provided some kind of tonic, or at the very least an uplifting experience, comparable perhaps to a local sighting of the Deadheads.

After his rest, he and his dad went fishing off a promontory above the ebbing tide of the river, a favorite place for the Bedfords for generations. They landed a couple of striped bass, one a keeper, twenty-eight inches long. Tommy caught it, and Mack expertly made a sharp cut along its shoulder, right behind the gills, then another in front of the tail before stripping the large tender fillets off the bone. He cut off the skin, discarded it, and packed the white fish sections on a tray in the cooler. This took care of supper for the Bedfords, and for a couple of circling black-backed gulls that instantly dived on the remains of the bass as it floated downstream.

Back at home Mack salted, peppered, and buttered the fillets, then wrapped them in aluminum foil, and cooked them on the barbecue with the lid closed. He'd been doing this since he was Tommy's age.

Meanwhile, Anne made some french fries and salad, and waited for her sister, the slim but much less beautiful and older Maureen, who was coming for supper and staying over to look after Tommy on Sunday. Aunt Mo was a local schoolteacher, and made a point of reading to Tommy from an inexhaustible supply of children's literature she had collected over the years. Tommy loved her.

But there would be no reading tonight. The little boy was out on his feet as soon as supper was over. Mack carried him up to his room, where Mo put him to bed.

The following morning, Mack and Anne went to the tall white-painted First Congregational Church of Dartford where both of them had worshiped since they were children, and in which they had been married. This would be the first public outing for Mack, and it would be the first time many local people had seen him for almost a year.

After a six-month tour in Afghanistan, leave had been cut short for all SEALs, and they had deployed rapidly to Iraq, to yet another insurgent emergency, scarcely having time to visit home. But now he was back, and back for good. And a lot of people he had known all of his life smiled greetings at him and Anne as they took their seats in the family pew, occupied by Bedfords for nearly one hundred years, third row from the front, right side.

At the conclusion of the service they walked outside to the place where Harry Remson and his wife, Jane, normally greeted parishioners, most of whom either worked for him or had some strong connection to the shipyard. Everyone in Dartford did.

When he saw Mack, Harry's face lit up, and he walked over to the big SEAL combat commander and said, "Hey, Mack, I heard you were home. I'm very glad to see you and really look forward to a nice long chat in the next few days. We got a lot of catching up to do. How ya been?"

Harry was so delighted to see Mack he clean forgot about Anne, and when he suddenly saw her standing just behind her husband, he exclaimed, "Oh, gosh, Anne, I'm so sorry—how are you? I was so thrilled to see Mack I lost sight of the most important member of the family! How's young Tommy?"

Harry Remson was a man in his early sixties. He was five-foot-ten with thick, prematurely white hair. He was never seen without an immaculately pressed suit. Like Mack Bedford, he had the rugged features of a genuine Down-Easter. But they had been softened by a family fortune of tens of millions of dollars, centered around the acres and acres of waterfront land the Remsons owned on the east side of the Kennebec River estuary. In the coming years, even if the shipyard declined, the land, with its sweeping views down to the estuary and marvelous high tides, would always appreciate in value, probably for one of the huge vacation development programs currently threatening this wild and glorious coastline.

Anne Bedford smiled at the lifelong family friend and said, "Good morning, Harry. It's nice to have Mack back, but Tommy is not so good and he doesn't seem to be getting any better."

"God, that's a real worry, Anne," said the shipyard owner. "Listen, if there's anything I can do—hey, I'm seeing you both later this afternoon, aren't I? At least I hope I am. Let's find time for a talk."

This particular Sunday afternoon had been on everyone's calendar for three months, the afternoon of the Remsons' summer party held on the lawn outside the biggest house in town, four hundred yards up the bay from the yard. The Remsons always threw a first-class affair, providing champagne, fresh seafood, and a couple of jazz bands from four o'clock until eight in the evening. No one ever needed dinner afterward.

"We'll be there, Harry," said Mack. "Looking forward to it."

By this time there were several local people lining up to shake Mack Bedford's hand and welcome him home. No one knew quite where he had been, but everyone knew Navy SEALs serve only in areas where there is optimum danger. And that meant either Afghanistan or Iraq. Hardly a day went by without television and newspapers reporting the death of American servicemen, but now Mack Bedford was home. Everyone knew he was one of the lucky ones.

Although there was no confirmation that he had left the United States Navy, rumors abounded that he was finished in dark blue and had returned home permanently. No one, of course, had one inkling that Mackenzie Bedford had been court-martialed and effectively forced out of the navy.

Mack and Anne stayed and talked to old friends for another twenty minutes, beneath the tall, white church spire that rose above the doorway to a point some twenty feet above the roof, where it then tapered into a high point with a cross at its pinnacle.

They walked home and found Maureen and Tommy sitting on the porch reading, and in Tommy's case trying not to go to sleep. They all helped prepare lunch, just soup, cold cuts, and Italian bread, before putting an exhausted Tommy back to bed.

The last thing on earth either Mack or Anne wanted to do was to attend the Remsons' party. But this was a duty. Harry was the most important man in town, and Mack could yet end up working for his company, as his father and grandfather had done. He would be too badly missed, and there was no question of skipping it. Mack and Anne had to report to the great-columned white colonial house on the banks of the river as close to four o'clock as they could. It was too far to walk, so Anne fetched the car from the garage before they changed.

Harry always stressed jackets, no ties, for this somewhat spiffy occasion around midsummer, but Mack always wore a tie as a mark of respect to the man who was responsible for keeping the town of Dartford alive.

They arrived a little after four to find there were already fifty to a hundred people on the lawn. Harry Remson and his wife were out there shaking hands, kissing cheeks, and speaking to people they had known for years, as if every family problem was theirs alone. The Remsons' attitude to their workers and fellow citizens had been ever thus for decades.

Anne and Mack found a quiet bench overlooking the water as a respite from the central area of the lawn where upwards of thirty people had come to talk to Mack, some merely to welcome the big naval officer home, others to thank him, sincerely, for everything he was doing for the country. Mack found it a bit wearing, as a matter of fact, and escaped to the bench with a plate of Maine lobster claws, which he did not want but could not resist. He used it as a shield from Dartford's chattering classes. Anne sat to his right, closest to the gathering, shielding him from the rest. Those who knew them well could sense the worry that pervaded their every expression. There were already rumors that the illness diagnosed by Tommy Bedford's doctors was not a trivial matter.

The dance floor, set up for the jazz band, had a wide canopy above to provide shade on this warm, sunlit early July day. George Bedford had just come over to ask Anne for the honor of a dance when Harry Remson arrived, put his arm on Mack's shoulder, and said, "Do you have a little time for a chat with your old friend?"

Mack looked up, grinned, and allowed himself to be steered across the lawn and over to the great house that had been built by Remson's grandfather Sam a hundred years before. They walked through open glass doors, across a bright, elegant drawing room, and into a darker green-painted, book-lined study. Harry poured them both a stiff glass of single-malt Scotch whisky and said, "Here you are, old buddy. You're going to need this."

Mack accepted the glass and sat down in front of Harry's wide antique desk with its polished red-leather top, a gift from the United States Navy for a destroyer built on time and under budget. Past times were ever-present at Remson's home.

Harry took a sip of his Scotch and said, "Mack, you have no doubt heard the rumors that the French may pull the frigate order, the one that's kept us going for close to fifteen years."

Mack nodded, and Harry continued. "You probably heard how serious this is. Not to put too fine a point on it, it could be the end of us. I can't keep running a shipyard with a thousand-strong workforce if we ain't building any ships, right?"

Mack nodded again.

"Guess you heard the reason they may pull the order?" asked the shipyard owner.

"Guess I did," replied Mack. "Some French guy. An ultraconservative Gaullist who will not allow any order for major military hardware to go abroad."

"You got it," said Harry. "He's a real hard-liner, and there are rumors he has big holdings in the French defense industry. In the upcoming presidential elections he's got a winning ticket, swearing to God French industry is for French workers, not foreigners. He's even ranting and raving about France buying inexpensive coal and steel from Romania. He makes it sound good, too. When he talks about military hardware, he never mentions he's almost certainly got a vested interest, as a major shareholder in one of the biggest arms factories in France."

"Jesus Christ," said Mack. "That sounds serious. France for the French, right? *Viva la France* and all that bullshit."

"Correct, and it ain't bullshit. I don't expect to receive another order from the French Navy. Ever."

"What's this bastard's name?"

"He's Henri Foche, a politician from Brittany. He has not yet started his campaign, but every political commentator in Europe is saying France is finished with left-wing government. Whoever carries the flag for the Right is a goddamned shoo-in, and this Foche character is like a French version of Ronnie Reagan or Margaret Thatcher, especially in the field of economics."

"Is there another runner for the Gaullists?"

"Yes, a kind of mild, intellectual Paris banker named Barnier. Jules Barnier, a man with no interest whatsoever in the defense industry and a great friend of the United States. He used to be head of Lazard Frères on Wall Street. Barnier's field is strictly economics, and he'll never tamper with an order for one navy frigate from us, from the French Navy. Especially if it might mean upsetting some powerful senator from the great state of Maine. But the commentators say he hasn't got a prayer against Henri Foche."

"Then I guess there isn't anything we can do," said Mack. "If the next president of France wants to cut us out of the game, he holds all the cards. We're like Barnier—haven't got a prayer either. I suppose there is no chance the U.S. Navy will give us another order for a warship?"

"I've been asking them every six months for more than ten years, and every time they tell me they are going to consider it, and every single time we hear nothing. One of the biggest problems is that Senator Rossow is thick as thieves with the chairman of Bath Iron Works. And God knows I understand their problems. BIW has a big workforce. Probably three times the size of ours. And every time the Senate Arms Procurement Committee in Washington even considers reducing the size of their ship orders in favor of anyone else, Rossow goes bananas and starts talking about layoffs in the shipyard that saved the U.S. in World War II. And it's a persuasive argument. Rossow always wins it, which kind of leaves us out in the cold. We lose the French frigate, and we're all done."

"That's a pretty morbid scenario in the middle of a beautiful party," said Mack. "And it feels like checkmate, which makes it worse."

Harry Remson took another sip of his Scotch and said, "Mack, I had a long talk with my dad today, and as usual he went on and on about what the yard means to the town and how its closure would destroy almost every family who lives here. He talks to me as if I don't understand that. I've only been running the place for thirty years since he retired. But just as I was leaving, he told me something that has stuck in my mind. He said, 'Remember, Harry, the simplest way is usually the best way.' I keep thinking about that sentence."

"Well, what do you think is the simple way?" asked Mack.

"I guess he means I gotta get rid of this Henri Foche," said Harry quietly.

"Get rid of him!" exclaimed Mack. "Get rid of him! You mean rub the bastard out?"

Harry Remson was silent for almost a half minute. And then he said, more of a murmur than a spoken sentence, "Yes, I guess that's what I do mean."

Mack Bedford puffed out both cheeks and blew air noisily through his lips, the universal expression of outright amazement. "Harry," he said, "I have known you all of my life. I have sometimes thought you were a bit rough with people, a bit hasty. I have often thought you were one of the funniest men I've ever met, and my dad swore to God you were the best boss a man could ever have. But I never thought the day would come when I thought you were totally fucking nuts. And here we are sitting in this old familiar house while you tell me you're considering the possibility of assassinating the next president of France!"

"Then you better raise your sights, Lieutenant Commander, because if I can't, this town is gonna die, and I don't want that on my conscience. As for rubbing out this French prick, I don't plan to do it myself, but I have the money to pay someone else. And I want you to help me."

Mack almost shouted, "Help you! What do you want me to do? Hold the ammunition? Carry the bomb? Anything to help!"

"Mack, I'm deadly serious. It may seem a wild outside chance. But people do get assassinated; it happens all over the world. And mostly no one knows who was truly responsible for the killing."

Mack stood up and paced to the door and back. "I don't especially want you to end up in the slammer, or worse yet in the electric chair, but I don't know where this conversation is going."

Remson looked thoughtful. "I think you'll find that in France, the assassination of a president comes under the heading of treason against the state. It's the guillotine, old buddy, and I understand it's swift and painless, a whole hell of a lot better than death by a thousand cuts watching my shipyard and my town die in front of my eyes after a hundred years."

"How many of these drinks have you had, Harry?"

"This is my first. And now let me come to the point. The kind of people I'm looking for are not criminals. They are people involved in the international security business. I'm looking for a couple of steel-eyed young guys who will track Foche and gun him down when no one is expecting it.

"I understand he is married, but there is a seamy side to his life, and he frequents certain nightclub establishments in Paris, where the dancers are beautiful but expensive. With a man like that, there is always going to be an opportunity to catch him off guard."

Mack put down his drink and spread his arms wide. "Well, what do you want me to do about it? You want to hire me to spy on this guy? Because I'm sure as hell not gonna shoot him. You might not care about the guillotine, but I'm not going with you."

"Mack, I would not dream of asking you to put yourself in danger. Jesus, I've known your family for longer than you have. But I want your advice. I want you to get me on a fast track to one of those international security firms. I've been reading about them. They are nearly all founded and staffed by ex–Special Forces guys, men from the Navy SEALs and the Rangers, from Britain's SAS, even French paratroopers, guys who've served in the Foreign Legion."

Mack looked doubtful. "I do know two or three guys who left the armed forces to join these types of corporations, but they're mostly based abroad. I wouldn't be sure where to start. But Jesus, Harry, these guys would want a fortune to take out a prominent French politician."

"I've got a fortune," replied Remson. "I'll offer one million dollars, but I'll go to two if I have to. A simple contract—no space for discussion; the money will be paid upon the death of Henri Foche. I'll advance expenses up to fifty thousand bucks."

"I can't guarantee anything," replied Mack. "But I'll make some phone calls for you, and try to get a lead. You may have to get someone else to be a middleman after that. I'm a naval officer, and I couldn't possibly be involved in such a scheme. But I'll do what I can."

Harry nodded, stood up, and offered Mack his hand. "Thanks, pal," he said. "Remember, I'm not doing this for myself. I'm doing it for the town, for everybody."

Mack shook his hand and replied, "I know you are, Harry. That's just about the one shred of merit this entire lunatic scheme has—but I'll do what I can."

The two men left the study and walked back out onto the sunlit lawn, where the party was gathering a head of steam. Harry walked up to the stage and signaled for the band to stop playing. Someone handed him the microphone to address his guests.

"I want to welcome all of you here for the thirtieth time since I took over the shipyard from my father. Believe me, I'm very proud to see how many of you have attended every one of these summer parties. I appreciate your loyalty, and although we are undergoing some very difficult times, you guys are never out of my thoughts, and I am doing everything I can to protect the futures of you and your families, and, of course, the shipyard. I do not want to make a long speech, and anyway it's not necessary, because you all know how I feel about every last one of you." At this point a spontaneous burst of applause rippled out across the Kennebec River.

Harry Remson continued, "I want you all to enjoy yourselves. There's about twenty cases of champagne out there. I don't want anyone to die of thirst! Up on the raw bar, there's seventy-five fresh lobsters Al and his son lugged up here this morning. The band I flew up here from New Orleans, and all this jazzy wine is because of my birthday—which isn't for three months, but who's counting? My family has been blessed through the years to have you working here. Without you, well, I don't know if Dartford would exist.

"But before I finish I would just like particularly to welcome home one of our most distinguished citizens. He has been serving this country in the most elite frontline battalion in the entire United States armed forces. He's served in the mountains and wild country of Afghanistan, he's fought terrorists in Baghdad, and up and down the banks of the Euphrates River. He's commanded his troops, he's led America's fighting men into the hellholes of the Middle East. And mostly he's come out on top. He's a United States Navy SEAL, ladies and gentlemen. He's our own Lt. Cdr. Mackenzie Bedford. Let's give him a real Dartford round of applause."

Everyone clapped and cheered the iron man from SPECWARCOM, and Mack looked about as embarrassed as any naval officer possibly could. Harry, however, stepped back up and said, "I'm not going to ask him to make a speech, because he thinks he's no good at it. So let's hear it one more time for a true man of action who has served his country long and well."

Again the crowd burst into applause and there were many cries of, *"Way to go Mack! Welcome home! Welcome home!"* Anne Bedford stood on her tiptoes and kissed him on the cheek. "Welcome home, my darling," she said. "This is where you belong."

And so the party continued on its noisy good-humored course until around seven-thirty, when Mack walked over to Harry Remson and put his arm around his shoulders, saying softly, "Harry, are you sure you are really serious about this French adventure?"

Harry turned to face him, expressionless, and murmured, "We do not have any other course of action. If this Henri Foche is allowed to live, this town will die. I believe it's an old battle commander's saying, 'When it comes right down to it, and it's a matter of us or them? Well, there's only ever going to be one answer, and it's not us.' I'm serious. I want Henri Foche removed, because that's our only chance of survival."

Mack replied, "I just wanted to check, but now I know. I don't think I can do much, but I will try to plug you into a group of guys who might know what you should do. I did not mention it earlier, but a lot of them left the armed forces in the United States and Great Britain and became mercenaries, guys who will fight for money, for the outfit that will pay them the most. It's a big business, and it's conducted mostly in Africa. I probably can find a way to key into them, but it'll take time."

"Quick as you can, Mack," said Harry. "We're right on the edge at Remsons. I have to lay off some of the steel cutters this week, because I have nothing for them to do and not much prospect of getting anything. If I can't get rid of Foche, I'm afraid we may have built our last warship."

Mack Bedford nodded. "I'll do what I can," he said again. "I can't do more."

Mack and Anne drove home quietly, both conscious of the stark contrast between the joyful camaraderie of the Remsons' party and the tragic circumstance that awaited them as soon as they entered their front drive.

The situation was, if anything, worse than either of them had expected. Maureen greeted them on the front porch with the news that Tommy had been very sick all afternoon and that she had spoken to Dr. Ryan at the hospital, who said Anne should bring him in first thing in the morning, nine o'clock. Maureen told them that Tommy was now asleep. And she kept repeating over and over, "It's just so sad. It's just so sad."

Anne Bedford, perhaps above all others, knew that Tommy was dying. All the symptoms she had been warned about three months earlier were slowly coming true. The tiredness, the sickness, the loss of memory, the weakening of once tough young muscles. It was all falling into place. Anne did not know how long Tommy could possibly go on getting worse by the week, and she also wondered, despairingly, how long she herself could go on, faced with this daily heartbreak. "I think I'll just go up and sit with him for a while," she said.

Mack told her he would walk down to the shore and back.

But when he reached the water's edge, he did something he had not mentioned to Anne. He took out his mobile phone and punched in the numbers to another cell phone, deep inside SPECWARCOM's headquarters at Virginia Beach. It answered on the second ring, and a voice said, "Hi, this is Bobby Rickard speaking."

Hey, Bobby, it's Mack. Guess they haven't killed you yet?

Sonsabitches tried their best, I can tell you that. I only got back last week. Wounded?

No. But one of them fucking tribesmen split my helmet with an AK bullet. Shit, I thought I was done for sure.

Not you, kid. Only the good die young.

Heh, heh, heh! Don't know about that—you're still here!

Mack laughed, and cut quickly to the point. "Bobby," he said, "do you remember Spike Manning? Petty officer. Left the SEALs about a year ago?"

"Sure, I remember him. I went through BUDs with his brother, Aaron. They came from Alabama, right?"

"Yup. That's the guys. You ever hear what happened to Aaron? Didn't he join some security outfit?"

"I'm not sure, but Spike took over his dad's road haulage business down in Birmingham. I might even have a number for him, if it'd help. He and I were in Kabul together. Crazy bastard got shot, remember? Wait a minute."

Mack sat down against a warm rock and stared at the water, muttering to himself, "This has to be the stupidest thing I've ever done."

And then Bobby was back on the line. "It's area code 205, then 416-1300. That's Spike's home."

"Hey, Bobby," said Mack, "I really appreciate that, but I'm in a bit of a rush. Let's get together, when you're up this way."

"Sure thing, buddy."

Mack punched in the numbers. A female voice answered.

Mrs. Manning? Hi, this is Mack Bedford. Do you think I could speak to Spike if he's around?

Oh, sure. He's watching the Braves, and they're getting wiped out by the Mets. He'd be glad to come to the phone.

Moments later, Spike Manning was on the line. "Hiya, Mack. Where ya been, buddy? Someone told me you'd retired."

"Yeah. I guess I'd worked in that madhouse for long enough, and my guys were getting wiped out three at a time, every darned week. I've had it with death. Done my share."

Spike Manning, an endlessly cheerful southerner, said, "Yup. I came to the same conclusion. You just can't go on getting beat up by a bunch of towelheads you don't even know. We lost six guys in Iraq on my last tour."

"Yeah. I hear they nearly got you as well?"

"Got hit in the right thigh, just missed the big vein. If they'd got it, I'd be gone. We were miles from help. Anyway, what's up, bro?"

Mack hesitated and then said, "I met a guy up here in Maine who wanted to contact Aaron. Didn't he join some security outfit?"

"Security! That was some mercenary outfit. Aaron's commanding some group of fucking maniacs in Niger, trying to overthrow the god-damned president, I think. They're paying him a fortune."

"Can he take a phone call?"

"Hell, no. He's living in a goddamned cave."

"Can he receive a message somehow?"

"Yes, he can. The organization he's working for is in Kinshasa. That's in the Democratic Republic of the Congo. Not to be confused with the Republic of Congo, which has been fighting against itself for damn nearly as long as anyone can remember. Kinshasa's a lot more stable. It's on the other side of the Congo River. And the outfit you're looking for is called Forces of Justice. You can get it through directory assistance, but they're always changing the goddamned phone number. They can get a message to Aaron."

Mack punched the letters into his cell phone memory and thanked Spike for his help. He switched off the phone and began to walk slowly home, not wishing to be missed by either his wife or her sister.

The following morning, Tommy seemed much better, but Anne decided to keep the doctor's appointment anyway, and Maureen had to leave. Mack sat on the screened porch and somehow found the phone number of Forces of Justice on avenue du Roi Baudouin, a throwback in name to the old king of the Belgian colonizers.

He placed the call and was unsurprised when the phone was picked up by an automatic message service—*Please state your name and the nature of your business.*

Mack replied, "Spike Manning, USA, trying to contact my brother, Aaron." Almost immediately, a British voice came on the line, saying briskly, "This is Major Douglas, commander central Africa. How can I help you?"

"Sir, I am trying to get some work done in France. Do you have an office there?"

"Our operation is based in Marseille. I can't give you an address, but there is a phone where you can leave a message—hit 33 for France, then try 491 2069. If you don't want to be called back, give them a time when you'll call again."

Mack said, "Thanks a lot, Major. I can handle that."

"You on the East Coast of America, old chap?"

"Yessir."

"They're six hours ahead. And you want to speak to Raul."

Mack checked his watch. It was 9:15, Monday morning, and he dialed the number. Again it was a message, and Mack spoke carefully. "I have some expensive work to be carried out in France. I will call in one hour. That's 1615 your time. The name is Morrison."

He walked slowly back up the road, aware that the next move he made, on behalf of Harry Remson, was fraught with peril because there were three clear and present dangers: (a) the traceability of his own mobile number, which had been originally issued to the United States Navy; (b) there may come a time during the conversation when money and methods of payment would have to be discussed; and (c) this next phone call would surely require the caller to identify the target. Once that was done, an international crime would most certainly have been committed.

These matters always have an elusive cloak-and-dagger aura, but sooner or later someone would have to come clean and state in words of one syllable what was required, plus the identity of the victim upon whom the contract was being taken out. There was no possibility Lieutenant Commander Bedford could allow himself to be identified as the caller, the mystery man who was planning to assassinate the next president of France.

Mack walked slowly up the road, wondering what to do. He could not go out on a limb for Harry Remson, not in a potential murder contract. He could not subject Anne and his family to the appalling disgrace if he should be discovered as one of the masterminds behind the killing of Henri Foche. So who the hell was going to make the call to this goddamned cutthroat Raul, tucked away in some backstreet of Marseille while carrying out some of the dirtiest business on the planet?

In Mack's mind there was already quite sufficient hidden disgrace in his own curriculum vitae, because just below the surface lurked the court-martial that had ultimately finished him in the navy. Not even Anne knew the details of that. But even Anne understood the enormous political agenda that had caused the navy essentially to throw him overboard. And the question would haunt Mack forever—had it all been his fault? Had that uncontrollable rage at the bridge over the Euphrates really been the Achilles heel of an otherwise exemplary officer? Blind rage it had most certainly been. He'd shot the twelve terrorists, no doubt. He would have shot a hundred of them if they'd been there. And despite the navy's best efforts to prevent him from being publicly identified, Mackenzie Bedford knew in his heart there would always be a suspicion about his motives. About the way he had stepped out from his troops and savagely gunned down his enemy, while they just might have been trying to surrender.

The words of Lieutenant Mason, spoken with such conviction at the court-martial, ran through his mind—*Lieutenant Commander Bedford was the best officer I ever served with.* But the short sentence uttered by the president of the judging panel, Captain Dunning, was also not so far from his psyche—*The court detected an element of panic.*

Yes, there was quite sufficient in the recent past to make all his future dealings a matter for great care and prudence. So how the hell could he make a phone call to an unknown murderer in France, requesting, on Harry Remson's behalf, the death of the next French president? No, it was out of the question. He could not make that call. He must instead explain to Harry the problem and, if necessary, hand over the number of the office in Marseille that may be prepared to carry out Harry's wishes, for a price.

And that too seemed to Mack almost insurmountable. How on earth was the shipyard owner going to transfer a massive sum like a million dollars to some bank account in France or Switzerland without it being immediately traceable? "Beats the shit out of me," he told a couple of low-flying seagulls. "Right here I'm badly out of my depth. International crime is a bit too tricky for me."

He reached home to find Anne and Tommy were not back. He felt a tug on his heartstrings, wondering if the little boy had been allowed to leave hospital. He made himself a pot of coffee and sat out on the porch, lost in thought. Maybe he should call Harry and explain this was just about as far as he could go. He had the organization, he had the office in Marseille, he had the name, he had the number, and he had never promised to do more. Just to plug Harry into the right channels, to people who might carry out his lunatic proposition.

He pulled out his cell phone and dialed Harry's private number. When the shipyard boss answered, Mack said, somewhat mysteriously, "I have made some headway. I think you might want to come over and see me. Anne has taken the car."

Ten minutes later, Harry Remson's dark-blue Bentley swept into the drive. Mack invited him in and poured coffee for them both. Then he explained the perilous nature of the next step that must be made if

Harry was indeed going to carry out his threat. Half expecting the Big White Chief of Remsons to bridle at the suggestion that he, Mack, could go no further, the former SEAL was astonished at the quiet, resolute way Harry took the news.

"Mack," said Harry, "I understand the enormity of what I am proposing, and I'm grateful for what you have done so far. However, your objections to helping me continue are mere pinpricks on the body of a giant scheme. When you are as rich as I am, all these minor matters can easily be taken care of. I would like you to make the call, and I will provide you with an untraceable phone you will use to contact Marseille, after which you will throw it into the sea. I would like you to inform them of our requirements, and to get a price. This is business, Mack, a nasty business, but still business. They're selling; we're buying. Don't get into too much detail. Suffice to say the money will be paid into a Swiss bank account by me. If they are, in your opinion, the right guys, offer them twenty-five thousand dollars immediately for reconnaissance. You know, find the target, establish addresses, make maps, locate regular routes. Have them e-mail that data, so we can make a judgment on whether we're buying."

Mack looked astonished and stared at Harry, eyebrows raised. "Could I ask you a question?" he said. "Where do you want this e-mail with a detailed blueprint of the murder to be sent? Remsons Shipbuilding? How about Anne's computer? Given a free rein, you could probably get us all locked up for the next twenty years!"

Harry Remson grinned. "Mack," he said, "that e-mail will arrive in my hands by such a circuitous route you'd get dizzy trying to understand it. In the end it will reach a computer that only I will see, and then the computer will be destroyed."

Mack shook his head and said, "Jesus, Harry, I didn't realize you were so sharp in the world of international gangsters!"

Harry stood up, finished his coffee, and said, "I am aware of the risks. And I cannot start this operation without taking some. Mack, I've gotta go. Do nothing until I've organized the telephone."

"But, Harry, I need to make that call in fifteen minutes. I think they'll be waiting."

Harry replied sharply, "Make the call, Mack. Tell 'em to stand by for another call at exactly the same time tomorrow. I'll be organized by then."

"Okay, boss. I'll do as you say."

He watched the Bentley drive away and hoped Anne would not return until after he had made the 10:15 call. He was lucky, because she was within three miles but stopped at the store before continuing home. Dr. Ryan had insisted Tommy remain under observation until later in the afternoon. He was sleeping now, and Anne would return to the hospital by one o'clock.

Mack dialed the number in Marseille, and a French voice answered, "Mr. Morrison? Right on time. This is Raul speaking. I understand you have some business."

Mack responded, "Raul, I need twenty-four hours. I'll call you at precisely this time tomorrow."

"Okay, Mr. Morrison. I'll be here."

If ever there was a place built and designed to house a lethal international center for mercenaries and hit men, Marseille, the second city of France, was surely the one. Its terra-cotta-roofed buildings, its warm, sultry, litter-strewn streets, its peculiar Mediterranean atmosphere of joie de vivre all provide an undercurrent of pure lawlessness. Those sprawling docks, wind-whipped seas, clandestine coastal coves, and rocky landing places all contribute to a cheerful, devil-may-care feeling that any crime on earth could be committed here and no one would ever know. Scarfaced Frenchmen and Moroccans in wide-striped T-shirts and berets give the entire place a piratical overtone. Every ramshackle old vessel in the Vieux Port looks like a getaway opportunity for men on the run.

Police sirens are always wailing. But their wail is somehow empty, as if no one is paying a bit of attention. The unseen beat of North Africa pervades the place. It's a melting pot, a crossroads to nowhere, where no one seems to belong and no one seems to care.

But whatever goes on in Marseille, it's working. The city is humming in a haphazard kind of way. The docks are pulsing with activity. Restaurants are full. The fishing fleet thrives, and the famous market has been there for more than two thousand years.

Forces of Justice was situated on a side street off the Place des Moulins, in the oldest part of the city, Le Panier Quarter, north of the docks. It occupied offices on the second and third floors of an apartment block. No phone was ever answered. There was no street-level doorman. Which would have been superfluous anyway, since Forces of Justice employed two machine gun–carrying guards on either side of the entrance.

There were four permanent staff members led by one former British army colonel who had managed to get caught with his fingers in the till during a stint with MI-6, Britain's international espionage operation. These days he went by the name of Raul Declerc, which sounded somewhat more cosmopolitan than Col. Reggie Fortescue, formerly of the Scots Guards. It was also more likely to throw London's Scotland Yard off the trail. The former Col. Reggie Fortescue had managed to transfer funds of almost two million pounds from MI-6 to his current account by what he described as an "administrative error." They'd never caught him, but in his absence he'd been formally stripped of his commission.

Raul was assisted by two ex-members of the French Foreign Legion, both of whom had served in North Africa. One was wanted for murder, the other on suspicion of wrecking an entire village near Algiers after a spat with his girlfriend, a retired belly dancer.

The fourth executive was a former French government prosecutor with international credentials who had been struck from the profession in France for accepting kickbacks from a criminal gang in Paris. There was also a hitherto unproven charge involving the blackmail of a senior French minister hanging over the head of the chief legal counsel for Forces of Justice. The lawyer had subsequently changed his name and identity to those of a former friend, Seamus Carroll, a retired (murdered) freedom fighter for the Irish Republican Army.

FOJ was very international, though it could not reasonably be described as a top-drawer operation. Lacked class. Nonetheless, like most of Marseille, it thrived, acting as a recruitment agency for African nations. It specialized in meeting the requirements of leaders whose armies needed training, or rebels who sought to take over the country.

These are incredibly dangerous paths to take, but there is huge money involved. African leaders have been known to ransack the accounts into which "aid" is poured from the West. Raul Declerc and his men were able to charge a fortune for highly trained Special Forces personnel, men who were finished with regular poorly paid national warfare and now wished to work at a proper commercial rate. FOJ had tentacles into all the crack Western regiments and specialized in recruiting ex-SAS, ex-SEALs, ex-Rangers, ex–Green Berets, or almost any of the British army's combat divisions. The most prosperous part of the business was certainly the Mercenary Operation. But the bedrock was security, providing many very tough ex-military men to heads of state of nations in which a sizable section of the population profoundly wished them dead.

All over the world there lived billionaires with almost as many enemies as dollars. A very large number of them had up to fifty, or even a hundred, bodyguards. And a large proportion of these were recruited through FOJ. Indeed, most ex-soldiers wanting employment were happy to settle for $100,000 a year running a specialist protection unit for a wealthy man. But those who were prepared to help train and command some African army might receive an up-front payment of $250,000. Those prepared to undertake an assassination, however, started at $300,000 but might charge $1 million, depending on the target and the level of security surrounding it.

The very last thing on Mack Bedford's mind was to become in any way involved with these international networks of edge-of-the-law cutthroats. Yet he now stood on the verge of a very evil organization.

The first moment Mack had announced his name as Morrison, Raul had put into place a set of routine procedures. He fired off an e-mail to all branches of FOJ, contacts and recruiters, to check if anyone might have recommended anyone of that name to the Marseille office. No one had. Then he redrafted the request to check if anyone had spoken to an unnamed American perhaps looking for contacts in France. Everyone shot back a reply saying, "Negative." Except for Major Douglas, commander central Africa, in faraway Kinshasa on the Congo River—*Affirmative. I had a Spike Manning on the line probably from Birmingham, Alabama, looking for his brother, Aaron, serving in Niger. Call came around 1515 French time.*

Raul immediately called Aaron on his cell and asked if he had heard from his brother in the past day or so. *Negative.* Raul proposed to bother the combat fighter no more.

So he called Major Douglas and asked if he had a number for Aaron's family, just the regular next-of-kin contact to be used in the event of the man's death. Major Douglas did, and he put in a call on Raul's behalf. He spoke to Mrs. Manning, mother of the two former Navy SEALs.

Yes, she had received a call yesterday from someone looking for Aaron, but her son Spike had dealt with it. No, she could not remember the name of the caller, but she thought it might have been something like Pat Stepford, "kinda like one of the wives."

"Huh?" replied Major Douglas, who last went to a movie when he was at prep school.

When Spike came home later that evening, he issued a very serious warning to his mom.

Do not ever mention to anyone the name of any one of my former SEAL buddies in any context whatsoever. Our work was top secret. Everything we did was highly classified. Not even the navy would release a name. Ever. Not even for a birthday card. We all have many enemies, and mostly we have no idea who they are. I repeat, never name anyone.

That evening, Spike Manning had the phone number changed at the family home. Mrs. Manning thought that was a bit excessive, but she was considerably chagrined at her very obvious near-blunder.

Anyhow, Major Douglas made no attempt to take the matter further. And Raul intended to do no more until the caller made contact again at 1615. He was, however, very interested. To the best of his knowledge no one was planning open revolution in France, which left the possibility of an assassination contract. Big money. These jobs were conducted "in-house" by the ex–Foreign Legion guys. The money would be split four ways, 20 percent each for the hit men, 50 percent for Raul the negotiator, and 10 percent for the lawyer, Carroll.

Perhaps Forces of Justice might be competent to carry out the operation against Foche. But the organization was nothing short of a bear trap for Mack Bedford. And his fears of disclosure were justified. He'd had a narrow escape on the phone to Spike Manning's home, and he didn't even know it. Now he was *almost* obliged to make contact again, and this time he might not be so lucky.

——— • ◆ • ———

Mack took Tommy fishing again that evening after Anne had driven him back from the hospital. It was one of those days that might seem strange to visitors, but to the residents of Maine it was just normal. It was a day when the clouds suddenly rolled in off the Atlantic, followed by fog banks. The summer heat seemed to evaporate in the mist. They stood on the shore listening to the deep baritone boom from the Sequin lighthouse. In the far distance, the ghostly chimes of the bells on the marker buoys clanged eerily, as they stood sentry over the great granite ridges that stud the inshore waters.

Mack didn't care. Tommy never gave it a thought, this total disintegration of a bright early July afternoon. Neither of them had ever known anything else. And they knew enough to bring thick sweaters.

It was low tide, and the channel leading outward from Dartford Bay seemed to run slowly. Sandpipers and sanderlings stepped through the shallows. There were arctic terns shrieking out near the middle of the stream, as they dipped and dived toward the slow-moving water. Large herring gulls dropped shellfish onto packed, pebble-strewn sand, trying to split them. The terns were very busy, and they were dive-bombing into a flashing shoal of porgies that meant the big bass and bluefish were right underneath.

Mack's eyes glittered as he made his first cast. "Tommy, these are great fishing conditions for us. Let's try to get one quick, and then dig out a few clams. Mom can fry 'em."

"I'll get a fish," said Tommy. "I'm good at low tide."

Mack chuckled. "Okay, let's see you do it."

Tommy cast, with a "popper." He hurled the lure way out and wound it in fast, watching it glitter across the water, waiting for the hit when a bass or a blue struck it.

Nothing happened. They both kept casting, trying to whip their lures way out toward where the terns were swooping. But they could not get a bite. Mack was on the verge of calling it a day when Tommy said, "Let's have two more goes. Those birds are still out there. There's gotta be fish."

"I can't understand it—maybe there's too much bait around. But . . . okay. You go first."

Tommy cast. He drew his rod back over his shoulder and flung the lure out toward the arctic terns. He let it sink a little, then he began to wind the reel in, faster, faster. And there it was, chopping across the surface, a silver streak right in Tommy's line of vision.

That was when the big bluefish struck. He ripped upward from the deeper water, spotted the darting lure, and powered forward, snapping his tough, toothy mouth right on it. The lure dived under, and Tommy felt the unmistakable jolt as the fish took it. Instinctively, he slowed the reel, then he jerked it back, setting the hook, as the fish came to the surface again.

"That's a blue, Tom!" yelled Mack as the glinting stripeless dark blue caught the sun. "Keep reeling him in! He's Mom's favorite."

Tommy adjusted his stance for the fight, and Mack, mindful of that unorthodox backward fall with the baseball, put down his own rod and wrapped his arms around the little boy's waist. He issued no instructions. Tommy knew how to do this, and he worked the bluefish into the shallows, where Mack took over.

He raised the rod, with the lure still in the fish's mouth, and lifted the head up, maybe a foot off the sand. Mack had to look sharp, because the blue was still flailing, trying to slacken the line to shake out the treble hook. Then, dodging the wicked line of teeth, Mack grabbed the fish in the only place you can grab a fighting blue: the little clear space between the head and the razor-sharp dorsal spikes. He gripped it like a carpenter's vice. "That's the old Bedford grab, kid," said Mack, grinning. "Never forget it!"

For a few moments, they both gazed at the thirty-two-inch silvery bruiser of the Northeast coast. Then Mack gave it a solid whack on the head with his "priest," killing it instantly. Even still, he used long pliers to remove the hook from its jaws. Then he placed the fish on a flat rock, four yards out into the water, and stood there in his waders, skillfully cutting and filleting it. He packed the two oily pink bluefish steaks on the tray inside the cooler and told Tommy, "That was outstanding, kid. Beautiful. Let's forget the clams. This is a great dinner right here."

He scooped the remains of the blue off the rock and into the incoming tide, below which he had no doubt hungry crabs were waiting. But even as Mack packed up the gear, the gulls were circling, wheeling, shrieking, dipping, preparing to dive. He turned to Tommy and then noticed the little boy was sound asleep on the sand.

Mack picked Tommy up and rested him over his shoulder, holding him safe with his left arm. With his right hand he picked up the rods, net, and cooler and wished to God they had brought the car. Still, fishing rods were lighter than machine guns. And he set off for home resolutely, one mile on a narrow beach road, with Tommy sound asleep. In a disaffected way, it was the saddest mile he ever walked. Worse than the Euphrates Bridge. He hadn't wept there.

They reached home and Anne took over, resting Tommy on the sofa while Mack prepared the fish. His method for marinating the blue was unlike that for any other fish, because of the high oil content. He placed the two fillets in a shallow pan and delved into the cupboard for a bottle of gin. He splashed the entire contents over the fish and left it to soak in the clear spirit that, in maybe an hour, would somehow suck out the excess oil. This was an old Down-Easter trick, and in a way it made dinner kind of expensive, even though the fish was free. But bluefish cooked on the grill after that marinade was sublime. Just butter, salt, pepper, and hot coals. That's all you need.

For all the disadvantages of Maine, the endless winters, the cold, the snow, the rough seas, and the northern New England bleakness, Mack believed that everything was worth it. Just to sit out there on the porch, eating the succulent bluefish, fresh out of those misty tidal waters. Especially since it had been landed with the old "Bedford grab," passed down to Mack through generations in this wild land of his forefathers. The bonus was, in his opinion, that he shared the table with one of the most beautiful women ever to reside on the banks of the Kennebec River. And his little boy, who was now wolfing down the delicious fish, kept reminding them both, "This is my fish. I got it, right, Dad? All by myself. Last cast, right?"

As ever, Tommy was every father's rookie, just sitting there reliving one of those unforgettable boyhood moments. For Mack Bedford, this was paradise. Almost.

———•◆•———

The focal point of Remsons Shipbuilding was a gigantic drydock, like a giant square cave, with one end open to the water, railroad tracks running from deep inside, all the way down to the low-tide mark. In the center of the dock, right above the railroad tracks, was a four-hundred-foot-long guided-missile frigate with a gunmetal-gray hull. Below the foredeck, painted black, seven feet high, were the identifying marks *F718*. The superstructure inclined at ten degrees to the vertical to reduce combat radar echo. This was a state-of-the-art Lafayette Class frigate, custom-built by Remsons for the navy of France. Its 21,000-hp diesels were already fitted. Its twin shafts were jutting from the stern awaiting the massive bronze propellers. The flat helicopter landing platform on the stern was being painted. The heavy foredeck gun was already in place.

The ship was encased in scaffolding and a jungle of electric cables. Sounds of heavy hammering muffled out from inside the hull. Two men with sledgehammers were slamming the wooden chocks, tightening the base upon which the great ship rested. Walking slowly down the port side of the hull was Harry Remson. His face was absolutely stricken.

He turned away from the ship and returned to the staircase that led up to his office. At the top he opened the door, walked in, and sat down, at the same desk, in the same red-leather-padded, curved captain's chair once occupied by his father and his grandfather. From here, the Remson-in-command had a view of the entire drydock. Old Sam had watched U.S. Navy destroyers being built from this very spot. And now it was over. At least it would be unless he, Harry, could take some drastic action.

Harry called for his longtime secretary, and niece, Maggie Tyler, to summon Judd Powell, his works foreman, to the office. Judd had worked in the shipyard since he left school and risen to the important rank of master shipwright. He was forty-eight years old now, and for seven years had been Harry's right-hand man.

At this particular time, he was testing the length of the bow and foredeck against the plans. Everyone knew of a recent British warship that had been inadvertently constructed four feet too short. The result had been an absolute uproar when it was discovered the bow dipped too low in a big sea. The breaking waves had come driving over and soaked the missile launchers. This ought not to have been a problem, except the unexpected saltwater had crusted a tiny switch, which then refused to function, leaving the missile system potentially out of action in the face of the enemy.

The shipbuilders were found to be at fault after a lengthy Admiralty Board inquiry in London, and the entire front end of the destroyer had to be rebuilt. In Judd's opinion there was enough goddamned trouble on the horizon without stupid foul-ups like that.

The yard sound system blared out—*Judd Powell to Mr. Remson's office. Judd Powell to the office.*

The master shipbuilder climbed over the rail onto the scaffold, moving expertly down the ladders to ground level. It was not an unusual request from the boss. It happened a couple of times every day.

But there was a hollow feeling in Judd's stomach as he made his way up to Harry's office. And he'd only just finished his breakfast.

One look at his employer told him plenty. Harry's face was a picture of misery. He never even said, "Good morning." He just looked up and said, "I've heard from the French, Judd. They mentioned the volatile political situation in France and the possibility of Henri Foche being elected. They also confirmed they were not able to order another frigate, but thanked us for all we had done over the years."

"Does that mean we're finished? Is it definite?"

"Nearly. You can hardly run a shipyard if you haven't got any god-damned ships to build. I'm paying out almost fifty million dollars a year in salaries. Barring a miracle, I have to start laying men off this week."

"How many?"

"Probably a hundred. Steelworkers first."

"Jesus Christ. I don't know what to tell these guys. If the yard closes, a lot of them will never work again."

"Don't remind me, Judd. I guess in a way I'm to blame. I should have known the score six months ago." An expression of bitterness crossed Harry's face when he added, "The French were stringing me along. And I should have realized it sooner."

"It's this guy Foche, right?" said Judd. "I read all about him. *Vive la France,* and all that shit."

"That's him. There'll be no more foreign defense orders from France. Everything will be made there under Foche. That's the problem. They're damn good at it—you know, the Mirage fighter jet, the Rafale guided-missile fighter, the Super Etendard, the Exocet missile, the Triomphant Class nuclear submarines, the Super Puma helicopters. The bastards know what they're doing. And they already build most of the Lafayette frigates."

Both men were silent for a few moments. Then Judd Powell said, "Sir, would you mind telling the men yourself?"

"Give me a break, Judd. This has already broken my heart. Isn't that enough? I'd do damned near anything to make things different."

Judd nodded understandingly. "I guess there's no chance this Foche will lose the election, is there?"

"None. Our only hope is if the French bastard drops dead."

"Is there a ray of light anywhere, Mr. Remson? Anything I could tell the guys, just so we still have a little hope?"

"There may be something, Judd. But it's a long shot. Just tell 'em I'm doing everything I can." Harry Remson already realized he'd said too much.

———•◆•———

The dark-blue Bentley came surging into the drive. Anne and Tommy had left for the hospital, where Dr. Ryan had promised to produce something to calm down the boy's bouts of violent sickness. Harry disembarked, carrying with him a small white cardboard box. He walked onto the screened porch and shouted for Mack, who came bounding down the stairs, clean-shaven and sharp before a superior officer. Like always.

"Okay, buddy, right here I got the cell phone, and it's ready to go. Got a special chip embedded inside it, makes it undetectable by any search agency in the world. Incoming or outgoing."

"Jesus, Harry. Where'd you get it?"

"NASA. Since you ask."

"Didn't tell 'em who it was for or why you needed it?"

"I might look stupid, but I'm not crazy," replied the shipyard chief. "Anyway, you can make the call and offer them the million for the contract."

"Do I reveal who we have in mind?"

"I'm going to leave that up to you, Mack. You may have to, in order to get a firm price."

"How about payment?"

"I think we'll agree to pay that twenty-five thousand for the recce. Then advance expenses of say fifty thousand. When Foche dies, we'll pay the balance. But I'm not paying a bunch of murderers a huge advance fee that they could keep and then say the plot backfired."

"No. That would be crazy. We'd never have a chance of getting repaid."

"It's our way or the highway. Tell 'em we'll go somewhere else."

"Harry, there may be a difficulty if they do not have the slightest idea who we are, or where to come, if their money does not arrive."

"Mack, they're in the high-risk, utterly illegal end of the business cycle. I'm betting they often have to take their chances on getting paid. But we're not handing out an advance. Screw that."

"Okay, boss. No names; no clues about identity. And how do we transfer the funds?"

"I've got a pretty big account in the city of Brest in Brittany, where the French Navy lives. It's not unusual for us to have tens of millions of dollars in there. I'll have the fee wired to an account in Switzerland, and from there it will go to the account of one of those Swiss lawyers whose sole purpose in this life is to hide identities, cash, bank accounts, and the rest. He will not know where the money came from when it lands in his account, nor will he ever have a way of finding out. The Marseille guys will contact him, and he will arrange their payment. No one will ever know who paid, and no one will ever know what it was for. If we get a deal, we'll request the name of the guy who'll pick up the check from the lawyer, and all he needs to do will be to identify himself at the office in Geneva. No problem." Harry glanced at his watch. "Christ!" he said. "I've gotta get back. And your call to France is in fifteen minutes. Keep me posted."

And with that Harry Remson was gone, leaving Mack holding one of the truly great cell phones of the world. *Anyone comes on the line, it'll probably be a fucking astronaut,* he muttered.

He decided to make the call away from the house, so he walked out of the driveway and jogged down to the lonely spot where Tommy had caught the bluefish. Just as he arrived, a local fishing boat, driven by an old-timer, Jed Barrow, was arriving back from a night in the fog in choppy waters. Mack could tell by the way the trawler rode low on her lines it had been a decent catch. "Hey, Jed," he yelled across the water. "Good job! Nice to see you."

Jed Barrow turned and stared across his starboard beam. Then he spotted Mack and yelled back, "Mack Bedford, you young rascal! I thought you'd taken over the entire U.S. Navy! Welcome home, boy!"

Mack waved. He guessed the old man had been out maybe three or four miles. Somewhere around the back of Sequin. It was very deep out there, and lonely. In the past men had disappeared without a trace in the long, rolling seas common to this part of the world. Out there in the night, with just a nineteen-year-old kid for company, was a tough way to make a living in a dragger.

But Jed knew nothing else. For him that short voyage out to Bell 12 was nothing short of a commuter run—there and back, maybe a couple hundred days a year. Coming home in the morning, cold, salt-encrusted hands, very often a decent haul, and then a short argument with the buying agent, summer and winter, sickness and health. And all because men like old Jed Barrow and his forefathers would rather have shot themselves than have someone tell them what to do.

Mack pondered the life of a fisherman. And wondered if he should get into it himself. He had the money with his navy payoffs, SEAL bonuses, and well-saved signing-on fees. He could navigate, he could fish, and he knew the waters. But then he stopped himself—because, subconsciously, he was thinking about forming a business for Tommy. Always for Tommy. And what was the point of that? Yet he could not stop himself.

He looked at his watch and mentally tore himself away from this world he knew so well, way down east on the Maine coastline. Instead he checked himself into a seamy, terrifying world of willful murder, a merciless, brutal place where he did not belong. He took out his super-sonic cell and tapped in 011-33 for France, then the number, which would ring in the office in the backstreets of Marseille, in the Assassins' Division. Raul's place.

CHAPTER 5

It was, possibly, the closest Mack Bedford had ever come to losing his nerve. At precisely 10:15, sitting against a rock above the ebbing tide of the Kennebec estuary, he suddenly snapped his cell phone shut and told a half-dozen busy sandpipers he simply could not manage this. Harry Remson would have to find someone else. Because he, Lt. Cdr. Mackenzie Bedford, could not deliberately place himself among the criminal classes. Particularly among this shady group of "murder for hire" brigands, lurking in the back streets of Marseille. It was entirely too much to ask of him.

Making a phone call to arrange the imminent assassination of the next president of France sounded pretty bad. About ten-years-in-the-slammer bad. Mack stood up and put the phone in his pocket and began to retrace his steps up the beach path. And then he thought again about the issues that were at stake, and about his old friend Harry. The Remson boss did not have to do this. He was an extremely wealthy man, and he could have just accepted the fate of the shipyard and let it go. It would hardly affect his life.

In fact, Harry's life would be a whole lot better without the shipyard. He owned a beautiful seventy-five-foot ketch he kept down in Saint Bart's in the Caribbean, and he could certainly spend much of the winter there instead of fighting the frost, the snow, and the endless problems of the Maine shipbuilding industry.

No, Harry was not, effectively, putting his life on the line for himself and his family. His wife, Jane, could have lived without Remsons Ship-building any day of the week. Harry was doing this for the people of Dartford. He was spending two million dollars and risking jail, just to keep everyone going with jobs, food, and comfort. Not one dollar for himself. Everything for the town. Everything to lose.

And here he was, Mack Bedford, shying away from making a phone call to help save his fellow citizens of Dartford. *The hell with it,* he muttered, and dialed the number in Marseille.

This is Raul. Mr. Morrison?

Right here, Raul. Mack felt a surge of confidence. The name was wrong, and the phone call could never be traced. He was safe. For the moment.

Raul stepped straight up to the plate. He dropped his faint French accent and reverted to English, in the kind of officer-class accent expected of a man called Reggie Fortescue.

"Okay, Mr. Morrison, old chap, let's not prolong this call because I have no doubt your business needs an element of security. Tell me what you need."

Mack was stunned at the straight-shooting Englishman's words. But he recovered fast and said quietly, "We need to have someone removed from the face of the earth."

"Uh-huh," replied Raul, as if he had just been asked to lend someone a ten-dollar bill. "Where is he?"

"France, probably Brittany."

"Uh-huh. Are you ready to reveal his name?"

"Not yet. That's a ways off," replied Mack. "Do you have rates for such projects?"

"Straightforward contract starts at three hundred thousand U.S. dollars. Goes up depending on the target's personal security. Could end up costing a million, and maybe more. Is he well known?"

"Yes."

"Then we start at a million and rising. Bigger the risk, bigger the price."

"I understand. Does this mean you'll undertake the project no matter what, if the money's right?"

"Almost. But we have turned down a couple of huge jobs. Mostly because both targets were heads of state, and that was a step too far."

"I see. Are you the biggest operation of this type?"

"Yes. I believe we are. But I imagine you're asking if there are alternative sources for you to try, and the easy answer is no. If we won't take it on, no one will."

"Raul, you have been very helpful, and you will understand my reluctance at this stage to go further. It would be remiss of me to have you and your colleagues fully acquainted with our plan, only for you to decide not to proceed. This would somehow leave you with knowledge that could place both myself and my colleagues in grave danger."

"Mr. Morrison. If we ever stooped to that level, we would not be very long in this business, or perhaps not even in this world."

Every instinct he had told Mack Bedford not to reveal the target. He also knew that if he was to make any progress whatsoever in this onerous project, ultimately he had to reveal the target. Harry Remson had specified that Mack alone must make this decision. If Harry had been here, he would have understood the quandary. This was the moment of truth. Either Mack Bedford was going to tell the mysterious voice in Marseille precisely what he intended to do, and who was to be assassinated, or he would ring off and call back another time.

He decided to swerve away from the critical path of the conversation. "Should you agree to undertake the contract," he said, "and we were able to settle on a price, what arrangements would you wish us to make with regard to payment?"

"Banker's draft or wire transfer, Swiss bank, numbered account."

"We had already thought along those lines. We would prefer to deposit the money in our Swiss account in Geneva, and then have the cash removed to a lawyer's office in Geneva, where your man would pick it up in person, subject to satisfactory identification."

"That would be perfectly agreeable to us." Raul knew when he was talking to the real deal, a genuine heavy hitter with the wherewithal to make something happen and the ability to pay the correct price. "There would, however," he said, "be the question of a first payment and then the final payment when the contract was complete. I imagine you have also considered that?"

"We have, and that may be a sticking point. My colleagues naturally would not forward to you a large down payment, with the chance that you could just keep it and not complete the work. In those circumstances we would have zero chance of recouping any of the money."

"Equally, Mr. Morrison, it would be unreasonable for you to expect us to undertake an operation in an area of the utmost danger that could see us all tried and executed, not without any compensation whatsoever to begin the project. We could easily end up either dead or incarcerated—or, worse yet, broke."

Mack Bedford chuckled. "Raul, I have no doubt you have tackled such stuff before. What's the usual drill?"

"Mr. Morrison, we will require minimum expenses of fifty thousand dollars. And if we are not to be paid until the completion of the contract, we must know precisely who we are working for. Which ensures clients pay us promptly for dangerous work."

"What if we could not risk you, or anyone else, knowing who we are? What then?"

"Fifty percent down, the other half on completion."

"And in those circumstances, you do not even want to know who we are?"

"Correct. Even though we run the immense risk of you knowing who *we* are."

"Checks and balances," said Mack. "The way of the modern world."

"The entire issue of us knowing your identity is our only security," said Raul. "Most people, perhaps unwillingly, stump up that first down payment to protect their anonymity. And we have never once failed to keep our side of the bargain. We are the acknowledged world professionals in the business."

"I guess I have to assess whether we are prepared to place our own futures in your hands," answered Mack. "And that's an awful lot of trust."

"Either that or pay the price up-front," said Raul. "By the way, may I assume you are calling from the United States?"

Mack's mind raced. His cell phone was untraceable. He could be anywhere. He answered the question in a strangely pressured manner. "No," he said, "I'm not. I am American, but right now I'm calling from London."

"Is that your headquarters?"

"Yes," said Mack. "Right here in London."

"And now you must tell me the identity of your target because we can progress no further. I must assess the risk and the price. You must assess your priorities—the secrecy, or the desire to protect your money until the last moment."

"I cannot make that last step without further consultation with my people," replied Mack. "I'll need time. Maybe two or three days. But I'll be back to tell you, one way or the other. Same time."

He snapped the phone shut and stood there on that lonely stretch of shoreline watching the Kennebec River flowing out toward the Atlantic. He dialed Harry Remson's number and asked to meet him at the house as soon as possible.

Harry arrived marginally after Mack and listened carefully to the account of the contact with the hit men from Marseille.

"It's a bit of a dilemma," said Harry. "Plainly, I don't want to hand over possibly a half-million dollars to a bunch of criminals who will vanish instantly and take the cash with them. And the alternative is to reveal my identity, which is more or less out of the question. If I'm going to do that, I might as well shoot the sonofabitch myself."

"I don't think you need to reveal your identity," said Mack thoughtfully. "But someone has to satisfy them that we are on the level, prepared to stand behind the contract."

"I was rather hoping, in the end, that might be you," said Harry. "But I had not thought it through properly, not at that point."

"So which of the two options do you prefer?"

"I'm not crazy about either of them," said the shipyard boss. "But I'd rather risk the cash than my name. And I'd sure as hell rather risk the cash than have the goddamned yard closed down."

"Which I guess brings us to the even more difficult question of re-vealing to them precisely who it is we wish to have killed."

"You got any thoughts on that?"

"Just one. We cannot get even to first base without telling them."

"And, of course, they might turn down the job as too risky?"

"Yup. They might. But I do get the feeling these guys are principally interested in the cash. If it can be done and they think there's a fair chance of getting away with it, they're gonna give it the old college try."

"Mack, I've mostly built my life on making tough decisions. And right now, I've just made one of 'em. We have to tell these guys who we want rubbed out. You didn't throw the astronaut phone away, did you?"

"Hell, no. It's right here."

"Then let's knock the ball right back into their court. And tell 'em now. We want them to hit Henri Foche. They can't trace us. NASA gave me their word on that. Let's go for it and tell 'em what we want."

"Okay. But I don't want to do it from here in case Anne comes back. I'll take a walk to a lonely spot down by the shore. And I'll call you right back. If it's a go, I guess we'll need that e-mail address, so they can show us a plan."

"See you later, buddy," called Harry as he climbed back into the Bentley and hurled gravel as he rocketed the slick dark-blue sports car out onto the deserted road.

Once more, Mack Bedford set off for the secret cove where he and Tommy had caught the bluefish. And there he once more dialed the number in Marseille. It was 10:45 now, not his call time in the French seaport, and the phone was answered by the machine.

"This is Morrison calling from London for Raul," he said.

Instantly, the familiar voice came on the line. "That was quick," said Raul. "We usually consider that a good sign."

"Raul, I want you to listen very carefully. First I am going to suggest a plan and a payment. And then I am going to tell you the name of the target. Is that agreeable?"

"Perfectly."

"Okay. This is going to require a recce and a plan of action that suits both of us. While you complete it, I am going to leave a payment of fifty thousand U.S. dollars with a lawyer in Geneva. When you have had time to consider the project, you can let me have the name of the man who will collect it. Meanwhile, the man we wish to eliminate is named Henri Foche. He is believed to be—"

"*HENRI FOCHE!* You have to be joking! That's like a contract on that Russian billionaire who owns Chelsea Football Club in London. He's got more security than the U.S. president. It'd take an army."

"Bullshit," snapped Mack. "He's not a head of state. He's just a politician running for office in a pain-in-the-ass European republic that is probably going broke."

Raul, a.k.a. Reggie Fortescue, laughed despite himself. "Not quite, Mr. Morrison. Henri Foche is going to become president of France. Trust me. And I have no idea which banana republic you are representing, or why. But I can tell you this. I can think of no more difficult person in the whole of France to kill and then escape afterward."

"Well, will you take it on?"

"Perhaps. But we are talking a very great deal of money."

"We have a very great deal of money, but we're not spending it stupidly. Gimme a price."

"Mr. Morrison. We would not even continue this conversation for less than a two-million-dollar flat fee—win, lose, or draw. I do not know whether you quite understand. Monsieur Foche is a very popular man here in France, but he has sinister connections. He is believed to be in some way involved with the international arms business at a very high level. You know—aircraft, warships, missiles. He is surrounded by bodyguards, men of a rather unsavory type. Not officers and certainly not gentlemen. Before I speak to you again, I need to have a conference with our most experienced and professional operators."

"I understand. By the way, where does Foche actually live?"

"He has a house in the city of Rennes. That's in central Brittany, where he also has a political office. When he launches his campaign on behalf of the Gaullists, it will be from Rennes. But like many men of his type, he keeps an apartment somewhere in Paris."

"When will you decide if the mission's go?"

"Give us twenty-four hours. Call at the usual time."

"Is the price firm? Two million?"

"Firm. If my colleagues will undertake the contract, it's two million U.S. dollars."

"If it's firm, it's agreeable."

"Oh, one more question, Mr. Morrison. Were you in the military?"

"Why do you ask?" replied Mack.

"Civilians don't normally ask if missions are go."

"Let's hope this one is. 'Til tomorrow." Mack disconnected, ducking the question, as if it had been a bullet.

In Marseille, Raul summoned his top men, the two rough, violent former Legionnaires and the crooked lawyer Carroll. Very calmly he told them someone was offering two million U.S. dollars for a contract. At which point there were smiles all around, especially from the Legionnaires, who stood to collect four hundred thousand dollars each from a successful hit. Then he revealed the target, and all three smiles vanished. Carroll blew coffee out of his nose in an involuntary act of pure astonishment. Jean-Pierre, the Legionnaire wanted for murder, accidentally tipped over his chair when he stood up and shouted, *"FOCHE? HENRI FOCHE? Even his fucking car's bulletproof!"*

Raul asked him how he could possibly know that.

Jean-Pierre, his voice still raised, said, "I've read stuff. Everyone's read stuff about Foche. Jesus Christ, he's supposed to be an arms manufacturer. His guys would probably take us all out with a fucking nuclear missile. Fuck that!"

"Does that mean you decline, Jean-Pierre?" Raul was all charm.

"Christ, no. I'll do it for the cash. What the hell have I got to lose? In the end the cops will catch me for the guy I already killed in that bar. This way I'll have the money to hide a lot better . . . and I'll be able to afford a lawyer." Jean-Pierre glanced over at Monsieur Carroll, whom he plainly hated, and muttered, "A better one than this asshole."

Carroll ignored him, having calculated that he stood to make two hundred thousand dollars if Jean-Pierre could shoot straight.

Which brought Raul to the second Legionnaire, Ramon, who was very much the henchman and number two to the wanted Jean-Pierre.

This was curious since Ramon was a huge man, exuding menace, possibly six-foot-five, fit, black-haired like a Moroccan, and a master with a knife. He just nodded and murmured, "I'm in. I'll kill him. Just give me an address."

"Ramon, I don't want you to oversimplify this," interjected Raul. "Henri Foche will have armed bodyguards with him night and day."

"Yeah, but I've read shit about him. Seen pictures of him with girls in Paris. He ain't got his guards with him when he's fucking, right? He'll be lucky I don't chop his cock off."

"Yes, er, quite," said Raul, who had never absolutely come to terms with the sheer low-life brutality of these two former desert fighters from the French Foreign Legion. "I understand entirely. But I want you to understand the importance of stealth, cunning, and vanishing without a trace. Quite frankly, the prospect of you two chasing the stark-naked Henri Foche through Montmartre trying to chop off his cock fills me with horror. This is a big man, the most important person we've ever tackled. We must be professional all the way—quiet, well planned, and very quick. This Foche is not going to be easy."

"Might even need a sniper rifle. Take him from a distance," said Jean-Pierre. "That way no one's going to recognize us."

Raul nodded. He understood the danger of letting these two brain-dead killers loose and the consequences of them being caught and charged with attempted murder. One wrong sentence could bring down the entire French operation of Forces of Justice, right here in Marseille. But Raul did not think that would happen. If Jean-Pierre and Ramon were caught, they would most certainly be shot dead by Foche's men, and dead men say very little. So far as Raul was concerned, there was much to be gained—in his case a million dollars—and almost no downside, to him at least. He wanted the mission to proceed, and he wanted Morrison's fifty thousand dollars in expense money in order to put together a professional-looking plan of operation that would impress the paymasters in London.

He could do no more than wait for Morrison to make contact tomorrow. Three times Raul had attempted unsuccessfully to trace the call. FOJ actually had a highly advanced military tracking system (stolen) in the attic of the building. This electronic satellite transmitter could trace any incoming call from anywhere in the universe. Maybe not the precise telephone number, but certainly the area of origin, any city in the world, accurate to within a couple of hundred yards. This was achieved by sending a second satellite beam on a replica wave length from the head office in Africa and then establishing the intersecting point of the two global lines. And it never failed. Except for Morrison's calls, when a high-pitched shriek darn near sent the operator deaf.

It was that, more than anything, that convinced Raul that this Morrison character was on the level, probably working for a government and using state funding. Not to mention this state-of-the-art telephone blocking system. If the money was good, Raul could put up with the anonymity of his client.

———•◆•———

Four hundred miles to the northwest of Marseille, in the heart of the city of Rennes, Henri Foche was looking at the newspaper. "Frowning" would be too mild a word. Henri was glowering at a front-page story that announced the burned-out wreck of a S500 Mercedes-Benz had been discovered in a deep green swamp in the middle of one of the most desolate parts of the flat, gloomy plain of Sologne, south of the Loire.

French police had called in Mercedes engineers from Germany, and they had pronounced the vehicle to be no more than eight months old. Forensic experts had been working on the car for several days in the police garages at Vierzon and believed the car may have been the one owned by the missing French missile scientist, Olivier Marchant. There was no trace of the rocket man, which was scarcely surprising since the automobile had been completely destroyed, almost certainly blown up by some kind of bomb, and it had been in the swamp for many weeks.

According to French police the vehicle was found by game wardens trying to rescue a deer from the muddy water who realized it was standing on a submerged platform. This turned out to be the hood of the

Mercedes, which the wardens considered to be an unusual parking spot for a car like that.

The nationwide search for Monsieur Marchant had yielded nothing, and police said the discovery of the vehicle had not provided one single clue as to his whereabouts. A spokesman from Montpellier Munitions near Orléans, where M. Marchant worked, said, "None of us has given up hope that Olivier may return. He was a very popular member of the staff here, and is missed every day on matters of high-tech aviation."

His widow, Janine, age thirty-four, was not called upon to identify the Mercedes, or even to see it. Last night she would say only, "I don't think we will ever know what happened to Olivier. He called home that day to tell me he would be here for lunch, and no one ever heard from him again. The discovery of his car makes me believe even more strongly that something very terrible has happened to him."

Henri Foche did some more glowering. "I said, 'without a trace,'" he grated. "I did not say to put Olivier's vehicle on the front page of every newspaper in France."

His face betrayed a level of exasperation unusual in ordinary mortals. No one could hate quite like Henri Foche. At least no one in the free world. And right now he was perfectly willing to have both of his loyal bodyguards, Marcel and Raymond, executed without trial.

He took a knife and spread strawberry preserves on his warm croissant, fantasizing that the thin puff-pastry end was Marcel's throat. His very pretty wife, Claudette, a former nightclub dancer, came into the room, took one look at him, and wondered whether he thought the known world was about to come to an end.

"Shut up, you stupid bitch," he growled.

"Such charm, such gallantry," she said. "The great Henri Foche, rude pig."

He put down the newspaper and turned to face her. "You don't think I have enough on my mind without the police trying to resurrect the mystery of Olivier Marchant? They'll be at the factory again soon I imagine, asking damn fool questions. How the hell do any of us know what happened to him? He left the parking lot that day, alone in his car, seen by several staff members, and vanished."

"Well, how come the police found the car in the swamp?" asked Claudette. "They say there's no trace of him. So somebody must have taken him out of the car and then blown it up."

"How the hell do you know all this?"

"Because I just saw it on the news. The car had almost been blown in half, but they've been looking for Olivier for weeks and still not found one trace of him."

"Maybe some crazy thief stopped him and robbed him."

"For a supposedly intelligent little man, you are remarkably foolish at times," she replied. "Crazy robbers do not go around with heavy-duty transporters, blowing up Mercedes-Benzes, and then driving miles and miles away to hide the damn thing in a Sologne swamp. This crime was planned and carried out by a professional operation."

"Okay, Madame Claudette Maigret. How do you know all that?"

"Because that's what the police inspector just said on television. And for the first time they are treating Olivier's disappearance as murder."

Foche looked up sharply. "Did he say that? It's not in the paper."

"That's because the stupid newspaper was printed at ten o'clock last night. The policeman was speaking on television about fifteen minutes ago in Vierzon."

"That's all I need. A murder inquiry involving a member of my board of directors, just as I launch my campaign for president."

"And that's not your only problem," said Claudette, an edge of spitefulness in her voice. "Last night while you were out I took a phone call from that little actress you've been seeing in Paris. I pretended I just work here, and took her number. She would like you to call her if you are going to the city on Friday. Which of course you are."

Foche pretended not to be listening, but Claudette had something to say. "I am prepared to tolerate your behavior because of the lifestyle you have given me. But I am not going to be humiliated. And if you become president, you will humiliate me with your endless affairs."

"So what are you going to do? Go back to the gutter where you were when I found you? 'Madame Foche, wife to the president of France.' Isn't that enough for you? Enough for any Saint-Germain whore?"

Claudette Foche was used to this. But this time she smiled and said softly, "Henri, I think you will find the shoe is on the other foot these days. If I decided to leave you, it would be a mortal blow to your chances of election. And then, of course, I could sell my story of your sex-crazed unfaithful tyranny to the nice little magazines for a very large sum of money."

"You couldn't give up this lifestyle—the glamour, the fame, the admiration."

"Not only could I give it up, but I'm only thirty-eight and I'd willingly start again. Perhaps you forget these days. . . ." Claudette carefully undid the top two buttons of her blouse, turned to face him provocatively, and added, "I can attract almost any man I wish. I'm still very slim and very sexy. And you have made me acceptable in French society."

"I guess once a whore, always a whore," he growled.

"Perhaps," she said, tossing back her long mane of blonde hair. "But I have never been unfaithful to you. Whereas your morals belong to an alley cat."

At this point the telephone rang noisily on the far side of the room. "Get that," he said sharply. "Hurry up."

Claudette walked across the room with the unhurried strut of a catwalk model, as if practicing for a new life back on the game in the expensive bars and hotels of the French capital. Foche could not help but admire her. And he agreed—she could have any man she wished.

"Hello," she said. "Yes, Marcel. He is here. Just a moment."

She stood by the phone and said, "Marcel."

"Well, bring the damn thing here, will you?" he rasped. "And then get out."

Claudette walked slowly back to her husband and handed him the phone. He snatched it rudely and repeated, "Get out."

His wife left the room, and Foche almost shouted, "I told you to get rid of that car—not have it all over the national news! Jesus Christ!"

Marcel, however, was no pushover. His actual words were, "Well, how the hell was I to know the stupid deer would find the fucking thing? I drove it into the swamp, damn near drowned myself and Raymond, somehow blew the bastard sky-high, and now you want me to act like a fucking part-time deer guard. For Christ's sake, sir. Be reasonable."

Henri Foche knew he had to be careful with Marcel, who knew his misdeeds even more thoroughly than his wife did. "But what about the fucking body?" he demanded. "Where's that?"

"In the foundation of that new shopping center about fifty miles east of Orléans. Buried in about a thousand tons of rock-hard concrete."

"How the hell did you manage that?" asked Foche.

"I got friends," replied Marcel. "Good friends."

"Anyone else know?"

"Of course not. I dumped it into the wet concrete. Drove the mechanical digger myself. Then my pal tipped about three truckloads of wet concrete on top of it. He probably guessed a body. But never mentioned it. I waited there until he'd finished the job. Gave him two thousand euros, like you said."

"Okay, okay. Sounds fine. I just wish they hadn't found the Benz."

"Million-to-one chance, boss. Can't fight that. We just keep our heads down."

"See you at midday, Marcel."

"No problem."

"*Claudette! Where the hell are you?*" Foche's voice rose in exasperation.

His wife came in and said, "I'm right here. What do you need?"

"First of all take this damn phone off my breakfast table. Then bring me some fresh coffee. After that I'll need a legal pad and a pen. And phone Mirabel. Tell her to meet me at the office right after lunch."

Mirabel, Foche's fifty-six-year-old secretary, a slim, plain local woman, was perhaps the only woman in Foche's life whom he had not attempted to undress. Although Claudette would not have put her life savings on that being entirely true.

"Will you be here for lunch?" she asked.

"No. I'm going out, probably locally."

The young girl he was seeing, Anne-Marie, had a small apartment near the canal, not far from his own home, which was set back behind a redbrick wall in the Les Lices area. They always met in L'Ouvrée restaurant and then walked to her home, from which Marcel collected him around three o'clock.

This weekly procedure was not without its perils. There had been one shuddering occasion when Foche and the girl had almost been caught, walking along rue de la Monnaie, with Claudette approaching on the other side of the street. Henri Foche had never raced into a church with such determination. Even the carved angels on the outer wall of the Cathedrale Saint Pierre looked startled at the sudden appearance of the serial adulterer, murderer, liar, and international arms pariah. But they would look startled: angels have superior insights to the rest of us.

And now Claudette was hot on his trail again. "Who are you seeing and where? I may need to contact you, especially if the police have more questions about Olivier." She should have known better. If there was one thing Henri Foche could not abide under any circumstances, it was interference with his plans. Particularly from a woman, especially from his wife.

He glanced up and said coldly, "Shut your damn mouth."

"I don't think you should speak to me like that anymore," she said. "I'm entitled to ask questions, and you are in a very vulnerable position politically."

Anger welled up inside him. No one thwarted Henri Foche, especially on matters involving illicit sex, to which he had been looking forward for several days. He stood up and walked over to her, drew back his right arm across his body, and whipped a backhanded smack right across his wife's mouth and nose. The blow sent her reeling across the room. She hit the sideboard and slid down the wall next to it, blood pouring down her face, dripping onto her still half-open blouse.

Foche stood looking down at her, fists clenched, as she cowered on the floor, sobbing and turning away from him. He lifted up his highly polished Gucci right foot and slammed a kick hard into her perfectly formed backside. "Remember," he said, "I am Henri Foche, the next president of France. You are a partially reformed Saint-Germain whore. If I were you, I would not forget that." With that, he walked back into his study.

It was not the first time he had hit her. But this was very bad. Claudette had been brought up on the wrong side of the tracks, the product of a baker's assistant and a violent dockworker who regularly beat her mother.

Madame Foche had not arrived at the gates of the Elysée Palace, as it were, by some kind of a fluke. She had been a calculating and careful hooker, very beautiful, very selective, with a high-class clientele. Like most members of her trade, she had a powerful instinct to fight back when threatened. She stood up and walked into the kitchen and selected a serrated bread knife made by Sabatier. She was shaking with rage, pain, and humiliation.

She walked into his study and said, very softly, "Henri, if you ever hit me again, I swear to God I will kill you. With this. I know what you are, and I know I am in danger. But you are a vicious bastard, and you deserve to die. And you won't find me as easy to get rid of as poor Olivier Marchant."

Foche looked up. His eyes narrowed. "Just so long as you remember your place in this world, there will be no more trouble. Step out of line again, and you will regret it. I have bigger things on my mind than you. So get out and stay out."

Claudette left the room, slamming the door so hard the eighteenth-century house shook on its foundations. She retreated into her bathroom to repair her cut lip and still-bleeding nose. Her display of bravado had left her unaccountably exhausted. She was afraid of her husband, and always had been.

She had seen some of his friends. She was aware of the reliance he placed on those two thugs, Marcel and Raymond. She not only believed he was capable of murder, she believed he had committed murder, and would not hesitate to murder her if he felt that was necessary.

Her dilemma was twofold. If she ran, Foche would hunt her down and have her eliminated, simply because she may prove a danger to him. No one would ever know what had become of her. Third wives elicit little sympathy. But if she stayed, that would be a different form of hell: a world of constant humiliation, sexual demands, fear, and the ever-present knowledge that her husband was in bed with another woman. She had long ceased to love him, or even care about him. But Claudette had some pride, and she did not consider herself worthless, just a sex object for a cruel and sneering husband. She thought she had value and a worthwhile mind. She sat on the bathroom chair and wept tears of pure helplessness.

She was a prisoner here in this perfect French provincial house, a captive of a truly bad person, and there was nothing she could do. Claudette understood she had not, by any means, led a blameless life, but she had been a good wife, and like many other people around the world, she fervently wished her husband dead.

She was not comforted by the prospect of becoming a twenty-first-century Queen Marie Antoinette, living similarly in the Elysée Palace in Paris, afforded every human luxury the French taxpayers' money could buy. Today she felt more like Marie Antoinette on October 16, 1793, trapped in her tiny cell in the Conciergerie, preparing herself to face the guillotine.

She heard her husband leave and debated the fairly simple possibility of having him followed and building a case for divorce on the grounds of his perpetual adultery. But for what? To end up like Olivier Marchant, wherever he may be?

———— • ◆ • ————

Mack Bedford decided to walk up to the shipyard for a final chat with Harry before they made their decision. He walked through the little town, occasionally stopping for a chat with local people he had known almost all of his life. But when he reached the big iron gates of Remsons Shipbuilding he saw what he thought might be a riot meeting. And in the middle of a throng of maybe a hundred men stood the proprietor of the yard.

Mack jostled through the crowd and stood next to Harry, who told him, loud enough for all to hear, "Hi, Mack, you find me on probably the worst day of my life. I have just laid off my principal steelworkers. There is no more work here for them, and I doubt there's going to be."

Judd Powell stood on the other side of Harry. He called out, "Guys, you know if there were any prospect of jobs, the boss would never have let you go. But all over the Western world the militaries are cutting back. Less ships are being built everywhere except Russia and the Far East. That may change, but it may take five years, and Mr. Remson obviously cannot fund a fifty-million-dollar-a-year wage bill until then."

"*But what are we gonna do, Judd?*" "*We got wives, families, mortgages—what now?*" "*This is all we know—and no one's been hired up the road at Bath for two years.*" "*There's nothing else here. . . . Are you saying we have to leave the town, move somewhere else?*" "*What about our kids, schools, grades, and everything else?*"

The questions rained in on Harry Remson and his foreman. It was nothing short of grief. As if someone had died. These hardworking men, men who came in and cut steel at seven on the coldest mornings. They were men who worked high on the hulls of these warships, forcing the cold steel into position. They were men upon whom the worldwide reputation of Remsons had been built. Men with wide shoulders, enormous strength, and a work ethic that would have made a New York longshoreman blanch.

They understood, albeit remotely, that Harry Remson and his family could not go on supporting them indefinitely if there was no work. But they could not rid themselves of the feeling they were somehow being cast out. Unfairly. Undeservingly. Unnecessarily. And now they had to go home and inform their wives they had been laid off and from now on they were officially unemployed. Just a government statistic, reporting to the benefit office in Bath every week, just to try to sustain family life. In some lessened form.

Most of these steelworkers were used to furnishing their homes, exchanging their automobiles, and buying new wardrobes for the entire family when the generous triannual Remson bonuses were paid out, upon completion of the French frigates. And all of them knew they were about to feel a financial draft in every possible sense, with rocketing winter fuel bills in one of the harshest climates in North America. A few of them, in the last riven hours, had already contemplated moving away, becoming strangers in a strange new place, perhaps somewhere warmer, where life might be less expensive.

For the steel men the loss of work coincided with a shattering loss of face. Because they alone form the bedrock of the workforce. The word "steel" has an extra connotation in the shipbuilding industry. No one states, "Work is about to begin on a new warship" or "Remsons expects to get moving next month on the new order." The phrase is traditional, and it appears in all naval lists of newly built warships: "First steel cut X months before the keel is laid."

And here they stood, one hundred men, each one of them with a lump in his throat, facing the day they thought would never come, facing the fact that their brutal hard work down the years had, in the end, meant nothing.

Harry Remson knew how they felt. He had been on the phone to his own father for two hours that morning, and the old man, eighty-six years old now and stubborn to the end, had started and finished the long conversation with the same sentence: "Son, you gotta do what's right for the guys. Don't give up. Please don't give up. It's your duty to save them and the shipyard. Give it one more try. See if you can pull something off."

Harry had put down the phone close to tears. And now Judd had laid off the steelworkers as instructed. And he, Harry, somehow had to provide them all with a ray of hope. And that ray of hope rested, he knew, in the breech of a sniper rifle, aimed by one of Raul's murdering bastards or, at least, someone comparable.

"Guys," he said, "I don't guess it would do much good for me to explain how I feel, and how sorry I am. Like you, I never thought this day would come. All I can say is that I am still doing everything I can to save that next French order. I can promise nothing, because we are right now dead in the water. But I have one last trick to pull, involving an extremely awkward meeting in France. It might lead to something. But it might not. Meantime, I have paid all of you three months' money, and your bonuses for hull number 718 are safe. You'll get those start of next year. And, as you know, your pensions, however big, however small, are safe here at Remsons. None of you will get one dollar short.

"But before you leave, I have one small request. Don't any of you bail out on me or the yard or the town for a month. Because I just might pull this off in France. And right then I'm going to need you back. And if that happens, we'll have a party they'll hear in Bath."

A few of the men clapped; a few grinned. But most of the older ones stood stoically before the chief, resigned to their fate.

Harry said simply, "I'm going to miss you guys. Every one of you. For me this is like the breakup of a family." He turned away and walked back into the yard, too distraught to continue.

Mack walked with him, while Judd stayed to talk to the men. The two international conspirators, joined now in a bond of clandestine intrigue, made their way to the office that overlooked the drydock.

Mack went in first, while Harry stayed outside the door, speaking to his secretary. The lieutenant commander stood for a few moments looking down at the French warship, and then he turned to a small framed poem on the wall, a verse by Henry Wadsworth Longfellow. The title was painted in an elegant, old-fashioned script—"The Building of a Ship." Beneath it were the lines:

> *Build me straight, O worthy master!*
> *Staunch and strong, a goodly vessel,*
> *That shall laugh at all disaster,*
> *And with wave and whirlwind wrestle.*

This was the creed of Remsons, words that inspired Maine shipbuilders back to the age of the clipper ships, which, for sailors at least, were forever the greatest sailing vessels of all. They kept building them right here on the Kennebec until the close of the nineteenth century.

Harry came into the office, all business now. No time for sadness. "What does he say, Mack? Did he turn us down?"

"No," said Mack. "He did not. He just said he needed a day to talk to his colleagues. I guess he meant the serial killers he employs to carry out this kind of high-risk contract."

"What's your latest take on it?"

"Oh, I don't doubt he'll say yes. It's going to cost you two million. I don't think they'd do it for less. And in a way we don't want them to.

When you've hired guys to do the unthinkable, it's gotta be an address changer. Otherwise, why should they do it?"

"Okay, let's say they accept—what then?"

"Well, we have to get fifty thousand for expenses to them. And that's a major worry, because we have to assume Switzerland is watertight."

"I'm happy with that end of the security. What I remain unhappy about is that 50 percent down payment. Because it remains a hell of a way to make a million bucks. Take the money and never even try; run no risk. That's what they could do. Just walk away with the mill, and never speak to us again."

"Don't think I haven't considered that, Harry. And you're right. It is a problem. But in the end, that's our risk. Theirs is getting shot by Foche's security guys. According to Raul, we're in it together, and we have to have some trust in each other."

"Okay, I'll tell you what, Mack. Let's see what they come up with. Meantime, I'll get the fifty grand into Switzerland, ready to be passed on to the lawyer for pickup. When that's in place we'll decide whether to go ahead."

"We're not going anywhere without it," replied Mack. "Because each side has a very definite objective. We want someone dead; they want big money to carry it out."

"When's the call, tomorrow morning?"

"Yup."

"Keep me posted."

———•◆•———

Mack's next stop was in the center of town, 342 Main Street, the New England Savings and Loan. The bank manager had agreed to see him, but neither man was very hopeful anything could be worked out.

The manager, Donald Hill, was relatively new, had come up from a branch in Massachusetts, west of Boston. He hated Maine, loathed the cold, disliked the ocean, had a wife who was allergic to seafood, and considered all Down-Easters to be rustic clamheads. Also, he missed seeing

the Red Sox and could hardly wait for a big-city promotion. On a man-
ager-customer charm scale of 1 to 10, he had not yet made the chart.

"Mr. Bedford," he said unnecessarily, "this is a very large sum of
money you wish to borrow. And your assets are not, shall we say, substantial. One house, owned in partnership with your wife, and a two-
hundred-thousand-dollar mortgage hanging over it on a twenty-year
basis. If my bank advanced you one million dollars and you managed
to pay back ten thousand a year, or two hundred a week, without interest it would take you a hundred years. From our point of view, that
would not represent a sound loan policy."

Mr. Hill hit the buttons on his calculator. "If we gave it to you on a 6
percent rate, it would never be repaid unless you won the state lottery,
which from our point of view would be unacceptable."

Mack Bedford gazed at him steadily. "Sir," he said, "I have a little boy
who is dying. He will die, unless I can get him to Switzerland for an extremely rare and difficult operation. The cost will be one million dollars. I am asking New England Savings and Loan for the money to save
my boy. My U.S. insurance will not cover foreign medical treatment."

"I understand the difficulty, Mr. Bedford, but I am afraid my company cannot be responsible for every hard-luck story that comes
through the door. You are asking for the impossible."

"For you this is so little," said Mack. "But for me it is life and death.
Would you consider asking your board of directors if they would
speak to me? My full name is Lt. Cdr. Mackenzie Bedford, United
States Navy SEAL, holder of the Navy Cross."

Mr. Hill looked up and nodded. "Sir, I would be more than happy to
do so. I will speak to our Public Affairs Department and get some kind
of recommendation from them. I mean, to whom you should speak. It
may mean a trip to Boston."

"Sir, I would gladly meet in the Hindu Kush if I thought it would help."

"The where?"

"It's the back end of the Himalayas. Not a bad place to get shot,
since you mention it."

Donald Hill sensed he was out of his depth with this tall SEAL commander with the Down-East accent. And he decided to terminate this

curiously embarrassing interview. He stood up and said, "Lieutenant Commander, I hope we can come up with something. Even in a bank as big as this one, there are still times when other considerations take precedence over purely financial matters. Don't lose heart."

"I won't," replied Mack. "It's not broken yet."

He walked out of the bank and retraced his footsteps toward home. It was lunchtime now, but he did not know whether Anne and Tommy were back, or even if the little boy had been detained at the hospital.

The sun had vanished behind a great rolling cloud bank, and there would be no fishing tonight, even if Tommy made it home. There was a weather front forecast to come in from the southwest over the Gulf of Maine, and in his seaman's bones he could feel the change, the slight alteration in wind direction, the cooler air, and the obvious onset of rain.

Mack walked on down to the shore, not to the fishing spot, just to a little cove with a pebble beach and granite rocks holding back the dark, encroaching pines. He picked up a few stones and hurled them hard, one by one, watching them bounce at erratic angles off the beach. He could see the chop building down on the estuary, and a fishing boat was making all speed to an upstream harbor, like a rust-colored seabird racing back to the nest. Mack guessed her helmsman had decided against the weather. The big SEAL considered that a shrewd decision. Behind the trawler he could see huge clouds rising far astern, and they were not white; they were pewter, with trails of falling mist behind them. Rain and rising wind, heading onshore. Not good, with a rising sea surging toward the granite rock guardians of the land.

There were still bright patches of light, the sun giving this July day one last chance. But Mack never thought of the land, not on days like this when the weather turned with such sudden venom. He thought of the ships out there, of those too far distant to make landfall by the evening. And he thought of the great white pillar of the Sequin light, still catching the dying rays of the sun, as the fishermen came slogging home against the hard sou'wester.

He was not a man accustomed to prayer beyond the confines of the family pew at the Congregational church. But today he looked up at a great gap in the cloud bank, perhaps at the final bright rays of the day, before the gray clouds engulfed everything. He envisioned his God in a faraway kingdom beyond the seething skies. He prayed for Tommy, and he prayed for the shipyard and the people who worked there. He prayed for the souls of his lost buddies, the guys who fell that day by the Euphrates River. And, as a last resort, he prayed that Raul's men would successfully assassinate the Frenchman Henri Foche.

This was, so far, a sad day, and it was about to get sadder. When Mack reached home, Anne was preparing coffee, but he could see she had been crying. Without a word he took her in his arms and held her close, and once more he felt her body racked with sobs. It took her a full minute to ask the question. "Tommy's worse," she said. "What did the bank say?"

"Well, they didn't throw me out. But they did point out that if they let me have the loan at 6 percent, the interest on the money would be sixty thousand a year. That's without paying off the principal."

Anne tore herself away and dried her eyes on a dishcloth. But when she turned around, they were blazing. "The interest!" she shouted. "The interest! Our beautiful little boy is dying, and all they can talk about is the interest on their money? Who the hell are these people—*Nazis?*"

Mack was more measured. "I guess we have to accept that Tommy is not their little boy. And they hear a hundred tough stories like ours every day. Anyway, they did offer one shred of hope. Donald Hill, the manager, told me there were certain unusual circumstances when other considerations were taken into account, not just the cash. He promised to speak to his public affairs people and then the directors. He told me not to lose heart."

Anne walked back across the kitchen and put her arms around him. "Everyone needs hope, darling Mack. Even when there's hardly any left. It's just that Dr. Ryan was so depressed about the whole thing. He said Tommy's particular strain of ALD was almost entirely exclusive to boys of his age. And when it took hold, it could move very rapidly."

"He's not still there, is he?"

"No, I brought him home and put him to bed. But something happened at the hospital that I think was very bad. Tommy had an absolute tantrum, the worst I have seen. He threw a teddy bear across the room, and then tried to rip its head off. That wasn't even the worst part. It happened with Joyce—you know, the nurse he likes so much. But Dr. Ryan came in immediately. I was trying to calm Tommy down, but I heard what the doctor said to Joyce."

"What was it?"

"He said, 'Damn, I'd really hoped this wouldn't start happening yet. Poor kid. He can't last six months.'"

"Didn't you say he'd reacted like that before?"

"Yes, a couple of times while you were away. But nothing like so bad as today. Anyway, I asked the doctor if this was as serious as it seemed, and he told me the disease was moving far too fast into his nervous system. He said the trouble was, Tommy was so strong and active and healthy. It seemed to get worse quicker in kids like that. He virtually told me that if we could not get him to this clinic in Switzerland, we would all need to accept that Tommy has a terminal condition."

———•◆•———

Back in Marseille, Raul was convinced he had a real live client for two million U.S. dollars on the hook, ready to be reeled in. He'd already hired a helicopter and dispatched Jean-Pierre and Ramon to take a fast look around Rennes. He'd instructed them to get the lay of the land, check out Foche's house, check his office, make a few local inquiries. When Morrison called back it was important that FOJ looked professional, as if they knew what they were doing.

Raul had just spoken on the cell phone to Jean-Pierre, who had done productive work. He had been across the street from the Gaullist Party's political office when Foche arrived. He'd checked out the Mercedes, written down the registration number, photographed both Foche and his two bodyguards, one of whom, the one wearing the brown suede jacket, was the driver. He thought the other one had a gun beneath his leather jacket.

While Jean-Pierre kept watch on the office, Ramon had located the Foche residence. It had taken only a few minutes to get the address, posing as a courier at the local delicatessen. The newspapers had published many times the area in which he lived. And now Ramon was busy with his camera, photographing the house from several angles, back and front. He snapped pictures from doorways, behind trees, from the front yards of other houses. He worked only when the coast was clear.

He waited in the area until Foche returned home, at around seven o'clock, not having noticed Jean-Pierre's tiny rental car following him back to Anne-Marie's apartment, where he had remained for around one hour. Ramon photographed him as he got out of the car outside his own home, and he noticed that Marcel did not walk to the front door with him. This pleased the FOJ hit man, pleased him a lot, and he once more considered whether a sniper rifle might be the best weapon to use.

The light was fading now. But in a very few hours, Raul's men had gathered some important data. There was much more to accomplish before one of them actually pulled the trigger. But there was not much more that could be accomplished this evening.

They checked into the comfortable Hotel des Lices and had dinner there, in readiness for an early start in the rental car right up the street from Foche's residence, first light. Their brief had been precise: Keep feeding data to the head office until four o'clock that afternoon. Then return to the Marseille base, by train.

———•◆•———

Henri Foche arrived at his political headquarters shortly after nine. The campaign staff was already there, trying to finalize slogans for the great Gaullist revival that they anticipated would sweep him to power. Stretched across the far wall of the big workroom was a twenty-foot banner: *HENRI FOCHE—POUR BRETAGNE. POUR LA FRANCE!!* For Brittany. For France. On the laid-out tables were large posters, each one dominated by a photograph of Henri Foche. Beneath each picture there were varying slogans—The Man Who Can Make a Difference; The Politician for Industry; The Politician for Jobs; Foche: The New de Gaulle; The Statesman Who Believes in France.

Foche gazed at the creative work with satisfaction. He'd master-minded almost every word himself, but he liked to give credit to his people, especially these people, who were doing it all out of unpaid political enthusiasm, trying to pull it all together in readiness for the national launch in two weeks.

Across the street, Jean-Pierre wondered whether a bomb right in the middle of that room, five minutes after Foche arrived, might be the cleanest and neatest way to accomplish the assassination. He realized it might unnecessarily wipe out a half-dozen other people—but the bomb had several major advantages. The first of these would be to deflect the attention of the police in their hunt for the murderer. A bomb is a much less personal weapon than an assassin's bullet. After all, it might have been thrown into the room by enemies of the Gaullists, by rabid left-wingers, furious that their grip on power was being eliminated. Also a bomb can be detonated by remote control. A timing device would not work, because no one knew if and when Foche might show up. The assassins would need to be on station and hurl it straight through the window or, alternatively, plant it carefully in the office during the wee hours and then detonate it from across the street as soon as Foche arrived.

Either way, the bomb eliminated the problem of passersby spotting a marksman aiming a bullet at the head of the next president of France. In Jean-Pierre's opinion, the assassination should be conducted from the open air. Rennes was a busy town, full of tourists, and the police would be on the scene very quickly. But no one would notice a man with a small detonator, pressing a red button and setting off a blast a hundred yards away.

And the six innocent people who would most certainly be killed or maimed when the device blew? Well, that had nothing to do with Jean-Pierre or Ramon, did it? Their task was to kill Henri Foche, pick up four hundred thousand dollars each, and make a clean getaway. A lot to do, right? No time for details.

Raul was delighted with their efforts. They phoned him and talked him through places on the tourist maps of Rennes. They had addresses, phone numbers, locations. They even had the address of Foche's local mistress, but not her name. If the contract went through, they would carry out a similar recce in the streets of Paris, if Raul could somehow come up with an address for Henri. The media usually referred to his home as "an apartment near avenue Foch, 16th *arrondissement.*"

Armed with his notebook and maps, Raul awaited the call, the big-money call, and Mack Bedford was right on time. Up in the attic two technicians worked feverishly to trace the cell phone, but, as ever, when Mr. Morrison came on, there was a total electronic blank-out. The trackers screamed, the technicians swore, and still no one knew, within ten thousand miles, from whence Mr. Morrison was calling.

Raul had long accepted the London base Morrison had first mentioned was probably accurate. London, with its new multiculturalism, its insane laws protecting criminals and terrorists, its dishonest, lightweight politicians, its totally out-of-touch police force, and its distinct lack of traditional Britishness was now Europe's hotbed of international intrigue. The British population had given up caring what happened, and mostly could not be bothered even to vote. The police were totally consumed with traffic offenses, and the left wing of the ruling government was more or less devoted to helping those who commit unforgivable crimes and are usually named Abdul, Mohammed, Mustapha, or Khaled. London sounded right to Raul.

"Hello, Mr. Morrison," he said. "On time as ever. And I have some interesting stuff to report, assuming you still require our services."

"You may take that as definite," replied Mack.

"Very well. I have spent a long time speaking to my colleagues, and we have decided unanimously that, while this project carries unusual dangers, it is not impossible, and my men are confident we can achieve the correct result."

Mack thought he sounded like a supermarket sales manager about to conduct a survey of the customers in the parking lot.

"We have already made a recce of the city of Rennes where the target lives. He has an accessible house, and is probably vulnerable two or even three times a day. He also has a girlfriend in the town and visited her twice yesterday, both times without his security men, who left in his car and returned to collect him around an hour later."

"The political office is in the central part of the town, on street level, with large windows and a staff of perhaps six people. Right now my men are inclined to favor an explosive device rather than a bullet. If you decide to go ahead, we will recce Paris this week, since the target does have a residence there, in a very public area in the center of the city. Paris would not be our first choice."

"Thank you, Raul. You have been very active. And you know what they say, 'Time spent on reconnaissance is seldom wasted.'"

"Yes, I have been sure from the very beginning that you were ex-military, Mr. Morrison."

"Have you now? But I expect you know I protect my identity with considerable care."

"I had noticed. Which brings us to the small matter of fifty thousand dollars in payment for our preliminary work. Have you given this some thought?"

"Raul, I've done a great deal more than that. The money is in Geneva in U.S. dollars, and will be available for you to collect starting tomorrow morning. I will let you have the lawyer's name and address within twelve hours. The bank has not yet decided which law firm to use. It's important the lawyer does not know either party and that the bank does not know you, correct?"

"Absolutely. And now perhaps I should mention that the degree of danger in this project is very high indeed. The target is under the protection of armed bodyguards almost all of the time, although we have not yet ascertained the level of security inside his house. My firm would be ruined if this went wrong, and in light of that we would be looking for three million U.S. dollars in order to complete the work."

"Guess you're going to have to look somewhere else, pal," replied Mack shortly. "I've told you from the very start we'd go to two mil, if we had to, but no further. And you said it was firm. I'll call tomorrow to give you the name of the Swiss lawyer—meantime, sorry it didn't work out. . . . See ya, Raul."

"*WAIT, WAIT, MORRISON!*" Raul was not actually panicking, but he was doing a very reasonable imitation of someone who was. "These matters are negotiable, and naturally I must try to obtain the best price for the men who are actually running the risks."

"No problem, Raul. But you're not getting it from me. We have already spoken to another operation like yours, based in Romania. They'll do it for one million. I don't think they have your finesse, but if you want three, then I'll take a chance on them. They *could* fuck it up, and then get him the second time, and I'd still be better off than I would paying you three million dollars. Sorry, Raul, you just priced yourself out of the market."

"Then perhaps you might allow me to price myself back in. Two million it is. I just thought that for a state-sponsored crime, we should be entitled to more."

"Raul, you don't know whether it's state sponsored or not."

"I'd be surprised if it wasn't. The target is an international politician, and in those cases it's nearly always a government that wants him removed."

"Okay, now we got the money out of the way. Tell me straight: can you guys really knock this target off?"

"Oh, yes, Mr. Morrison. You can count on us. We have a very hard-earned reputation to protect."

Mack Bedford stared at the rough, dark water at the end of the slipway in Remsons' yard. And he looked back at the remainder of the workforce completing the painting on the hull of *F718*. But there was a note of caution that was bothering him.

"Raul," he said, "when I call tomorrow to give you the law firm's name, I am going to consolidate this deal. But I need time to consult. I'm disappointed you became greedy and tried to change the terms. Because it's affected our friendship. But perhaps we can overcome that."

"I hope so, Mr. Morrison. Because in the end I believe we can work together to rid you of your problem."

Mack hoped so. For the sake of his hometown. But he did not like people who reneged on a firm deal. He did not have a warning bell in his head. He had a blaring fire alarm.

CHAPTER 6

The freight train running south across the great plain of Khuzestan, down toward the hotly disputed estuary of the Shatt-al-Arab, was not on the regular schedule. For a start, it was the middle of the night, and in the silence of Iran's enormous southwestern farmlands, the diesel locomotive made a harsh, discordant racket as it clattered through the soft, warm air, causing pastoral nomads and their cattle herds to stir in their slumbers. Tribesmen, wrapped in rough desert blankets, sleeping in the lee of their camels, heard the noise and recognized it as a locomotive. But they could not see it, because this train displayed no lights; dark eyes strained through the moonless night, but the jet-black shape of the train was invisible, and quickly the sound of its thundering engine was lost in the vastness of the dark landscape.

If the journey was unscheduled, the stop was really off the charts, way out there on the long southern curve of the main line from the oil-refining, flame-belching city of Ahvaz. The locomotive was about four miles from the little station at Ahu, when it quite suddenly slowed, gently came down to walking pace, and then came to a halt. Up ahead were lights on the track, and alongside was parked a truck bearing the insignia of the Iranian army.

Altogether there were sixteen armed military personnel alongside the train when it stopped, but the greetings were cheerful. Both train drivers, upon closer inspection, wore army uniforms, and they disembarked and moved back down the freight cars to assist in the operation. The truck was backed up just a couple of feet from the railroad, and a gangway was placed from its flatbed rear end across to the freight car.

In the still of that almost silent Iranian night, a mechanical winch in the truck began to haul the first of the twenty-seven unmarked crates out of the train and across the little steel bridge. The crates were five feet long and weighed three hundred pounds. It took four men to manhandle each one into a stack, and the whole operation took two hours.

When it was completed, the men shook hands and said their farewells, and the train pulled away, heading south down to Khorramshahr, still heavily laden with Diamondhead missiles, all of which were scheduled for a long sea voyage down the Persian Gulf, out through the Gulf of Hormuz, and on to Afghanistan, to the waiting Taliban warriors.

The truck on the plain of Khuzestan headed due west, nineteen miles, to the border with Iraq. The landscape was rough, cross-country all the way to the sharp right angle where the frontier zooms into Iran, away from the wide flow of Iraq's Tigris River. But for the last four miles the route became treacherous, marshy, with deep water on either side of the track, and it needed expert scouts to find a safe route to the Iraqi line. Fortunately, the Iranian army had at its disposal many such men.

These lands were attacked, hit with missiles, and occupied for two years by the marauding armies of Saddam Hussein during the 1980s war. These days, however, they were quiet, still the grazing grounds for the herds of the plain's nomads, but very safe for the Iranian army to run armaments to both the beleaguered al-Qaeda and Shiite terrorists in Iraq.

Iraqi troops patrol this border, but it has for centuries been the weak point of the unseen line that separates essentially implacable enemies. Beyond this border, to the west, lie the ancient lands of the Madan, the Marsh Arabs, which for hundreds of years provided a safe haven for escaped slaves, Bedouin and others, who had offended the state. These historic Arab marshlands are accessible only to boats. No army has ever operated successfully in the treacherous swamps. Indeed, the marshes were such a supreme irritation for Saddam, mostly because of deserters, that he drained hundreds of square miles, all the way down to the confluence of the Tigris and Euphrates. He drained rivers and built two enormous canals to carry away the water. Saddam destroyed an entire ecosystem, reducing the marshes to silted-up, arid flatlands, devoid of wildlife and water birds. After thousands of years, the Marsh Arabs were obliged to leave, some heading north, others east. Saddam then laid down huge causeways to permit his heavy armored vehicles to roll to the Iranian border and then to attack.

However, after the overthrow of the dictator in the opening years of the twenty-first century, the Americans and the British restored the flow of water, and the Marsh Arabs began to return. Tonight, as the Iranian missile truck drove through the eastern marshes to the frontier, the dark wetlands looked much the same as they had in biblical times. But the unseen modern frontier was engraved upon those desolate lands, and the Iranian guards came to a halt with about six GPS bleepers issuing a warning.

The guards stepped out to scan the area with Russian-made night glasses. They were secure in the knowledge that this country was just about impossible to patrol, but the hair-trigger tensions between the two nations were never far from anyone's mind.

On the Iranian side of the border there stood one stone bunker, not much different in appearance from those Hitler's generals constructed on the coast of Normandy. It was low, made of solid concrete, but with a lookout, or patrol, area on the roof. However, to its northern side was a long, deep storage bunker, underground and hard to detect. Into this cunningly concealed space, the Iranian guards loaded twenty-five of the crates, using the truck's winch to control the speed of each one as it slithered down the ramp into the cellar.

It was 0330 on the Iranian captain's watch when the twenty-seventh was secured underground. Only then did a small donkey cart driven by two young Arab men, Yousef and Rudi, come slowly down the track to pick up the last two crates. Both boys were Bakhtiaris, pastoral nomads from the foothills of the nearby Zagros Mountains, but somewhat displaced in the modern world after various governments of Iran tried to discourage their nomadic way of life.

The cart was loaded with bales of wheat, and swiftly the soldiers pulled them off and placed the two crates, end on end, in the flatbed. They piled the bales back, all around the missile boxes, and immediately the donkeys began to walk steadily to the west, crossing the border within the first hundred yards. They were now three miles from the wide Tigris River that needed to be crossed. It was essential they made the riverbank before first light.

Yousef's cry of encouragement, and the sharp swish of his whip, urged his donkeys on toward the tiny boatyard where Iraqi fisherman kept their dhows. They were there by 4:15, and the two crates were offloaded and lifted onto two flat-bottomed riverboats.

Yousef and Rudi, Iranians on a dangerous Iraqi shore, turned away, and the sound of the donkeys' hooves were all that was heard as they clip-clopped across the hard sand, away into the night, having made possible a truly lethal missile delivery.

On the far bank of the Tigris, now between Iraq's two great rivers, the crates were loaded onto yet another donkey cart and again piled with bales of wheat. This one would travel even less distance than Yousef's, just far enough to reach one of the first small navigable waterways of the Marsh Arabs.

Right here, on this slippery, reed-choked riverbank, eight men, four of them terrorist commanders, sweated, strained, splashed, and heaved the crates on board two long, slender poling canoes, the Marsh Arabs' legendary *mashuf.* This is probably the only vessel ever built that could run through these long lagoons and shallow lakes so efficiently that no one has changed the design in six thousand years.

The three-foot-wide crates would not lie flat and needed to be propped diagonally between the gunwales of the narrow boats. Once the crates were packed and tied down, the boatmen slipped their moorings and began their long journey, poling ever northward, through the almost hidden waters of the overgrown marshes, guided only at night by the bright light of the North Star.

Even with modern GPS it would be impossible to navigate through here. Long waterways suddenly became six inches deep, and quite often it was impossible to turn around. The Madan, with thousands of years of history and navigational knowledge behind them, knew every yard of their territory. They could pole those boats blindfolded, and for this immense skill they were rewarded by the al-Qaeda cutthroats with ten U.S. dollars a day. A four-day journey up to the northern end of the marshes, 125 miles, thus earned each boatmen forty dollars, which was not much considering the value of their cargo—three hundred thousand dollars. But with four voyages per month, a father and son were paid more than either they or any of their ancestors had ever earned in any one of the preceding six thousand years.

Out to the east the sun was rising above the Zagros Mountains. The canoes slipped through the reeds, with the morning light astern. There were times when the boats were completely invisible from only thirty yards away, as they floated past small clusters of *sarifas,* houses set on poles above the water, with strangely ornate latticework entrances. At this time in the morning the boatmen cast long shadows, but they were miles from the Iraqi road system, and the great overhanging reeds of the marshes camouflaged the insurgents' deadly missiles well.

No noise betrayed them as they slipped through the water, just the soft splash as the poles came out at the end of each long push. The boats would scarcely slow until they reached al-Kut at the north end of the marshes. From there the two missile crates would travel in an old farm truck to the southern suburbs of Baghdad, stacked between a cargo of dates and driven by former disciples of Saddam Hussein.

This was the tried-and-trusted route of illegal arms from Iran to Baghdad—as elusive to the Western military powers as Saddam's nuclear program and chemical weapons had been. Elusive but no less real for that—hidden in the endless sand-swept wilderness, transported from one site to another, and finally across the desert to Syria.

———◆———

Mack Bedford and Harry Remson met at eight o'clock in the shipyard office. There, over coffee and danishes, the ex–Navy SEAL tried to explain his grave misgivings about the conduct of the Forces of Justice, and in particular that of Raul, the headman. "Harry," he said, "I am just not used to the goddamned shenanigans of civilian life, and I guess I better get used to it if I am going to survive. But I have just categorically dealt with a man who tried to rip us off for a million dollars. He made a deal and broke it. When I said we'd walk away, he collapsed, which means he was just trying it on. But I'm damned if I think it's a great idea to entrust this fucking villain with a million bucks that we have no hope of getting back."

"You know, Mack," replied Harry, "it may not have been that bad. He was just trying to up the price when he thought he had us eating out of his hand. It happens all the time."

"Not where I come from," said Mack. "I recently retired from an organization where it was considered damn near illegal to tell a lie."

"Mack, he didn't lie, did he?"

"No, but he reneged. We had agreed on the project, agreed on the price, a kind of handshake over the phone. And then he backed down on that agreement, with no thought for the project, or our bond of trust. It was just a shitty little attempt to gouge more money out of us."

"And for that you want to fire him? Because you'd never quite trust him again, and you don't want to hand over a million bucks in case he goes AWOL, knowing we don't dare come after him?"

"Correct."

"Okay. I can't really argue with that. A million greenbacks is a lot of cash to mislay. What do we do now?"

"I have another old buddy who went into some foreign-based security outfit. I'm going to try to find him."

"And what about Raul's fifty grand?"

"I sorted that out last night. He'll have his money by now, and I took accurate notes on the information he gave me about Foche and his hometown and all that. Give me twenty-four hours, and I'll see if I can get something moving."

"Let's have another cup of coffee," said Harry, and then he reached into his drawer and pulled out a magazine. "Someone sent me this," he said. "It's a London magazine. A big article on Foche. It's interesting. Give it a read later, and let me know what you think."

Mack took the magazine and stuffed it into his jacket pocket. He sipped his coffee and admitted, "Harry, I'm in this a lot deeper than I ever wanted to be. Which I guess is inevitable, since there's only you and me, the only two people in the world who know what's going on. But it's a worry, and I don't really want to get in much deeper."

"These hoodlums in Marseille have no idea who or where we are, do they?"

"Definitely not, so long as your space-age cell phone holds up."

"Look, Mack, I know that in the end, this is my problem, and I guess you'll never know how much I appreciate what you've done so far. All I can say is, if I have to, I'll go it entirely alone. But any help you can give me, I'll never forget it."

"It's just that right now I've got a whole lot on my plate," said Mack. "Tommy's so ill, Anne's on the verge of a nervous breakdown, the bank won't help me, and the insurance company is out of the game when it's a foreign clinic."

"Hey! I just solved it," chuckled Harry. "Why don't you pop across to France and hit Foche between the eyes with a bullet, and then I'll give you all the cash, and we can save Tommy?"

"Great idea," said Mack. "Can you save something for Anne and Tommy to fly over to Paris and visit me in the fucking Bastille, where I'll be locked up for the rest of my life like the goddamned Count of Monte Cristo?"

"Mackenzie Bedford," replied Harry mysteriously, "may I remind you, the Count got out."

"And may I remind you, the Count was fiction," laughed Mack. "And the one thing we know about this Foche character, is, he's real. And I have to get moving."

"Okay, Mack, great to see you. Do your best, and if you could just get me the phone number, I'll go the rest of the way by myself."

Mack made a dismissive gesture, which meant, *Get out of here, Harry. I'm still in your corner.*

He drove back through town, picked up the mail, and arrived home in time to see Tommy and hand over the car to Anne for the drive to the hospital.

"I wish I'd seen the game with you last night, Dad," Tommy said. "I just saw the paper—the Red Sox beat the Yanks by 15 to 1. That must have been great."

"Guess so. I only lasted through the seventh, and they scored twelve runs in the final two innings. Didn't finish 'til way after eleven o'clock. Too late for you."

"And you, right?"

Mack laughed and picked up the little boy. "We going fishing tonight?" he asked. "Save Mom buying our supper."

"Sure. You want me to catch another one of those blues?"

"Darned right I do. So does Mom."

"Hey, what happens if there's no fish? Does that mean we don't get anything to eat?"

"Hell, no. Not us. We'll just dig out a bucket of clams and get Mom to fry 'em."

"Can we get french fries as well?"

"I bet we could, if we ask her nicely."

Mack carried Tommy out to the car, lowered him into the backseat, and fastened the seat belt.

"See you around noon," said Anne. "I'll bring sandwiches back from the store."

Mack wandered disconsolately back onto the screened porch. He could see there was a letter from the bank, which was not a regular statement. He opened it with dread, and the news was bleak. After due consideration, the directors felt that Lieutenant Commander Bedford's was a case in which they could not intervene. The bank's normal policies must be upheld in accordance with Federal Reserve guidelines—no loans for customers with little possibility of repaying the money.

His heart sank. This was their last hope. All they could do now was to wait for some kind of a medical breakthrough, some miracle cure that would arrest Tommy's ALD, the satanic disease that seemed to be eating him alive. All he could do this morning was to hope to hell the news from the hospital was better. Whether it was or not, he would have to tell Anne the bad news from the bank, and he was uncertain how much more bad news she could take. Anne was on the edge. Anyone could see that. If Tommy died, he did not know how she could ever recover. Come to think of it, he was not sure how he could recover himself.

He leaned back on the comfortable wicker furniture and absent-mindedly turned on the radio. He was just in time to hear the precise kind of news bulletin he did not wish to know about:

Twenty-three U.S. military personnel were either killed or injured in the northern suburbs of Baghdad last night. A U.S. marine convoy making its way back to base after a successful mission against insurgents was hit by two tank-busting missiles. Reports coming in suggest several of the men were burned to death.

The missiles, which hit two armored vehicles, were believed to be Diamondheads, the ones banned six months ago by the United Nations Security Council. This is believed to be the fourth instance of Iraqi insurgents opening fire on U.S. personnel with a weapon that the UN unanimously declared to be a crime against humanity.

The supply line is believed to lead from southwestern Iran across the Tigris and then to Baghdad. The missile is French made, and the Pentagon is uncertain whether there were stockpiles in Iran or whether there has been an illegal new delivery.

Last night the French Ministry of Defense stated that export shipments of the missile have been deemed illegal in France, and, so far as they know, there have been no shipments leaving any French airport, or seaport, for many months. Certainly not since the UN ban was formalized.

U.S. military commanders in Iran confessed they were mystified by the continuing onslaught of this missile. But they were perhaps even more mystified about their own inability to locate and break the supply line if such a system exists.

A U.S. Marine colonel, unidentified because he is still serving in Iraq, last night stated, "This is the fifth or sixth time we've been hit by this outlawed weapon, and every time, I guess we think it's the last of them. And every time they come back at us with more. I can say that the U.S. High Command in Iraq is convinced there are still Diamondheads coming into Baghdad. But we don't know whether there is a large supply still in Iran, or whether new ones are coming in from elsewhere."

The U.S. secretary of defense has sent an official complaint to the United Nations protesting in the strongest possible terms. A spokesman for the Defense Department said earlier today, "Perhaps the Iranian government should remember we went to war against Saddam Hussein because he consistently defied edicts from the United Nations." He added that U.S. Navy SEALs recently returned from Iraq have been ordered to pack down in readiness for immediate redeployment to Baghdad. It is understood that veterans from SEAL Team 10 will be the first to leave.

"Jesus Christ!" snapped Mack to the empty porch. "Those sons-abitches. Those goddamned sonsabitches!" And even as a civilian, here on this tranquil North American shore, he felt within him the rising of the "hours of the wolf." It was only the second time he had been aware of burgeoning rage since the bridge. But he could not control it.

Right now he could not tell for whom he was most concerned—Anne, Tommy, the shipyard, the town, or "his guys" going back to that cauldron of pure hatred around the Tigris and the Euphrates. He knew he should remove himself from the situation, but all the years as a Navy SEAL had forged him into a part of this steel-rimmed brotherhood of men, who, when the bugle sounded, would come out fighting. Barry Mason and Jack Thomas were as much a part of him as Anne and Tommy and Harry. And now they were going back to the battlefield without him. And none of it was his fault. But if anything happened to either of them, he would somehow blame himself for all of his days. He would blame himself for not being there for them. He would blame himself for being unable to take command, to issue the orders, and if necessary to face the enemy right up front on their behalf.

It wasn't rational. He was perfectly aware of that. But the hearts of SEAL commanders aren't rational. They're not supposed to be rational. They're just supposed to care. And Lieutenant Commander Bedford *really* cared. The memories of "his guys" stood stark before him. And still there surged the burning flame of the "hours of the wolf."

He turned off the radio and checked his watch. It was almost time to call Raul. He had told him either today or tomorrow, to remain on standby for the final plans. But he was unable to rid his mind of the man's dishonesty. Raul had attempted to renege. Which meant he ought never to be trusted. It reminded him of an old joke of Charlie's, the one about the very pretty young secretary riding on a train and her copassenger, a handsome, slightly older man asking her, "Would you go to bed with me for one hundred thousand dollars in cash?"

The girl looked suitably shocked, but then smiled and said, "One hundred thousand dollars. I suppose I would."

"Well," said the man, "would you go to bed with me for five bucks?"

The girl almost yelled at him, "What the hell do you think I am?"

"I thought we'd already established what you are, and now we're just haggling about the price."

Mack was not absolutely certain which end of this moral outrage he was on. But he definitely considered Raul to be a whore, and not a man to whom he should entrust one million dollars of Harry Remson's money. Not today, at any rate. Maybe tomorrow he might feel differently. But not today.

He slipped the super–cell phone back into his pocket and mildly congratulated himself for never having revealed one single detail about either himself or Harry, or even which country they were in, throughout the negotiations with FOJ.

He passed the remainder of the morning on the house phone trying to locate the two ex-SEALs he believed to be either mercenaries or involved in security. The trouble was he did not want too many people to know he was trying to locate these men, because words leave a trail, and names leave an even bigger one.

It took Mack one hour to discover his first choice, a chief petty officer named Dave Segal. He had never gone into security, but had been offered a job training combat troops in the Israeli army. He had gone with the blessing of the U.S. military, relocated his family in the Holy Land, and been presented with a full commission. Colonel Segal was now a very highly paid and aboveboard Israeli officer, well regarded and expected to rise even further in that perpetual war zone.

Mack's old buddy Segal was out of the running. But the second SEAL had left the military entirely, and had returned to his home state of Colorado, where he was a partner in a new and productive coal mine, and fully expected to make a financial killing.

Both of them were an entire waste of time, and Mack decided to make no more calls today. Instead, he'd just have a cup of coffee and read the papers until Anne brought Tommy home. Generally speaking, he was rapidly arriving at the view that locating some foreign-based Murder Incorporated was not precisely his game.

Harry Remson stopped by shortly after eleven and wondered if Mack had made any progress.

"Not yet," he replied. "But I'm on it." Mack did not think Harry was ready for the double whammy of losing FOJ and then not finding a replacement. And this was important to the former SEAL, because this town could not afford for Harry to go into some sort of decline. Nonetheless, there was a profound sense of relief in Mack's mind now that he was a few steps further away from going into some insane partnership with a band of international assassins.

"Harry," he said, "I feel like a racehorse trainer who has just been told his owner is considering a gigantic bet on his horse for Saturday's big race. The trainer doesn't want to say, 'Great idea—we can't get beat,' in case the horse finishes seventh. Neither does he want to say, 'Don't do that, for Christ's sake,' in case it wins. The first instance would be bad, the second about fifty times worse."

"You mean you're kinda loath to hand over Raul's number for me to go right ahead, by myself. Because if it works, you end up looking like a wimp!"

Harry was laughing. Mack was not. "Something like that," he said. "But I guess my real problem is that if this bastard steals your million bucks and vanishes, then I look like a real fool. There would be some people who'd think Raul and I somehow shared it."

"I would not be one of them," said Harry, no longer laughing. "Because I trust you completely. And I do see the problem. But if we can't find anyone else, my back will be hard against the wall. And I may have to ask you for that number. Then the problem would be entirely mine."

Mack poured the Remson boss a cup of coffee, but he could not stay for long. Just before he left, he asked, "You read that magazine I gave you yet? The one about Foche?"

"Not yet. I'll read it tonight."

"You'll find it interesting," said Harry. "Talk to you later."

———•◆•———

Anne and Tommy returned from the hospital just before noon. Tommy was cheerful and wanted to play some ball. Anne looked stricken. "Dr. Ryan gave us some new medicine, some kind of an oil that has been effective in other cases, just at arresting the process. It's not a cure." Tommy was well out of range when she said this. Mack held her in his arms, neither of them with one word to say to the other.

When Tommy came back out to the porch he had already pulled on his glove. Mack took a couple of baseballs from the basket, grabbed his own glove, and took Tommy out into the front yard. Anne could see them throwing the ball to and fro, catching it in the gloves, finding different angles. It had always been a total mystery to her why men found such fascination in this pointless activity, but today she had no room for empty thoughts.

While Joyce had taken Tommy to the playroom, she had a very serious consultation with Dr. Ryan and two surgeons. All three men pointed out the dangers of drastic surgery on such a young boy. One of the surgeons was very attuned to the activities of the Swiss clinic and told her they had enjoyed one success in the past two weeks, but another operation had been a disaster and the child did not survive the week. All three men told her that Switzerland was the only hope, though not that good a hope. The success rate was, in their opinion, unimpressive, perhaps three victories in five attempts. They all thought this was a very good reason to wait for the U.S. medical profession to make the breakthrough that could happen at any time and eliminate most of the risk.

As far as Anne was concerned, three in five sounded fantastic since she and Mack currently faced zero in five, with no apparent possibility of a reprieve. Before she and Tommy left, Dr. Ryan had taken her aside and said flatly, "Anne, Tommy is in very bad shape. This thing is spreading. Never mind the odds—that Swiss clinic is the only game in town. If you can get him in there, take my advice and go. And remember, the toughness and good health that make him so vulnerable to this virulent disease are still the qualities to get him through the operation."

Quietly, she prepared the sandwiches for lunch and a small salad for each of the three plates. She poured three glasses of fruit juice and summoned her ballplayers to the table on the porch. Tommy charged into his tuna fish on rye and wondered if he could get some potato chips with it. Anne told him certainly not, especially if he and his father hoped to have bluefish and french fries this evening.

"Mom," said Tommy, grinning, "I think the chief fisherman ought to have a few chips if he needs 'em. When you think, supper is up to me."

"The chief fisherman can have an apple after his sandwich."

"But the chief fisherman doesn't want an apple. He wants potato chips."

Tommy Bedford was an endearing boy, but he'd met his match in his cholesterol-concerned mother. "Perhaps he does," replied Anne. "But the chief cook has rules about how much fat the chief fisherman is allowed to eat in one day. You may have some potato chips, but then there will be no fries with the bluefish."

This was too much for Mack. "Don't you bargain away our french fries, Tom," he said. "We might need 'em for strength after we fight the blues."

"Don't worry about that, Dad. Chips are okay, but fries are awesome. I'll take the apple."

Anne changed the subject and, absently, asked Mack who had been visiting that morning. "I saw the second coffee cup," she added.

"Oh, just Harry. He didn't stay long. He's always in a hurry."

"No news about the yard?"

"Not really. He's still trying to have one last go at the French, maybe get in under the wire with a new frigate before the new government gets in. But he's not hopeful. I'm telling you, laying off the steelworkers really got to him. I never saw him so despondent."

"It's caused a lot of fuss in town," said Anne. "So many people are affected. I was talking to one of the young guys in the store, and he thinks his grandparents will have to move away, somewhere south. They've been here for five generations."

"It's awful," replied Mack. "And in some ways it's as bad for Harry as for any of them. He thinks he's somehow let everyone down—in a way neither his father nor his grandfather ever did."

"Do you think he has?"

"No. Although I think the writing's been on the wall for a lot longer than he believes. The trouble is, Remsons has become a specialized yard, warship experts, with an expensive staff who are good at electronics, radar, sonar, weapons guidance. The Dartford guys really know what they're doing. And once the French Navy even suggested they would not be coming back as clients, that left Remsons high and dry. Harry should probably have begun drastic changes, offering designs for oceangoing freighters, maybe even cruise liners, because aside from the U.S. government, there are hardly any customers for an American shipyard trying to build warships."

"I suppose not," replied Anne distractedly. "Who knows what will happen now."

Mack smiled and said, "I'll say one thing. Harry does have a plan, and I think it has a chance. I can't tell you about it, or anyone else. But he has confided in me, and I'm optimistic for him."

"Will you end up working for him—in some capacity?"

"It's not impossible, and he keeps telling me that the closure of a medium-size shipyard takes years to clear up. He says he wants to work with a lifelong friend whom he trusts. Someone who has held positions of trust. Guess it would solve our problems."

"Some of them," replied Anne.

After lunch, Tommy became very sick. Anne looked after him for more than an hour and then put him to bed. "He may sleep for three or four hours," she said. "But this is all part of it. I don't think he should go fishing, because it will just exhaust him more."

"Okay," said Mack. "I'll go off by myself now and see if I can find us some supper. He might be upset if we're not going, though. I don't want to tell him."

"You may find he won't remember," she said. "Then maybe twenty minutes of throwing the baseball would be all he wants. He can watch the Red Sox with you for a little while, at eight o'clock."

Mack took his fishing gear to the car and drove down toward the water. This was not some cheerful outing with Tommy. This was a mission. This required watchfulness and split-second decisions. He chose a road running east, where the water would become silvery as the afternoon wore on, and the sun slipped lower in the sky. As ever, he was watching for the arctic terns, those Ted Williams of the deep, those rock-steady little fishermen who never swung at a bad pitch and came in hard when the porgies betrayed their presence. They knew what they were after, tiny silver flashes swarming to and from the surface. Mack knew what he wanted, the big fellas, swimming right below the porgies, the bass and the blues.

Slowly he cruised along the shore of the long Kennebec bay below the shipyard. He stared out of his side window all the way. There was no traffic, and no arctic terns. He swung the car down the estuary to a spot five miles south of Dartford, where granite rocks jutted from the water at low tide.

There was a bell buoy out there, but the tide was flowing in and had already covered the rocks. The bell clanged in the light summer breeze, and all around, settling on the red structure of the bell supports, were the outriders for a flock of arctic terns.

They were diving, about eight of them, diving the way terns do when they hit porgy pay dirt. Deep below them, circling, Mack knew, were the big fellas, cutting through the cold depths of the estuary, scattering the porgies, grabbing, snapping, in a nightly feeding frenzy, like little sharks, and just as vicious.

Mack stopped the car and lovingly selected a silver lure, triple hooked, the same popper Tommy had used a couple of nights ago. He tied it to the line, leaned back like a javelin thrower, and hurled it clean across the channel and out toward the bell buoy. It was by any standards one heck of a cast. At this game, Mack had the arms of a longshoreman and the hands of a violinist. He began to wind in his reel, just past the limit of the eight terns, who were by now dipping and plunging into the choppy little patch of water. At least it looked little from where Mack stood but in truth was probably twenty yards across.

The lure came skittering along the surface, bumping and plunging, hardly ever out of sight, but it came all the way, with no sudden jolt when a big fish took it.

Mack cast again. Nothing. And then again. Nothing. But now he noticed the silvery splashes in the disturbed water were just a little closer. And with his fourth supreme cast he dropped the lure bang in the middle of the shoal of porgies. Wham! A big thirty-six-inch bass took it the first time, and Mack's reel screamed as the striped devil swerved away and dived. The trouble here was that the line might snap. Mack whipped his right arm back at a forty-five-degree angle behind his shoulder to set the hook. This was a big fish, and Mack felt him dive to the base of the rocks. Immediately, Mack loosened the spool, giving the bass more line because the fish could break it by sheer force, with its own weight and the power of its struggle to get free.

Mack let him run, for around thirty yards, and then carefully raised his rod to eleven o'clock, then lowered it. He quickly reeled in the slack. With a fish this big, he could not let it become a straight test of strength because the line might not take it.

This was shaping up to be a serious battle, not of muscle, but of guile. Again and again he lifted the rod high, then dipped it, and carefully reeled in the slack. The trick was to fool the fish, not letting him understand he was being drag-hauled into the shallows. Mack kept it up, and the contest was going his way, until the bass finally cottoned on to the fact he was in foreign territory, away from his buddies, near rocks that were strange to him. And looming above was the gigantic shape of Mack Bedford.

The former SEAL commander waited for the last titanic effort of his opponent. And when the fish was a mere twenty yards out, it happened:

the fabled second wind of a fighting bass. The fish turned. And dived away once more, heading back out toward the rocks. Mack's reel screamed again, but he was ready. He loosened the spool a fraction, gave the bass some line, and only then began to reel him in.

Mack could feel the strength of the big fish fading away. He guessed it was a bass, because of the ebb and flow of the contest. His fish was fighting like a bass—diving deep, steady and powerful; totally unlike the erratic, aggressive, surface-breaking efforts of the innately vicious bluefish trying to spit out the lure.

A shoal of blues has a lot in common with a pack of wolves. They have been known to bite a line in half just to save a friend. There is no fish in all of North America's coastal waters that is quite such a warrior as a threatened bluefish.

A bass is strong, but not like a blue. And Mack knew that last dive of the fish on his line had been, in a sense, the last attack. The fish was defeated. And Mack knew defeat when he stared at it. He'd seen it in the eyes of a hundred al-Qaeda warriors in the backstreets of Baghdad. And now he could see the fish, with its stark stripes along the silvery body. He'd reeled it into shallow water now, and he could see it was swimming on its side, but it was barely swimming, just flapping in the water. Slowly, the willpower of the fish drained away, and almost in slow motion it veered slowly from side to side, with the last of its strength, a sad, final reflex for survival, a reflex that echoed back for a million years. The tail became still, and Mack leaned over with his net and landed the fish. It was one of the biggest bass he'd ever caught.

"Now that," he murmured, "is a high-quality sonofabitch." He killed it with one swift crack on the head with his priest and then laid it out on a flat rock while he selected his filleting knife. Three minutes later he'd cut the two long, white bass steaks off the bone and thrown the remains of the fish back into the estuary. The gulls were already circling. "Little bastards don't miss much," said Mack to no one in particular. And then he packed the Bedford dinner into the cooler, loaded the car, and left.

His thoughts immediately turned to Tommy resting in his bedroom, so sick, so tragically sick. "I guess it's a good thing he didn't come today," he muttered. "He would have loved it, but that big striper might have hauled him straight across the estuary, because Tommy wouldn't let go. That's the thing—Tom's a Bedford through and through. He'd never let go."

He arrived home, washed off his rod, dumped the ice onto the lawn, and took the fish into the kitchen, where Anne was making him iced coffee. A couple of miles away there was a spot on the coast road where she could see for a few yards. He knew she'd been watching, and he knew she'd seen the car coming home.

He took her in his arms, and only then did he notice she'd been crying. "We can't give up," he told her gently. "We just have to keep doing our best, and praying for Tommy."

Anne did not answer for a couple of minutes, and then she asked him if he'd caught a fish.

"I caught one of the biggest bass I ever saw," he said. "Must have been three feet long. We'll only need around half of it this evening. Might as well freeze the rest." But for the second time in a few minutes, Mack sensed she was not really listening. He'd seen this before in men who had been engaged in combat, and for whom fear was beginning to creep into their psyche. All combat troops have to fight this, but for a few of them the problem is more defined. And slowly the fear begins to dominate. These men were no longer attacking the enemy; they were just trying to survive.

Experienced commanders spot these battlefield subtleties and are usually sympathetic, moving such men to less onerous parts of the operation, possibly Intel or Strategic Planning. In World War I, they would have been shot for cowardice.

All of these thoughts ran through Mack's mind as he gazed at his very lovely, very distracted wife. It was so unlike her to lose her focus. But Tommy's illness was taking its toll after so many weeks of disappointment following disappointment.

Upstairs, Tommy yelled. Anne immediately left the kitchen, and Mack took his iced coffee out onto the porch, where he sat and stared out toward the coastline. It was curious, but in a way the battles in Iraq had shielded him from this other mental battle that was taking place in his own home: two people trying still to love each other, trying to hold it all together while their little boy was dying in front of their eyes. As colossal strains go, this one was right up there. Mack could never remember, even in his darkest hours along the Euphrates River, feeling this sad, this helpless, this melancholic.

He heard Tommy yell again, a yell of temper through the open upstairs window. He heard Anne raise her voice, the first time she had raised it since he had returned from Iraq. He decided to remain out of it, but he could not help but hear the raging tantrum Tommy was having and the difficulty Anne was having trying to get him under control. Finally, Tommy dissolved into crying, long, racking sobs of pure anguish.

"Jesus Christ," thought Mack. "I just hope he doesn't know."

A half hour went by, and he stepped outside to prepare the grill for the bass. Tommy and Anne finally came downstairs, and he looked absolutely normal. Anne, on the other hand, was white-faced and very much within herself.

Tommy came over to see his dad and said, "Wanna play some ball after you fix the fire?" Mack grabbed him and managed to put a sooty handprint on Tommy's clean T-shirt.

"Hell, Mom will think you've been hit by the Black Hand Gang."

"No, she won't. She'll think it's the Invasion of the Deadheads. They've got black hands." And the little boy raced around the garden shouting, "Watch out, guys! Here come the Deadheads!"

Mack lit the fire and then took Tommy back inside to pick up the baseball gear. He returned to the kitchen and selected one of the bass fillets, prepared it with oil, salt, and pepper, and wrapped it in tinfoil. He decided to leave it in the fridge while he and Tommy played catch, but before he went outside he heard a crash from the porch, followed by a scream from Anne.

He moved swiftly out to the porch only to see that Anne had dropped and broken an empty milk jug, but she was crying hysterically—the kind of distraught sobbing that usually occurs when someone's house has burned down.

Mack went over to her and again took her in his arms, saying, "Come on, Anne, it's only a milk jug, and not even very big. Don't get upset. Who cares? We'll replace it tomorrow." But Anne could not be consoled, and she cried for ten minutes. Even Tommy came in and said, "What's up, Mom? Are you really crying because of the stupid milk jug?"

Mack ruffled his hair and whispered to him, "It's not the jug, kid. Mum's suffering from battle fatigue."

"What's that?"

"It's what the Yanks had last night when the Red Sox beat 'em 15 to 1. Acute depression."

"Well, what's that got to do with the milk jug?"

"I think it belonged to Mom's grandmother," lied Mack. "It's kinda sentimental."

"Senti-what?"

"Shut up, Tommy, and get your glove on. I wanna see some power throwing from you."

Tommy bounced down the steps, saying over and over, "Senti-menti. Senti-menti. Mom's got senti-menti." Even Anne laughed. She brought out the bass and supervised the cooking, which took twenty minutes, grill to table. The french fries were already in the warming oven.

The fish tasted about as good and fresh as any fish can ever taste. The french fries were pretty good, too. The meal seemed to energize Tommy, who announced that he wanted to go fishing right then, wanted to catch another bluefish like last time.

Mack was secretly thrilled that he remembered last time, because loss of memory was one of the known symptoms of adrenoleuko-dystrophy. But the thrill did not run to another fishing trip today. And anyway, the light was fading fast. "It's too late, Tommy," he said. "It'll be dark in fifteen minutes."

"But you said the early darkness is sometimes the best time of all to catch fish. Come on, Dad, you said we could go. You said we could."

Without a word, the big SEAL commander walked around the table, hoisted Tommy clean out of his chair, put him up on his shoulders, and hanging onto both ankles ran out of the house with Tommy cling-ing onto his hair, laughing his head off. Mack raced around the garden, with Tommy perched on his shoulders, hanging on grimly and yelling, "You said we could go! You said we could go! You said we could go!"

Eventually, Mack stopped and pulled Tommy down into his arms, and already he could feel the little boy becoming tired and submissive.

"Come on, let's go and find some ice cream," said Mack. "Would you like that?"

Tommy opened his eyes, nodded, and muttered, "You said we could go," laughing despite himself.

Tommy lasted about another hour, then wearily asked his mom if he could stay up and watch the baseball game with his dad. But his eyes were closing. The Red Sox had barely sent down three Yankee bat-ters in order at the top of the first when Tommy fell fast asleep on the sofa. Mack carried him up to bed between innings.

It might have been the general elation of a 4–0 Red Sox lead, but Mack decided he must tell Anne about the bank's rejection. They could not have secrets from each other, and he heard her come slowly down the stairs. "Is he okay?"

"For the moment. I've given him some of the new medicine, and hopefully he'll sleep through the night."

Mack stood up and suggested they have a glass of wine together, but he noticed she answered "okay" with the same enthusiasm she might have offered for a glass of strychnine. He poured two glasses from a new bottle of California red anyway, a four-year-old merlot from the Napa Valley, and offered one to his wife, who took it as if her mind were a thousand miles away.

"Anne," he said, "it's not the end of the world, but I did hear from the bank today."

"They turned us down?"

"They did. And it was a computerized letter. They never had any in-tention of giving us a million."

"I just wonder who these people are," she said. "Here we are, faced with the most adorable little boy, who is dying of some incurable disease, and no one will lift a finger to help. The stupid doctors have been outwitted by a nation that basically makes cuckoo clocks, the insurance company won't provide coverage the only time we have ever needed it, and the bank has better things to do with its money."

"I know," replied Mack. "It's as if the whole darned world is indifferent to everything. Billions of dollars being made every day. And no one will do anything for us."

Quite suddenly, Anne began to cry again, just sitting in an armchair making no attempt to hide her tears. But her voice was raised when she spoke. "It's just so unfair!" she almost shouted. "And I don't know how much more I can take. I do everything I can, all day, every day, and in the end nothing matters. Because in the end Tommy will die, and no one will give a damn, except us."

Mack put down his glass and stood up. But he was too late. Anne literally screamed at him, "All I have is Tommy and you! And you can't help! For years they've told me you were the best this, and the best that, and then they threw you out, and now you're just helpless, like everyone else!"

This was the moment Mack had been dreading. The day when Anne blamed him for being unable to raise the money for Tommy to go to Switzerland. He understood he was her protector and provider, and now in the hour of her greatest need, he had somehow failed her. No one understood the cold truth better than Mack Bedford.

And Anne was not through. "I have nowhere to turn. Even your Mister High and Mighty Harry Remson can offer nothing. But most of all I come back to you, my husband, Tommy's dad. Because if ever there was a moment in both our lives when you had to do something, it's now. And the best you can do is advise prayer. I don't need prayer. I need a million dollars to save my little boy's life. And you can't get it. You're no different from the rest—*I HATE YOU! I CAN'T STAND THE SIGHT OF YOU! WHAT GOOD ARE YOU IF YOU CAN'T DO ANYTHING FOR TOMMY?*" She smashed her glass of wine off the side table next to her chair and ran out of the room. All the way up the stairs she never stopped raging: "If not you, WHO? If not now, WHEN? WHAT ELSE IS THERE?"

Mack did not for one moment think he was merely watching a highly strung woman at the end of her tether. He was watching the total mental breakdown of his own beautiful wife. And he had no idea what to do about it. He tried to think, to step back mentally from the problem, away from the heartrending emotion of Anne. But there was no stepping back. Tommy's illness lived with them both, night and day. It had already torn his wife apart. He did not know if she could ever recover. And he thought it was entirely possible she did hate him for his inability to solve the problem of Switzerland.

Carefully, he took the glass off the floor and tipped a bottle of club soda over the red stain on the carpet. He tried to watch the Red Sox but could not concentrate, not with Anne upstairs, hating him. He poured himself a second glass of wine and turned off the television. Then he remembered the magazine Harry had given him, which he had promised to read. He went out to the hall closet, retrieved the publication from his jacket, and wandered back into the living room.

He spread out along the length of the sofa, and then stood up again and decided to give the Red Sox one more try. The game was tied 4–4 at the bottom of the fifth, and he decided to watch the Sox pitch one more inning, whether Anne hated him or not. Mack ended up watching it through eight, when the Sox finally managed a 9–5 lead and he decided he'd better read the magazine in case Harry showed up early in the morning.

He switched off the television and sat down again on the sofa, turned inside the publication to the spot where Harry had placed a little yellow sticker, and there before him was the face of Henri Foche, alongside a big black headline that read:

THE NEW LEADER OF THE GAULLIST PARTY—
THE NEXT PRESIDENT OF FRANCE?

The main story read:

France is preparing to welcome to the Elysée Palace the most right-wing president certainly since Giscard and probably since de Gaulle. Henri

Foche, the forty-eight-year-old native of Brittany, has accepted the party leadership and will fight the election three months from now under the banner of "Pour la Bretagne. Pour la France." For Brittany. For France.

Heavy industry all over Europe will feel the draft. Insiders say he has already made up his mind on a drastic cut in imports. "If it can be made in France, it will be made in France" is one of his most quoted slogans. He is expected to install an immediate ban on imported coal and steel, which will send a very chill blast through the industrial heartlands of Romania and parts of Germany.

Of course, many French politicians are advising against this quasi-protectionist policy, reminding him that even the American president who tried to protect U.S. steel had finally been forced to change his mind. But France is different. These kinds of "Viva la France" outbursts from French leaders strike a chord that is echoed nowhere else in the free world.

The French parliament long ago decided to wean itself off foreign oil with a massive nuclear power program, which today provides France with almost 80 percent of its electricity.

Monsieur Foche is believed to have a heavy interest in the French ship-ping industry, although details of his business activities have traditionally been very well concealed. But he has recently made major political speeches in the shipyards around Brest and Saint-Nazaire, all of them assuring the workers that new ships—passenger, freight, or navy frigates—will be cut from French steel.

Nothing will be imported. The French shipping industry, and indeed the French Navy, will rely solely on French-built vessels, from aircraft car-riers to submarines.

There followed almost two columns of detail about Foche's politics, his flirtation with capital punishment, and his determination to reduce taxation.

The story finished with the following paragraph:

Whether you agree with him or not, Foche has struck a nerve in France. Left-wing and liberal moderates in Paris society are openly nervous of the fire-eater from Brittany, who cares nothing for advice.

At the bottom of the story was an arrow pointing overleaf, and there, printed in a box, white type on black, was a rundown of Foche's reputed business interests. It was plain the researchers had come up with little. Nonetheless, there was a paragraph in the middle of the box that stated, *Henri Foche is believed to hold a significant interest in the guided-missile corporation Montpellier Munitions, located in Orléans, along the Loire Valley.*

There was not one word of confirmation, save to assure readers that two of the biggest holdings in Montpellier were recorded under the names of Paris law firms, the inference being they were front men for Henri Foche.

The article continued:

Montpellier is, of course, the French arms factory suspected of manufacturing the banned tank-busting missile, the Diamondhead. But last night a spokesman for the corporation said, "We do make an advanced version of Aerospatiale's MILAN–5, but we know nothing of the Diamondhead, and certainly would not dream of exporting such a missile to anyone in the Middle East after an official ban by the United Nations."

Mack Bedford read it all with some interest, but his attention was mild compared to the moment when he glanced over to the right-hand page and saw a large picture showing three men standing beside a black Mercedes-Benz outside the Montpellier factory. The caption below pointed out that the man in the center was Henri Foche himself. But Mack Bedford did not need the caption. He took one look at the photograph and almost jumped off the sofa, because there, right before his eyes, was a familiar balding, middle-aged Frenchman in a pinstriped suit, complete with the bright scarlet handkerchief in the breast pocket of the jacket.

Mack Bedford had spotted the man and his clothes distinctly, through binoculars on the far side of the Euphrates River, just before his friends were incinerated by a Diamondhead missile. In that split second, standing alone in his own living room, Mack realized that he, above all other men, knew that Henri Foche was the mastermind behind the most hated guided missile on earth. He, Mack, had seen him plainly, in sharp focus, standing with the Arab terrorists across the river. He'd been peering through the sights of the missile launcher, for Christ's sake. Mack had watched those turbaned killers talking to Foche in the moments before the Diamondheads had ripped across the water and smashed into his tanks, burning his men alive. That was him, Foche, standing there, large as life, with a black Mercedes at his beck and call, and several Arab missile men hanging on his every word. Mack had watched him, with his own eyes. And he'd never forget that scarlet handkerchief, sharp beneath the desert sun.

The answers to a thousand questions posed by the reporters suddenly sprang into focus. Was Foche the owner of Montpellier Munitions? Of course he was. Had they made the Diamondhead and sold it to Iran? Of course they had. And were they still doing it? Given this morning's shattering news bulletin? In Mack Bedford's mind there was no doubt. *Yes, they fucking well were.* And who could he tell? Who would listen? No one was the answer to that. And into the mind of the former SEAL commander, there began creeping forward a thought that he had never in his most unlikely dreams considered possible.

Once more the images of his best friends stood starkly before him. The SEAL team gunner, Charlie O'Brien, who died in the tank with Billy-Ray Jackson; Chief Frank Brooks and Saul Meiers, who never had a chance when the second tank was hit. In his mind he could see only the searing blue chemical flames as they demolished the best people he had ever known. That unusual crackling sound as the heat devoured everything inside the cockpits and then melted the fuselage of the tanks. The Diamondhead was a weapon from the dark core of hell, a man-made, laboratory-honed missile that belonged to the black arts.

For a few moments he just stood staring at the face of the man who produced it—Henri Foche, who, in just a few short seconds, had become not just a politician who was somehow going to close down the local shipyard. He had become the most hated figure in Mack Bedford's life, in the entire chronicle of Mack Bedford's life.

He rolled up the magazine and stuffed it in his pocket. He paced back and forth across the room, checked to see the final score at Fenway Park, and then had one more look at the pictures of Henri Foche. This was the man he had somehow pledged to have assassinated on behalf of Harry Remson. He'd been doing his best for almost a week, but hitherto for no reason. Certainly not a personal one. Just Harry's determination to save his shipyard. But now things had changed. Very drastically.

Again he put the magazine in his pocket, and he walked out to the hall table and picked up the car keys. Then he selected a small piece of paper from a notepad and scribbled ten numbers on it. He left the house and wondered whether he should drive, because the hours of the wolf were upon him. Carelessly, he dismissed the thought, and strode up to the garage, hauling open the door and firing up the Buick. He eased out of the garage, then hit the gas, swerving out of the drive, hurling gravel.

Upstairs, Anne was curled up on the bed with just a quilt over her. She was not asleep and heard the car start. *Oh, my God, he's left me. Oh, my God!* She flung off the quilt, ran to the open window, and yelled through the screen, *"Mack! Mack! Darling Mack! Please, please, don't go!"*

But she was not in time. She watched the car hurtle out of the drive and disappear. And she just stood there, repeating over and over, "Darling Mack, please don't go, please don't go. Don't leave me. You can't leave me. No one could ever love you like I do." But no one was listening. She was used to that.

Mack sped through the quiet coastal road to the western end of the town, and was making about seventy-five miles an hour as he flashed past the gates of Remsons Shipbuilding. Still racing, he reached Harry's drive and pulled in, almost sideswiping a stone lion that was supposed to be on guard at the gate. He glanced at his watch, just eleven o'clock. Harry might be in bed . . . *but he'll get up for this.*

Mack pulled up outside the front door and without hesitating hit the front doorbell. Hard. There was no answer for at least two minutes, and then a light was switched on in the front hall and the door was pulled open.

Harry stood there in a very snazzy dressing gown, dark red velvet, with the golden crest of the shipyard on the breast pocket. "Jesus, Mack," he said. "Do you know what the time is?"

"Of course I do. You don't think I'd be knocking on your door at 2300 hours if it wasn't important, do you?" Mack knew Harry loved to converse in the language of the bridge. "One hour before eight bells, right? End of the First Night Watch."

Harry chuckled. "Come on in, buddy," he said. "Let's have a glass of Scotch whisky."

They walked to Harry's study, and the shipyard boss poured them each a double shot from a crystal decanter. He opened the fridge door below and selected a bottle of club soda, from which he topped off each glass. "Your good health," he said.

"And yours," replied Mack.

"And now perhaps you'll tell me what's so important you need to be here at six bells? Before the watch change!"

Both men chuckled. They'd been going through this routine since Mack first joined the navy.

"Harry, you understood my reluctance to continue with our highly illegal project this morning? And you said all I needed to do was provide you with the telephone number of a competent assassin who would carry out your wishes and take out Henri Foche?"

Harry nodded, and Mack handed him the piece of paper on which were written the ten numbers. Harry stared at the 207 area code. "Jesus," he said. "This is a local Maine number."

"It's closer than that," said Mack. "It's mine."

CHAPTER 7

Harry Remson did not know whether to stand up and cheer or reach for his blood-pressure pills. Men have won the Olympic 200 meters with heart rates slower than Harry's was at this particular moment. He tried to remain calm, considered, and businesslike. He took a long pull on his Scotch and soda. "Mack," he eventually said evenly, "are you saying what I think you're saying?"

"I believe so, Harry. I've fired Raul, who I don't trust one inch, and I'm volunteering to undertake the contract myself, for the same money."

Harry stood up and walked across the room to refresh his dwindling drink. He lifted up the decanter, but before he poured, he said quietly, "It's Tommy, isn't it, Mack? You'll do it for Tommy."

"Mostly," replied the former SEAL commander.

"That's good," said Harry. "Anyone can be a hired killer. But it takes a real man to put his life on the line for his little boy."

"I guess you know the situation, about Switzerland and everything?"

"I do. I was talking to your dad yesterday. They want a million, right? To do the operation—the bone marrow?"

"That's their price. Fixed. No extras, and a room for Anne for up to six months if necessary. One million U.S. dollars."

"Mack, they just got it. If you'll take this on, I'm coming up with the first million right away. I'll have it wired from the account in France, direct to the clinic. Book their tickets."

"And what if I fail?"

"The money's a nonreturnable deposit. But I know you won't fail."

Mack smiled. "You do?"

"Sure I do. As far as I'm concerned, Henri Foche is living on borrowed time." Harry Remson looked as if the weight of the world had been lifted from his shoulders, as if the sudden recruitment of this battlefield commander had solved his every problem. "Mack," he said, "remember one thing. Until this moment I had no one who could be trusted to carry out the project. I know you had leads, but they were full of dangers and suspicions. And you were right to be concerned— these Marseille villains could just as easily have bolted with the greenbacks and done nothing."

"I just didn't trust them, Harry."

"The difference is, I trust you. I know you will undertake this venture as if you were still a SEAL. I know you will plan carefully, and then carry it out. For the first time I feel my money is going to buy me something of value. Guaranteed."

"Harry," said Mack, "I can't guarantee my success."

"I don't want you to guarantee success. But to me your handshake is better than a thousand contracts. You are a United States Naval officer, a gentleman, and a lifelong friend. I know, without you saying it, you will give it everything . . . for yourself, for Anne, for me, for the town— and above all for Tommy."

"On that," replied Mack, "you do have my guarantee."

"Knowing you, you've already thought about how this is going to work—the time frame, expenses, and so forth."

"I've been thinking about it for a week now. Not for myself, for Raul. But the same basic rules apply."

"Go on."

"He was to be paid two million dollars for the project. There was no mention of expenses. So I assume whatever they were came out of his share of the money. In my case, the money for Tommy, I thank you from the bottom of my heart. My expenses will come out of the second million, same as Raul. But I'm poorer, so I'll need a substantial advance against the second payment."

"Okay," said Harry. "Where do we stand?"

"I will need two hundred thousand dollars, maybe ten thousand in U.S. currency, the rest in euros and British pounds. I intend to enter France via southern Ireland and England. And I have some quite serious purchases to make."

"Such as?"

"A sniper rifle that I will need to be made especially for me. Plus some rather expensive underwater equipment."

"What's that for?"

"Foche has major financial interests in shipbuilding. That magazine says he has made most of his important speeches to workers in that industry. That's where I may nail him, in a shipyard, and my only way of escape will be the water."

For the first time, Harry Remson felt the project shifting gears, like a blurred photograph, suddenly becoming clear, jumping into the realm of stark, hard-focused reality. The assassin, the bullet, the victim, the blood, the headlines.

"Holy shit!" said the shipyard owner. He took another quiet gulp of his Scotch and soda. He looked at Mack and thought he could see a difference in the man. This was no longer the cheerful young guy who'd made it big in the military yet was always ready to offer the hand of friendship. This was a deadly serious professional. And a professional killer at that, the way all U.S. Navy SEALs are ultimately professional killers. If the American government did not want them for that, then there was no purpose in their existence. They were men trained specifically to carry out that which no one else would even dream about.

Here he was, Mack Bedford, outlining the precise nuts and bolts of the operation, the absolute anatomy of an assassination. And Harry was financing it, making it possible. For a split second he wondered whether he ought to turn tail and run, but then he thought about the family business and the men he must cast out onto the cold streets of midwinter Dartford. No, he wouldn't fail them. He must not fail them.

He turned again to face the assassin, Lt. Cdr. Mackenzie Bedford. "How long before you can leave?"

"Two weeks. I'll need three expensively forged passports and three matching driver's licenses, one American, one Irish, and one Swiss. I'll need you to take care of that, but I can give you contacts, CIA freelance guys. Expensive but perfect documents."

"Will they have time?"

"Sure. They'll damn nearly finish them overnight if they have to. They've got plenty of blanks, for damn near any country in the world."

"You'll give me details of your other identities?"

"Tomorrow. Send 'em e-mail. They'll come back by courier, five thousand dollars each."

"Airline tickets?"

"Business class return, Boston to Dublin. Aer Lingus. Book in the same name as the new American passport. I'll pay my own way to and from the local places. Cash."

"Anything else?"

"Negative. I'll take care of the rest."

"Do I need to know how, where, and when?"

"Absolutely not. You will never know, and hopefully neither will anyone else."

Harry Remson vacillated somewhere between blind admiration, outright shock, and general disbelief. This was actually happening. Standing before him was the man who would assassinate Henri Foche.

He tried to look at the man objectively, as if he had never known him. He saw a big and obviously very fit person. There's something about guys like that. Military guys. Hard-trained, controlled diet, no excesses of alcohol. They radiate an understated power, toughness, as if they could instantly turn into Godzilla, which Mack Bedford most certainly could. The face was strong, with laugh lines around the deep gray-blue eyes, with no malice in their gaze. There was a steadiness in the expression. This was a man not easily thrown off his chosen course, and not easily intimidated. In Harry Remson's opinion this was not the face of an assassin. It was the face of a born commander, a man whom other men would follow. Harry wondered how Mack would settle into his new role, operating beyond the law, seeking out his target with precision and ruthlessness.

On reflection, he considered there was no better man in all the world to save the shipyard. This was Harry's lucky night, and right now he did not give a damn if it was midnight. He would not have given a damn if it had been 4:00 A.M. on Christmas, eight bells, that is, end of the Middle Watch.

He turned to Mack and offered his hand. "No contract, old buddy," he said. "Just take me by the hand. That's all we need."

"One question, Harry," said Mack. "What happens if I should be shot by French security forces, when I'm trying to get away? What happens to Anne and Tommy?"

"I will take care of everything. The second million belongs to Anne. Do you need an IOU in writing?"

"Negative."

"Will we meet in my office tomorrow morning to finalize those passports?"

"Start of the Forenoon Watch—0800 hours."

Harry Remson felt nothing short of a wave of elation sweeping over him. He was somehow in the middle of a military operation, so secretive, so highly classified, he felt darned near legal. Well, not quite that. But self-righteous, certain he was doing the correct thing.

They walked to the door together, and Harry let Mack out into the night. He watched the Buick slide noiselessly away, turning right, back toward town. He stood there for a few moments, shook his head, and said quietly, "Jesus Christ, what have we done?"

— ◆ —

It was six o'clock in the French seaport of Marseille. Almost everyone in the area around the old port was somehow connected to the sea. Trawlers were still unloading cargoes of fish; others were gassing up in readiness to leave. The chefs on the yachts that lined several of the jetties were up and about, starting preparations for breakfast for both crew and guests.

One man, however, was not connected to the sea, and he was headed north along Quay des Belges, past the fish market, walking at a very steady pace, wearing an expression like a lovesick bloodhound. Raul Declerc was not happy. And the reason for this was simple: he had not heard from Mr. Morrison, the man, apparently, with the two million bucks. Raul Declerc had no idea what had happened to his seemingly reliable new client. The initial expense payment had gone off without a hitch in Geneva. But Morrison had now missed two calls, and there was an empty feeling in the stomach of Monsieur Declerc. He had a disquieting instinct that this particular feeling might shortly transfer itself to the Declerc wallet area.

He was mostly furious at himself. He should never have tried to grab an extra million dollars from a man like Morrison. Even the voice had betrayed a dangerous edge. In that split second, after he had suggested extra money, and reneged on his agreement, Raul knew he had gone too far. Morrison had come back at him like a striking cobra— *You're not getting it from me.* The words had stayed with him. And now Morrison had vanished and taken his bloody two million with him. And he, Raul Declerc, had probably sent staff, helicopters, and God knows what else all over France for absolutely nothing. "Fuck it," said Raul.

The worse part of all was he had no idea who this Morrison was, no idea whom he represented, no idea where he was calling from, except it was quite possibly somewhere on the planet Earth. "Fuck it," said Raul again.

In his particular trade, assassination and killers for hire, there was often a spin-off for deals that went wrong. Priceless information. Details about a plan. But in this case, the level of information was so low, so devoid of anything even resembling a fact, he feared there would in the end be nothing. Nothing to sell, trade, or barter.

He swung northwest away from the Old Port and, still walking swiftly, headed up to the Place des Moulins. He wanted to be at his desk early in case Morrison decided to make contact. There might even be a message on the machine. But he was not holding his breath.

Every intuition he had told him he'd blown it with Morrison, and there would be no second chance. Not with a man like that.

———•◆•———

Mack Bedford arrived at the shipyard a little before eight o'clock. Harry Remson was already at his desk. He instructed the boss to open up his laptop and take down the following details:

Jeffery Alan Simpson. 13 Duchess Way, Worcester, Massachusetts. Born: August 14, 1978, Providence, Rhode Island. U.S. passport no. 633452874. Issue date: February 2004. U.S. driver's license. Issue date: March 2009. Photographs to follow.

Gunther Marc Roche. 18 rue de Basle, Geneva, Switzerland. Born: November 12, 1977, Davos, Switzerland. Swiss passport no. 947274902. Issue date: June 2005. Swiss driver's license. Issue date: July 2008. Photographs to follow.

Patrick Sean O'Grady. 27 Herbert Park Road, Dublin 4, Ireland. Born: December 14, 1977, Naas, County Kildare, Ireland. Irish passport no. 4850370. Issue date: January 2008. Irish driver's license. Issue date: May 2009. Photographs to follow.

"Okay, Harry," said Mack. "E-mail those details to these guys in Bethesda, Maryland. Here's the address on this card. Put a line in telling them you're sending these requests on behalf of Lt. Cdr. Thomas Killiney. He's already called. Tell them the photographs will be sent by courier tonight. And have your bank in France wire thirty thousand dollars directly to their bank—right here on this card, all numbers and details."

Harry turned out to be a top-class secretary, firing off the information in all directions. Then he said, "Anything else, Captain?"

"Yup, fire up the Bentley and drive me to Portland. Right away."

Harry Remson had not hopped to it that smartly for years. But he did so today, heading down the stairs, into his car, and out onto Route

127, north to Bath and then Brunswick, before heading down the coastal highway to Portland. Twenty-seven miles, all fast.

In the city, Harry was a mere chauffeur, driving Mack from an optician to a hair stylist and then to one of those photographic shops that specialize in passports. He assisted with a disguise that he thought made Mack look ridiculous, a blond wig and mustache, with rimless reading glasses. Mack went inside and purchased six photographs, which took care of the Jeffery Simpson passport and license.

Then he went to another branch of the same store and had Harry fix him up in a wig of long, curly black hair and a bushy black beard—this latter piece of gear being a remnant from Mack's SEAL days when he sometimes worked among tribesmen. Once more he had six photographs made, which put Gunther Marc Roche right on the map.

Then they went back to the first store, and Mack had a half-dozen photographs done of himself without disguise, thus creating a perfect look-alike for Patrick Sean O'Grady.

They immediately headed back to the shipyard, where Mack carefully captioned each picture and Harry had his own secretary whistle up FedEx and then check that the e-mail had arrived at the French bank. After all that, they strolled into town, to Hank's Fish Shack, down on the wharf, and treated themselves to a couple of lobster rolls and iced coffee.

They had said little since they left the yard. It was Mack who finally broke the ice. "Getting yourself shot by your enemy is more or less an acceptable risk in my trade," he said. "But to fuck up the paperwork would be regarded as kinda silly."

Harry laughed. "Mack," he said, "you have no idea how confident I am that you are going to pull this off and everyone's problems get solved."

Mack took a deep and luxurious bite of his lobster roll and muttered, "That's why I didn't want to fuck up the paperwork, right?"

At around two o'clock Harry drove back to the shipyard. Mack elected to walk home with his disguises crammed into his pockets. He was feeling tired, having hardly slept. The sofa was nothing like as good as his bed. Anne had called down just once to check he was there, and he took this to mean some kind of truce. But the hurt of her words had stayed with him, and while the truce was okay, he felt too wounded to go for a full reconciliation. He hoped she had not meant it, but the sting of her attack had not left him, and he had thought of little else when he walked over to Remsons at seven thirty that morning. And now, as he turned onto the long country road where they lived, a feeling of dread settled upon him. Had she perhaps meant it?

And then he saw it. Parked way up the road, maybe four hundred yards, right outside the house, blue lights flashing, was an ambulance, its rear doors open with a stretcher being loaded in by two paramedics.

Mack broke into a run, pounding up the lane, terrified that Anne had tried to commit suicide. But then he saw her come running out of the house and saw the doors slam shut with the two assistants in the back, presumably with Tommy. He raised his arm and shouted, *"WAIT!"*

But the ambulance accelerated away, and as Mack came thundering into the front yard there was only Anne, standing by herself, desolate, inconsolable. She did not throw herself into his arms, but simply stood there, repeating, "He's so ill, he's just so ill. And I'm supposed to just stand aside and watch him die."

Mack walked up to her and embraced her at last. He said quietly, "Tell me what happened."

"I could not stop him from being sick, and he was getting frightened. I didn't know where you were, so I called Dr. Ryan, who said it was not that bad, but he was bringing Tommy in immediately. He told me to leave for the hospital one hour after the ambulance left."

Mack steered her toward the house and decided to play his ace right now. "Anne," he said, "Tommy's going to Switzerland. I've raised the money. So get the brochures and make the calls. He can leave right away if they'll take him."

Anne turned around in disbelief, and for the first time in days, a smile lit up her tear-stained face. "He's going?" she said. "He's really going?"

"You're both going," said Mack. "Everything's arranged, paid for in advance. Call them and get the dates, and I'll fix the tickets. And get their bank details; the money's being wired from France."

Anne Bedford stood there in shock, trying to pretend this was not just a dream. Finally, she said, "It's Harry, isn't it? I know it's Harry."

Mack replied, "There's just one condition to this. You must never again ask me how I raised the money. And you must never mention to anyone that the money was raised. Say nothing. Because it's no one's concern except ours."

Anne came toward him slowly and wrapped her arms around his neck. "Did I ever tell you, Mack Bedford, that you're the most wonderful person I ever met?"

"Coupla times, I think. You also mentioned that you hated me."

"Well, I don't, and I spent the entire night wishing I'd never said it."

"Amazing what a million bucks will do, right?" he chuckled.

Despite everything Anne laughed, slapped him playfully on the arm, and went to find the brochures.

"It's after eight o'clock in the evening in Switzerland," called Mack. "They might not answer."

"Yes, they will. It says in the brochure their phone is 24/7—anyone can call anytime, and there will be staff to take care of you."

"At a million bucks a pop, I guess they can afford a few extra staff," muttered Mack as he prepared coffee in the kitchen.

"What did you say?"

"Who me? Nothing. I'm just trying to work the coffeepot."

Mack could hear Anne on the phone. He took the coffee and mugs out onto the porch, and waited quietly, his mind full of details about his forthcoming mission. His first concern was fitness. He had done little hard exercise for a week, and for a Navy SEAL that was a long time. He needed a program that he would draw up this afternoon.

Then Anne appeared, her face lit up with joy. "He's going," she said. "They'll take him. They even had his diagnosis from Dr. Ryan on computer. We're leaving on Tuesday. The clinic will send a car to meet us at Geneva Airport. The lady I was talking to said if she ever had any disease with similarities to leukemia, and she could have any surgeon in all the world, she'd have Carl Spitzbergen. And that's who Tommy's having. I'm just so happy, Mack. And thank God."

Privately, Mack was not absolutely certain God would have been thrilled about the way the money was being raised, but he replied softly, "Thank God is right. Will you be okay going to the hospital without me, or do you want me to come?"

"No, you stay here. I can do the journey blindfolded. Here's the bank details you wanted. I'd better drink this and go, but it won't be too bad. Dr. Ryan said Tommy would be much better and can come home with me. They can't do everything, but they can stop nausea."

Thus, Anne went her way, and Mack went his, walking back to the shipyard and handing the Swiss bank address and numbers to Harry, who promised to have the money wired "this day."

The next part took some serious willpower. Mack walked back to the house and pulled on his combat boots and canvas shorts. Maine did not have long, sandy beaches like Coronado, and he settled for the coastal road, setting off at a slow jogging pace and then hardening his stride. He came through the first mile easily, but this past week of soft living immediately started to take its toll. There was a dull pain in his upper thighs, and his breath was shorter. He knew the signs. He was coming up light— no longer at the level of fitness expected of a SEAL commander, who had also served a couple of terms as a BUDs instructor. Mack could feel it, a deadening in his stride, and he solved it the way he solved everything, pushing harder, driving through the pain, pounding across the ground, making every stride count, making every stride the toughest he ever ran.

Coming to the little bay that washes up to the granite cove on his right, the ground began to rise, and as it did so, Mack hit the gas pedal, accelerating, driving forward with strength he had to find. He was pushing, punishing, pumping, going for the hilltop with every ounce of power and determination he had. And that was a lot. Even in his present state of fitness, he would still have finished out clear of any BUDs Class fighting its way along the Coronado beach. But that was not the level he wanted. Mack wanted Superman, mountain lion, sinews like blue twisted steel. He wanted the level of supreme conditioning that made him unlike other men, the way he had always been: Honor Man, right? The best. Ever since he was selected by his peers, in his own BUDs Class, the first year he became a SEAL.

He reached the brow and glanced right to see the glistening Kennebec bay on this calm July day. For a split second he considered stopping just to see the seascape of his youth spread before him, the waters where he had learned to sail, to fish, and to swim. But he cast the thoughts from his mind and faced the downhill run with suitable grit. Again he accelerated, running fast, covering the ground at almost top speed, trying to keep the jarring at bay, trying to keep his balance, knowing the faster he traveled downhill the easier it was. He reached the bottom without falling and slowed slightly along the flat ground at the head of the bay.

He had covered two miles and had still not achieved his second wind. He was breathing hard, feeling tired, and not at all relaxed in the run, as he knew he should be. But he pushed on until he reached the end of the bay, and there he hit the rising ground, a steep hill that he and every one of his boyhood buddies had hated on their bikes, hated it every time they had to pedal up it. Dead Man's Hill, it was called, because sometime, a couple of hundred years ago, a ship had wrecked right here in the bay after grounding on the granite ridges. Somehow, while they were attempting to get off, a powder keg had blown and killed most of the crew. The bodies were brought on shore, and the local carpenters had constructed coffins on the hillside, ready to transport the deceased to the local cemetery.

Mack faced up to Dead Man's Hill with misgivings. He had traveled fast and was still blowing hard, but as he began to climb, he growled, "HIT IT, MACK! LET'S GO!" He surged forward, arms pumping, combat boots hitting the blacktop. Up ahead he could see a cyclist, wearing Olympic spandex shorts but struggling. And in Mack's mind this was Osama Bin Laden trying to get away. And this put a fury into his stride. He was charging up the hill, running each stride as if it were his last, catching the cyclist, driving on, making every yard the hardest yard he ever ran.

The cyclist, who was not even a member of al-Qaeda, was a young local schoolteacher, and he stared in astonishment as Mack Bedford came pounding past him. It crossed his mind that whoever the hell this was, he'd probably committed some kind of crime. Ordinary joggers do not normally run with that kind of desperation. He watched

Mack storming up to the brow of the hill, and was still pedaling disconsolately when the former SEAL commander vanished, hurtling down the other side, heading for the three-mile mark, checking his watch, trying to make up for the lost week of easy living.

Somewhere on the far side, Mack found his second wind, and the running grew slightly less painful. He settled down and made the four-mile mark in twenty-six minutes. Not bad. He turned around immediately, without stopping, and set off for home, sweating hard, but pleased he was done with that first lap.

About a half mile down the road he met the cyclist and raised his right hand in salute to a fellow athlete. But the rider was more exhausted than Mack, and did not return the greeting in case he fell off. It did occur to him, however, that whomever this lunatic might be, he was almost certainly returning to the scene of a crime.

Mack kept going, running steadily, but still making the yards count, stretching out, testing his body, building his lung strength, the way he'd taught so many young tigers out there on the sands of Coronado. There was no other way to do it, except to keep striving, keep forcing himself onward, taking the pain, knowing that there will come a day when it would all come together, when you ask truly searching questions of your body and get the right answers—*Make it count, Mack, all the way. Make it count.*

He already had a plan for the last quarter mile, and such was his iron-clad determination that he was already dreading it. Of course, a normal person would have decided that was an exercise too far, and jogged home cheerfully. That, however, was not the Bedford way. Mack swung into the home stretch with a slightly uphill climb before him, and let it rip. He stepped it up into a lung-bursting, uncontrolled sprint, the fastest he had traveled during the whole eight miles. He pounded up the road, driving himself to the point of blackout, swerving into the front yard and collapsing on the ground, gasping for breath. Anne thought he was dead. Well, she would have, had she not seen him do it so many times before.

Tommy, however, had not, and he came bolting out of the house yelling, "Mom! Mom! Dad's dead! I think the Deadheads got him!"

At which point Mack jumped right back up and grabbed Tommy, lifting him high and shouting, "They never got me! I killed the god-damned Deadheads!"

Tommy thought this was approximately the most important thing that had ever happened. But Mack would not lower him, and Tommy kept laughing and demanding to know where the bodies of the Deadheads were. Mack told him they were all under the bed. And so it went on, just a little boy and his dad, the one acceptable face of a diabolical international scheme.

They played baseball for a while after that, and then while Anne put Tommy away for his late-afternoon rest, Mack went to the garage and took out a four-foot length of metal pipe, like a short piece of scaffold. He took it to an apple tree out in the backyard and jammed it horizontally between two branches about two feet above his head.

This was a killer SEAL exercise, the pull-ups, where a trainee grasps the pipe and hauls himself up, chin high, holds, and slowly releases and lowers. A normal untrained person probably could manage to do it twice, a young sportsman perhaps nine times, and a fit member of the Special Forces possibly fifteen. Mack Bedford could do thirty-two, though today he may have dropped back to twenty-nine. This is a discipline you need to assault every day, preferably twice.

He tackled the exercise slowly, moving through the first ten with long, steady pulls, each time his chin clearing the pipe. The next twelve were hard but not that hard. Number twenty-six was absolute murder, the pain stabbing through his biceps, his lower back throbbing. Grimly, he hauled himself up again, the pain now ripping through his shoulders. But he made it. And then he made it again, almost crying out with the agony, but still keeping his feet off the ground, and going for his target twenty-ninth. But this was a heave too far. The strength in his forearms and fingers was sapped, and he slipped back onto the grass, never having seen over the bar for the final time. "FUCK!" he roared.

"Sorry?" called Anne from the back doorway. "I didn't quite catch that?"

Mack looked up. "This sucks," he gasped.

"Yes, I thought that was what you said. I wasn't sure."

She came over and brought him a large glass of water, having watched him torturing himself on the pipe. "I can't quite see why you need to prepare yourself for another combat mission," she said. "You're home now, and you're not going back."

"Fitness is just a bad habit," he grinned. "I've had it for a long time, and it's hard to kick."

"I know. But there's fitness and fitness. One of them has to do with general well-being and health. The other kind is what people do before trying to throttle a polar bear with their bare hands."

"That's my kind," said Mack. "You haven't seen any polar bears locally, have you?"

Anne laughed at him, as she always did. Well, nearly always. She gazed at him with admiration. He really was the most incredible specimen of a man. Thirty-three years old, tall, without one ounce of extra weight, broad shoulders, and a manner that could charm the stony heart of a highway state trooper. Anne did, however, suspect there were certain Middle Eastern terrorists who might not wholly go along with that view.

"I'm making a fish pie for dinner, with the other half of the bass and some scallops I picked up at Hank's."

"Plenty of cheese in the sauce," said Mack. "With hot French bread and a baked potato. That's my girl."

"Anything else?"

"One nice cold beer, and I'll go to bed happy. If you'll have me."

"Yes, please," she said sassily, heading back to the house with a spring in her step Mack had not noticed since before his last tour of duty in Iraq.

He chugged his pint glass of water and stared at the bar, which in his mind had defeated him. Temporarily. "You bastard," he told it. "I'll get you tomorrow."

He pulled out his super–cell phone and checked in with Harry, just to make sure the money was in place.

"All done, Mack," he said. "Money's gone. One million smackers to the clinic. No bullshit."

"You're a goddamned hero, Harry," he replied. "They're leaving Tuesday night."

"Yup. I already checked. Boston to Geneva. American Airlines, 9:30 P.M. I'll have business-class return tickets here tomorrow morning. Want to come and pick them up? We can have a chat."

"I'll be there 1100 hours, six bells. We'll have coffee on the Forenoon Watch." He heard Harry Remson chortling away as he put down the phone.

Mack flexed his arms and decided he had recovered. He walked to the side door of the garage and stepped inside, walking across to a small storage area to the left of the Buick. And there he found the packing crate he had shipped to Maine from Coronado. He'd meant to unpack it last week, and there were items in there that he wanted to move to the house—books, memorabilia, and of course his uniforms, which would hang in his bedroom closet until he died. There were also a few items he did not wish Anne to know about—not for the moment, anyway. This was SEAL stuff, things that spelled out a thousand words to him but were meaningless to anyone who had not done what he had done.

He hauled out the books and uniforms, walked back, and placed them on the hood of the Buick. Then he delved into the box and pulled out his SEAL underwater goggles, top-of-the-line scuba diver's gear that had once been bright red but was now colored the dullest gunmetal gray, with not a glint of light reflecting off them. Every SEAL had a mask like that.

Then he pulled out his state-of-the-art wet suit, a truly superb piece of modern underwater equipment, light but incredibly warm, with layers of a plastic/sponge compound insulating the wearer. It was jet black in color with a fitted hood, tight across the back of the neck, forehead, and chin. At the top of each leg were four black metal "popper" studs, and to them were attached Mack's special SEAL flippers, too big for ordinary mortals. On the instep of each one was painted his BUDs Class number, 242, precious numbers that signified the sun and the moon and the earth to Mack.

BUDs 242. Seven little marks, the marks that reminded him of a grim black-top square in Coronado where a legendary SEAL admiral had pinned on his chest his golden Trident, which would forever confirm that out of 168 starters, he, Mack Bedford, was one of the 11 chosen to step forward into America's most elite fighting force. Only then was he able to have the class number painted on his flippers. BUDs. The Basic Underwater Demolition course, where they test the mettle of would-be SEALs. It was ten years ago now, but he remembered it as if it were yesterday. He just stood there in the garage, cradling his wet suit, the one he had worn when he led them through the depths of the Persian Gulf to capture Saddam's offshore oil rig.

He glanced again at the numbers, and the memories shed a mantle of sadness over the former commander. They were memories of the best of times, when he had tackled every obstacle they threw at him and then punched that BUDs indoctrination right on the nose. He'd run that beach until he'd darn near passed out, he'd swum the laps, on the surface and under it. They'd tied him up, ankles and wrists, and shoved him in the twelve-foot deep end of the pool. They'd made him row the rubber boats until he thought he'd die. He'd dragged those boats, run with the goddamned things on his head. He'd hauled those boats up rocks, he'd hauled tree trunks, and he'd sure as hell hauled ass. They'd yelled at him, insulted him, called him a faggot, driven him to the limit of his endurance. Once they'd kept him in the freezing Pacific for a couple of minutes too long, and then had to ship him to the hospital when he passed out from hypothermia. And had he quit? Nossir. He told the ambulance drivers to take him right back to the beach, where he dived right back into the water.

BUDs 242. Those numbers told him everything he needed to know about himself. And when they made him one of the youngest lieutenant commanders in the history of the SEALs, he felt for the first time in his life that he had achieved a worthwhile ambition. Because that promotion was bigger than BUDs. Ten other guys had made that and stood alongside him when the Tridents were handed out.

Lt. Cdr. Mack Bedford. That was priceless, a singular honor, just for him . . . and then they took it all away. At least they took as much away as they could. But they could never take away the words that were written on his heart:

> *My country expects me to be stronger than my enemy, both physically and mentally. . . . If I am knocked down, I will get up, every time. I am never out of the fight. I am here to fight for those who cannot fight for themselves. I am a United States Navy SEAL.*

Carefully, he reached down in the packing crate and retrieved another of his most cherished possessions, his "attack board," the kind they issue to SEAL commanders launching underwater assaults on the enemy. The board was light, made of strong polystyrene, around eighteen inches square, weightless in the water. Into its flat surface were set three instruments: a clock, a compass, and a global positioning system. The board is held out in front, with both hands, as the SEAL leader kicks through the water with those massive flippers. It saves him having to stop to check either the time, the direction, or the team's position. All of it stands right in front of him, softly illuminated but betraying no glare to enemy searchers or sentries on the surface. Mack had located the Iraqi oil rig using this personal attack board.

He leaned down and found his battle-scarred leather bag. Into the bottom he packed the attack board, covered it with his carefully folded wet suit and flippers, and tucked the big underwater mask alongside. The suitcase had a concealed false bottom, and in the space beneath it Mack would pack passports, driver's licenses, and two hundred thousand dollars worth of cash, euros for Ireland and France, pounds for England, and dollars for a U.S. emergency. Everything below the false bottom would be paper or cardboard, and none of it would show up on the X-ray machines in airports. The leather grip would be his only hand baggage. It would never be more than three feet away from him.

He put the bag down, behind the packing crate, and carried the books and uniforms into the house. They had a family supper, and afterward Mack and Tommy watched the Red Sox. Anne was upstairs packing for the journey to Switzerland.

At around nine Mack drove over to Harry's house and apologized for the late, unexpected visit. Harry, who had just finished dinner with his wife, Jane, was unfazed. "Come on in," he said. "We'll have a nightcap, and you can give me the news."

Mack followed him into the study and handed him a piece of paper. On it, for the first time, he had written down his date and time of departure, six days from now—a Saturday, arriving Sunday morning in Ireland, when customs and immigration staffs would be less diligent. He hoped.

"Tickets in the name of Jeffery Simpson," he said. "Open return. Better make it first-class. That way I can pretty well guarantee I'll get a seat anytime I want it, and I might be in a hurry."

Harry nodded. "No problem, pal," he said. "I had a call this morning—the documents will be here by FedEx Monday. Cash, Wednesday morning."

"Perfect. And I just wanted to let you know I will take the cell phone, but it's only for dire emergency. I know the number cannot be traced, but after I hit Foche, there'll be a nationwide manhunt for the killer. And a phone can be traced by the police. Not the number. But the area where it was utilizing the satellite signal. And that might put me in more danger than I need."

Harry Remson poured two Scotch whiskies with soda. Then he said slowly, "Mack, is the exit the hardest part?"

"Yes. Incoming, nobody's looking for me. At least I hope not. Outgoing, the whole fucking world's looking for me. I need to get away in the seconds after I pull the trigger—before Foche hits the ground."

Harry nodded as if he were an expert on high-profile assassinations. And then he stated something that had been on his mind for a few days. "Mack, I've never asked you. But from the very start of this proposal you shied away from any deep involvement. By the time you decided to fire Raul, you wanted to stay at arm's length. Jesus, at one point I thought you were going to bail out on me altogether. And then that night, something happened. You arrived here at Christ knows what time and announced not only were you in on the project, you were actually going to carry it out. Jesus, that's a big turnaround. What happened? Because it wasn't just Tommy, was it?"

Mack smiled ruefully. "No, Harry, it wasn't just Tommy. It was the magazine."

"What magazine?"

"The one you gave me, the Foche magazine."

"Interesting article, right?"

"Harry, it was more than that. There was a picture of Henri Foche standing outside his arms factory. I recognized him right away. Because I'd seen him before."

"You had? Where?"

"He was standing on the far side of the Euphrates River in Iraq. The far side from us, that is. I had my glasses trained on him for about five minutes. He was instructing the fucking towelheads how to fire the missile from its launching post. Looking through the sights, showing them how to aim it. I'd recognize him anywhere."

"And then?"

"Two missiles came in. We all saw 'em flying across the river, and they hit my tanks, burned three of my best friends alive, just incinerated them in some kind of a blue chemical flame. Both missiles ripped straight through the fuselage of the tanks."

"And what kind of missile was it?"

"It was the Diamondhead, the one the United Nations banned in all countries as a crime against humanity. My guys were not attacking anyone, and they were killed by a missile that ought not to be used in any war. So they weren't killed in battle, were they? They were murdered in cold blood."

"The Diamondhead was mentioned in the article, correct?"

"Yes, Harry, it was. There's an accusation that Foche was the manufacturer, but no one seems able to prove it. In all the world, only I know the truth, because I saw him, just before my guys were burned to death. He was plainly the manufacturer, standing there next to his fucking Mercedes, wearing his pimp scarlet handkerchief, instructing Iraqis how to murder American soldiers."

"He was wearing that handkerchief in the magazine," recalled Harry.

"That handkerchief was the one deciding factor. When I saw that, I had him. But I'd have known it was him even without it."

"Mack, you have as big a reason to take him out as I do."

"I have a bigger reason. Those guys were like family to me. We'd fought together all over the place. And to watch them burn like that—it was as if I'd died and gone to hell. I don't have a better way to explain it."

"Has this become a mission of revenge for you?"

"You're damn right it has. This Foche murdered my guys. And in France he already seems to be untouchable, because he's going to be the next president. But I am going to make sure he never becomes president of France. You can bet on that. Because I'll find him."

Harry was thoughtful for a moment, and then he said, "Mack, we're equal partners in this. My money; your brains, skill, and planning. Just don't let it get in the way—that rising red mist of anger about the guys. Stay cool, and stay focused."

"That's the way I've been taught, Harry. This is just another mission—Taliban killers, al-Qaeda killers, insurgent killers, missile killers. They're all the fucking same to me. But this one won't get away."

Harry Remson put out his right hand, and Mack took it. "Partners," said Harry.

"Partners," replied Mack, and they shook, with a new unspoken warmth.

The two men walked to the front door together, but after Mack had left, Harry was faced with a brand-new problem. His wife, Jane, walked into the study and asked him why it was necessary, these days, for Mackenzie Bedford to arrive at this house at unusual hours.

"Oh, we were just talking about some business deal that may come to fruition. If we have to close down the yard."

"Oh, were you? Well, I'd prefer to put my cards on the table. And I heard you and Mack discussing the possibility of having this French politician, Henri Foche, murdered."

"Are you crazy? We did no such thing."

"Didn't you? Then I'll quote you two or three phrases I heard Mack use: 'after I hit Foche,' 'nationwide manhunt,' and 'after I pull the trigger—before he hits the ground.'"

Harry turned to face his wife of thirty-two years. "Jane," he said, "neither Mack Bedford nor I had a choice in this matter. You must believe me, and you must trust me."

"Trust you! Trust you? You mean I should just sit here quietly and watch you two plan to assassinate the next president of France, which will, without question, put us all in jail for the rest of our lives? Do you really think you could get away with it? My God, Harry! The FBI would be in our front yard within a week. In all the years we have known each other, I have never once heard you suggest anything quite so utterly unreasonable."

Jane Remson, at the age of fifty-eight, was a very good-looking lady. She was svelte, petite, and chic, always beautifully turned out, with a mane of lustrous natural-looking blonde hair. The combined process of this dazzling example of twenty-first-century preservation was privately estimated by Harry to have cost somewhere in the region of seven billion dollars.

He appreciated her and loved her as she loved him. But she had never before spoken to him quite like that. Still, he reasoned, he had never decided to assassinate the next president of France before.

And Miss Jane, as the household staff still called her, was not finished. "Harry," she said, "I am asking you to call this whole insane thing off."

"I cannot do that," he said. "And perhaps you should keep in mind that I am not going to assassinate anyone. I'm staying right here. And I shall never breathe one word about such a plot to anyone. And I would be obliged if you would do precisely the same. It has nothing to do with you, and, in a way, nothing to do with me."

"*HARRY!* How can you be so naive? I stood outside that door and heard you and Mack Bedford discussing the killing of Henri Foche. And in my view you will both be caught by the police and charged with his murder."

"Eavesdropping is a very dangerous game," said her husband. "And no one should do it. Because you only hear about one-tenth of the truth. It is obvious, and has been for some time, that if Henri Foche should win the presidency, this shipyard will have to close. There are many options. And Foche has many enemies. You happened to hear one tiny snippet of the conversation, just a fraction of the discussion."

"Well, it did not sound like a snippet to me. It sounded like a very sinister piece of planning. And I can't understand why Mack would even be talking about it. It's not his shipyard, and you cannot be so stupid as to be paying him to murder Foche. That's fairyland. And what if he gets caught, or shot by Foche's security guards? How long do you think it would take the police to trace him right back here to Dartford, and in a matter of days associate you with the crime?"

Harry had rarely seen his wife so fraught with anxiety. He knew, of course, she had only his best interests at heart. But there was a clarity about Jane's assessment that was beginning to unnerve him. And he decided to pull rank. "Jane," he said, "you have lived very well off my family business for several decades. Every comfort I could provide you came from Sam Remson's shipyard. I have never thought of myself as the owner, just the custodian for future generations. I know we have only two daughters, but that has not changed my thinking. I owe it to this family, these workers, and this town to do all in my power to prevent Henri Foche from becoming president and closing us down. If we could land just one more order from the French Navy, I could hire a couple of top international salesmen and send them out looking for new business. We have never in one hundred years had to do that. What I cannot survive is three or four years with no work. . . . "

"But Harry," interjected Jane, "we aren't getting younger, and we don't need the yard. The land is worth a fortune—we could sell it off and be fine for the rest of our lives, spend winters on the boat. What are you thinking, getting involved in some hideous international crime?"

"Jane Remson, if I sold this shipyard and cast almost the entire town out of our lives, I could never look at myself in the mirror again. I'd never get over it. I'd end up sitting in Saint Bart's or somewhere, drinking too much, and waiting to die. And that I won't do. I'm in this fight. And I'm staying in."

"But you can't be serious about Mack Bedford and this killing . . . ?"

"No one ever said Mack Bedford was doing any killing. But he has friends, ex–Special Forces, guys who work for international security firms, hiring mercenaries and the like. He is trying to give me some advice. And now I want you to promise me, you will never again, for the rest of your life, mention one more word about what you think you heard—not to me, certainly not to Anne Bedford, or to anyone else. Ever. As far as you are concerned, you never heard anything."

"I still can't understand why Mack Bedford is involved."

Harry Remson's face betrayed more anger than his wife had ever seen. He stood up and walked toward her, not quite threatening but sufficiently unfriendly to make her literally catch her breath. She'd never seen him look like that before.

He stood over her and said very slowly, "Not one more word, Jane. I'm sorry. But there's too much at stake. Not one more word."

———— • ◆ • ————

Mack Bedford drove Anne and Tommy to Boston's Logan Airport on Tuesday evening. In the end, Harry had purchased first-class seats to Geneva and arranged for an American Airlines representative to take them to the lounge immediately after they had checked in and cleared security.

There was no need to park and wait, and they said their good-byes outside the terminal. Tommy was in tears because he would not see his dad for the next month, and insisted on wearing his baseball glove to the check-in area. Anne just wanted Mack to get back on the road, because the drive home was close to 150 miles, the last third through slow, winding, lonely coastal roads.

And so, in the gathering summer darkness, Mack drove out of the airport and headed northeast back up the highway to Interstate 95, which cuts a swath up the short New Hampshire coast, and then scythes its way parallel to the rocky shores of Maine. The journey took him more than three hours, and the house seemed very dark and remote when he arrived home. While Anne had spent months on end here, alone except for Tommy, Mack had never spent time here by himself, and he was not sure he was looking forward to the next four days.

He put on some lights and made himself coffee. He was starving hungry and not tired, so he fixed himself a ham sandwich, stole some of Tommy's potato chips, and rummaged around in the freezer for some ice cream. Zero.

He poured the coffee and opened the big envelope that he had picked up from Harry earlier in the day and examined the documents that had arrived from Maryland. There were three passports, and he looked at them carefully. They were absolute masterworks of their type. He checked the dates, the photographs, and the quality of the printing. Then he checked the driver's licenses, all three beautifully forged. He checked each license against the relevant passport, searching for discrepancies. But there were none.

Mack took his sandwich and coffee into the living room and watched the postgame roundup from Baltimore, where the Red Sox had, unaccountably, been beaten 4 to 2. Tomorrow morning he would pick up the cash from Harry, before finalizing his departure on Saturday evening. But right now, Mack was suddenly tired, too tired to watch the Orioles–Red Sox replay on NESN, and he took himself wearily to bed.

He missed Anne here, more than he missed her when he was away, perhaps because he had never been without her in this house. Their king-sized bed seemed vast and hollow, and he curled up on one side and fell instantly asleep.

Five hours later the alarm on his clock radio went off, and Mack awakened fast, like all SEALs. He rolled out of bed and pulled on his canvas shorts, his navy-blue instructor's T-shirt, socks, and combat boots. This morning he had a plan, and he needed to be on the move before first light in order to carry it out.

He went downstairs, fired up the Buick, and hit the road six minutes after he first awoke. Mack needed a beach, and they didn't have any in his particular neck of the woods. He needed a beach because that was where SEALs trained. There were only two SPECWARCOM garrisons in the United States, one at Virginia Beach and one on the beach at Coronado, San Diego.

For all of them, there was something about training on sand. It was harder to run over, more demanding, and it sapped energy quicker. It also kept a top combat SEAL sharper because he was always looking for the firm ground at the top of the tide where the sand was not too deep.

Out there in Coronado, often at first light, the BUDs trainees were subjected to the most grueling regimen of physical fitness. And the one truly awful moment was when the instructors yelled at someone to "get wet and sandy." Which was a schoolboy euphemism meaning, "Run into the goddamned freezing Pacific Ocean, boots and all, then come out and roll in the sand." This was essentially torture because no one was allowed to stop. Boots filled with water, and the men had to squelch and chafe their way through the miles, in diabolical discomfort, with feet that were suddenly made of lead. But it honed them into fighting men, gave them an edge, because everything else was kid stuff compared to the rigors of BUDs training.

Mack's part of Maine, and all the way up the coast to Canada, was devoid of long beaches. It comprised hundreds of coves, bays, harbors, islands, and rocky inlets. The entire Maine coast is only 250 miles long as the crow flies, but it has a convoluted coastal length of well over 3,000 miles, hardly any of it straight. Except in the most southerly stretch, from the Isles of Shoals, past Kennebunkport, and up to Richmond Island. Along there are some magnificent stretches of wild sand, some of them miles long, places like Old Orchard Beach, Wells, and Scarborough.

It was to this summer paradise that Mack was headed, maybe 40 miles from Dartford. He needed to be there before the tourists and vacationers showed up. It was still dark when he crossed the bridge at Bath and headed down to Interstate 95, where he'd been only a few hours before.

The sun was just rising when he pulled into the parking lot on the long beach and emptied his pockets. He pulled on a baseball cap and sunglasses, locked the car, and walked down the sand to the water's edge. It was a calm day, just little wavelets lapping the shore.

Mack looked to his left and right. It looked a hell of a way in either direction. He set off, going east, into the rising sun, which reminded him of Coronado so long ago. It was a cool morning, much cooler than California, but the temperature of the sea was comparable. Cold. Darned cold. Maine had a lot of charms. The temperature of the ocean was not one of them. Unless you happened to be a walrus.

Mack had been training for several days now, on the road, but within a half mile he could feel the difference, the extra effort required, as he splashed along the tidal limit—*just like old times with the guys, banging our way along the beach past the old Hotel del Coronado.*

He decided to make his first challenge after two miles, and he kept on going, driving forward like always. He was already asking questions of his body, and he was getting the right answers. His breath came easily, his legs had no ache, and at the two-mile mark, he closed his eyes tight. He tried to imagine Instructor Mills running alongside him, on an easy stride—*"YOU'RE NOT PUTTING OUT FOR ME, BEDFORD— YOU'RE RUNNING LIKE A GODDAMNED FAGGOT!"* That had usually been yelled at him when he was right up with the leaders, going for his life. Around him there was a ripple of suppressed laughter among the guys at the sheer mind-numbing unfairness of it, with possibly ninety men laboring behind the leaders.

And then the quietly uttered payoff—"Bedford, get wet and sandy." Mac heard it then, and he heard it again now, echoing down the years, into his mind, those dreaded words that had contributed so much to the man he now was. He turned sharp right, and, in the glare of the rising sun, Mack Bedford rushed into the freezing Atlantic. Boots and all. This was BUDs revisited.

The shock of the water brought back a thousand memories as he plunged beneath the surface, swimming hard, keeping his head down, feeling the icy water numbing his face. He kept going, driving through the water, swimming with one of the most powerful overarm strokes the instructors had ever seen at Coronado. On the first day in the SEAL training pool, he had overheard an instructor asking, "What the hell is this guy, some kind of a fucking fish?"

Mack swam out for a quarter of a mile and then turned back, still going hard, all the way to the beach. He climbed out of the shallows and walked to the deep, dry sand and threw himself down, rolling in it, back and forth. Finally he stood up, rigidly to attention, and somewhere in the deepest recesses of his mind, he heard the far-lost cry of the faithful—*HOO-YAH, MACK BEDFORD!* How could he forget that? How could anyone ever forget that?

Once more he turned to face the east, and he set off again, pounding forward, checking his watch, counting off the miles. Back at the top of the beach, a state parking lot attendant came on duty, and watched Mack's exit from the water. He shook his head, confident he was staring at a person who had almost certainly gone stark-raving mad.

Twice more on the run, once at the four-mile mark and then again at the end, Mack hurled himself into the ocean, the last time washing away the sand that had made the exercise so uncomfortable. Then with a cheerful grin on his face, he strode back to the car. He could still do it, right? Like always. No problem. HOO-YAH, Mack.

He'd packed a couple of big towels in the back of the car, and he removed all of his soaking clothes and used one towel as a sarong and the other to cover the seat. The place was still deserted, since it was only seven o'clock.

Mack reached home at around eight thirty, took a shower, and put on dry clothes. The past few days had made him feel great, as he reached the kind of peak fitness known only to those who have spent a lifetime achieving it. His muscles felt supple, he knew his reactions would be razor sharp, and there was an inner strength deep inside that gave him supreme confidence.

Mack, in just a few days, had regained the old SEAL swagger, the feeling of physical and mental supremacy that rendered him, in his own mind, indestructible: the way all SEALs must feel when they go into combat.

He had prepared for this mission, because he understood there may be adversity. He must somehow steal into France, and he must be prepared if necessary to cope with armed security men. For a normal person, this would be a nerve-racking, tense operation. For Lieutenant Commander Bedford it was an extension of what he had always done. He was not nervous, and he was unafraid. Indeed, he was gratified to know his opponents at least would not be trying to hit him with a Diamondhead missile, even if their fucking boss did manufacture the damn thing.

He hit the parallel steel bar shortly after eleven and stared right over it thirty-two times, no sweat. It was, he knew, a superhuman performance. He'd never seen anyone beat that in all his years in the navy.

At noon he went to Harry's office to collect the cash, and his partner had everything ready, the bank notes packed in bundles amounting to four thousand dollars each, fifty of them packed into a leather briefcase, three lines of six, in each of three layers. Crushed down tightly. Mack knew there was more room in the secret compartment in his own leather bag, under the attack board.

They had a cup of coffee together, and Harry handed over the first-class return Aer Lingus ticket to Dublin. Both men agreed not to meet or speak again. It was better that way. They should not be seen together anymore, not at this stage of the proceedings.

Mack had only one last request, that Harry arrange for him to use the near-Olympic-sized pool at the private golf and country club outside Portland. In the remaining days he did not want to run on the roads, and swimming represented the safest way to work out hard without straining or jarring joints, muscles, or tendons.

This was no time for accidents or mistakes. Mack wanted to swim more than fifty laps every day, to stay right on top of his game. And every day he drove to the country club, signed in as Mr. Patrick O'Grady, an Irish friend of Harry Remson's, and completed his workout.

On Saturday afternoon, he finished packing and stowed the reservoir of cash under his underwater gear. He took barely any clothes, just underwear, shaving kit, toothpaste, and socks. He was unarmed, for the opening stage of the journey. He was wearing his light-blond wig, with the thin mustache, and rimless glasses. It was astounding how different he looked. He wore dark-gray slacks, black loafers, and a dark tweed sport coat. A blue shirt with a maroon necktie completed his innocuous appearance.

At four o'clock a black limousine pulled up outside the house, sent from a private car-hire firm in Portland, to be charged to the account of Mr. Harry Remson, chairman, Remsons Shipbuilding, Dartford, Maine.

"Good afternoon, Mr. O'Grady," said the driver. "Logan Airport, right?"

"You got it. Aer Lingus. Terminal E."

"May I take your bag, sir, and put it in the trunk?"

"No thanks, pal. I prefer to keep it with me."

They pulled away, up the long country lane to the main road where Mack had arrived by bus, just a couple of weeks previously. They turned left, and neither of them noticed a dark-blue Bentley parked about a mile along the road outside the local garage.

The driver of the Bentley did, however, see them. Because he'd been waiting for almost an hour, half in disbelief, half in almost unbearable excitement. But he fought the feeling down as the limo swept past.

"God go with you, Mack," breathed Harry Remson.

CHAPTER 8

Mack checked in with his Jeffery Simpson passport. The Aer Lingus girl, neatly dressed in her emerald-green uniform, glanced at it briefly and allocated him a seat at the front of the aircraft, which she said was not full tonight.

Mack thanked her and walked upstairs to the security lines and put his bag on the conveyor belt for X-ray. The dials on the attack board instruments showed up like small travel clocks, and did not strike the operator like possible dangerous weapons. The rest of the contents were mostly paper and soft rubber, and the old leather grip came straight through.

The chimes did not spring to life as Mack walked past the metal detectors, and three minutes later he was in the newspaper shop, purchasing a copy of the French daily, *Le Monde.*

He found the first-class lounge and settled in an armchair at a corner table, near the television. The Irish attendant said she would bring him coffee, and a sandwich if he wished, and there was no need for him to take any notice of any announcements. She would escort him to the aircraft at the appropriate time.

This particular lounge was very quiet since the flight to Dublin was the only Aer Lingus departure at night. There were perhaps six other people in residence, but Mack was the only one watching the ball game from Fenway Park.

The smoked salmon sandwich, wild Irish salmon no less, represented probably the best meal he'd eaten since Anne left for Switzerland. When the Red Sox loaded the bases and then jumped to a 3–0 lead, bottom of the first, he decided life was not really that bad after all.

They called the flight early, and Mack settled into his roomy green-patterned seat with the Red Sox still holding a 5–3 lead. It was warm on board, and Mack took off his jacket. The first-class attendant asked him if he'd care for a black velvet before they left.

"What's a black velvet?" he asked.

"Guinness and champagne," said the girl. "The lifeblood of Ireland."

Mack declined, as he was resolved to decline all alcohol until Henri Foche lay dead, and he was safely home.

They took off on time, and Mack had a medium-rare Irish fillet steak for dinner. He read for a while, practiced his French with *Le Monde*, and noticed a photograph of Foche on page 8 of the newspaper. "Sonofabitch," he muttered, and tried to fathom what the story said about the French politician. The answer was not much, except that he seemed to be making a speech in his hometown of Rennes the following day. The newspaper was dated *mercredi*, so he'd probably made it already. But Mack was gratified to see that a speech by the man he sought was now considered news on a national scale—*stop the sneaky little bastard hiding from me, right?*

Mack slept for most of the transatlantic crossing. Five hours later he was still asleep when the flight attendant awakened him and suggested a few scrambled eggs and Irish bacon with soda bread for breakfast. They'd be landing at Dublin in thirty-five minutes.

Revived by a tall glass of orange juice, "Jeffery Simpson" adjusted his wig and enjoyed one of the great airline breakfasts. *The hell with cereal and yogurt*, he thought. *This is the game for me.*

They landed in Dublin on Sunday morning at 9:30 A.M. local. Mack picked up his bag and moved into his first serious test at a foreign immigration desk. He lined up and presented his U.S. passport. The official in the booth smiled and opened it, checked the photograph against Mack's face, and asked, "How long will you stay in Ireland, Mr. Simpson?"

"Maybe a week."

The official stamped the passport, confirming a Dublin port of entry, and said, "Welcome, sir. Have a grand visit."

Mack moved outside and joined the short line for a taxi. He jumped aboard the first available cab and asked to be taken to the Shelbourne Hotel in St. Stephen's Green. Traffic was light, and after seven miles and twenty minutes, they were moving through the outskirts of the relatively small city.

They crossed the Liffey, turned left, and ran along the south bank toward the outskirts of Ballsbridge. Up ahead Mack could see precisely what he was seeking—a large used-car dealership with a lot of flags flying and obvious activity.

He allowed the driver to drive perhaps four hundred yards farther, and then said in the best Irish accent he could manage, "Will you stop right here, sir? I've decided to have a quick cup of coffee with my aunt."

"No problem. That'll be twenty-four euros."

Mack pulled a few notes out of his pocket and gave the man thirty. He climbed out of the cab and walked back to the car dealership, strolling slowly down the line of cars, not wishing to attract the immediate attention of an overeager salesman.

That represented his first failure of the journey. Michael McArdle, the owner, was upon him, telling him the Ford Fiesta at which he was currently staring was probably the greatest buy in the entire history of motorized commerce. "I'll tell you something about this particular car," he said. "It's four years old and used to be owned by a local lady. It's got only sixteen thousand miles on the clock, and I've serviced every last one of 'em meself. This particular car represents one of the great bargains of me life.

"Am I asking twenty t'ousand for it? Nossir, I'm not. Am I askin' fifteen t'ousand for it? Nossir, I'm not. I'll tell you what, twelve t'ousand buys it! And could anyone ever be fairer than that?"

"Depends," said Mack. "How about ten thousand for cash?"

"Well, I'd have to let the check clear first."

"I said cash. Bank notes. Ten thousand euros," said Mack.

"I'll take dat," said Michael McArdle. "I'll take dat, even though it's like a dagger to me heart, to part with this car for that money . . . When do you need it?"

"Now."

"Now! Christ! I have to do the paperwork, register it, fill in the forms. That'll mean tomorrow."

"Guess I came to the wrong place. See you," replied Mack.

"Now wait a minute, sor," said the proprietor of McArdles. "I'll have to see what I can do. But I need to fill out a government form. I'll want good identification."

"No problem. I got a passport and a driver's license right here. I don't have to get my photograph done?" asked Mack.

"Jaysus, no. They don't need that. Just the numbers."

"You sure this thing runs okay?"

"I'm sure enough to give you the two-year McArdle guarantee," he said. "And we've been here for half a century. This car breaks down in the first five t'ousand miles, you can have your money back and you can keep the car."

Mack laughed. "Come on, Michael, let's get this thing done."

A half hour later, the Ford Fiesta in "moondust silver" with AC pulled out onto the road and swung left for Lansdowne Road. It was registered with the government authorities in the name of Patrick O'Grady who (a) did not exist himself, (b) had an address that was also nonexistent, and (c) possessed an Irish driver's license that had never been issued to anyone.

Mack had managed to coerce a map of Ireland out of Michael McArdle, who confirmed that deals as generous as this would most certainly be the death of him. But nonetheless he hoped the wind would always be at Mr. O'Grady's back.

Mack hit the gas pedal, and was happy to discover the Ford engine was as sharp and fine-tuned as Michael had claimed. He swung up to the Merrion Road, turned right after crossing Ballsbridge, and cut through to the main road to the southeast, heading straight for the Wicklow Mountains.

In the whole of Ireland, he had but one contact, a man named Liam O'Brien in the little Wicklow town of Gorey. And he came by that name only by the luckiest of circumstances. In the final days of his life, before he died in the tank, Charlie O'Brien had mentioned that he and his wife were planning a vacation in Ireland. Mack had asked him where they were staying, and Charlie had responded by telling him he had a long-lost cousin he had never met, in the town of Gorey. "He keeps a hardware store," said Charlie. "But my father swears to God he was a senior member of the IRA. Liam's father, who died years ago, was my dad's brother."

Mack had somehow remembered that, and in the long days he spent alone after Anne had left had decided that here was a man who might know a gunsmith in England, because there was no question of trying to acquire a rifle anywhere else and then attempting to bring it through Britain's red-hot customs and immigration.

To his great delight he had seen that Gorey was on the main Dublin road south, the N11, and in that moment had decided to take the ferry to England from Rosslare in County Wexford, rather than from Dun Laoghaire on the south side of Dublin. Gorey stands thirty-four miles north of Rosslare Harbor.

The trouble was, O'Brien's hardware store was unlikely to be open, and Mack elected to get into the town, locate the store, and then try to get a number for Charlie's cousin. He would not call from the magic cell phone, because he was already thinking like a man on the run. Mack actually found it hard to believe that no one had yet committed a crime, except against the Irish motor taxation authorities. And he did not really count that.

He drove through the Wicklows, running east of the Great Sugar-loaf Mountain, which rose above the highway. The Ford Fiesta then whipped past the range of hills that led up to the Devil's Glen. It was a fast new road, and swept straight around the historic old port of Arklow, County Wicklow's busiest town, with history dating back to the second century.

Mack crossed the River Bann and ran into quiet little Gorey at around two o'clock Sunday, lunchtime. "Quiet little Gorey" is, however, a mild deception, because in this hillside town in southern Wicklow, there beats the heart of Irish Republicanism. It was for years a stronghold of the IRA. Indeed, when they blew that double-decker bus to smithereens in London a few years back, the perpetrator was from Gorey.

Mack Bedford did not, of course, know this; otherwise, he might have stepped more carefully. He could see there were a few shops open, and several bars, the iron grip of the Catholic Church having been released somewhat in southern Ireland in recent years. However, there was no luck at the hardware store, which he located on a small side street forty yards off the main road that ran through the middle of town.

It was very definitely closed, and the only information Mack acquired was the name, L. O'Brien and Sons, Hardware and Paint. Mack headed up the road to the church and found a telephone kiosk. He could see the phone book in there, and parked and scanned down the columns. He found the store, and right below it, he located another L. O'Brien of the same address. Plainly, this was the private number, and the family lived above the store. Mack considered this a stroke of good fortune because there were about seven thousand O'Briens in the phone book.

He went back to the car and boldly dialed the number of one of the most dangerous former IRA commanders in the country. A somewhat gruff voice answered, a noncommittal, "Yes?"

Mack decided to speak in his regular American accent and said:
Is that Mr. O'Brien?
Who's asking?
I was a close friend of your American cousin Charlie O'Brien.
Oh, you were?
I was. I was with him in Iraq just before he died, and I told him I was coming to Ireland and then to England.
And what can I do to help you?
Well, sir, I am going shooting in England this fall, and I was trying to locate a gunsmith in London. Charlie said you might be able to help.
Who you planning to shoot? Liam O'Brien laughed.

Just a few pheasants and grouse.

Of course. Well, why not try one of the main gunsmiths in London, Holland and Martin? Maybe even Purdey's?

I . . . I suppose I could. But I was hoping for something kinda unobtrusive.

Well, if I'm any judge, you're looking for a different kind of a gun. And it's not against anyone's law for me to steer you right.

I wouldn't want to break the law, Mr. O'Brien.

No, of course not. I never wanted to meself. But I'll tell you what, I'll come downstairs at an agreed time, and I'll hand you a piece of paper with your man's name, address, and number on it. I'll have to phone him, and give him a name. It's going to cost you two thousand euros, and I don't want to see your face, or know your real name. Take it or leave it.

I'll take it. As for the time, how about now? I'm in Gorey.

Park yourself outside the shop in five minutes. And do not look at my face. Do you have the cash?

I do.

Men who want illicit rifles usually do, eh? Mr. O'Brien chuckled again.

Mack Bedford liked doing business here in Ireland. No bullshit, right?

He drove back around to O'Brien Hardware and Paint and parked outside. One minute later, a figure moved fast out of a side door and positioned himself next to the car. One piece of paper was handed to Mack Bedford, which he swiftly read. The hand that gave him that piece of paper was still there, slightly open, and Mack pressed twenty 100-euro bills into it.

"Very trusting of you, sir. Especially as you don't know the value of the information I just gave you."

"It better be good," said Mack.

"It had?"

"Yes, O'Brien. Because if it's not, I'll come back and probably kill you."

"It's good," said the Irishman. "There's still a little bit of honor among thieves." He chuckled again, the same distinctive merriment Mack had heard on the phone.

"And what name shall I give him, for identification when you get there?"

Mack still never turned his face toward the man, and he said, without hesitation, "McArdle, Tommy McArdle."

"I'll make the call. Your man's about a half hour west of London. He's the best private gunsmith in England. . . . Stay safe, Tommy, and for Jaysus' sake, shoot straight."

"See ya, Liam," called Mack, chuckling as he pulled away, still staring dead ahead, never having cast his eyes on the roguish Liam O'Brien, and never having allowed the Irishman to see him.

He pressed on south, heading directly to the ancient town of Enniscorthy, with its mighty round-towered Norman castle and spectacular Roman Catholic cathedral, designed by Augustus Pugin, who also designed the Houses of Parliament in London.

He ran through Enniscorthy, which was much more tourist-busy than Gorey, and he crossed the River Slaney on the one-way bridge. He turned right and followed the meandering course of the river on the fast, flat, wide road to Wexford town. There's a bypass here, and the road hooks right on a split highway, moving traffic swiftly down to the port of Rosslare.

Mack Bedford stopped at a garage on top of the hill above the harbor, gassed up the car, and bought himself a cup of coffee, which he drank slowly on the forecourt, gazing across the road, out to sea, at the calm waters of the St. George's Channel.

He drove down the steep hill to the ferry port at around half past four, parked, and walked to the Stena Line desk to inquire about a ferry to England.

"Actually, it goes to Wales, sir," said the clerk, a young man whose name tag identified him as Seamus. "And it doesn't sail 'til 10:15 tonight. You can go aboard around half eight."

"Not before?" asked Mack.

"Well, before that she's in the middle of the Irish Sea," said Seamus. "So I'd say not."

"What time does it get in?"

"Just before three. Fishguard, South Wales, and you can drive off right after that. But if you take a cabin and decide to stay in your bed until six thirty, that's fine too. Just tell us when you want to disembark so we can put your car in the right place."

"Okay, Seamus. Give me a round-trip first-class ticket, for a cabin and a Ford Fiesta car."

"No one else traveling with you?"

"No."

"And when will you return, sir?"

"Leave it open, will you, because I'm not sure."

"That'll add twenty euros to the cost, sir, without a firm date I mean."

"I can handle that," replied Mack.

"Name?"

"Patrick O'Grady."

"Irish passport?"

"Yup."

When Seamus asked for the color and registration number of the car, Mack told him dark blue, and then altered at least three of the numbers on the registration, hoping no one would notice, which they didn't.

"Which card will you be using for payment?"

"No card. Cash."

"No problem."

Mack handed over three hundred euros, took his tickets, and left. He considered it, so far, a good day's work. He was leaving the American Jeffery Simpson behind in Ireland, and he was driving onto the ferry with a ticket made out to the Irishman Patrick O'Grady, who had never been born, and lived nowhere. The false Irish passport had been noted, and the return ticket would never be used.

The car Mack was driving was recorded in the ferry office in the wrong color, with vast discrepancies in the registration, thus rendering it, and its driver, untraceable by any police force in the world. If anyone ever came after him, that is.

Mack retired to the parking lot, which was quite busy, and settled himself in the front seat with the windows open, and a copy of the *Irish Sunday Times* he'd bought in the garage. He decided not to join the line of cars waiting for the 10:15 sailing until around half past seven, because right now he'd be the only one there. What Mack wanted in the line was a car behind him and one in front.

The two-and-a-half-hour wait passed slowly. Mack slept for a half hour, but he had a lot of time to think. And one worrying truth kept crossing his mind. On every mission, no matter where, from the Afghan mountains to the backstreets of Baghdad, there are surprises, sudden unexpected problems and downright bad luck. There is also apt to be one stroke of very good luck. Amidst all the horror, something almost always breaks for a top SEAL commander. What worried Mack was that, on this mission, he'd already had his one bit of real good luck, and its name was Liam O'Brien. From now on, he pondered, things might not fall right for me. . . . *I'd better be real careful, or I'm going to end up dead.*

He joined the long line at around a quarter of eight. They boarded on time, no one asked for any further identification, and he placed his car among the very few first-class ticketed vehicles. He checked his cabin, which was small, but neat and spotless. The steward told him he was welcome to go up to the first-class lounge, where he could have a drink and some dinner if he wished.

He took his bag and climbed the stairs to the upper deck, found the lounge, and poured himself some coffee. He ordered, on the steward's recommendation, a fresh Dublin Bay sole, off the bone, with french fries and spinach. He drank only orange juice, and finished his dinner with a plate of Irish apple crumble with fresh cream.

The huge ship sailed at 10:15, running slowly along the jetties and out past the great hooked harbor wall. They stood fair down the channel, running out toward the flashing light on the jutting rocky ledge, which marks the maritime roads in and out of Rosslare.

Mack took his bag and left as soon as he sensed the changed beat of the engine, when the ship began to move. He went outside and leaned on the rail, watching the harbor lights disappear, feeling the old familiar roll of the ocean, which would increase as soon as they came out of the shadow of the land and sailed into the rough open waters of the Irish Sea, with the Atlantic swells surging in from the southwest. He saw the high light flashing on the ledge and guessed as they passed that they were making fifteen knots. It reminded him of home, and the towering light on Sequin Island.

But ahead of him was only darkness, and he decided to go to bed. Back down in his cabin he took off his jacket and shoes, locked the door, and crashed under a couple of blankets. The ship was warm, and he slept almost immediately, awakening at around two thirty, after three and a half hours.

The night was still dark, but the ship was rolling less than it had been after they passed the Rosslare ledge. Mack climbed out of bed and stared through the starboard side window. About a mile off their beam he could see the light on Strumble Head, the first rocky point on the British mainland, a famous old lighthouse flashing four times with a seven-second gap, stark in the night on this Pembrokeshire headland.

Mack knew the ship was due to dock in a half hour, but his old seaman's instincts caused him to consult the complimentary map of the Welsh coastline, which Stena placed in all first-class cabins. On any ship, Mack Bedford always assumed he was either driving or navigating, and he didn't want any mistakes; he needed to check his bearings. He was the everlasting lieutenant commander.

He went back to bed, resolving to sleep again at least until it was light. He heard the ship dock but then drifted off until six. He stripped off his shirt and shaved, dressed, and walked along to the car deck. He'd been on this ship long enough, and he did not wish to be remembered by anyone, in any way.

He drove straight off the ferry, over the wide steel bridge, and onto the British mainland. He drove down the long exit road from the ship, and up ahead there were tall sheds, plainly a customs checking area. There were also two kiosks, with uniformed security men standing out front. There was only one other car near him, the rest having plainly rushed out of the ship in the small hours.

Mack slowed down and saw the man look at his license plate. "Irish passport, sir?"

"Right here," said Mack, waving the one that belonged to Patrick O'Grady.

"Straight on, sir," he replied, without even looking. Mack Bedford thus entered the United Kingdom with a minimum of fuss and total anonymity. He planned, in a few days, to leave the United Kingdom in much the same way. But right now he needed to reach London, and the gunsmith, as fast as this fine-tuned, McArdle-guaranteed Irish automobile would take him.

He climbed the steep cliff face from Fishguard Harbor on the new road, and then turned right, away from the ocean, onto the A40. He drove quickly at this time in the morning, on a long, winding road, almost deserted except for ferry traffic coming the other way. He sped through the spectacular farmland of West Wales, passing villages named in the ancient native language with about three hundred letters and hardly any vowels.

At seven he passed Wolf's Castle, an extraordinary jagged-rock fortress set high on a hill, silhouetted against the sky. It took another hour to reach the M4 motorway, which runs all the way through South Wales, past the old coal mining valleys, and then on to London, a fast three-hour drive, from end to end of Great Britain's busiest highway.

Mack crossed the Severn Bridge at nine and stopped for breakfast at the first service area he found. He gassed up the car and then went inside to order a couple of English sausages, toast, and scrambled eggs. He lingered for a couple of cups of coffee, carefully studying a London A–Z guide. He located the gunsmith's street, and hit the M4 again, running hard, due east toward the capital.

The map had proved extremely useful because it confirmed that he did not need to move into London. He could stay outside, possibly at one of the many hotels that surround the airport out here on the M4. He could deal with the gunsmith from here. Southall, where Mr. Kumar lived, was less than five miles from the airport.

This was all extremely good news, because hotels next to big international airports are the most impersonal organizations in the world. Everyone's in transit, everyone's in a hurry, and no one has much time for anyone else. For pure anonymity, they were the perfect answer. All Mack had to do was find one.

He took the London Heathrow exit and turned left, the wrong way for the terminals. Within a half mile he found precisely what he needed, a big commercial hotel, owned by an American chain, with shuttle service to the terminals, running, by the look of the congested forecourt, every ten minutes.

A doorman opened his car door and inquired, "Are you staying, sir?"

Mack nodded his assent. He walked inside and took a large single room for a week, told them he'd be paying in cash, and handed over two thousand British pounds.

The receptionist counted it and told him, unnecessarily, "No problem." He handed Mack the card key to Room 543, and asked if he needed help with the bag.

Mack declined and was told the boy would bring his car keys to the room when the doorman had parked it.

As it happened the boy was at the room before Mack and was waiting for him. Mack gave him a fiver and took the keys. He removed his shaving kit and other toiletries from the bag and placed them in the bathroom. Then he re-created his Jeffery Simpson persona, and almost immediately went out again.

He followed the map and found Merick Street in nearby Southall, one of the western suburbs of London with a largely Indian and Pakistani population. The place was as busy as downtown Bombay on this Monday morning, and Mack had no trouble locating a hardware store.

There he purchased a workman's toolbox, metal, eighteen inches long, a foot high and a foot wide, with a central handle set into the lid. Inside were folding racks, built for hammers, screwdrivers, and wrenches.

"Very fine box, sir," said the Indian in the store. "Very fine indeed. Good box for excellent workman."

Mack was not certain he looked like an excellent workman in his Jeffery Simpson disguise—more like an unemployed bank clerk. Nonetheless, he smiled and paid the sixty-two pounds for the toolbox, which he thought, privately, was plenty of money.

Outside he aimed the Ford Fiesta into a maze of side streets, searching for the address on the piece of paper handed to him by Liam O'Brien. Eventually, he found it, a wide residential avenue, nicer than any other street in the area, and he turned into number 16, which was a big double-fronted Victorian house in its own grounds.

The garden was overgrown, and the wide driveway was greatly narrowed by overhanging trees. But the house was in excellent repair, with white trim around the windows and a jet-black pair of front doors, glossy, recently repainted.

Mack rang the bell and was shown in by a uniformed Indian butler. "Whom shall I say has called?" he asked.

"Tommy McArdle," replied Mack.

A few minutes later the butler returned and announced that Mr. Kumar would like his visitor to go down to the workroom. He was led along a short hallway to a padded leather door, which the butler opened and then led him down to a bright workshop.

There was a central table and three working bays around the outside, each one of which was illuminated by a shaded light slung low over a workbench covered in dark-red baize. It looked a lot more like a jeweler's workroom than an arms factory.

A tall, slender Indian came toward Mack and held out his hand. "I'm Prenjit Kumar," he said. "I hope I can be of service. You come recommended by a man who was once among my finest customers."

Mack Bedford stared at him. Mr. Kumar was dressed in dark-blue pants, with a dark-blue sweater over a white shirt. He wore a green apron and carried a small jeweler's glass in his left hand. He had eyes that were almost jet black. Mack put him at around forty-five.

"I presume you are here to purchase a firearm, Mr. McArdle," said the Indian. "And before we even start I must ask you how you intend to pay for it. I take no checks, and I accept no credit cards. I also leave no trails for anyone who might be interested. No rifle or handgun leaves here with any form of identifying marks, which is against the law. However, I am more concerned with the well-being of my clients than foolish English bureaucracy."

Mack liked what he was hearing. He liked it very much. Liam O'Brien had been a stroke of luck. Kumar was a professional, the definition of which is, in its purest form, a person involved with the total elimination of mistakes. Professionalism has nothing to do with money. Well, not much anyway.

"Mr. Kumar," said Mack, "I am happy with all that you have said. Of course, I realized you would need to be paid in cash."

"Then I imagine we have reached the point where you tell me what you need," said the gunsmith.

"I require a sniper rifle, but I am uncertain precisely what type. Also, I am in a real hurry, so I must accept your recommendation."

"Range?"

"Around 100 yards, no more than 150."

"Single-shot bolt action or a five-round feed magazine?"

"Single-shot bolt will be fine. I do not expect to fire more than twice."

"Silencer?"

"If possible. And a telescopic sight."

"Six-by-twenty-four 2FM?"

"Perfect."

"I can give you shot grouping of less than 40 centimeters over 800 meters, 7.62-millimeter caliber with a muzzle velocity of 860 meters per second."

"That's outstanding. What kind of rifle will it be?"

"I'm thinking of an Austrian-built SSG-69. A lot of people have tried to build a better sniper rifle, but in my opinion no one's ever improved it. The British SAS used it for years; some of them still do."

"Will it take long to get?"

"Mr. McArdle, I am assuming you will want this rifle tailored to your precise measurements, and perhaps shortened, while retaining its accuracy?"

"That is what I need."

"The time is a matter for you. I can only go so fast with a precision instrument like this."

At this point Mack Bedford produced his very fine toolbox. "My biggest problem may be that it has to fit in here," he said.

Mr. Kumar was in no way disturbed. He opened the box and produced a tape measure, swiftly measuring each dimension.

"The SSG–69 is sufficiently long, but it will restrict you to a hard-
ened, cold-forged 13-inch barrel. On a rifle like this, it's a perfectly
adequate length."

Mack nodded, understanding the language.

"I do have two of those rifles here, and I could probably begin work
immediately. Let me measure you right now." He handed the former
SEAL a black rod.

Mack took up his shooting stance, right hand on the spot where the
trigger ought to be. The gunsmith measured him down his left arm
length, and then measured the distance between his right shoulder
and his trigger finger, across the hypotenuse formed by Mack's elbow
and forearm.

"Yes, that ought not to be too much trouble," he said. "The stock on
these rifles is made from some form of cycolac, which I will cut out
and remove. That will leave you with an aluminum stock, formed by
two struts with a wide, fitted shoulder rest. I presume you favor your
left eye?"

"Correct."

"Well, Mr. McArdle. You may leave the rest to me. I am presuming
you will want high-velocity bullets that explode on impact—chrome,
slim entry point? Are you intending a head shot?"

"Possibly two, if the rifle's sufficiently quiet."

"Your toolbox has ample room. I think we can oblige you in every
respect. There will, of course, be no serial numbers on the rifle, which
is illegal, but it is the way things like this are done. No one will ever
know where you got the rifle, or who made it. Mr. Liam O'Brien liked
that very much."

"And the price?"

"Depends on how soon you want it, whether I need to drop everything for this one job."

"It's Monday today. How about Saturday?"

"Saturday! That would be a very great rush. If you want it then, it
will cost you thirty thousand pounds. If you will give me another

week, it will be twenty-four thousand. Either way, it will be half down now, and the balance when you collect the rifle."

"Saturday. I will pay you fifteen thousand pounds right now."

Mr. Kumar looked suitably impressed but not amazed. "You will not regret this, Mr. McArdle. This is a superb sniper rifle and, in the right hands, cannot miss. Also, I will engineer it to screw together very quickly with no room for error."

"Will it come apart just as easily?"

"No problem. A matter of seconds."

Mack turned away and dug into his bag, searching for his bundles of English cash. He found them quickly and produced five stacks of fifty-pound notes, neatly bound, sixty in each. He handed them over, and then he made two more requests of Mr. Kumar.

"Could you get me a Draeger rebreathing apparatus?"

"Of course. Direct from Germany. How far do you intend to travel under the water?"

"Maybe a long way. Two hours."

"Then you'll need the Delphin I. It's their best, state of the art, standard issue, U.S. Navy."

"Oh, really?" said Mack. "That good?"

"The best. They'll ship to me FedEx. Be here in two days. But it's not cheap. Do you want it to be filled and ready to go?"

"Of course."

"I only ask because some people are nervous walking around with a small tank of compressed oxygen. You're not going to take it through an airport, are you?"

"Christ, no!" said Mack.

Mr. Kumar smiled. "I will get it for you, and I charge a 20 percent commission on the retail price."

"It's a deal."

"Pay me when you pick up the rifle on Saturday."

The two men walked back to the staircase and made their way to the front door.

"Are you from India, originally?" asked Mack.

"Oh, yes, but I hardly remember it. My family is from a small town on the north bank of the River Ganges up near the Bangladesh border. Place called Manihari."

"West Bengal?"

"How could you possibly know that?" replied Mr. Kumar, smiling.

Mack, who like many naval officers had an encyclopedic memory for geographic facts, told him, "Well, I don't know the exact town, but I know that West Bengal hugs the frontier with Bangladesh, and I know the Ganges floods into the Bay of Bengal."

"Ha, ha, ha. You're like Sahib Sherlock of Baker Street. Very good detective."

Mack wasn't too sure about Sahib Sherlock, but he found himself chuckling with the tall Bengali.

"And how did you get here?" he asked.

"Oh, my father emigrated here when I was only four. He was a mechanic in the army, and then he started a garage here in Southall. He still has it, and he does not approve of my business. But he drives a small Ford. I have a very large BMW. Big difference. Ha, ha, ha!"

Mack shook the hand of the Indian gunsmith. "There's usually bigger money for men who take bigger risks. But be careful. What time on Saturday?"

"Come at noon. Ha, ha."

———— • ◆ • ————

Raul Declerc sat in his Marseille headquarters, still depressed about the way he'd had the big fish on his line, and then failed to land it. Damn Morrison.

It was the second time in his life that greed had been the downfall of Raul Declerc. The first had caused him to run for his life from the watchdogs of MI-6, who were wondering where the hell their two million pounds had gone. The former Col. Reggie Fortescue had thus been obliged to race from London to Dover and board a cross-Channel ferry to flee the country. He had left with a few hundred thousand pounds, but he was only forty years old, and now lived with the fact that he had brought disgrace upon himself, his family, and his regiment.

He would never return to his native Scotland, and in the intervening three years he had spent his time looking for another big hit to make him a million. The mysterious Morrison had appeared to be that opportunity. And now Morrison had vanished, leaving Colonel Reggie to rue the day he had asked for another million.

He knew it, and Morrison plainly knew it. Greed had yet again been Reggie's downfall. And now, with his new French identity and his fourth cup of Turkish coffee of the morning, he racked his brain to come up with a salvage plan.

There was only one. He had information, and, in a sense, it was priceless information. At any rate, it was to one person in all of France. He told the secretary to find him a number for the Gaullist Campaign Office in Rennes, Brittany, and then to connect him.

It took five minutes, but the connection was made, and an automatic recorded voice came on his line saying, "Vote for Henri Foche, *pour Bretagne, pour la France.*" Almost immediately another voice, human, female, came on, and confirmed this was indeed Henri Foche's campaign headquarters, and what could she do to help?

Raul spoke carefully, asking to be put through to Henri Foche. He was told that Monsieur Foche would not be in the office for another hour, but could she tell him what the call was about?

Thus suitably screened, Raul said quietly, "I have some very valuable information for him. And it is of a highly dangerous nature. It is important that I speak to him in person. I will call back in one hour." Before M. Foche's assistant had time to ask him for his name and number, Raul rang off.

He called back in one hour and spoke to the same woman, who asked him to hold the line. Two minutes later a voice said, "This is Henri Foche."

Raul, giving himself his old title from the days when he was respectable, replied, "My name is Col. Raul Declerc, and I am the managing director of a French security corporation in Marseille. I am calling to inform you that we have reason to believe there will be an attempt on your life sometime in the very near future."

Henri Foche was silent for a moment. And then he said, with the practiced realism of a man not entirely unfamiliar with the dark side of life, "Are you selling, or are you merely a good Gaullist with genuine concerns for my future?"

"I'm selling."

"I see. Is this because you feel you might be able to prevent this from happening? Or are you just trying to make a fast buck?"

"Monsieur Foche, we have been offered two million U.S. dollars to carry out the killing. And of course we turned it down. I am calling partly out of a sense of decency, and partly because this kind of knowledge is hard-won. We occasionally receive such information, which in this case was costly to us. And we always charge for our services."

"I see. And why should I believe what you tell me is true? How can I be sure you are not simply making something up? Just a pack of lies designed to defraud me of money?"

"Very well, Monsieur Foche. I'm sorry to have bothered you. Good afternoon to you."

Raul put down the phone, having deliberately taken no precautions to hide his identity, or that of the phone from which he was calling, a landline on the main Marseille exchange.

Four minutes later his phone rang. He picked it up before the answering machine intervened and said, "Yes, Colonel Declerc speaking."

"Colonel, did you just call me? This is Henri Foche."

Raul knew precisely who it was. And he understood the value of the thunderbolt he had just delivered to the Gaullist front-runner: that someone with a very great deal of money was out to assassinate him. He knew Henri Foche could not let that one go by, because this was plainly not a nutcase. This was almost certainly a state-sponsored intention.

"Obviously," said the politician, "I need to know everything you can tell me."

"Only if you intend to remain alive," replied Raul. It was an answer that owed more to the droll, understated men who walk the sinister corridors of his late employers, MI-6, than to the French killers on his payroll.

"Tell me your price."

"I have two requests, if I am to give you all of my information. First, the sum of one hundred thousand euros. Second, that if there is an attempt on your life, as I believe there will be, you will hire either me or my people to protect you until the threat is removed."

"I do not have a problem with either of those conditions," said Henri Foche. "I will either send you a check or wire the money, whichever is the faster. I assume you will not part with information until the money is secure in your account?"

"Not so, Monsieur Foche. Unless I am wrong, we have a deal. We may even have a long-term partnership. And I believe there is a certain urgency to this matter. I fully intend to tell you everything I know right now. Because I believe you are a man of your word. I am happy to take your check. It is in both of our interests to move swiftly."

"I appreciate that. Please proceed."

"I received the first call a couple of weeks ago. Character called Morrison, said he was calling from London, but he spoke with an American accent. At first he offered a million dollars for a straightforward assassination, and I kept him on the line while we tried to trace the call. In the end he agreed to two million. He wanted immediate research on you and your movements. He lodged fifty thousand U.S. dollars in cash for expenses with a lawyer in Geneva. We were to collect it."

"And did you?"

"Er . . . yes. We did. It was supposed to be for research, and I told him some totally innocuous facts—you live in Rennes and have interests in shipyards—nothing he could not have ascertained from any newspaper or magazine. Monsieur Foche, I want you to be in no doubt. This character was not joking."

"You are certain he was not in France?"

"Yes, I am. We arranged a time for his calls. And he once said something about the time difference, you know, from him to me. He was abroad, very definitely. And he did tell me he was in London. So, if we were undertaking your protection, we would assume the threat would emanate from Great Britain."

"But he was not British? And you could not trace the call?"

"No, we could not. I'm assuming he was American. But I believe he was calling from London."

"Any idea how he found you?"

"Yes. He reached us through our office in Central Africa, Kinshasa, in the Congo. He may have had military connections. The only good news was he did not appear to have a shred of information about France. No local knowledge. However, I am afraid the most you can do at this moment is to step up your personal security, and keep us posted if there are any developments. And I must warn you, this Morrison wanted us to move on this right now—you should take immense care not to place yourself in harm's way."

"But what can I do?"

"Vary your routes to and from the office. Do not walk alone from your front door to the car. Keep an armed guard in the campaign office all night just in case someone wants to plant an IED in there. Put your present bodyguards on high alert. I am assuming you have ample security in place when you make public appearances?"

"I do. But I would like to place you on standby to move in if there is a definite threat."

"Always at your service," replied Raul Declerc. "For Brittany and for France."

The irony was lost on Monsieur Henri Foche.

———— •◆•————

Mack Bedford was more or less confined to barracks. For hours on end he waited alone in his hotel room, planning, going over his strategy, reading the newspapers, studying maps and charts, sleeping, doing one hundred push-ups on the floor every four hours. He was always wearing his Jeffery Simpson disguise—the Jeffery Simpson who was still in Ireland, that is.

He used only room service for meals, and was always in the bathroom when the waiter came in and placed the dishes on the table. Mack went to no public places in the hotel, he made no phone calls, and he never asked the doorman to fetch the Ford Fiesta from the parking garage.

The days passed with agonizing monotony, and Saturday, when it came, was gloomy and overcast. He ordered a power breakfast—scrambled eggs, bacon, a couple of sausages, mushrooms, and toast—because he was uncertain when he would eat again.

He packed his bag, and at eleven thirty in the morning went down to settle his hotel bill. There were room service charges but little else. Mack handed over another sixty pounds and asked the doorman to bring the car to the front entrance.

He took a quick look at his map, and memorized the route to Southall. He did not return to the M4 motorway but drove a half mile south and picked up the old A4, a busy two-lane road that skirts London Airport. Ten minutes later he was in Prenjit Kumar's drive. It was raining steadily.

The same Indian showed him down to the basement workrooms where the gunsmith awaited him. And there, laid out on the dark-red baize of the first workstation, glinting in the bright overhead light, was the SSG-69. Mr. Kumar was looking at the spot where the telescopic sight fits. He had a jeweler's glass in his right eye, like a monocle, and he was using a tiny file, applying a finishing touch. He stood up to greet his client, and said deferentially, "Welcome to my humble workshop. I have built you the most superb sniper rifle, pure precision, and as accurate as any rifle you will ever own."

Mack replied, "And I have brought you another fifteen thousand pounds, plus cash for the Draeger. Has it arrived?"

"Of course it has, Mr. McArdle. In my trade we don't make empty promises. I've had it since Wednesday. And I tested it for you. One of the valves was very stiff, and I fixed it. I also constructed a place in the bottom of the toolbox for the Draeger to fit. No problem."

"Is the rifle ready to test?"

"Of course. And that we will do first. Then, if you are happy, we will take it apart a few times just to get familiar with the procedure."

He handed Mack the rifle, which was light and beautifully balanced. The stock looked strange, like a skeleton with its two struts and angled shoulder rest. The former SEAL took up his firing stance, and the rifle felt like a part of his right arm, comfortable, secure, made-to-measure.

They walked into a different room, and there before them was a long, well-lit tunnel about forty yards from end to end. There was a regular target about eighteen inches square in the distance and a high wooden bench to lean on in the firing area.

Mr. Kumar told Mack there was a bullet in the breech plus five more in the magazine. But he could already see he was selling the rifle to an expert. Mack prepared to fire, leaned forward, and stared through the telescopic sight, until the crosshairs dissected the bull's-eye. He was motionless as he squeezed the trigger, and there was the faintest dull pop as the silenced SSG-69 sent the practice bullet away at a speed of a half mile per second.

Mack pulled back the bolt, loaded the breech, and fired again. And again. Then he straightened up and said, "Better take a look at the grouping."

Mr. Kumar wound in the target on rope pulleys, and handed it to Mack. There was only one hole, right in the center of the bull's-eye.

"Very nice, Mr. McArdle, very nice indeed," said the gunsmith, smiling. "Perhaps you have used such a rifle before."

"Perhaps I have," said Mack. "But I've never used a better one than this."

"You would like to take three more shots?"

"I will. But I'd find it tough to improve on the first three."

Again he fired, a little quicker this time, and when the new target was pulled in there was the slightest variation on the right side of the hole in the bull's-eye.

"I wouldn't say you'd lost your touch," grinned Mr. Kumar. "That's very fine shooting."

"I varied the second bullet just slightly right, only a fraction just to see the margin of error. It's a superb job, Mr. Kumar. Outstanding."

They spent the next hour testing the assembly of the rifle. Taking it apart and then putting it together, screwing the wide chrome bolt of the aluminum stock into the area behind the trigger, then sliding the telescopic sights, Russian made, into the tight metallic grooves Prenjit Kumar had engineered. The screw-in barrel, cut down to thirteen inches, had an attachment for the silencer, and when dismantled, the rifle could be placed easily in the toolbox on specially built velvet-covered racks with safety clips to stop it from moving. Precious jewels have been transported with less delicacy, and Mack stared down at the stored sections of the weapon, snug in the very fine toolbox, bright against the black velvet, above the Draeger. In a separate section, the six chrome bullets were set in a line, each one capable of blasting a hole the size of a melon in Henri Foche's head.

Mack Bedford turned to Mr. Kumar and shook his hand. Then he handed him an envelope containing the fifteen thousand pounds, plus another four hundred for the Draeger. They said their good-byes, and Mack carried the toolbox and his bag to the car.

Before he left, the Bengali reminded him, "You should practice with another dozen bullets at the approximate range from where you intend to fire. There may be a fractional variation, and the new sights should be adjusted. But I can tell you know all this, and I have placed the practice bullets in the toolbox."

"Thank you, Mr. Kumar," replied Mack. "And be careful."

He started the Ford Fiesta and this time made straight for the M4 motorway, the great east-west artery of southern England. Ahead of him lay a two-hundred-mile journey to the southwest, to an area known in England's more optimistic circles as the Devon Riviera. This spectacular stretch of coastline is supposed to be where the sun shines more often and the rain belts down less often than anywhere else in the country. And there were times when both of these tourist "facts" may have been true. But Mack Bedford doubted whether they applied today.

The spray was flying and the rain stayed heavy when he hit the M4. Even though it was Saturday, there seemed to be as many enormous trucks as ever, sending a tidal wave of flying water, left and right, as they screamed through the grayness of a July afternoon.

Mack, of course, had been on this road before, for many hours, on his journey from the port of Fishguard to Southall. He would, however, remain on it for only a little more than an hour, veering left before the great bridge over the River Severn and heading down the M5 into Somerset and then Devon.

Right now he had a lot on his mind. Four hundred and fifty miles away, Tommy had had the operation at the peerless Nyon Clinic, located a dozen miles from Geneva, along the north shore of the lake. He had told Anne it would be very difficult to make contact since he was due to attend a private meeting with navy pension officials in Norfolk that day. Anne did not believe him, but having been the wife of a SEAL commander for so many years, she knew better than to ask her husband what he was really doing.

Mack had seen pictures of the clinic, which was set in rolling country right on the edge of the lake. The views were marvelous, but above all, this place specialized in children's diseases and they were confident of their breakthrough in the curing of ALD. The surgeon, Carl Spitzbergen, was the acknowledged world master at the long operation, and Mack could do nothing but hope, his only comfort being that Tommy was in the finest hands.

Out here on the rain-lashed M4 he was doing his level best to uphold his part of the bargain with Harry Remson. But he had to admit one thing: the McArdle-guaranteed Ford Fiesta was also doing its part, tearing along the highway, wipers flashing across the windshield, a tough, powerful little car, about half the size of the Buick but gutsy as hell, the way Mack had hoped.

He broke clear of the airport traffic and aimed the car west, watching the rise of the hills as he raced toward the Berkshire Downs. Out here on the high ground the rain was if anything worse, sweeping diagonally across the highway, and not letting up until the road swooped downhill, off the Downs and into Wiltshire.

From here it was a straight thirty-mile run across a flat plain of open farmland to the junction with the M5, which veers right around the north side of the port of Bristol. Mack pushed on through the rain, turning southwest, all along the coastline of North Somerset, with the River Severn estuary to his right.

The M5 then ran inland, running north of the Black Down Hills into the heart of Devonshire, and finally ran out of steam just south of Exeter, the most important city in the entire southwest of England, once walled by the Romans, and then conquered by the Normans a thousand years later.

The rain had stopped by the time Mack reached the end of the motorway, and now he ran onto another divided highway, the A380. This took him almost the whole way inland down to his destination, the ancient fishing port of Brixham, which sits in the great shadow of Berry Head, jutting out into the English Channel at the southern tip of Torbay.

Mack ran into the old part of the village, a half mile above the harbor, a little before five o'clock. He drove around for a half hour and finally settled on a small, unobtrusive hotel, with views to the sea. Saturday is traditionally changeover day in this part of the west country, and Mack was in luck.

The hotel was full, but they'd just had a cancellation. Yes, they could give him a single room with a bath for just one night, but after that they were once again full. Mack accepted and went outside to park his car in the small area at the back of the hotel.

He picked up his workman's toolbox and his bag, locked the car, and came in to sign the registry. He was still in his Jeffery Simpson disguise, but signed his name Patrick O'Grady. The girl did not ask to see his passport.

He told her he would pay in cash, in advance, and the girl said their front rooms with the sea views were ninety-five pounds per night, plus tax, and that included breakfast, which was served from seven on. Mack gave her two fifty-pound notes and said he may be gone before breakfast, but understood the way things worked.

The girl gave him a key to Room 12 and told him it was on the second floor, straight up the stairs. She very much hoped he would be comfortable and let him know if there was anything else he needed.

They did not do dinner, but there were plenty of excellent places in town, easily within walking distance.

Mack thanked her and carried his toolbox and bag up the stairs. He crashed onto the bed for an hour, weary after the long drive. When he awakened he called and asked if someone could bring him some coffee, which arrived after about twenty minutes. His room had a small balcony on the side rather than directly overlooking the harbor, and he leaned on the rail and sipped quietly.

Out on the northern edge of the port there was obviously some heavy construction in progress, because looming over the jetties on that side was a very high crane, maybe 150 feet. Mack stared up at it, went back into the bedroom, and began to assemble his sniper rifle, fixing all the components together except for the aluminum stock, which was the easiest piece of all to screw into place.

He loaded the rifle with six of his practice bullets, then packed both sections into his leather bag, pulling out a stack of British pounds for himself. At this point he prepared to go out for the evening and walked downstairs, still in his Jeffery Simpson disguise.

There was no one at the reception desk, and Mack walked straight out and around to the parking lot. He dumped his bag into the trunk and slammed it shut, knowing it could not be opened except with a key. Then he sat in the front seat and very carefully turned himself into Mr. Gunther Marc Roche, a Swiss national residing at 18 rue de Basle, Geneva.

He removed the blond wig, thin mustache, and rimless spectacles. He placed the long, curly black wig on his head. Then he affixed the bushy black beard to his face, combed it all into reasonable shape, and stepped out of the car, carefully locking it behind him.

In the soft summer light he glanced at himself in the wing mirror and was astounded by the transformation. No one could possibly have recognized him. He took a stroll down to the harbor, which took him about twenty minutes, and inspected the trawlers moored on the jetties.

This was a historic fishing fleet. It was the fishermen of Brixham who *invented* trawling for their catch, dragging the nets along the floor of the English Channel, way back in the eighteenth century. So far as

Mack could see, they were still doing it. He counted fourteen draggers moored in the harbor, and he spent more than an hour observing both the boats and their masters.

There was not much activity, but it looked to Mack as if at least three of them were going out tonight. He assessed this from the boats parked on what Americans call the gas dock, where an attendant was loading them with diesel.

Mack walked past, stopping just once to practice his Swiss accent. "Nice night to go fishing," he said to one of the skippers. "Calm sea and a good forecast." In truth the accent was closer to Trinidad than Geneva, but the man turned around and grinned.

"I hope so," he replied. "'Aven't had that much luck this week. I'll need to catch a ton just to pay for the bloody fuel."

Mack smiled. "What time do you go?"

"There's about three of us leave around ten o'clock in the summer. It's about an hour out there to the best places. Old Charlie thought there were plenty of haddock around. So we're just 'oping."

"Good luck to you anyway," said Mack, and walked slowly back down the jetty, trying to look casual. He hung around for another half hour, just watching the boats, watching the harbor master's office, and noting the general quietude of the famous old port.

At around eight thirty he walked back up to the town, stopping to look at All Saints parish church in Lower Brixham, where Henry Francis Lyte had been the first vicar in the late eighteenth century. A well-kept notice board informed tourists that the Reverend Lyte had been the poet who wrote the bittersweet hymn "Abide with Me."

Since Mack had only ever heard the hymn played at funerals, he was not 100 percent certain this was a particularly good omen. He hurried back up the long hill and went into a local pub, which was quite busy and served grilled steak, chicken, and fish. He ordered a tall glass of sparkling water and a medium-rare fillet of Angus steak. He positioned himself at a table close to the center of the beamed dining room, in full view of as many people as possible.

The steak was delicious, and Tommy would definitely have approved of the fries. Mack ordered another pint of water, and then a soft French cheese and crackers to complete his dinner. He was deeply tempted to have a large glass of port with the cheese, as Harry Remson almost always did. But he remembered his mantra—*Not one drop of alcohol, until Henri Foche lays dead.*

He sat for a while, until he could see through the window that it was dark outside, then he paid his bill, and tipped the waitress generously. "Thank you very much, sir," she said. "Come in again. Goodnight, Mr. . . . er . . . "

"Roche," said Mack. "Gunther Roche. I'm from Geneva, but I'll be back."

The waitress, a dark-haired young girl, obviously a local student, replied, "Before September—that's when I go back to university. I'm Diana."

It was such a short exchange, but both parties had established something important. The girl had demonstrated that she was not just a waitress but an intelligent academic doing a summer job. Mack Bedford had established in the village a very definite identity for the tall, bearded Swiss visitor.

He walked through the crowd and out into the street, making his way another two hundred yards up the hill to his hotel. But he did not go in. Instead, he walked around to the parking lot, unlocked the door, and fired up the Ford Fiesta.

He drove quickly out onto the street and turned right, climbing high above the little town on a lonely road all the way to the cliff top. From there he headed farther to the right, for almost a mile, until he was directly above the harbor. Way out to sea he could see the lights of a ship steaming east up the English Channel.

But those were not the lights he was interested in. The ones he had come for were high atop that crane that loomed over the jetties. He had guessed it would have a couple of warning lights, but in fact it had three, two directly above the driver's cabin, one more out at the end of the rig. From where Mack stood, the high point of the crane was pretty much at eye level, about six hundred yards distant.

The road was deserted, and he pulled over onto the grass shoulder and drove forward maybe fifteen yards on a slight hill. He switched off the lights and opened the trunk. He unzipped the bag and retrieved the rifle that lay in two pieces. Carefully, he screwed the stock into place and checked that the weapon was tight. Then he leaned forward onto the roof of the car and drew a steady bead on the red light at the end of the crane's forward rig.

With the light right in the middle of the crosshairs, he fired. Instantly, the crane had only two red lights instead of three. Mack lined up and fired again. And the small glowing red bulb high on the rig above the cabin was obliterated, showering glass onto the driver's roof. Mack lined up his final target, the remaining red light set on a metal strut around ten feet above the cabin, the highest point of the crane. And once more he fired, shattering the bulb. It was a superb exhibition of marksmanship, Olympic-grade shooting, but standard procedure for a U.S. Navy SEAL sniper. Especially one who had finished Honor Man at Sniper School, out there on the rough desert ground of Camp Pendleton, the 125,000-acre U.S. Marine Corps Base, south of Los Angeles.

What truly pleased Mack was the quietness. The silencer fitted to the barrel with such immense precision by Prenjit Kumar was the best Mack had ever used.

"Tell you what," he murmured, as he put the bag back in the trunk. "Sonofabitch knows how to make a rifle."

CHAPTER 9

Mack sat in the car for a few minutes, mostly getting rid of Mr. Gunther Marc Roche. He removed the wig and beard and replaced them with the lighter, much more comfortable Jeffery Simpson disguise. Then he drove back down to the town and parked behind the hotel.

There was a different receptionist on duty, and Mack, who was carrying his leather bag, smiled and said, "Room 12, please."

She handed over the key, glanced at the register, and said, "There you are. Thank you, Mr. O'Grady."

Mack climbed the stairs to his room and went to bed. As he switched off the bedside light, his last thoughts were, *If I can just get a clear shot, I can't miss, not with this rifle.*

He slept soundly but only until six. He awakened and immediately climbed out of bed, showered, shaved, and dressed. He wore a clean black T-shirt, the same jacket, and pants. And once more he fitted his Gunther Roche disguise, the black curly hair and beard.

His plan was to escape the hotel without being seen, and the place was deathly quiet as he opened the bedroom door. With the toolbox in one hand and the bag in the other, he slipped along the corridor and down the stairs. There was no one on duty yet, and the kitchen staff was making no sound. He actually had to unlock the front door to make his exit.

Once outside, he walked quickly to the parking lot, stowed his gear in the trunk, and drove down to the harbor. In this fabled fishing port, Patrick O'Grady was history, Jeffery Simpson had been seen but not recorded at the hotel, but Gunther was marching around large as life, the way Mack wanted it.

He drove down to the harbor and found a small town parking lot. It was positioned right next to the jetties, separated by a three-foot-high wall. There was no gate, but there was a charge for remaining there up to two hours. At least there would have been, had the attendant been on duty, but he was not scheduled to show up until eight o'clock.

Mack parked in the corner, locked the car, and took a walk around the harbor. There was some activity, trawlers unloading, boxes of fresh fish packed on ice. He could see a couple of guys with clipboards, talking to the fishermen, making notes, signaling for a couple of truck drivers to start loading. Buying agents for the big supermarkets. They'd been here since midnight, since the fleet began to arrive back from its nightly labors out there in the Channel.

Mack could see the old skipper he'd spoken to earlier, and he looked busy, talking to the agents, pointing back at his boat. Mack hoped his luck had turned. He walked past the harbor master's office, nodded a greeting, and then strolled to the end of the harbor wall.

He made notes of the boats he thought had come in during the small hours, about seven of them. For the moment he was assuming they went out to the fishing grounds most nights. Four of them were far too big for his purposes; two of them were still busy with at least four men working. But one of them had unloaded, and the crew, probably just two men, had gone home.

Their boat was a sixty-five-foot trawler, with a dark-red hull in need of a coat of paint. The name *Eagle* was painted in faded black lettering on her bow. She was already being gassed up, which Mack took as a sure sign she'd be going out tonight. With diesel at its current prices, no one filled up until they needed to.

He walked back past the harbor master, who was standing outside his office. "Good morning," said Mack, trying to sound Swiss, but doing a fair imitation of Papa Doc, the president of Haiti.

"Hello, sir," replied the harbor master, not knowing whether he was speaking to the owner of a one-hundred-foot oceangoing yacht. "Nice morning."

"Did they have much luck last night?"

"Some of 'em did. That big trawler there ran over a shoal of cod about twenty miles offshore. And cod's fetching a lot of money just now. We'll be busy tonight."

"How about that boat there, *Eagle*? I met the owners a couple of nights ago. Did they do okay?"

"They found the cod as well, but they're usually first out in the summer. Old Fred Carter don't miss much. He's fourth generation out of Brixham."

"I see they're fueled and ready to go again."

"They'll clear the harbor wall by ten o'clock tonight. You see if they don't. Rest of the boats aim for eleven."

Mack wandered off up to the street that runs along the harbor. He found a small café that opened at eight o'clock, five minutes from now, and then he walked farther to find a newspaper shop. That was open, and he picked up a *London Daily Telegraph* plus a copy of Monday's *Le Monde*.

Armed with his reading, he went back to the café and ordered breakfast from the menu—poached eggs, Devonshire smoked ham, and buttered brown toast. Mack liked it here; he liked the people, and he definitely liked the breakfast.

He noticed that within twenty minutes the café was quite full, which was good. He ordered more coffee and sat reading until around nine thirty. He paid his bill and walked up to the town's main street, where he spent his time looking at the shops.

Once he was absolutely stunned at his bearded appearance, which, with his tweed jacket, made him look like a vacationing college professor. He actually thought it was someone else and turned around to check who might be looking over his shoulder. As disguises go, this one was sensational.

By eleven o'clock the sun was climbing high to the southeast. The sky was very blue, and so was the sea. Mack could see what they meant

by the Devon Riviera. He found an empty bench overlooking the water, took off his jacket, and decided to tackle *Le Monde,* brushing up on
his French as he went.

On page 5 there was another major article on Henri Foche, with a
picture. He translated the headline to mean:

GAULLIST LEADER APPALLED AT
NEW DIAMONDHEAD MISSILE ATROCITY
DESCRIBES LATEST HITS ON AMERICAN TROOPS AS "OUTRAGEOUS"

"You little bastard," muttered Mack under his breath. Though it was
difficult for him to translate word for word, he got the drift of the
story—that Foche had no idea how these illicit missiles were finding
their way to Iraq. And he fervently hoped the illegal manufacture of
the "inhuman" Diamondhead would swiftly be stopped.

His United Nations Security Council partners, the USA, had all of
his sympathy. They could count on him, as president of France, to remove the suspicion that any factory in his country would ever stoop to
such criminally dishonest behavior.

"Jesus Christ," said Mack to a passing fish truck. "Is this guy something or what?"

He tossed *Le Monde* into a trash bin and walked on to find a small local supermarket, and there he bought a high-squirting, medium-sized
plastic carton of Great Britain's most powerful window cleaning fluid.
He had once been told that if you want something really cleaned spotless, this was the stuff. It had the same name in America, so he knew
what he was looking for. He also purchased a packet of soft dusters.

At this point just before midday, he returned to the parking lot to
find the attendant about to issue him an official town fine. Mack did
not wish that to happen, and he walked swiftly over to the man and
told him, in a foreign accent that no nation in the world could possibly
have recognized, how sorry he was, but his wife had been taken ill at
the hotel.

The attendant was sympathetic, and Mack told him he would have
to go back and forth to the hotel all day, and would these two 50-

pound notes pay for the day's parking? This was, without question, the biggest cash payment, or quasi tip, the Brixham parking lot chief had ever seen. He stared at the banknotes for a few seconds and allowed thoughts to cascade through his mind before he said, "Why yes, sir. I think that will take care of it very nicely." He then asked the question that separated an honest council employee from a dishonest one: "Will you be requiring change, sir?"

"Certainly not. I'd like you to give special attention to the safety of this car. I'll probably be around for the next couple of days. Same payment tomorrow be okay?"

"Oh, very much, sir. That would be very much in order."

Once more Mack wandered away, but he watched the parking lot, and at 12:45 he saw the man walk across the street to a pub, probably for a beer and a sandwich.

Mack moved quickly back into the parking lot, unlocked the car, and went to work with the high-squirting window cleaning liquid. He shot it everywhere, especially on the steering wheel, gear stick, hand brake, door handles, window buttons, and leather(ish) driver's seat. He hit the center console and the windshield. He hit the driver's side windows and the armrests. He power-squirted it all over the backseat, and on all the dashboard controls, radio, and air vents. Men cleaning New York skyscrapers have used less window fluid.

And then he rubbed and polished, destroying every semblance of a trace that he had ever been inside that car. By the time he finished, if there had somehow been a tiny smudged suggestion of a fingerprint, it would have died of loneliness. But Mack knew there was nothing, not one single clue that he had ever driven the McArdle-guaranteed Ford Fiesta.

He would leave the outside work until later, and now he shoved open the passenger door with his elbow, made his exit, and pushed it shut with his knee, locking it with the remote-control key. The attendant was not yet back, and Mack walked up to the main street and found a "menswear" store that sold thin leather driving gloves. He purchased a pair of these, and also a top-of-the-line pair of Reebok trainers. Then he crossed the street to a hardware store and purchased a screwdriver.

It was a very warm day now, and he strolled back down to the harborside bench, which was still unoccupied. He decided to skip lunch but to have an early dinner, because he was uncertain when he would have an opportunity to eat again.

For the next hour he just sat and stared at the ocean, thinking about Tommy and Anne, knowing he could not dare risk a call. He could risk nothing that might at some time be traced and betray the information that Lt. Cdr. Mackenzie Bedford had left Maine and had come to England. Nothing.

At four o'clock he walked back to the newspaper shop in search of a better guidebook to France. The one he had bought in the hotel near Heathrow was okay, but not sufficiently detailed for his mission. At the back of the store he found a shelf with several guides to European countries, and right in the middle was a thousand-page tome, *The Lonely Planet Guide to France,* the traveler's bible, containing enough information to conquer France, never mind visit it.

Hardly a city, town, or village in the entire country escapes its scrutiny. There are vast area maps, local maps, street maps, hotels, restaurants, train stations, bus stations, airports, cathedrals, churches, post offices, shrines, government buildings, and God knows what else. It was probably the easiest sale that Brixham store ever made. And Mack was reading before he stepped back out into the street: *Rennes, Brittany's capital, is a hive of activity . . . a crossroads since Roman times . . . sits at the junction of highways linking Northwest France's major cities. . . .*

He took the book back to his still-vacant bench and combed through the section on Brittany, the great westernmost promontory of France, jutting defiantly into the Atlantic, with thunderous rollers crashing onto its granite coast, its back to the rest of the country. In a sense, a lot like Maine.

Mack checked out the big shipbuilding area around the French Naval port of Brest and wondered whether Foche might be planning a political speech somewhere along those vast dockyards. Then he came south to the Atlantic Coast and checked out Saint-Nazaire, another huge shipbuilding center in France. He'd read somewhere that Foche had major holdings in one of the yards.

His *Lonely Planet* revealed that Great Britain's massive new trans-atlantic cruise ship, *Queen Mary II,* was built there, and the mighty plane maker Airbus had a factory in Saint-Nazaire. *Sounds like Foche's kind of place,* he muttered.

But this perusal through the industrial and military strongholds on the French coast was the lightest possible piece of reconnaissance. The part with which he was most concerned was the southern shore of the Gulf of Saint-Malo, that yachtsman's paradise stretching from the mast-filled twelfth-century walled seaport of Saint-Malo itself, east through Dinard, beloved of Picasso, and then past the headland of Cap Frehel, down to Saint-Brieuc.

This was the other side of the English Channel, around 135 miles due south of this particular Devonshire bench upon which Mack sat and studied. As the afternoon wore on, his lifelong association with the sea kicked in, and he sensed a change in the weather. There was just a little coolness to the gentle southwesterly breeze. He could sense it on the back of his neck, and he had not noticed it before.

Mack stared ahead to the horizon, and the crystal-clear line, which all day had separated sea from sky, was now less defined, as if someone had run a misty gray paintbrush along the far edge of the ocean.

He glanced at his watch: half past five. And he checked again the parking lot where the Ford Fiesta was still standing. The attendant was back, just placing a ticket on the windshield of a Jaguar that had remained there too long without paying.

Carrying his book, he walked again onto the harbor jetty and checked for activity. A couple of the trawlers were being fueled, but this was a quiet time in the fishermen's day. He could see *Eagle* still moored in the same spot. Her decks were deserted.

At six the parking attendant, wearing a light red windbreaker, came out of his kiosk and locked the door behind him. He walked up toward the town, and Mack immediately came over to finish wiping off the Fiesta. He pulled on his driving gloves and took the cleaning fluid off the floor in front of the driver's seat. Then he hit the area all around the door lock and handle, rubbed hard, and removed all traces. He did the same to the rear door and the driver's side; remembering his check in the wing mirror the previous night, he attended to that, too. He knew he had never opened the doors on the passenger side, nor had he touched the other wing mirror.

Finally, still wearing his leather driving gloves, he used his key to open the trunk and placed his French guidebook in his bag. He took out the new trainers and a navy-blue sweater. He placed his black loafers and tweed jacket inside, zipped the bag up, and backed off, leaning over to put on his new footwear. He rammed down the trunk lid with his elbow. Then he squirted the liquid onto the lock, polished around that wide area, and the car was clean.

Mack walked to a trash bin and dumped the plastic carton and the remainder of the dusters. As far as he was concerned it was now dinnertime, and he walked to a new pub one street off the seafront, and ordered fish and chips with a pint glass of sparkling water.

He already missed his French guidebook, but although he did not mind being recognized by local people, he did not wish to be seen planning a trip to France. When he blew out of this fishing port, he wanted his destination to be a total mystery for as long as possible. He also knew that particular mystery might not stay secret indefinitely.

His fish was perfectly fried cod, and he accepted the landlord's advice of sprinkling salt and vinegar, the way the English prefer it. Professor Henry Higgins would have been perplexed at the strangeness of Mack's accent, and the landlord, a retired fisherman, doubtless wondered whether he had ever eaten fried fish before.

As good as the cod was, the fries were not to Mack's taste; they were too heavy-cut, too big, and he did not wish to weigh himself down with that kind of food. Not tonight, when he would need to be sharp and agile. So he ordered another piece of delicious cod, and somehow had to leave two large portions of fries.

He lingered for a while, sipped his water and ordered more, plus a large cup of black coffee. He could see outside the clouds were moving in. The bright summer day was gone, and if he was any judge there would be rain before midnight. By a quarter of nine he could see it was very gloomy, and the clouds caused night to fall early. He paid his bill, pulled on his driver's gloves, and walked back to the deserted parking lot. There were lights along the jetties near the boats, but nothing was obviously preparing to get under way.

Mack went straight to the parking lot, opened the trunk, and pulled out his toolbox and leather bag. He placed them close to the wall in the shadows and then went around to the front of the vehicle, pulled out his new screwdriver, and removed the license plate.

He walked back down the side of the car and suddenly noticed the tax disk stuck in a clear plastic holder on the lower-left windshield. "Fuck," he muttered, noting that the car registration was written on that disk. He reached for his key, gloves still on, opened the door and whipped the plastic off, and shoved it in his pocket.

Then he moved to the back of the car and unscrewed the rear plate. Leaving his bags by the wall, he walked down to the water and skimmed both metal plates like Frisbees into the middle of the thirty-five-foot-deep harbor. He took the tax disk out of its holder, and ripped the red colored paper into about a thousand pieces and placed half of them in one trash bin and half in another.

It was nine when he pulled on his driving gloves, gathered up the toolbox and bag, and walked down onto the deserted jetty. He could see the harbor master was not in his office, and he passed no one as he walked toward the section where *Eagle* was moored.

The trawler was close in, no more than three feet off. Swiftly, he tossed the bag aboard and jumped across the gap, holding the toolbox. He made straight for the lifeboat, an inflatable Zodiac with an outboard, which was attached to a davit on the starboard side. He shoved the bag and box under the cover, and then clambered in himself, taking care not to dislodge his black wig.

And there in the dark of this Sunday night, Mack Bedford waited. It was almost nine thirty when things began to liven up on the jetties. Mack could hear fishermen talking about the weather to the harbor master.

Sea's getting up out there—shouldn't be surprised if we got a bit of a storm.

Forecast's not bad—the glass is falling, but they don't think it will amount to much.

Probably worse farther south—they're saying it veered off toward the Channel Islands.

Damn good thing too—stop the Spanish stealing our bloody cod.

Evenin', Fred. This weather putting you off?

Not me. I've been out in a lot worse, and I need the money! Ready, Tom?

Mack heard two men come aboard. Fred Carter and his first mate, Tom, who sounded much younger. They checked their gear for a few minutes, and then the rumble of twin diesels shuddered the boat.

The wheelhouse was in a raised for'ard upperworks, with the engines astern, a deck below. Mack heard a door slam shut and guessed that Fred was at the helm while Tom was casting off. In fact, he heard the harbor master shout from the jetty, "Stern line comin'," and he heard it drop on the deck as it was thrown over.

Then Tom shouted, "Okay, Teddy, I'll take it"—and again Mack heard a mooring line land, this time on the foredeck. The boat trembled slightly as Fred Carter opened the throttles very slightly with the wheel hard over. Then *Eagle* leaned to her port side, before straightening and moving dead ahead.

The harbor was still flat calm, despite the rising wind, and the trawler moved slowly between the other boats, heading to the harbor's outer reaches before coming a few degrees to starboard and making directly for the inshore waters down the south Devon coast.

It was dark now, and Mack knew the flashing light on Berry Head was somewhere up ahead. He felt the rise of the ocean as they stood fair down the Channel, leaving the land behind, making around fifteen knots now toward the bad weather and, Fred hoped, toward those big shoals of cod or mackerel.

The ebbing tide would be with them for the next thirty minutes until they crossed the estuary of the River Dart, hugging the shore until they reached the lighthouse at Start Point, fifteen miles from Brixham. Right there they would head out to the open sea.

With the wind gusting from the southwest, Mack was certain he would know when they reached the lighthouse, and, simultaneously, the end of the shelter from the land. Conditions would surely deterio-rate as *Eagle* began to take a buffeting from the hard Atlantic wind.

He had not heard the wheelhouse door slam for a second time, and he was uncertain whether Tom had joined Fred. In a good-sized drag-ger like this, there were always a hundred different tasks to complete before the nets were dropped, and Tom could easily be in the hold preparing gear for the night's catch.

In any event there was not much Mack could do about it. So he just lay very still, awaiting the change in sea conditions and then making his move. It was almost twenty minutes past ten when he felt an un-mistakable increase in the size of the swell. *Eagle* started to ride up and then wallow as she rode down into the trough of the wave.

They were clear of Start Point now, no doubt in Mack's mind. He risked a peep out from under the tarpaulin, aware that he might be looking straight into the eyes of Tom, the first mate, and then he would have to kill him, which he did not wish to do. He pushed the tarp higher and looked up into the wheelhouse. There were two men in there, and one of them had to be Tom, steering the ship.

Mack climbed out of the lifeboat and made his way to the bottom of the short flight of steps, where there were two round white life pre-servers clipped to the bulkhead. He removed them and placed them on the deck. Then he climbed three steps until he could reach the door handle, opened it, and yelled, "Fred! Get the hell out here!"

He heard Tom shout, "Who the fucking hell's that?"

At which point big Fred Carter came into the wheelhouse doorway and leaned out. Big mistake. Mack Bedford grabbed him by the balls and heaved. Fred roared and fell forward. Mack took him by the throat and, with an outrageous display of strength, using the full forward weight of the *Eagle*'s skipper, hurled Fred Carter over his head, straight over the side, and into the English Channel.

Before Fred hit the water, Mack had the life preserver in his hands and dropped it about one foot from the powerful hands of Captain Carter. Instantly, Mack turned around to see Tom, with one hand on the wheel, standing gaping in the wheelhouse doorway, in shock at what he had just seen.

Mack came up the steps like a panther, grabbed Tom by the belt, and hauled him forward. Mack dropped down to deck level, and Tom's hand was torn from the wheel. Overbalanced, he fell forward, and Mack caught him, hurling him over the side into a full summersault, exactly like the boss. Tom hit the water with his backside, and plunged under the waves. The other life preserver almost hit him on the head as he came to the surface.

Mack leaped into the wheelhouse and hauled back on the throttle, slowing down and sliding into reverse. He backed the trawler up forty yards to where the two fishermen were swimming, secure in the big life preservers. "Sorry, guys," he yelled in his latest Leeward Islands accent. "I need boat. Don't panic. You'll be rescued. Warm water, eh? Very good."

Tom could not believe what he was seeing, and for the second time in as many minutes he demanded, "Who the fucking hell's that?"

"'Ow the hell do I know?" bellowed Fred. "He's a fucking pirate, that's what he is. And he's not getting away with this. No bloody way."

"Have we been hijacked?" asked Tom. "I mean like you see on the news?"

"Hijacked!" cried Fred. "We've been robbed, that's what's happened! That bastard up there with the fucking black beard has nicked the fucking boat, that's what he's done!"

"He was as strong as a bear," said Tom. "He just threw me up in the air. Talked funny as well, didn't he?"

"Never mind all that," said Fred. "We have to get home. If the clouds break, we can follow the North Star—it's got to be back there, the opposite way to *Eagle*. She's headed for France; we have to swim to South Devon."

———————— • ◆ • ————————

Mack checked the compass and held course at 135 degrees. He flicked on the GPS electronic map, which showed the south coast of England and the north coast of Brittany. The black triangle was just off the English coast. Speed on the sidebar showed 17.2 knots.

He opened the throttles until the trawler was lurching along at around 20 knots, rolling with the swells, occasionally taking silver water over her bow.

She felt very seaworthy, as Mack had been sure she would. She had a good motor, and she was definitely full of gas. Before him was a run of well over 110 miles, which at 20 knots would take him almost six hours. If the sea flattened out on the far side of the Channel, he could probably wind her up to 25, driving the motor hard in a completely empty ship.

The trouble was he needed speed, as much speed as he could muster, because Fred and Tom in the busy sea-lanes off the coast of Devon stood a very fair chance of being rescued within two or three hours, and the ship-to-shore radio would take only moments to alert both French and English coast guards that a Brixham trawler had been hijacked by a pirate. It was even possible that someone would find the two fishermen by midnight. All stations would be alerted, and satellites would be sailing through the stratosphere looking for the *Eagle*.

But none of it would be easy for the searchers, not in the dark, trying to scan a "possibility-zone" area of 110 miles by 110—that's more than 12,000 square miles, and no one had the slightest idea in which direction this bearded monster was going. Especially since Mack intended to transmit nothing. He would steam to France with no running lights, no radar, and no sonar. He had his map of the south coast of England, the English Channel, and the north coast of Brittany. With the compass to guide him, Mack could find his way across the pitch-black, and probably rain-swept, Channel. But he needed to be in French coastal waters before first light around five thirty. That gave him seven hours' running time.

At 20 knots she could make it with time to spare, but if the sea slowed her badly, it would be touch and go. *Eagle* could run at 20, and Mack prayed the weather would not get much worse. His prayers, however, were not answered, and Mack presumed this was because the Almighty took an extremely bleak view of his hurling two perfectly honest, hardworking fishermen into the English Channel.

The sea got up almost immediately after he took the wheel. The rain from the southwest belted down, but he found the windshield wipers easily, huge blades that swept water away, left and right, in great slashing arcs.

Eagle was comfortable at 20 knots in this long, quartering sea, but any increase would have caused her to ride up and wallow too steeply. Boats are strange creatures, and a lifelong seaman like Mack Bedford, even after only fifteen minutes at the controls, knew precisely where that speed gauge should be. But it was not a comfortable journey; he was unfamiliar with the pull of the tide, and he needed to concentrate fully to hold course on 135.

The wind was howling, and waves were breaking over the bow almost the entire time, hitting hard and cascading heavy water across the foredeck, with spray lashing the windshield. But this was a very tough trawler, as good as Mack had ever driven, and she shouldered her way defiantly through the heavy seas. She cleared the water quickly, and Mack could see it parting in two powerful surges, port and starboard, running down the length of the ship and out over the transom. Battened down, this thing was damn nearly as waterproof as a submarine.

And her diesels were not complaining. Mack could hear them throbbing, sweet and steady, as they drove her forward, and Mack eased their task by slicing the bow head-on into the waves, splitting them asunder wherever he could. After an hour of pitching his wits against the weather, Mack flicked on the sonar and tried to work the section that gauges speed over the ocean floor rather than across the surface. But it was too complicated when he was trying to hold course in these conditions, so he gave up and kept going.

This southeasterly course would bring him to the northern edge of the Channel Islands, close to the island of Alderney, and from there he would change course suddenly, coming 60 degrees right and cutting through the dark seaway east of Guernsey. There was nothing quite so baffling for pursuers than a sudden course change in the dead of night. Mack knew also that periodic stretches of land like these big British islands can play havoc with radar.

The GPS showed Alderney was fifty miles away, two and a half hours. It was eleven thirty. He ran his finger south to the French coast to a little place called Val André and muttered, "That'll do for me."

———•◆•———

By midnight, Fred Carter was cold, bloody cold. His first mate, Tom, was colder, and they were still a mile and a half from the Devon coast. That was the bad news. The good news was they had plainly been spotted by a three-thousand-ton freighter heading east and now coming directly toward them. Twenty minutes later they were on board, wrapped in blankets, still shivering but drinking hot cocoa with a dash of brandy. A couple of young crewmen were sitting with them, astounded at their story.

"Piracy on the high seas, right here off the English coast? That's unbelievable."

"I mean it's like being up the fucking Amazon or somewhere," said Fred. "And he was a big bastard, bearded, foreigner."

"Strong as a bear," added Tom.

"Shut up," said Fred. "I'm telling it."

"I'll let the skipper know," said one of the crewmen. "We have to report this. You can't have a bloke like that running around loose."

"And what about my boat?" raged Fred. "I mean, Christ, what's going to happen about that?"

"It's well insured, right, Fred?" said Tom.

"Yes, but that's not the point. No one wants their trawler loose in the English Channel, being driven around by a fucking madman."

"I'll see the boss," said the crewman. "You're out of Brixham, right? And I shouldn't worry—the coast guard will find him. You can't hide a sixty-five-foot fishing boat."

"He could scuttle it," said Tom unhelpfully.

"Shut up," said Fred.

This is the freighter Solent Queen *out of Southampton calling Brixham harbor master.*

Copy that. Brixham harbor master receiving.

We're at position 50.12 North 3.35 West. Reporting we just picked up Brixham trawler skipper Fred Carter and his first mate, Thomas Jelbert. Their boat Eagle *has been hijacked by a pirate who threw them both overboard.*

Teddy Rickard had been a resident of Brixham all his life. An ex-trawlerman, he was fifty-two years old and had been harbor master for fifteen of them. Yet never had he heard anything even remotely as wild as that.

Please repeat. Did you say hijacked? Pirate? Fred and Tom overboard?

Solent Queen *repeat. Fred Carter and Tom Jelbert rescued from the sea. The Brixham trawler* Eagle *has been hijacked, and is now missing. We're heading into Brixham to bring them home.*

Anyone have the trawler's last known?

Fred Carter says about one mile south of here, two hours ago.

That's 50.12 North 3.35 West, correct?

Correct. Solent Queen *ETA Brixham one hour.*

Copy that, and thank you, Solent Queen. *I'm calling the coast guard right now. Over.*

———•◆•———

The coast guard station at Dartmouth was as astonished as the harbor master at this apparent piracy on the high seas. At first they thought it was a joke. But there was nothing amusing about two Brixham trawlermen being thrown overboard and a British fishing boat in the hands of a criminal. They put out an all-stations alert, and they sent an urgent e-mail to the French coast guard at Cherbourg, the gist of it being that a black-bearded foreign pirate had hijacked the Brixham trawler *Eagle* and appeared to be heading their way. The e-mail added that only the prompt action of the crew of *Solent Queen* had saved the lives of Mr. Fred Carter and Tom Jelbert, *Eagle*'s two-man crew, who had both been thrown overboard.

With the possibility of a dangerous criminal about to enter France, it was a matter of pure routine. Cherbourg Coast Guard Station automatically sent a copy of the e-mail through to Brittany Police Headquarters in Rennes. The police chief, Pierre Savary, a short, tough-looking, stocky character, balding, midforties, was still at his desk sipping espresso so strong the spoon would almost stand up.

The light on the computer screen immediately began to flash, and Pierre touched a button on his own keyboard to pull up the message.

He read it with great interest, because earlier that day he had had lunch at the home of Henri Foche, not with the great man himself, but with his security men, Marcel and Raymond. The purpose of the meeting was to review the protection surrounding the next president. Henri Foche was without question the biggest and most important issue in the life of Pierre Savary. If anything happened to Rennes's most celebrated citizen, there was absolutely no question, Pierre Savary would be blamed.

He had listened with immense interest to Marcel and Raymond, in particular to the suggestion that there may be an attempt on Foche's life. And that it may come from England. And now we have a violent criminal, in a stolen fishing boat, crossing the Channel from England in the small hours of a dark and stormy night. If Pierre Savary missed that, and anything befell the legendary Gaullist leader, Rennes would be looking for a new police chief, and he, Pierre, would spend the rest of his life in disgrace. He glanced at his watch, shuddered, and dialed Marcel's cell phone.

Foche's security chief answered on the first ring, and Chief Savary did not procrastinate. "Get down to headquarters right away, *mon ami*. It's important."

Marcel, who slept in a downstairs bedroom at Foche's house, flew out of bed, dressed, and hurried through the drawing room into the wide hall. There was an armed night guard on the door these days, and Marcel snapped as he went by, "I'm with Chief Savary. Call if you need me."

He gunned the Mercedes through the dark streets and was with the police chief inside of five minutes. And there he was shown the e-mail from Cherbourg. Marcel read it thoughtfully, and then said quietly, "You were right to call, Pierre. God knows where this man is, or who he is. But we're expecting some kind of attack, emanating from England. And this man might be heading for the coast of Brittany. We need to stay on this until he is caught, right?"

"Those are my thoughts," replied Pierre. "I'll put in a call to the coast guard, check for developments. Meanwhile, I'll tell them to keep us posted, blow by blow, until they find the trawler."

"Where's that last known position?"

"It happened just off the coast of Devon a few hours ago. And no one's certain which way that trawler is headed."

"Shall we stay here until they do?"

"I think so. Because this might be a real problem. They'll hang me if anything happens to Monsieur Foche."

"What do you think they'll do to me, award me a medal?"

———•◆•———

0200. English Channel
49.39 North 2.20 West

Eagle's GPS put Mack Bedford four miles west of Alderney. The radio that had been silent all night suddenly crackled into life:

Alderney Coast Guard here. Alderney Coast Guard. Marine navigation four miles to our west making course one-three-five—repeat one-three-five—please identify yourself.

Mack immediately hit the transmission switch and without hesitation called out in response:

This is the fishing boat Tantrum *out of Plymouth, England, bound for the port of Saint-Malo. We suffered satellite and radio transmission difficulties in the storm. Will report harbor master Saint-Malo on arrival. Wave band nine-three dead . . . over.*

Mack switched off the radio, and instantly made his course change coming right sixty degrees. He flashed on the GPS screen and checked he would run somewhere between the island of Guernsey and tiny Sark, which were lonely waters at this time of night.

The wind had died, and the sea was calmer. Sheltered by the big island he would make all of 20 knots through here, running toward the coast of Brittany, every yard of the way. Course: one-nine-five, sou'sou'west.

The Alderney Coast Guard had received a signal from Cherbourg that a hunt was forming for the missing British trawler. But they accepted that *Tantrum* out of Plymouth was having radio difficulties and would berth in Saint-Malo within three hours. Nonetheless, they re-ported the radar sighting on the coast guard link, confirming the pres-ence of the Plymouth-based British fishing boat and requesting a confirmation from the Saint-Malo harbor master when it arrived at around five o'clock.

Cherbourg was more interested, having been given a very strong warning from the head of the Brittany police that anything, repeat anything, pertaining to an unknown boat in the sea-lanes approaching Brittany was to be treated with the utmost diligence.

Coast Guard Cherbourg instructed the little station at Alderney to get on the case. But two hours later they had been unsuccessful in making contact. The young officer trying to reach Mack Bedford by radio was obliged to observe, "Of course she won't answer—her radio is up the 'chute; she already told us that."

And now *Eagle* was out of radar range, as Mack Bedford drove her farther south, comprehensively "wooded" by the little island of Hern. All she needed to do was move swiftly down the nine-mile channel be-tween St. Peter Port, Guernsey, and the island of Sark. At which point Mack faced a sixty-mile straight run across the Gulf of Saint-Malo in open water all the way, then down into the deep V of Saint-Brieuc Bay. And there was not a whole lot anyone could do about it, since there was not an active French Coast Guard boat within a hundred miles. And, anyway, it was still pitch black, and Mack Bedford was still with-out running lights, and he was still transmitting nothing. The coast guard no longer knew his course, and, better yet, no one knew whether the mysterious radar "paint" that appeared on the Alderney screen was *Eagle* or not.

The weather worsened as the trawler came out of the protection of the islands, and once more *Eagle* was pitching and rolling, but still pushing along, throttles open, making 20 knots or just below.

By this time, Teddy Rickard had made out a much more detailed signal, which he fed to the coast guard station at Dartmouth, and now at 0300 this latest intelligence went on the international link, and im-mediately Cherbourg Station began transmitting urgently:

All stations alert . . . North coast Dieppe, Gulf of Saint-Malo to Saint-Pol-de-Léon. Searching for British fishing trawler Eagle, *dark-red, sixty-five-foot hull, black lettering. Maybe running under false identity as* Tantrum *out of Plymouth.*

This is Cherbourg. Repeat, Coast Guard Cherbourg. English fishing trawler Eagle *running under illegal master. Big, black-bearded male. Caucasian. May be dangerous. Hijacked* Eagle *off English county Devon.*

All coast guard boarding parties to be fully armed. Alert all coast guard vessels in your area. Last known position Tantrum: *49.39 North 2.20 West—four miles west of Alderney. Course and speed unknown.*

That kind of signal from the normally restrained and careful coast guard operations on both sides of the Channel sends an electric shock through the service. And right now sleeping officers were being awakened and told to head to the jetties.

To Pierre Savary and Marcel, who were both wide awake and looking at the police computer screen in Rennes, however, it sent a tremor well up the Richter scale. These two had, of course, more to lose than anyone else. Except for Henri Foche.

Chief Savary hit the open line to the coast guard station at Cherbourg and demanded some fast answers, which he did not get. The duty officer told him they had every available man on the case, and there were three possibilities in their area: (1) a fishing boat apparently headed for Saint-Malo, (2) another heading for the same coastline but more westerly, and (3) a small freighter that may have switched course to Le Havre. Even with helicopters it was a vast area to search in darkness. If Chief Savary could just be patient, they'd have a far better idea how to proceed when the sun came up and boats could be seen.

With something less than good humor, Chief Savary put down the phone. "It seems to me," he said, "the two fishing boats are our concern. If there's some kind of murderer on the freighter going into Le Havre, that's Normandy's problem, not ours. But if he's in one of those fucking trawlers and he really is after Henri Foche, we'd better start moving."

"Well, we can't do anything from Rennes, that's for sure. This place is so far from the ocean, half the population has never even seen it." At this time of night, with sheeting rain and high winds, the forty-five miles up to the northern shore seemed a hell of a long way to Henri Foche's number-one bodyguard.

"Marcel," said Pierre, "I think you should round up Raymond, get into the car, and get up to the coast. Because that's where this bastard is going to show. By the time you arrive it'll be four thirty, and the coast guard will be tracking both boats inshore. Why not go for somewhere like Ploubalay? That way you can double back to Saint-Malo or head more west."

"And what do we do if they catch the guy, or we catch him?"

"In the interests of French justice I'd be inclined to act fast, with as little fuss as possible. The way we usually do in operations of this kind where there may be some embarrassment to people of grand stature. Remember, he's foreign, and if we stay legal there'll be enough red tape to throttle a stud bull."

"Pierre, you can leave it to us. If he lands that boat, he won't get five meters. Because there is only one fact that matters: Foche lives in Brittany, and anyone who wants to assassinate him is coming to Brittany. That narrows it down to the fishing boats. We'll stay in touch."

Marcel hurried out of the police department and once more hit the road, bound for the apartment block where Raymond lived. He called his cohort on his cell phone, and the two of them were on the road in ten minutes, both armed with the powerful French Special Forces handgun, the Sig Sauer 9mm. Chief Savary's wishes were clear to both of them.

———— • ◆ • ————

0500
48.42 North 2.31 West

The storm had veered inshore, and *Eagle* ran on south through the dark. The sea was now choppy, but without those long, rolling swells. Mack switched on his radar only in ten-second bursts, just to check he was not yet being tracked by the coast guard. Right now he was eight miles offshore, just north of the great jutting headland of Sables d'Or les Pin.

He flashed on his depth finder and saw one hundred meters below the keel. He wanted to move in closer to the land because the backdrop would confuse coast guard radar. And he'd already chosen his spot to come ashore, the little town of Val André, about six miles southwest of Sables d'Or. He thus had about fourteen miles to make landfall and an hour to do it before six o'clock when the sun would be above the eastern horizon. Mack knew he was too late to land in darkness, but he wanted the cloak of the night to shield him for as long as possible.

What he did not know was that at four thirty, three coast guard boats, one from Cherbourg and two from Saint-Malo, had cleared the jetties and were out there searching for *Eagle,* reporting in with signals that were relayed to Pierre Savary in Rennes, and onward to Marcel and Raymond.

Thus far, one of them had located the suspect fishing boat heading into Saint-Malo itself and had discovered only that the perfectly legal Spanish crew had switched off the radio and were listening to flamenco. Their boat was not named *Tantrum;* it was *La Mancha.* The master was a slim five-foot-six baldheaded fisherman of some sixty-eight summers. No, *La Mancha* had not been hijacked, but she was low on fuel.

Those were very moderate events for Lieutenant Commander Bedford because he was by now the only suspect, and deep in his combat-trained soul he guessed there might be some kind of a dragnet closing in on him. But in his mind he knew there had been no other way. He could not possibly have risked coming through a French airport or ferry port with a portable Austrian sniper rifle in his metal toolbox. That would have been suicide. So therefore he had to land in France anonymously, bringing his rifle with him. He could not have hired a boat because everyone in Brixham would have known. He could not have stolen a boat, because it would have been reported missing about three minutes after he left. And he could not have purchased a boat because of the rigid British rules about registration. A car was one thing, a boat, from a working, gossipy seaport, quite another.

The hijack route had been the only route. It gave him time, a head start of several hours, leaving behind a gigantic search area to confuse his enemy. Right now, however, the chase was coming down to what Mack called the short strokes. They must be closing in now. But so far he had not seen another ship. And, thank God, it was still dark.

He rounded the Sables d'Or headland and found himself in much more open water. He switched on his radar, and five miles to the north was a "paint" on the screen. Whatever it was, it was coming dead toward, and it was moving fast, which was unsurprising since this was a brand-new navy cutter, state of the art, with electronic telescopic sights that could pull up a bumblebee on the moon.

Mack slammed open the throttles and aimed straight for the beach at Val André six miles to the southwest, flank speed. *Eagle* shuddered up to 21 knots, but Mack knew if his apparent pursuer was in a coast guard cutter, it would make 35 knots. They'd be alongside as he came inshore. Not good.

He ran hard for ten minutes. Dawn was breaking, and he used Fred Carter's binoculars to check over his shoulder. He could see plainly the running lights of his pursuer, both red and green. She was still coming dead toward. Fast.

0530. This is coast guard cutter P720 two miles north of Sables d'Or. We have POSIDENT fishing trawler Eagle *making 20 knots southwest heading toward Val André.* Eagle *is four miles ahead. We are in hot pursuit, repeat hot pursuit. All personnel armed.*

Saint-Malo station to Chief Pierre Savary: coast guard cutter P720 located British fishing trawler Eagle *making 20 knots southwest, toward Val André. POSIDENT 0530. ETA Val André 0600. We are in hot pursuit.*

"Marcel, make straight for Val André. *Eagle* is being chased in by the coast guard. Expected to make landfall at 6:00 A.M."

Mack Bedford could see the beach as the sun began to climb into the eastern skies. He snapped the helm onto automatic pilot, cutting back the throttles as he did so. Then he ran below, to the engine room, hoping to high heaven *Eagle* had a plug stopping the drain hole, which he knew most fishing boats have, ready for power-flushing the bilges and fish holds in drydock.

It took him a half minute to find it, a wide brass screw-in about eight inches across with two jutting arms. He grabbed and heaved, trying to turn the plug. But it was too tight. He ran to the fire cupboard and found a hefty sledgehammer next to the hydrant. He took aim and hit that plug harder than it had ever been hit in its life, so hard it swiveled a full turn.

Mack spun it out, and seawater cascaded in. He dodged some of it, but got mildly soaked and charged back up the ladder with tons and tons of water gushing in below. He reached the wheelhouse and cut the throttles to all-stop.

His bag and the toolbox were still in the lifeboat. Mack ripped off the cover and lowered away. The lifeboat hit the water on the starboard side, and Mack took one final look around. Then he remembered the binoculars and went back to the wheelhouse, retrieved them, and grabbed a fishing rod. He hit the deck running and vaulted over the side, landing in the lifeboat and damn nearly falling overboard. He was about two miles offshore, and *Eagle* was sinking fast. He loosed off the lines, and started the outboard the first time with the pull cord. *Say one thing—that Fred Carter keeps a tidy ship.*

He chugged around to the port side and trained his binoculars on the oncoming *P720*, now about three miles and six minutes away. The water was up to *Eagle*'s gunwales, and now the sea was surging in over the top. Mack watched her roll left, and then the stern began to go down. Water rushed over the transom, and she went under stern first, her bow rising and then sliding down into sixty fathoms. As she did so a massive air bubble broke the surface. But Mack was too busy to notice. He ripped off his black wig and beard and stowed them in his bag. Then he took the Jeffery Simpson wig and mustache out and changed his appearance beyond all belief.

He took one of the fishing rods, which already had a heavy lure on the line, and cast it over the side. And there, quietly chugging along in the morning sea fret, leaning back without a care in the world, Mackenzie Bedford awaited the arrival of the coast guard.

On board *P720* there was pandemonium.

What do you mean, she's vanished? She can't have vanished!

Give me a moment. There's a lot of mist around, and she's two miles ahead—I'll pick her up in a minute.

Well, where the hell is she?

I don't know, sir. I just can't see her.

Let me look. . . . There you are, right there—I can see a ship!

Sir, that's just a dinghy. Not a sixty-five-foot fishing trawler.

Well, what's a fucking dinghy doing there?

I'm not sure, sir.

Helmsman, head for that dinghy, full speed.

P720 came thundering into the waters where Mack was fishing. A curving white bow wave on the cutter probably frightened the life out of any fish that might have been tempted to have a snap at Mack's lure.

"Bonjour, monsieur!" the coast guard officer called from the foredeck.

"Bonjour, mes amis!" responded Mack. And of course the officer knew in an instant the fisherman was not French.

"Anglais?"

"Non, American."

"Ah, oui, monsieur. You have caught anything today?"

"Couple of small bass. I've only been out here for twenty minutes. My wife's still asleep."

"Everyone's still asleep except us!"

Mack wound in his reel, conscious of the word "Eagle" stuck on in adhesive red letters on the inside of the lifeboat's gunwales, visible only to him. But he grinned cheerfully.

"Monsieur, did you just see a fishing trawler go past? Moving quickly?"

"Yeah, real close, dark-red boat called *Eagle*." Mack pointed to a rocky promontory, maybe a half mile to the south. "She went straight toward that headland over there, moving real quick."

"You didn't happen to see who was driving, did you?"

"Sure I did. She passed only about forty yards away. He was a big guy. He had a black beard and long hair. Looked like a fuckin' buffalo."

"A buffalo, huh? You Americans. So funny. Bon chance, monsieur. Merci."

Coast guard cutter *P720* surged away, making for the headland, throttles open.

Mack decided to hang around for a while, in case they came back his way. So he wound in the reel and cast again.

———— • ◆ • ————

The black Mercedes belonging to Henri Foche was being gunned along a straight country road behind the picturesque Côte d'Emeraude. At the wheel was number-two bodyguard Raymond, who was apt to drive as if he were eighty-five miles to the southeast in Le Mans.

Marcel was on the phone to Pierre, who informed him the coast guard was having problems in the mist behind the fishing trawler, but the ETA at Val André was the same, six o'clock. "For Christ's sake, slow down!" yelled Marcel. "You'll kill us both!"

"It's after five thirty, and this fucking place is still another six miles," retorted Raymond. "We gotta get there. Shut up."

"We're not going do much good if you wrap this thing around a tree," said Marcel. "And I'm still worried about our orders. Pierre wants the job done quickly and quietly, no mess. But Jesus Christ! What do we do if the guy shows up on his own? Just shoot him down in the street, like fucking *High Noon*?"

Raymond chuckled. "No, we just take him somewhere quiet and shoot him, like *The Godfather!*"

"Either way, we have to take him out," said Marcel. "But I can't help wondering if he really is trying to kill Monsieur Foche. I mean, what if he's not? What if he's never even heard of Monsieur Foche?"

"I guess they don't like the coincidence. The warning about the assassin coming in from England. The sudden theft of the trawler, men being thrown overboard. This guy's a desperado, the kind of killer who would accept that two million dollars to pull off the job."

"I suppose so. But we're not supposed to ask questions. They want this Blackbeard character taken out. And we've got the chief of police for Brittany plus the next president of France on our side. Let's just kill the sonofabitch, get rid of the body, and go home."

"Guess you're right."

By now the Mercedes was running at eighty-five miles per hour into the outskirts of Val André. Marcel thought it was entirely possible this crazy prick Raymond might just drive straight into the ocean, since he obviously had no idea where the brakes were.

Meanwhile, back in Brixham the police had awakened half the town at four o'clock in a local dragnet designed to identify the big man with the beard who had stolen Fred Carter's trawler *Eagle*.

They'd roused pub landlords and café and restaurant owners all over the area trying to get a handle on the villain who had very nearly sent Fred and Tom to their deaths. There were two landlords who remembered him, his size, his hairiness, and his accent.

One of them recalled the waitress who'd served him, the live-in student, Diana, and she too was aroused from her sleep. "I do remember him," she told the young detective constable. "He was very nice and gave me a good tip. He said his name was Gunther Rock, I think. He lived in Geneva. I'm sure he didn't steal the fishing boat."

"Did he have some kind of a foreign accent?"

"Gosh, yes. French, I think. But it could have been German."

Within five minutes, the added information on the hijacker was being e-mailed to the French coast guard and on to Brittany police: suspect believed to be Gunther Rock, a resident of Geneva, heavy foreign accent. That last part tallied with the description supplied by Fred Carter and Tom. And of course with that provided by the Brixham harbor master, Teddy Rickard, who had spoken to Gunther twice.

Pierre Savary dialed Marcel's number and passed on the new information. "He's Gunther Rock from Geneva, and he speaks English with a French or German accent, which doesn't affect you. The description's the same. Big, bearded, and probably dangerous, like most assassins."

"Okay, Chief," replied Marcel. "We'll be ready for him when he comes ashore. I expect we'll see the trawler."

Raymond had finally slowed right down, and he came quietly down the main street of Val André, looking for a place to park unobtrusively. He settled for a side street on which no one was awake. The two men rammed new magazines into their pistols, slid them into shoulder holsters concealed under their jackets, and walked down toward the beach.

And here, of course, there was a problem. No trawler—just an almost empty expanse of sea; no sign of life except for a tiny dinghy way out there, hardly moving, and what might have been some guy fishing. The problem was, of course, a natural but tiresome reaction by coast guard *P720*, who did not wish to call headquarters in Cherbourg and admit they'd just lost a seventy-ton fishing trawler in broad daylight. Right now they were around the headland, helpfully pointed out to them by Mack Bedford, and they had a pretty well uninterrupted view of the ocean for five miles in every direction. No trawler. *C'est impossible!* yelled the coast guard captain.

"Sir, the only thing I can suggest is he turned back to the northeast and ran back up the coast toward Cap Frehel, and we somehow lost him in the mist along that shore." Privately, Lieutenant Cartier thought he stood a fighting chance of being fired for this. And he was more mystified than the captain, because he'd had the electronic sight trained on the *Eagle* for five minutes. He had turned away to speak to a crewmate and then gone below to see the captain, and when he'd returned the trawler was gone. Or at least it was gone so far as he was concerned. In fact, at that point *Eagle* had been lower in the water but still floating. The four-mile distance and the choppy sea state had merely rendered it impossible to see. She did not sink for another six minutes, but now they were right in the area of her last known, and the *Eagle* really had vanished.

"No other course to take," agreed the captain. "Helmsman, turn around and steer zero-four-zero. Back up the coast. Full speed."

"Shall I report in, sir, explain what's happened to headquarters?"

"Lieutenant Cartier, have you finally gone crazy?" demanded the captain. "Are you really anxious to explain to the admiral that we are in the process of proving we are the most incompetent ship since Villeneuve got his ass kicked at Trafalgar? Get back on that glass, Lieutenant, *AND FIND THAT FUCKING TRAWLER!*"

"Aye, sir."

Two minutes later, Marcel and Raymond saw the government boat come hammering out from behind the headland and speed across the bay. She was a mile out, but in this thin morning air, they could hear the growl of her engines.

"What the hell's going on?" said Raymond. "That's the coast guard, not the trawler. Are we in the wrong place?"

"I can't say," replied Marcel. "But our orders are to wait here for the trawler, locate her master, and eliminate him as a dangerous criminal and a threat to the security of France."

And so they waited, leaning here on the seawall, staring out at the Bay of Saint-Brieuc, waiting for Pierre to call with new instructions. But nothing happened. Because the coast guard did not know what was going on, and neither did the police HQ at Rennes.

And poor old Lieutenant Cartier was searching the surface for a ship that was not on it. Mack Bedford carried on fishing until the coast guard had gone past. He gave them a quick wave as they went by, and then he tied the heavy binoculars to the fishing line and dropped the rod over the side. He changed his disguise, reinstating himself as Gunther Marc Roche of 18 rue de Basle, Geneva. He turned the Zodiac around and ran lightly through the calming sea, making around six knots on his two-mile, twenty-minute journey to the beach at Val André.

Still patrol boat *P720* did not report in to Saint-Malo. Pierre Savary heard nothing. And the two hit men leaning on the seawall were completely in the dark. Both of them could see the return of the fisherman, but took little notice. Their eyes were trained on the horizon, compulsively looking for the dark-red shape of *Eagle* trying to make landfall.

But there was only the fisherman, chugging ever nearer in his little Zodiac, a matter of such underwhelming indifference that Marcel and Raymond scarcely noticed as the inflatable came running easily into the shallows, 150 yards away.

Just then, Marcel's phone rang. And the message complicated what was already complicated. "There appears to be some doubt as to the landing place of *Eagle*," said Pierre. "The coast guard has asked everyone to stand by until they issue a definite location."

"Well, what do we do?" asked Marcel.

"Better stay right there until further orders," said the police chief.

"Does this mean they've lost the fucking trawler?" asked Marcel.

"I don't know that. But it's beginning to look that way. Stupid bastards."

"Well, how the hell can anyone lose a sixty-five-foot trawler? It's bigger than the fucking police station," snapped Marcel.

"Who knows?" grunted Pierre. "Better hold it right there till we finally get organized."

He rang off and left Marcel wondering what was happening and staring down the beach as the fisherman came onto land. The sun was up now, but still low in the sky, and it had the effect of silhouetting Mack as he raised the little outboard engine and beached the Zodiac, casting no light on his face whatsoever. He hopped adroitly over the bow and hauled on the painter, catching the next incoming wave, which helped shove the boat up the beach. Mack pulled some more, then walked around and gave an almighty heave on the side handles, which hauled the boat around to face the water, its bow rising slightly with the incoming tide.

He leaned over and pulled out his leather bag and the metal toolbox, and placed them on the sand. Then he took out his sharp screwdriver and punctured and ripped the inflatable hull of the boat in about ten places close to the waterline. Marcel and Raymond, watching from afar, thought he must be some kind of a nutcase.

But Mack was not done. He rolled up his pants and took off his trainers and socks. He waded out and started the engine, which roared and sloshed water everywhere as he eased the boat through the shallows. Then, with one movement, he smacked the engine into gear, and opened the throttle wide. In the shallow water the motor almost died, spluttering, gasping for depth and space for the prop to spin. Mack gave it one last almighty heave, and the Zodiac took off, growling its way straight out to sea. It couldn't be stopped. Better yet, it couldn't float. At least, not for long.

Mack pulled his socks on, over his wet feet, put on his shoes, and adjusted his damp driver's gloves. Then he set off up the beach, holding the box in his right hand and the bag in his left.

At which point, Marcel almost had a heart attack. "Jesus Christ, Raymond!" he gasped. "Look at this guy. He's not only a nutcase, but he's big with long dark hair and a black beard. I think it's him."

"Are you kidding me?" exclaimed Raymond. "What do we do?"

"Let him get close and then call out his name—Gunther. What else can we do?"

"It's gotta be him," said Raymond, sliding his Sig Sauer service revolver out of its holster. "Let's take him right now, soon as he gets close enough."

"No. No. I want to check. We can't just gun down the local grocer or someone. I wanna know it's really him."

By now Mack was within thirty yards, and Marcel shouted, "Gunther! Right here!"

"You talking to me, pal?" said Mack, still striding toward them.

"Gunther Rock, we are from the French police because you answer the description of someone who has committed piracy on the high seas, and attempted to murder the crew. Put down both those bags and raise your hands."

Raymond, meanwhile, standing just ten feet away, drew his revolver, and aimed it straight at Mack Bedford's heart.

CHAPTER *10*

Mack made his very best effort to look resigned to his fate, and adopted a downcast look, nodding his head to confirm he would do precisely as he was told. Wearily, he leaned forward and placed the toolbox and the bag on the ground, as if they were precious. As he straightened up, he raised his arms into the surrender position, staring all the while into the eyes of Raymond the gunman.

And then Mack Bedford struck with dazzling speed, snapping both hands around Raymond's right arm, swaying sideways, and smashing the arm on the sharp edge of the wall, breaking it in half at the elbow like a rotten stick.

Raymond screamed with pain, and the gun flew over the wall and onto the beach, at which point Mack delivered a stupendous kick to his groin that knocked him flat on his back, writhing in agony.

Marcel had no time even to draw his revolver, and he leaped at Mack from behind, ramming his forearm around the former SEAL's throat. But Marcel was simply not strong enough. Mack twisted and brought his right arm around in what looked like a haymaker delivered by a boxer.

But this was no punch. This was unarmed military combat, a lifetime of training. And Mack's right hand was traveling at the speed of light as he rammed two fingers into Marcel's eyes so hard he would have been blinded for life. But that was not relevant. Marcel tried to veer away from the monster who now faced him, but he never had a chance. Mack grabbed him by the ears and sharply twisted his head right around, first left, then right, snapping the neck almost in half.

Marcel was dead before he hit the ground. And before he did hit the ground Mack had hauled Raymond by the ears into a sitting position and done precisely the same thing to him. It had taken him 9.7 seconds to kill them both. And now he heaved them both over the wall.

Mack could hear Marcel's phone ringing as the body thudded onto the beach, but this time Pierre Savary would receive no reply. He did not, of course, know there were two vacancies this morning on Henri Foche's security staff. Which was just as well, since he was already fuming, fit to explode at the pathetic failure of Marcel to answer his goddamned phone.

Mack picked up his bag and toolbox and muttered, "Fucking amateurs," as he considered the sheer futility of the two killers who had been sent to murder him. The image of his beloved Tommy stood before him, and he added quietly, "Guess that one was for you, kid."

The street that led up to the village of Val André was deserted. Mack's watch showed a few minutes past six, but France was an hour in front of England, and he knew it was just after seven. Thus far, he had been operating purely on matters of darkness and lightness, sunrise and sunset. But now he moved officially onto French time, six hours in front of Maine, but the same as Switzerland.

Mack knew perfectly well he had to stop torturing himself over Anne and Tommy, because there was nothing he could do, and while he did not give a rat's ass for the late Marcel and his dimwitted cohort, he could very easily have sat down and wept helpless tears for his wife and their little boy. Deep down he was sure the great Carl Spitzbergen was going to save Tommy, and they would go fishing again together, and they'd throw the baseball and watch the Red Sox. He wasn't going to die. Mack was struggling for control, just to stop his tears, which were rolling into his beard as he strode toward the village. It's often that way with the bravest of men.

The street narrowed as he walked, and high above, slung right across the road between the shops, were two huge banners proclaiming, *HENRI FOCHE—POUR LA BRETAGNE, POUR LA FRANCE.* There were already one or two early customers buying warm baguettes from the *boulangerie,* but no one paid much attention to the big bearded man carrying his toolbox up the main street.

Mack was resolved to walk through the town until he came to a garage, and it turned out to be a fair distance, just less than a mile. But there it was, with a Foche banner strung across the forecourt—Laporte Auto. It was really a gas station with a half-dozen cars lined up for sale outside.

There was a dark blue Peugeot for fourteen thousand euros and a red Citroën for nineteen. In any event, the garage was closed, and a notice said it would not open before eight. Mack put down his bag and box and leaned on the doorbell, and he heard it ring loudly inside the building.

No response. So he hit it again. And again. Two minutes later, a sleepy, unshaven, and very angry Frenchman opened an upstairs window and shouted, "Are you crazy! It's seven fifteen in the morning, and we don't open until eight o'clock. Go away! We're closed."

Mack stared up at him, and in the most desperate German accent, which sounded like a Punjabi peasant, he shouted back, "You see this Peugeot right here? I'll give you twenty thousand euros for it, in cash. So long as you're down here in sixty seconds."

"Go away. I'm in bed with my wife. You must be a pervert! I call the police."

He slammed down the window. And Mack waited, still looking up at the building. The window flew open again.

"How much?" yelled Monsieur Laporte.

"Twenty thousand."

"I'll be right down."

One minute later the garage owner unlocked the front door. "You want the car now?" he asked.

"Right now," said Mack, delving into his bag and removing seven bundles of euros. "How many miles has it done?"

"Eleven thousand. It's a good car. Belonged to a local man. I serviced it myself."

"I'm paying you this much money to get the documents signed and to get me out of here inside of ten minutes, so get buzzing."

M. Laporte got buzzing. He produced registration documents and said he needed, legally, to see Mack's passport—"Photo identification, *n'est ce pas?*"

Mack pulled out his scarlet Gunther Marc Roche Swiss passport and handed it over, complete with the photograph taken in Portland of the bearded Swiss national. This was laminated onto the page, with a small white computerized cross set onto the right side of his face, the way all Swiss passports are designed.

The Frenchman wrote down the details carefully—"Passport number 947274902 . . . 18 rue de Basle, Geneva—and I need to see your driver's license, if you want to drive away from here on French roads."

Mack gave him the Gunther Marc Roche license, and watched M. Laporte add it to the document, complete with date of issue—July 2008. He handed over the money and signed the registration documents for the French government—*Gunther M. Roche.* Monsieur Laporte dated it, and stamped it with the authentic seal of Laporte Motors.

"No bullshit," said Mack.

"Pardon, monsieur?"

"Do I get a guarantee?"

"For a cash deal like this you get my personal guarantee that I will repair this car free no matter what, for a period of six months."

"One year, you stingy little prick," said Mack, confident that a man who was unable to translate the word "bullshit" would have real trouble with "stingy little prick." Anyway, he felt better for saying it.

"Okay, one year," said Laporte, and Mack refrained from calling him a stingy little prick again. Instead, he patted him on the back and told him to send the official documents to his address in Geneva when they arrived from the government. They went outside, and Monsieur Laporte washed the price off the windshield of the car. He gave Mack the key and asked if he would like the tank filled.

"Good idea," said Mack, and sat in the driver's seat while twelve gallons were pumped in.

When this was completed, he said to the garage owner, "Remember, with a cash transaction like this, you will never breathe one word about it to anyone."

"Never," said M. Laporte, who now had the twenty thousand euros stuffed into his pocket. "That will be sixty-two euros for the petrol."

"Why don't you go fuck yourself?" said Mack cheerfully, accelerating away into the street and heading east, fast, away from Val André, away from this parsimonious little sonofabitch and the bodies of the two hoodlums he'd just killed.

"Fuck it," said Mack. "I'll be darn glad when this French bullshit is over."

For the moment, he concentrated on what the navy describes as leaving the datum. He drove fast along a lonely country road headed in the general direction of Rennes, remembering how his guidebook on the bench at Brixham had informed him that Brittany's main city had been a crossroads since Roman times. In his opinion crossroads were good, because he was uncertain in which direction he may need to travel, uncertain where Henri Foche might suddenly show up. However, he guessed the city of Rennes, where the politician lived, would consider him to be permanent news. The Foche travels and speeches would probably be easier to find there than anywhere else.

But first he had tasks to complete, and the first of these involved another killing . . . well, a killing off. *Lt. Cdr. Mackenzie Bedford is pleased to announce the death of Mr. Gunther Marc Roche of rue de Basle, Geneva.*

He found a deserted stretch of road and pulled off onto a rough farm track with trees on either side. And there he ripped off, for the last time, his black curly wig, his beard, black T-shirt, and navy-blue sweater, and stuffed the disguise items into the deep recess of the false bottom of his bag, along with the red Swiss passport and the driver's license.

He pulled on a clean white T-shirt and his lightweight tweed jacket, and then carefully fitted his light-blond wig, the neat mustache, and the rimless spectacles that contained only plain glass. It was just about impossible even to equate him with the black-bearded hijacker who was currently being hunted by the English police, the British coast guard, the entire French government Maritime Services, and the police department of Brittany.

Mack had laid a sensational trail. There were confirmed sightings of him just about every yard of the way from the pub opposite his Brixham hotel to Laporte Auto, now ten miles astern of his new Peugeot. There were waitresses, harbor masters, parking lot attendants, booksellers, trawler captains, even some guy out fishing who'd done his best to help the Saint-Malo coast guard officer. And then there was the garage boss who had dutifully filled in the government forms, inspected his passport and license. In Mack's view Interpol would be knocking on the door of 18 Basle Street within four or five hours. Gods knows what they'd find, especially since he'd made the address up. He did not even know if there was a Basle Street in the entire mountainous Swiss Confederation.

As far as Mack could tell, there would be a general murder hunt and panic in Geneva, and there'd be a real panic and murder hunt in Rennes, and another in Val André. There'd be a massive alert and attempted-murder inquiry in Brixham, especially when the parking official blew the whistle on the bearded guy with the weird accent, the one who'd left behind a Ford Fiesta with no license plates, no tax disk, no registration, and no fingerprints.

Mack smiled to himself. "And all for a man who never existed, and could never be found—a Swiss ghost."

He supposed that in the end the English police would strip down the car and find its chassis number, which would, perhaps, lead them to Dublin. And there they would meet Mr. Michael McArdle, who would tell them all about Patrick Sean O'Grady, of 27 Herbert Park Road, Dublin 4, a fair-haired Irishman, slim mustache and rimless spectacles, born in County Kildare, passport number and license registered with the proper authorities.

Mack almost burst out laughing at the compelling thought that Mr. O'Grady had never existed either. And neither did his address or his passport and license.

But the entire exercise was too serious for laughter, and sometime in the next few hours he would destroy the evidence that could link him to Gunther Marc Roche. Right now he needed to complete his second task. Clean-cut in his Jeffery Simpson mode, he drove out onto the road and set forth again, urgently now looking for a French café.

Five miles later he found one, a small country restaurant with a large parking lot and several cars sharing the space with a couple of enormous trucks. He pulled in and parked the Peugeot at the back of the lot, then walked around his vehicle with his screwdriver and swiftly removed both plates. He put them on the backseat and walked to the café for breakfast.

It was a bright, clean, inexpensive place, and it was busy. Mack was shown to a small table for two next to the window. He ordered orange juice and coffee and took a copy of *Le Monde* from the newspaper rack. When the waitress came for his breakfast order he glanced down at the menu and settled for an omelet and bacon with a croissant and fruit preserves.

He turned to the newspaper, and the lead story's headline on page 3 read:

SECURITY ALERT AS HENRI FOCHE FACES
SAINT-NAZAIRE WORKERS TOMORROW

Mack sipped his coffee and grappled with the French language, trying to grasp the gist of the story. In the ensuing ten minutes, before the arrival of his omelet, he learned that there had been unrest among the workforce in the Saint-Nazaire shipyards. *Le Monde* assumed that Foche himself held a substantial shareholding in this sprawling industrial complex, and he was nervous that the dissatisfaction might cause the entire workforce to vote against him in the forthcoming election.

Foche was essentially going to Saint-Nazaire to put out a fire, but he would disguise it with an inspiring political speech designed to convince everyone that life would improve dramatically, for everyone, if they would sweep him to victory and install him in the Elysée Palace. *Pour la Bretagne, Pour la France!*

He planned to address the great throng of workers in the Saint-Nazaire yard shortly after five, at the end of the shift. The executive had agreed to postpone the start of the next shift for one hour, with no loss of pay. There was a picture of a wooden stage being constructed with a lectern and microphone, beneath a patriotic red, white, and blue striped awning, and a huge Foche battle banner, as above. The workers interested Mack, all dressed in standard royal-blue overalls.

Mack stepped once more to the newspaper rack, where he could see a selection of road maps of France on the lower shelf. He helped himself to one of these and took it back to the table, just as his breakfast arrived. He told the waitress to add the cost of the map and his newspaper to the bill.

She replied that of course she would, and was there anything more she could bring him? Mack confirmed he was fine for the moment and attacked his breakfast, the first food he had eaten since the fried cod with the overweight chips back in the pub on Brixham harbor thirteen hours before. And he'd been up all night, fighting the elements and local villains.

The omelet was supreme among all omelets, flavored with Parmesan cheese, tarragon, and chives. Mack assessed, conservatively, that he could probably have eaten about twelve of them. But he did not want too much food, because he needed to stay sharp. He ate the delicious French bread with strawberry preserves and said yes to a coffee refill.

Then he asked to pay the bill, and for a large black coffee to go. The waitress brought both, the coffee in a plastic container with a lid. Mack paid, left a tip, and said he'd sit there for a few more minutes and finish his second cup. The waitress privately thought he must be a coffee addict and would probably become a basket case sometime in the next half hour. Wrong.

Two minutes later, Mack watched a small Citroën drive into the parking lot. Two men got out, walked the short distance into the café, and took a small table across the room. Instantly, Mack stood up, took his second cup of coffee with him, and hurried out the door, helping himself to a small book of matches as he went.

He walked casually to the parking lot, where the Citroën was out of the sight line of the café's main serving area. And then he went to work.

He knelt down at the front and rear of the car, swiftly removed both plates, and screwed them onto his dark-blue Peugeot. Then he took the other plates off the backseat and screwed them onto the Citroën. He poured the fresh black coffee into the hedge, kept the container, jumped into the driver's seat, and gunned that Peugeot onto the highway at a pace that would have made the late gunman Raymond gasp.

Ten miles later he stopped on a long, quiet stretch of tree-lined road and consulted his map. Saint-Nazaire was about eighty miles to the south, but he no longer needed to head for Rennes. He needed to cut across country to Lorient, and find Brittany's great coastal highway that runs straight past the ancient city of Vannes down on the Morbihan coast. From there it was a straight shot down the highway to the French shipbuilding hub.

Mack checked his watch and the gas gauge. It was nine o'clock on a bright July morning, and he had plenty of fuel. At least old Laporte had pumped in the right amount, though he had not filled the tank, probably because he guessed he was giving it away to the man who had just paid him six thousand euros over the odds for the Peugeot.

The car would probably take two or three gallons more, and Mack pulled into the next service station and filled up, also pouring a pint of four-star into his empty coffee container.

Three miles farther on, he pulled off into a rest area, retrieved the black curly wig, beard, and black T-shirt, ripped up Gunther's passport, and wrapped up everything in the pages of Le Monde, including the false Swiss driver's license. He walked over to a metal garbage bin and pushed it all down to the bottom. Then he upended the pint of four-star into the bin, struck one of his matches, and tossed it in, ducking away as he did so. The bin blew with a dull WHOMPF! Flames leaped high as it became an inferno, and Mack could feel the intense heat as the last remnants of Gunther were cremated on this desolate French country road.

Leaving the metal bin shimmering hot, he reboarded the Peugeot and headed south.

———— • ◆ • ————

At 9:15 A.M. a couple of schoolboys on vacation found the bodies of Marcel and Raymond. In fact, they did not precisely find the bodies; they found Raymond's loaded revolver, safety catch off, lying on the sand. The bodies were strictly an afterthought, and anyway the boys thought the two men were asleep.

Discovery of the heavy revolver was just about the most exciting thing that had happened on this vacation, and one of them, young Vincent Dupres, aged eleven, took aim up over the seawall, pulled the trigger twice, and blew out someone's upstairs window. The resultant rumpus, which is apt to emanate from gunshots and a shower of broken glass, led to a surge of neighbors swarming out onto the beachfront street of Val André and the subsequent discovery that the owner of the gun was dead and so was his pal.

The police were called immediately, and twenty minutes later two white cruisers from the Gendarmerie Nationale arrived from Saint-Malo. Detective Constable Paul Ravel was temporarily in command, and this was a fortunate move for the police:

Ravel was a quiet, contemplative, often overlooked thirty-four-year-old career police officer. Many of his colleagues thought he should have been promoted much higher, long ago. But Paul Ravel, married with two children, looked at the world with a wry smile, the kind of smile that is often backed up by a heavyweight brain, which his very definitely was.

He was an athletic man of medium height, originally from the southwestern city of Toulouse, where he was educated, and considered to be a rugby fullback destined perhaps to play one day for one of the great French teams. Toulouse scouted him when he was only seventeen years old, the owner of the safest pair of hands schoolboy rugby in that city had seen for years.

But Paul Ravel gave up everything for love, falling for a dark-haired beauty from Brittany, the daughter of a coast guard officer. He left his busy native southwestern city for the soft farmlands and spectacular coastline of the North. He never went back, and he married Louise at the age of twenty-two. They lived in a small house on the edge of Saint-Malo and had no wish to live anywhere else. Ever. Paul's ambitions to become a detective had started swiftly but somehow stalled. He had not yet reached the point where he was resigned to his modest status, but he was close.

No one yet understood this was the most important murder investigation of his career. And right now, pending the arrival of someone very senior, he was in charge of the initial police routine. He immediately discovered that not one but both of the dead men had been armed with very powerful revolvers, same make. Marcel's was still in its shoulder holster. The policeman searched the bodies and found driver's licenses belonging to Marcel and Raymond. They also found in Raymond's jacket pocket a set of car keys and a cell phone, switched on.

Since none of the local people had ever laid eyes on the two bodyguards, it was obvious they were complete strangers in the area. The policemen asked if anyone had seen a strange car arrive that morning and park somewhere in the beach location.

No one had seen it arrive, but someone had noticed a large black S-type Mercedes-Benz parked on a side street about two hundred meters away. The detective constable and one other officer went to check, and found that Raymond's push-button keys easily unlocked the vehicle, with a little display of flashing lights, front and rear, and wing mirrors swiveling into place.

He checked inside, but there was very little in the way of possessions, just a road map and a couple of coffee cups. He wrote down the registration number of the car and walked back to the two cruisers, which were now parked diagonally, completely blocking the road from either direction.

He sat in one of the cars and punched the Mercedes registration number into the onboard police computer. Four minutes later the screen flashed up the name and address of the registered owner—Montpellier Munitions, in the Forest of Orléans. The detective had heard that name somewhere before, and quite recently. But he could not recall where and why. Nonetheless, it would be the work of moments to call Montpellier and check out precisely who was driving their car.

Meanwhile, he had the cell phone, and with little anticipation of success he pushed the redial number, and, slightly to his surprise, heard a number being connected. On the third ring a voice answered and said, crisply, "Marcel, where the fucking hell have you been?"

Paul Ravel said evenly, "This is not Marcel. May I ask who is speaking?"

"What do you mean it's not Marcel? You're using his damned phone! It's showing on my caller ID. Where the hell is he?"

"Sir, this is Detective Constable Paul Ravel of the Saint-Malo Station. May I ask again to whom I am speaking?"

"Ravel, this is the private telephone of the chief of police for Brittany. My name is Pierre Savary. I'm in the Rennes headquarters. And may I ask again, where the hell is Marcel?"

"Sir, I have no way of knowing whether or not I am speaking to Monsieur Savary. I am going to call the police headquarters in Rennes and ask to be put through to you."

Before the chief could protest, Paul Ravel had clicked off and was dialing Brittany HQ on the police cruiser phone. Paul told the officer who answered that M. Savary was awaiting the call, and moments later the same voice came back on the line.

"Sorry about that, sir," said the Saint-Malo detective, "but I had to be certain. You see, Marcel and his colleague Raymond are both dead. They are lying on the beach here in Val André, but we've only been here for ten minutes. I have few details."

The blood drained from Pierre Savary's face. He almost went into shock, since the words of the detective contained such overwhelming ramifications that he momentarily lost the power of speech.

"Sir? Are you still there?"

"Yes, Detective Constable, I'm still here. What details can you give me?"

"Well, sir, the bodies contain several signs of physical violence. We have not conducted a proper investigation yet. But Raymond has a badly broken arm, and his body was curled up, almost in the fetal position, as if he was trying to protect himself from an attacker."

"And Marcel?"

"Sir, he had some terrible damage to his eyes, one of them had been bleeding, and they were somehow pushed back into their sockets. You could not see the eyeballs. And I noticed both men had their heads at a strange angle, lying there on the sand. I've never seen anyone with their head twisted around like that."

"Had they been killed in the place where you found them?"

"Oh, definitely not, sir. They had been thrown over the seawall. There were major indentations in the sand. I can't imagine what kind of man did this to them. But maybe there were two, or even three. It's hard to think this was the work of just one person. Remember, sir, both Marcel and Raymond were armed."

"Did you check whether either of their weapons had been fired?"

"Yes, sir. Marcel's revolver was still in its holster, fully loaded. Two shots only had been fired from Raymond's gun, both by the kid who found the bodies."

"Kid?"

"Yessir. A couple of eleven-year-olds found the bodies and discovered the gun lying on the sand, about five meters from the two dead men. Little devil fired it up over the seawall and knocked out someone's bedroom window."

"Christ, he could have killed someone."

"Don't I know it. I've got one of the young officers giving them a right bollixing about handling loaded firearms. Explaining how dangerous they are."

"Well, Detective Constable, I cannot explain to you how serious this is. Get a full murder investigation team over from Saint-Malo: forensics, ambulance, police doctors, pathologist, photographers, and the most senior detective they have. Even though you seem to be doing a very thorough job yourself."

"Thank you, sir."

"Meanwhile, I'm coming up to Val André myself, by helicopter. And there is something you should know, because I do not wish anything to get out to the media, certainly for a few hours: Marcel and Raymond were the private bodyguards to Henri Foche."

"Jesus Christ," said Paul Ravel.

———— •◆• ————

Pierre Savary dialed the private cell phone of Henri Foche, and he spoke in his most measured tones. "Henri," he said, "I want you to drop everything you are doing immediately. And come over to my office on a matter of extreme urgency. Now."

The Gaullist leader knew a major problem when he heard one and asked Mirabel, his secretary, to drive him to the police headquarters. There, in his large but plain office, Pierre Savary told Henri Foche precisely what had happened, right from the beginning. He outlined the story of the bearded Swiss hijacker who had hurled two English fishermen over the side of their own trawler. He described the chase across the Channel, during which all the resources of English and French law enforcement were brought to bear on this elusive, murderously strong international criminal. He told Henri how the fishing boat *Eagle* had eluded the French coast guard, and how the man had somehow vanished. In Pierre's opinion, the boat had been scuttled. He told Foche how he, Pierre, had been sitting here through the night with Marcel before advising him to go to Val André and be on station when the Bearded One landed. And then he outlined how the bodies of the two security men had been discovered dead on the beach, having both been murdered, by "someone with the strength of a fucking grizzly bear."

Henri Foche was visibly shocked. The loss of his friend and most reliable confidant, Marcel, was a terrible blow to him, because he valued the hit man a lot more highly than he did his wife. He'd traveled miles and miles with Marcel, to all corners of France. He'd laughed with him, had dinner with him, and above all had relied on him 100 percent. And now he was gone, and by Christ someone was going to pay for that.

"Do we know yet whether this Swiss character actually did land at Val André?"

"Not yet. But I have a murder investigation team in there combing the entire town for clues. Sounds like he's a very ostentatious kind of a guy. People must have seen him."

"And if he got off a boat he would not have had transportation, eh?"

"Not unless someone was there to meet him," said Pierre.

"Let me ask you something, old friend," said Foche. "Do you think this guy has really come to kill me?"

"Well, we don't have anything in the way of hard evidence. But the coincidences are beginning to stack up in a rather unpleasant way. We get a very dependable warning that a high-priced assassin is being hired, another warning that he's liable to come from England. Then we get this desperado on the fishing boat, crossing the Channel, trying and succeeding to break into France with no passport or records. And then he proceeds to murder both of your personal bodyguards within about ten minutes of his arrival."

"I agree, *mon ami*," replied Foche. "You certainly couldn't love it."

"Especially as the fucker now seems to be on the loose, right here in France," said Pierre, "where he is able to read newspaper reports that pinpoint every move you make on a day-to-day basis."

"There was no sign that he either shot or stabbed my men, was there, no sign of a weapon?"

"Absolutely not. The only weapons were the revolvers belonging to Marcel and Raymond. And now it is obvious you must increase your personal security."

"I already had, as soon as we heard there may be an attempt on my life."

"But now Marcel and Raymond are dead, you must do something else."

"I already know what I'm going to do. I'm going to hire a private security firm. Because I cannot restrict my own movements. With this election coming up I have to address the people of this country—and no fourth-rate killer is going to prevent me from doing that."

"Actually, Henri, I have to correct you there. So far, we know of only four direct opponents this man has faced. Two of them he hurled into the middle of the English Channel, and the other two he took out with some kind of deadly unarmed combat. I'd put him at first rate, not fourth. Let's not start by underestimating him."

Foche nodded. "What strength of security do you think I need?"

"Four armed men to accompany you at all times. And you need men in the house, on duty outside your bedroom, inside and outside the front door. And your car, is it bulletproof?"

"Yes, it is. And would you get someone to drive it back for me, from Val André, that is?"

"No problem. Meanwhile, I'm going up to Val André right now. If I see anything of interest, I'll call you right away. I might even drive the car back myself."

"Thanks, Pierre. I'd appreciate that."

———•◆•———

Henri Foche was driven back to his campaign office. He retreated into his private room at the back of the operations room, and dialed the number in Marseille of Col. Raul Declerc.

The ex–Scots Guards officer saw the ID system kick up the number of the Foche campaign headquarters and picked up the phone immediately. He was, of course, delighted to hear the voice of the Gaullist candidate, because that could mean only one thing, cash. And Raul liked cash more than anything else in the world.

Foche told him he was proposing to bring Raul and his team on board for the duration of the campaign. He did not wish to relay the details of the two murders over the phone, but explained he thought it important they meet as soon as possible, in order that everything could be explained.

"Have you thought about money?" asked Raul.

"Yes. My police advisers think I should have four highly trained ex–Special Forces men, armed to the teeth, on duty twenty-four hours a day."

"I wouldn't dispute that, sir," replied Raul. "And we're looking at three months. That will cost me a minimum of five hundred thousand euros, because you're going to need ten of them on permanent duty or standby. They'll work shifts. I'll come myself as team leader, and there'll be substantial expenses. My price for the entire operation, everything included, will be one and a half million euros. Wouldn't touch it for less, especially as someone might get killed, hopefully not you, sir."

"I'll pay you one million up front. But if I should die, you will not receive the last half million, because you will have failed me."

"You want a floating commission of one-third, on a flat fee?" said Raul. "That's a harsh bargain."

"If I get killed, that will be somewhat harsher, for me, that is. And remember, if anything happens to me, your duties are over, and you walk off with a very large sum of money with no further expenses."

"Yes, I suppose so," replied Raul. "I accept the terms. But I want the full payment, and I will do everything in my power to ensure nothing happens to you. My staff will be top-of-the-line, ex-Legionnaires, ex–British SAS, two former Israeli Special Forces men."

"Can you get up here by tonight, then travel to Saint-Nazaire with me tomorrow?"

"I could by air, sir. Marseille to Rennes. Probably a private plane."

"No problem. On my account. Just get here. I'll have someone meet you at the airport. Call me back with an ETA."

———•◆•———

Pierre's police helicopter touched down on the beach at Val André at a quarter past eleven. It landed about twenty yards from where Mack Bedford had touched down five hours earlier. But Mack had landed on a lonely rural stretch of sand on the lovely northern coast of Brittany. Pierre found himself in something resembling a city riot. The entire population of the town seemed to be gathered, and the Saint-Malo police were fighting a losing battle trying to keep the murder site clear. The crowd kept pushing forward as if to find a better view of the action, even though there were large screens surrounding the little area where Marcel and Raymond had thumped down off the seawall, already dead.

Detective Constable Paul Ravel hurried over to meet the Brittany police chief as he stepped down from the helicopter. "Good morning, sir," he said. "I'm very glad you're here, because I think this is looking a bit more sinister than we first thought."

Pierre Savary, of course, knew precisely how sinister it was. He was also damn nearly certain the perpetrator of this crime was in France specifically for one objective—to assassinate Henri Foche. The coincidences were too compelling.

He offered his hand to Paul Ravel and said above the howl of the dying rotors that were still whipping up a sandstorm on the beach, "Let's get behind those screens and talk to the staff."

The two men walked to where the body of Raymond was being lifted into an ambulance. Marcel was still behind the screens, and Ravel and Savary walked over to talk to the police doctor who was still examining the body.

"Sir, this is a most unusual killing," said the doctor. "Both men died from badly broken necks, instant and terrible damage to the spinal cords. And I've found abrasions on the back area of the ears. All four, both men.

"If you want to take a look under that white cloth, sir, you'll also see that this man was more or less blinded. Basically, someone rammed something into his eyes and forced the eyeballs so far back almost every working part was ripped and destroyed."

"And then he broke his neck?"

"That's my reading of it, sir. Because it's doubtful he broke his neck and then bothered to blind what he must have known by then was a mere corpse."

"Agreed," said Pierre. "How about the other man? Tell me about his injuries."

"Sir, he had probably the worst broken arm I've ever seen, and I've done a lot of car wrecks. It was snapped in half, right at the elbow. It's hard to imagine the force required to break a big man's elbow that comprehensively. I doubt he would ever have had proper use of that arm again."

"Was it the right elbow?"

The doctor hesitated, and thought carefully. He then said, "Sorry, sir, just trying to get my bearings. Yes, it was the right elbow."

"I imagine he was carrying that gun in his right hand," said Pierre. "Paul, how far was the gun from the body when it was found on the beach? I think you mentioned five meters?"

"Yes, sir. It was exactly five meters. I had the kids walk back to where they picked it up, and the mark where it fell was in the sand, clear as daylight."

"I'd guess it came from up there by the seawall. Both the bodies and the gun made big indentations, correct?"

"Very much, sir. The bodies definitely fell off the top of the wall, and the gun flew down onto the beach from a similar height."

Pierre turned to the doctor. "I suppose there's no way of knowing which of the men died first?"

"Not really. But the bodies landed almost together, and I noticed the left leg of Raymond was under Marcel's hand. Which suggested that the man who had held the gun was first over the wall."

Pierre nodded and turned to Paul. "We should remember," he said, "there were two Frenchmen here, and I know they were both trained bodyguards detailed to protect Monsieur Foche. We know why they were here, and what they may have been doing. Either helping the police, for which they would not be thanked, or perhaps to ensure the threat to the life of their boss was . . . er . . . well, eliminated."

Paul looked extremely thoughtful. "Sir," he said, "you know a great deal more about this than I do. And I accept what you say is the gospel truth. Don't you think it's looking like the two bodyguards found themselves in some kind of a confrontation and came off worse?"

"That is precisely how it's looking," replied the chief of Brittany's police. "I already have a vision of a big black-bearded defendant standing in a French courtroom and explaining how these two men jumped him, and that he was in fear for his life, and was forced to fight them off."

Detective Constable Ravel looked quizzical. "Black-bearded?"

"Sorry. I didn't mean black-bearded like a pantomime villain. But the man the coast guard was seeking, the guy who stole the fishing boat and threw the crew members overboard, was officially described as a man with a big black beard."

"I just haven't had time to get into the details about the killer," replied Paul. "I think there's a briefing on the computer, and I'll get to it as soon as I can."

"That's probably a good plan," said Pierre Savary. "Because if we don't move fast, this character is going to be out of our area, and on the loose somewhere in France in search of the next president. Paul, we've got to find him. Soon as the second body is cleared out, put every available man into a search of Val André. Remember, we think the killer had no transportation, and he may still be here, hiding out, under someone's protection."

"Sir, I do not have the authority to instigate such a huge police action. I'm just a detective constable."

"Not now you're not. I'm making you up into a detective inspector right now. And I'm putting you in command of this case, with immediate effect. From this moment on, you answer only to me."

"Well, thank you, sir. I'll do the very best I can."

"Leave the formalities to me. I'll inform Saint-Malo personally."

"Yes, sir."

Pierre grinned at him. "Paul," he said, "I may not be the greatest police chief who ever lived, but I know about people. And this morning I have developed some very definitive opinions about two of them. You and this bastard who's after Henri Foche. We must find him, whatever the cost. Because if I'm any judge, this man is dangerous, skilled, smart, and determined."

"Sir," said Paul Ravel, "just one thing before you go. It looks to me as if this guy is a professional trained killer, very possibly military, maybe even Special Forces. I'd like to get a couple of experts to take a look at the bodies, check out the killing method, see if it rings any bells."

"Good idea. You have my permission. Go right ahead. Anything for a lead. Just don't take your eye off the ball. We have to find him."

"Okay, sir. And what do you want to do about Monsieur Foche's car?"

"Have someone drive it back to police HQ in Rennes. I'm sure I can count on you."

Pierre Savary was, of course, confirming that the Toulouse rugby scouts were not the only people who recognized a safe pair of hands when they saw them.

———— • ◆ • ————

Upon the departure of the police chief, Detective Inspector Paul Ravel, suddenly commissioned in the field, as it were, headed immediately to one of the cruisers. He picked up the open line to Saint-Malo and asked for two numbers to be located and then connected.

The first was to Direction Generale de la Securité Exterieure (DGSE), France's successor to the former internationally feared SDECE, the counterespionage service. DGSE was located in a bleak ten-story building over in the twentieth *arrondissement,* which is about as far west as you can go and still be in Paris. The second call was to one of the most secret compounds in the whole of Europe, the Commandement des Opérations Speciales (COS), the joint service establishment that controlled special ops conducted by all three of France's armed forces. COS was located in the outer suburb of Taverny, and is generally regarded as the home of the French equivalent to Great Britain's SAS, or the United States' Navy SEALs.

Ravel spoke to DGSE first, and immediately the duty officer went on high alert. This was clearly important. "We'll have someone come over to Saint-Malo right away. Are you also contacting COS?"

"My next call."

"Well, speak to the First Marine Parachute Infantry. And then tell them to get back to us. The guys can share a helicopter. What is it? 'Bout 220 miles to Saint-Malo?"

"Yeah. 'Bout that. One and a half hours' flying time."

"Tell Saint-Malo we'll be there by one thirty."

Paul Ravel called COS and explained the circumstances. They said they'd send over a military doctor who could provide an expert opinion on the method of killing. Yes, they'd pick up the DGSE guy en route. They'd land on the Saint-Malo police HQ roof.

"Good luck," said Paul Ravel. "It's sloping. Tell 'em to stick it on the beach."

The duty officer at COS chuckled. And said, "Don't worry, sir. We've landed in a lot tougher places than Saint-Malo *plage!* We'll get there."

Detective Inspector Ravel exited the cruiser and saw the final ambulance on its way out of Val André. Then he began to organize a house-to-house search for the missing killer, detailing as many as twenty police officers to operate road by road, but to start at the one where the Mercedes had been found.

He took two assistants with him and decided to concentrate on the question of transportation. There were few buses and no trains. No cars had been reported stolen, and that meant the suspect either had acquired one or was still in the vicinity. He could not possibly have tried to hire a taxi.

By this time there were several police cars parked near the beach, and the DI took one of them and drove through the village in search of a garage. He pulled up outside Laporte Auto, the only establishment of its kind for several miles, and asked to speak to the proprietor.

M. Laporte sensed trouble, and he was not about to delve deeper into it. Yes, very early this morning, around seven o'clock, there had been a customer in the garage, bought a dark blue Peugeot for cash. Yes, he seemed to be in a very great hurry, and wanted the car immediately. Yes, the registration documents were accurately completed, and yes, he, Monsieur Laporte, had seen the man's passport and license.

And did he have copies of the documents? *Absolutement.* In fact, he still had the originals, personally signed by the purchaser. Right here, *Gunther Marc Roche, 18 rue de Basle, Geneva, Switzerland.* The registration number of the car was also written down, plain as day.

"And what kind of a man was he?" asked Paul Ravel.

"He was tall. A powerful-looking man with long curly hair and a big black beard. Spoke in a strange accent; wore gloves all the time."

"Was the accent European?"

"It might have been. But it sounded more like a black man to me, and this person was white."

"Not Swiss—I mean German Swiss?"

"Not really. But he didn't say much. He just wanted to get the car paid for, and be on his way. He ripped me off sixty-two euros for petrol."

"But he paid for the car in banknotes, right?"

"Yes, he did. And I think he had a lot of them."

"Be careful with all that money lying around," said Ravel. "And if he happens to come back, call me at once."

"Okay, sir. But what has he done?"

"He's wanted for murder."

Monsieur Laporte stood wide-eyed as he watched the two policemen drive away, back to join their two dozen colleagues down at the beach. Once there, they switched on their onboard police computer and pulled up the background on the Swiss hijacker. Paul Ravel stared with some satisfaction at the screen. Big. Curly haired. Black beard. It tallied with M. Laporte's description. That was good. So was the new address. No one had that.

But the innate detective in the heart of Paul Ravel knew it was all bad. Because by seven thirty this morning the Swiss suspect was out of here, in a nice, reliable French car. That was almost six hours ago, and there was still no national alert to apprehend him.

Paul hit the button to the Brittany Headquarters and relayed the car's make and registration number. He understood that if the car had been making a steady 60 kilometers per hour, it could be darn nearly 300 kilometers away. That's 200 miles. He could already be in Paris, probably without the car. This wasn't just bad, it was actually diabolical.

Before he signed off, he added, "The suspicion that this man may be attempting to assassinate Henri Foche has become very real. Suggest extra vigilance in the Saint-Nazaire area where the Gaullist leader is due to speak tomorrow afternoon."

Paul's cell phone suddenly rang, and it was the station sergeant in Saint-Malo to say, "Sir, we have been informed by Rennes of your promotion. And everyone here congratulates you. This call is just to confirm that we will not be sending another detective inspector to join you in the investigation, because Monsieur Savary advised against it."

"Thank you, Freddie," said Paul. "See you later."

By the time he replaced the cell phone in his pocket, every police department in France was on the lookout for the dark blue Peugeot, but they were too late. Much too late.

The only break came at around one o'clock that afternoon when a Citroën, displaying the Peugeot's license plates, was pulled over on the N12, just north of Dinan. Since the numbers tallied precisely with the registration officially recorded in Monsieur Laporte's garage, the police assumed the make of car they had been given was inaccurate. And more to the point, they assumed the two plumbers driving it were guilty of some heinous crime.

The airwaves rippled with confusion. The plumbers were not believed. In fact, they were arrested and taken into the police department in Dinan, where they were questioned until it became obvious to everyone that their plates had been stolen. And that the dark blue Peugeot was at this moment charging through France bearing the Citroën's plates, with a possible assassin hunched over the wheel.

"Sacre bleu!" sighed Paul Ravel when the news was broken to him. "May I assume someone did update the nationwide search for the same car, just with different license plates?"

"Oh, sure," said the station sergeant in the kind of world-weary tone that comes when you know there are about ten thousand dark blue Peugeots out there, and that license plates are not that easy to read accurately in the oncoming darkness.

"Maybe they did, maybe they didn't," muttered Paul Ravel. "I'd better call Pierre Savary."

He punched in the same numbers that had located the Brittany police chief when they had first spoken. Pierre answered instantly. "Hello, Detective Inspector. What's moving?"

"Too little, sir. We picked up the right license plates on a southbound Citroën on the highway north of Dinan. Right plates, wrong car. Now we got two very angry plumbers in the Dinan station. Anyway, we now know the numbers on the Peugeot, so I hope we'll get a breakthrough sometime this evening."

"As the coast guard lost the fucking trawler, so my staff have lost the getaway car. Not a good day for us, eh, Paul?"

"Not really, sir. But we've still got chances. Every police officer in France is looking for that Peugeot."

"Do you know the time, Paul?"

"Yessir. It's one thirty."

"That would be six hours since Monsieur Roche drove out of Val André. He could be a very long way away by now."

"Yes, he could, sir. But I don't think so. I think he's somewhere along the road to Saint-Nazaire, biding his time, waiting for Monsieur Foche to arrive tomorrow afternoon."

"I can't disagree with that," replied Savary. "Keep me posted."

Paul switched off his cell phone and called for someone to drive him back the twenty miles to Saint-Malo. He arrived a little after two and asked to see the doctors from the French Special Forces as soon as they had completed their examination.

That had apparently not taken long. Both men, who had the military rank of colonel, were in agreement. The killer blow, which had killed both Marcel and Raymond, was a specialist neck break, as practiced, when absolutely necessary, by Britain's SAS, the U.S. Navy SEALs, and the French First Marine Parachute Infantry.

"Does this mean the man we are seeking must have served in one of those military organizations?" asked Paul.

"About 80 percent certain, yes," replied the doctor.

"How about the other 20?" said Paul.

"Well, I think the Israelis are capable of such extreme life-ending violence when necessary. But this stuff is really SAS, SEALs, and French First Marine. They train for this, and they're complete experts. I should also say the action requires enormous strength. Just imagine how hard you need to twist a man's neck with your bare hands to break it almost in half."

"Could he have whacked them with something—maybe a rifle butt or something?"

"Out of the question," said the doctor. "The necks of these men were snapped, using a method that would require them to be twisted first one way and then the other. One single twist would not have done it. This killer was a specialist—you can count on that. The abrasions behind the ears of the dead men confirm it."

"So he was probably British, American, or French?"

"Yes," replied the doctor. "I only mentioned the Israelis because we know there is a suspicion that the same man may be here to attack Henri Foche, and he has Middle Eastern connections."

"How do you know that?" asked Paul Ravel, smiling.

"You will discover in your new position, we almost always know more than anyone else," said the doctor.

"And how do you know this is my new position?"

"As above," smiled the man from COS.

"I have another question I hope you can help me with," said Paul Ravel. "I am disturbed by the way our killer decided to blind one of the two Frenchmen. Why would he bother?"

"That looks like a classic Special Forces reaction to an attack. It's the quickest, most deadly form of response. Render your enemy instantly blind, and then kill him. It was the same with the other guy, Raymond. Looks like he pulled a gun on our killer, who disarmed him by snapping his right arm in two, before killing him."

"So you believe Marcel and Raymond attacked him first?"

"Oh, no doubt, Inspector. And we also noticed the man with the broken arm had been kicked very severely in the balls. There's still fantastic swelling."

"And what does that mean?" asked Paul Ravel.

"I cannot be certain. But I will give you a professional opinion. Obviously, the man with the gun was leveling it at the Swiss hijacker, who reacted by breaking his arm and then slamming him in the balls with colossal force. That dropped attacker number one to the ground.

"By this time I'd say the second man had somewhat foolishly attacked to save his friend. He would have been no match for a trained Special Forces guy, who we both believe rammed his fingers into Marcel's eyes, then killed him instantly with the neck break."

"Jesus," breathed Paul. "And then?"

"Well, he plainly could not let Raymond live, perhaps one day to talk and identify him. So he killed him by the same method, and dumped both bodies over the wall and onto the beach."

"And who threw the gun over the wall?"

"No one. It just flew out of Raymond's hand when the killer snapped his arm, probably right on the edge of the wall."

"How the hell can you know all this—the reactions and methods of such men?"

"Well, Inspector, I used to be pretty good at it myself before I took up medical studies full-time."

"You served in the First Marine Parachute Infantry?"

"We both did. They don't recruit their doctors from just any old source, you know."

"Plainly not," laughed Paul. "And gentlemen, you have been extremely helpful. But one last thing—could a normal person have been taught to employ these tactics, perhaps by a friend who served in Special Forces?"

"Not a chance, sir. This stuff takes years to learn. And you really can only learn it by training endlessly with other such men. A normal person could not possibly have the strength, the skill, and above all the cold-blooded ruthlessness. Not to kill like that."

All three of them were silent for a few moments. Then the senior doctor said quietly, "Your man, Inspector, served in either the SAS, the U.S. Navy SEALs, or the First Marine Paras. I'd bet the farm on that."

Detective Inspector Ravel saw the two men out, inquiring, "Where are you parked?"

"On the beach, just as you said, sir. You need anything more, we'll be back in Paris two hours from now."

Ten minutes later, Paul heard the clatter of Aerospatiale's Alouette III swooping low over Porte St. Thomas, then heading due east, straight for the northern suburbs of the City of Light.

Paul sat in deep contemplation, wondering how his new information could possibly help him solve this double murder case. And after about five minutes of soul-searching, he decided it was essentially a blind alley.

He checked on his computer, Googled the SAS and the SEALs, and added up the number of serving personnel, combat troops trained in this level of violence. In Great Britain and the United States alone there were a few more than three thousand. In France he thought there were another one thousand maximum. If he took a ten-year assessment, there were probably around ten thousand such men in all the world, only four thousand of whom could be accounted for. The rest could be anywhere. And it was a million-to-one chance that any commanding officer would have a sudden memory flash identifying a former combatant who might have gone into France to murder the next president. And anyway the Americans and the Brits would not be so likely to tell him details about their most secretive personnel.

"This is fairyland," he murmured. "But I better call Pierre Savary and tell him the opinions of the doctors."

This took just a few minutes because the Brittany police chief realized it was a wild goose chase pursuing such avenues. Besides, there was so little time. "You're not planning to chase down the Special Forces commanders and question them, are you?" demanded Pierre.

"Absolutely not," replied Paul. "That would be a monumental waste of time. It's the type of stuff that would be damning evidence against a defendant charged with these murders in a court of law. You know, 'The guy once served in the SAS. He'd know how to do it,' etc. But it's never going to help us find him."

The more Chief Savary heard from Paul Ravel, the better he liked him. He said, "My thoughts precisely. Let's just concentrate on finding the goddamned car. Hopefully, the bastard will still be in it."

"I doubt that, sir. But when we find it, it will be the biggest break we've had so far. I'll stay right on it."

Pierre Savary liked the "when" rather than an "if." He liked that a great deal. His mood of mild self-congratulation ended, however, as soon as he put down his phone. Because it rang again, almost immediately, and he thought, correctly, there was an angry edge to the ring.

Henri Foche was not pleased. "Have your guys found this Peugeot yet?" he asked. "Because if they haven't, I am obliged to wonder, why the hell not?"

"Mostly because not one of the hundreds of police officers I have on the case has seen it. If anyone had, we'd probably have this Gunther character under lock and key."

"All I know is, first we have him trapped on a red fishing boat sixty-five-feet long a mile offshore, and he manages to vanish, with his boat. And then, with all the resources of one of the biggest, most modern police forces in Europe, we can't find his car."

"Well, Hans Blix couldn't find Saddam's atom bomb, but no one held it against him."

Henri Foche chuckled. He and Pierre Savary had known each other a long time. And he believed that if the Brittany boys could not find that car, then it was far away.

"You'll understand I'm getting slightly jumpy about all this," he said. "I mean, it's apparently me this character is trying to kill. And unless he's blind, he must now know I'm due to speak in Saint-Nazaire tomorrow afternoon."

"I'm sure he does, Henri," replied the police chief. "And I am afraid I have some even more alarming news for you—this Gunther Marc Roche is almost certainly a former member of the Special Forces, either the U.S. Navy SEALs, the British SAS, or the French First Marine Paras. We've called in military specialists from Paris. And they are quite certain Marcel and Raymond were killed by a highly trained member of such an organization. Just because no civilian could possibly have killed quite like that."

"Well, now that I am probably as good as dead, perhaps you can tell me if anyone is planning to do something about it."

"We are doing all that we can, Henri. You know that. And we have made progress. We know the guy's name and address; we have a description. We have his car number."

"Perhaps I should remind you, all four of those assets you just listed can change inside a very few minutes—his name, address, description, and car number. Right now we have almost nothing. Have the Swiss checked in about his address?"

"Not yet, Henri. I'll try to keep you up to date."

Even as they spoke, there was chaos on the rue de Basle in Geneva. Especially outside number 18. The police had decided to cordon off the busy street a few blocks west of the downtown area of Switzerland's greatest city. There were police cruisers at either end of the rue de Basle, positioned alongside ambulances, in case this confrontation became violent. No one knew whether Gunther Marc Roche was a member of a group of international assassins, all armed to the teeth.

When the police went in, they went in hard, fifteen of them, racing out of their cruisers and straight through the front door, machine guns raised. Which came as something of a shock to the three elderly ladies trying to draw their pensions in a local branch of Geneva Credit and Savings.

It was a relatively modest door on the street, and there had been no time to check what lay behind it. The Swiss police, rigid with embarrassment, put down their arms, and apologized for the intrusion. They did speak to the manager, who explained that the whole of the street-level floor was occupied by his bank and there were no apartments in the three floors above, just offices. No, he had never heard of anyone named Gunther Marc Roche.

The police conducted a routine search of the building, speaking to various secretaries and office managers, but this was not a residential building, no one lived here, and the entire fictitious credentials of Gunther Marc Roche were blown dramatically over the Alps in about twenty minutes.

The head of the Geneva Police Department only just stopped himself from firing off a memorandum to the French police in Brittany, warning them to be much more careful in the future about wasting his valuable time. He did not even bother to send a standard police report about the "raid." He simply sent an e-mail to Detective Inspector Paul Ravel, confirming there was no Gunther Marc Roche at 18 rue de Basle, and neither was there anyone else. Number 18 was just a regular small office block, no residents.

The signal from Geneva gave Paul Ravel no comfort. It only confirmed what he already knew, that this trained killer from the SAS, or somewhere like it, was a master of deception. Monsieur Laporte had been definite; he'd seen the passport and driver's license.

In his heart he believed this investigation would soon switch its base to Saint-Nazaire. He was nearly certain that's where "Gunther"

CHAPTER 11

Mack reached the coastal town of Vannes in the early afternoon, roughly around the time when Detective Inspector Paul Ravel was discovering the Swiss hijacker had almost certainly served in the Special Forces. Mack had no idea how much the French authorities now knew about him, whether they had discovered the scuttled *Eagle,* and whether Monsieur Laporte had shot his mouth off to the gendarmes.

As far as he could tell, there was little else to link him to any kind of crime. The key was Laporte, and if the garage owner had handed over details of the Peugeot, it meant that the French police had by now organized a nationwide dragnet to hunt him down. However, they were looking for the wrong number plates. Mack glanced at his watch and decided that if the bodies had been found around nine o'clock, Laporte would have been cooperating very soon afterward, and anytime now the police would be picking up the two guys in the Citroën. Which meant they would soon know the replaced plate numbers on the Peugeot, and despite the fact he was yearning for a cup of coffee, Mack hit the gas pedal, and drove on hard toward Saint-Nazaire, another forty-two miles.

He arrived on the outskirts of the shipbuilding city at three o'clock and took a quick tour around the main streets in order to establish his bearings. He found what he was looking for, a large hardware store, and then a central public parking garage. He drove very carefully down the slope of the latter, looking for the closed-circuit television cameras.

Taking his ticket from the machine, he deliberately drove the wrong way, against the white-painted floor arrows, and hoped to hell no one came the other way. At the end of the line there was a wide circular ramp leading down to the lower level. He took that, and again drove the wrong way down the lines of parked cars.

He found a space, parked the Peugeot for the last time, and retrieved his toolbox and bag from the trunk. He checked again the closed-circuit cameras, and was confident none of them was aimed at the Peugeot. Using his trusty screwdriver, he swiftly removed the license plates, locked the car, and left.

On the upper level he tossed the plates and the keys into a trash bin, which was lined with a black plastic bag, and counted on his luck that no one would ever search it. And then he left, carrying his toolbox and leather bag, abandoning the car for which half the police patrols in France were searching: the one parked in a remote corner on the lower level, away from the cameras. The one with no plates.

Mack knew where he was going. And he was in a major hurry to get away from that car. No one knew what he looked like, or who he was. But they knew about that Peugeot. It thus took a considerable amount of self-control to hang around near the entrance for almost twenty minutes until the attendant was heavily engaged with another driver, who had perhaps mislaid his ticket.

At that point Mack, who still looked like Jeffery Simpson, walked very quickly up the slope and out into the busy streets of Saint-Nazaire. It took him ten minutes to locate the hardware store, and he wasted no time once he was inside. He found the area where regular tools were sold, hammers, wrenches, chisels, pliers, and so on. At the end of the display he found a shelf stacked with both gardener's and workman's boots and overalls. Green and blue. And the blue was the shipyard blue, the same as he had seen in the picture in *Le Monde.*

Keeping his driving gloves tightly on, Mack selected XXL overalls and a pair of the largest black work boots. He then moved to the elec-

trical area and chose a small, powerful flashlight, a slim pocket calculator, and three small batteries. Just along the aisle was the sporting
goods section, which offered shotguns (all padlocked), fishing rods
and knives, and some clothing, including green gum boots, socks,
caps, and belts. He chose a sheathed fishing knife, one cap, and two
pairs of socks.

He moved to the counter to pay and pushed the knife into one of
the boots. He stuck a pair of socks into each boot, and paid for everything except the knife, which the shop assistant did not notice. On his
way out he gave the cap and socks back, slipping them onto their original shelves, which he considered to be a fair exchange.

There was a sense of relief in his mind as he left the store. For several
days now he had been essentially unarmed, except for the sniper rifle,
which, in an urgent situation, would of course be hopelessly too slow.

Mack was not used to being unarmed. He never went into combat
without at least a service revolver and a knife, and while this French
operation was rather different from his normal SEAL missions, he
needed something. Mack was happy to face two assailants with machine guns, just so long as he had a decent blade with which to . . .
well . . . in a way . . . defend himself.

But he did not need some assistant to be telling the French police a
tall foreigner had just purchased a potentially lethal fishing knife in
the Saint-Nazaire hardware store. Thus the elaborate deception at the
counter, where the girl had been friendly and only too happy to give
him some two-euro coins instead of a banknote.

He stuffed the knife, overalls, boots, and electronics into his bag and
walked on to a newspaper store, where he purchased a detailed street
map of Saint-Nazaire. Then he found a coffee shop, and settled at a
corner table to study the lay of the land. He lingered for only ten minutes, purchased a *jambon et fromage* baguette with a bottle of Perrier
water, and then went outside. He flagged down the first taxi he saw and
asked for the bus station at Saint-Brevin-des-Pins on the south bank
of the river, a distance of almost four miles.

It was only when they set off on the two-mile-long span of the
Saint-Nazaire Bridge, to cross the Loire, the greatest river in France,

that Mack fully appreciated just how wide the estuary was. Looking back both left and right he could see the enormous sprawl of the ship-yards on the north bank. He thought of the sunlit tidal waters below and the task that almost certainly would face him tomorrow night. When they reached the bus station he paid the driver and climbed out, holding the toolbox and the bag.

Immediately, he walked over to the departure schedules that were displayed in huge glass cases on one wall. There were two or three people making similar checks on the frequency of the service, and Mack had to wait to get a clear run at the listings for the evening buses to nearby Nantes. The times were not important. The regularity of the service was.

When he had finished this minor detail, he went in search of a public telephone and checked the directory for the number of the railroad station in the city of Bordeaux. Using his euro coins, he made the call, a simple inquiry to find out what time the last train from Nantes arrived in Bordeaux.

À douze heures et demie, monsieur. Gare St. Jean, à Cours de la Marne.

"Et départe Nantes?" struggled Mack.

Huit heures et demie.

"Merci beaucoup, madame," replied Mack, and then to himself, *Eight thirty Nantes. Jesus, I'd better not miss that bus.*

He walked out of the bus station secretly pleased he had assessed the transportation problems between here and Nantes, bus and train, without making a telltale phone call or speaking to anyone in Nantes about his requirements. There would be nothing anyone could ever remember, even under searching police questioning, about a foreigner trying to leave the city.

And then he set off along the road that ultimately ended up in Nantes, forty-two miles away. But Mack was going only two miles. He kept walking until he broke free of the houses and came to a long wooded area on the right-hand side of the road, with the river to his left. He reached a bus stop and waited. Not for a bus, but for the road to be clear of traffic and pedestrians. There was very little of either, and after five minutes he suddenly turned right and went straight into the woods.

There he established a small private camp, well out of sight of the road, and, so far as he could tell, everyone else. He explored the trees around him on a hundred-yard radius and decided he was safe. He selected a bush with wide fronds and eased his way underneath. There he ate the baguette, drank some water, and checked the time. It was almost five o'clock.

Using his new knife, he began to dig out a shallow hole sufficiently large to contain his leather bag. When he'd completed this, he pulled out his black wet suit and stripped down to his undershorts. Carefully, he pulled on the trousers and then the close-fitting top, keeping the hood rolled down. Then he took out his two oversized SEAL flippers and clipped one on each thigh.

He unpacked his new overalls and pulled them on, over the wet suit, fastening the buttons and stuffing a pile of euros into his pockets. He put on the work boots, fastened the laces, and slipped his new combat knife, sheathed, into one slim side pocket of the overall trousers. Into the other he placed his flashlight and the calculator.

Then he hollowed out more dry dirt from the hole and made sure everything was packed into his leather bag—street clothes, passports, licenses, cash, and Perrier water—and pushed it down, before covering it with earth. He then cut two bushy branches and arranged them to obscure the disturbed surface completely, with the two cut stems rammed into the ground.

He checked his watch and waited for the 6:15 bus to arrive at "his" stop. He heard the doors open and then heard it pull away along the road to Nantes. Three minutes later, he grabbed the toolbox, wriggled free of the bushes, and headed back to the riverside road.

Hot in the wet suit–overalls combination, his heart unaccountably pounding, Mack Bedford was nonetheless ready to go.

———— • ◆ • ————

Henri Foche's Mercedes, now being driven by one of the missile men from Montpellier Munitions, collected "Colonel" Raul Declerc from

Rennes Airport at six o'clock and drove him directly to the home of the Gaullist leader.

It was a day when things had moved extremely rapidly, and Raul was obviously shocked at the pure brutality of the two murders. He had never served with Britain's Special Forces, and although he had heard many a tale of their ruthless execution of duty, and anyone who got in the way, he had not experienced anything this close to home, as it were.

The first thing that crossed his mind, unsurprisingly, was cash, and he wondered, very sincerely, if he had charged Foche sufficiently. A million euros was one thing, but grappling with this apparent monster from the black lagoon was entirely another.

But Raul had a sense of duty, and he understood he had pursued, and then struck a deal with, the man who would become the next president of France. Foche was a man who had a slightly shady background, and in the opinion of the former Colonel Fortescue, he was not a man to be fooled with. In Raul's view, an angry Foche might prove pretty damn similar to an angry Gunther Marc Roche. *Christ, even their names are similar,* thought Raul, who was unaware of the pantomime on Basle Street that day, which almost certainly rendered the Swiss killer nonexistent.

At least that was the current opinion of the French police. Pierre Savary had called his friend Henri to express it a couple of hours ago. He did not think it meant the black-bearded hijacker/assassin was nonexistent. There was too much hard, widespread evidence for that, from Brixham to Val André. But the name was false, the address was false, and that Swiss driver's license, recorded by Monsieur Laporte much earlier that morning, was also false.

"The man is obviously real," said Foche, "but we have no idea who he is. The police think it unlikely he is Swiss."

"As you know, sir, my own opinion is that the threat comes from England, and there is a fair chance the killer is English," offered Raul.

"But there are several people in England who swear to God he spoke in a very foreign accent."

"Sir, I could speak in a very foreign accent if I so wished."

"Yes, I suppose so. But let us look to the future. How do you and your team intend to protect me from this assassin?"

"Right now I am assembling them in Marseille. My two SAS men are flying in from central Africa. Both of them served with the British in Sierra Leone. Two of the best Israeli commanders I ever met are leaving Tel Aviv tomorrow morning. I have five ex–French Foreign Legion commanders. All of them have seen active service in North Africa. I intend to place a steel cordon around you, sir. A cordon of armed men ready to shoot on sight any assailant who sticks his head above the parapet."

Henri Foche liked the sound of that. "And what do you intend to do about tomorrow afternoon's speech in Saint-Nazaire? Can you be assembled by then?"

"Sir, you have explained to me how this Gunther character has so far given everyone the slip. And right now with every police officer in the city searching for him, he still hasn't shown up in Saint-Nazaire. Since he has only been in France for less than a day, we might be overreacting about tomorrow. I'd be surprised if he could get himself organized in under forty-eight hours for a serious attempt on your life. Those ex–Special Forces men are notoriously long-winded about detail. We in the regular old British regiments always think them a little slow."

"Oh, really," replied Foche. "Well, that's encouraging, but I will not cancel Saint-Nazaire. It's too important, both for me and for the people of southern Brittany."

"I will of course have a substantial part of our plan in operation, if you are concerned."

"Which part?"

"The Foreign Legionnaires and the SAS men can fly directly from Marseille to Saint-Nazaire. I do not think the Israelis can get here in time, even if I divert them via Paris. Besides, they'll need a briefing, and there won't be time, if you want us to go operational as early as possible tomorrow."

"That means you will have eight men, including yourself?"

"That will constitute your personal bodyguard, sir. Men whose only task is to watch for danger. Men who are trained to do it."

"I will naturally have state-provided security all over the shipyard," said Foche. "Probably a busload of them. But they are not specialists. They are merely numbers to provide an intimidating presence."

"Sir, I need to ask you about the chain of command."

"As my new chief of security you will exercise total control over all personnel except for the French police. They will be under the command of my close friend Pierre Savary, the chief of police in Brittany. But tonight the three of us will dine together, and I am certain you and he will work as a team."

"No problem, sir. Who will travel with you from Rennes to Saint-Nazaire tomorrow afternoon?"

"I would prefer you and your men to be in the shipyard as early as possible. Therefore, I will arrive later under police escort. Probably two cruisers, front and rear of my own car, plus two motorcycle outriders in the lead, and two others behind the last police car."

"That sounds fine. Because I need time in that shipyard, combing every inch of it. Even though I consider it so unlikely that this Gunther is going to be in there. I think it's far more likely he will attempt to strike two or three days later, when he's organized."

"Well, it's in the papers every day," replied Foche. "I'm speaking in Brest at two different locations on Wednesday, and in Cherbourg in three different locations on Thursday. On Friday I have business to attend to in Orléans, but on Saturday I have a major Gaullist rally to address in Rouen."

"He's got a lot of choices," said Raul. "If he's serious. But I'd be looking hard at Cherbourg. It's a Channel port, with easy local access to the ferry back to England."

"I just have a feeling, Raul, that our lives would be so much simpler if the police could locate his car."

"I agree. It would at least mark his trail for us. Right now the bastard could have gone in any direction. Saint-Nazaire, Brest, Cherbourg, anywhere. Even Rouen."

———•◆•———

It was seven o'clock, just as Mack Bedford turned onto the north-bound walkway over the gigantic Saint-Nazaire toll bridge, when the French police got their first break. The incoming night attendant at the parking garage noticed the Peugeot. On a normal evening, be-tween five o'clock and six, there was a mass departure of cars owned by shoppers and businesspeople. This usually left the lower level al-most bereft of vehicles. And the new man always walked down to see what was still parked. If there was nothing, he cordoned it off with heavy wooden barricades, thus restricting his duties to one single level. Tonight there was just the Peugeot, and he strolled down the line to check it out.

The first thing he noticed, of course, was that it had no plates. So he walked back up to his kiosk and phoned the security line direct to the head office of Français Nationale Parking in Paris. It took him just a few moments to report: *suspicious car, dark blue Peugeot, no registra-tion plates, parked on its own, deep in the underground section, Place des Martyrs de la Resistance, Saint-Nazaire, Brittany.*

The duty officer thanked him and punched the information into the computer link, sending the warning instantly to the antiterrorist desk at the Prefecture de Police on the Quai Marche Neuf on the banks of the Seine River. Automatically, the e-mail ripped through cyber-space into the police headquarters at Rennes, with a copy arriving si-multaneously in the Saint-Nazaire Commissariat de Police.

The antiterrorist men in Paris immediately requested Saint-Nazaire to investigate, while the duty officer in Rennes almost had a heart at-tack since he'd heard nothing but the words "dark blue Peugeot" for as long as he could remember.

Every available city police patrol was ordered to the garage on Place des Martyrs. Four of them arrived within five minutes, and a bomb disposal squad from Nantes had already been dispatched.

Because of the shipyard's close proximity to the town, the Saint-Nazaire police had a number of resident experts in the field of high explosives. Every last one of them was ordered to Place des Martyrs. They swarmed all over the garage, surrounding the Peugeot. But it took an hour to establish that the vehicle was clean, and not in any way likely to blast the city to smithereens.

The police then drove a tow truck into the garage, and hauled the Peugeot out onto the street and on to the station, where they were tasked with finding out whether it was indeed the one sold to Mr. Gunther Marc Roche in faraway Val André that eventful morning.

They opened the door with a master key and permitted the forensic department to search every inch for fingerprints. There were none. But under the hood they located the chassis number, and checked in with Monsieur Laporte that it matched the official registration certificate he still had in his possession. This was the car. This was the vehicle purchased by the bearded hijacker, who was wanted for two murders in Val André, and was suspected of intent to murder Monsieur Henri Foche.

The head office of Brittany Police telephoned the home of Monsieur Foche to impart the gravest possible news to his dinner guest, Pierre Savary. . . . *Sir, the Peugeot has been found. It's in Saint-Nazaire.*

"Jesus Christ!" As far as Pierre was concerned, the roof just fell in. He walked back into the dining room, where Raul and his host were sipping superb burgundy, Corton-Bressandes Grand Cru from the Domaine Chandon de Briailles. He apologized for the interruption but felt that everyone needed to know the dark blue Peugeot had been located in a public parking garage in Saint-Nazaire, the license plates removed.

"That, Henri, heightens the danger tomorrow, probably by about 1,000 percent," said Pierre. "Because that Peugeot means that Gunther, or whoever the hell he is, is headed for the fucking shipyard, which is only about eighteen miles long with about thirty-seven thousand places to hide."

Pierre paused, and then said gravely, "I am asking you to call the Saint-Nazaire speech off."

Henri Foche stared at him, betraying just a little of the character that may one day make him an extremely effective president of France. His expression was serious, but his eyes were blazing. "Nothing," he said, "nothing in this world, would persuade me to call off that speech. This is my homeland, I am from Brittany, these are my people. And a very great deal is expected of me. There are hundreds of jobs in that shipyard, hundreds of men dependent on those jobs. I am going to Saint-Nazaire to assure them personally that when I reach the Elysée Palace, those jobs are safe. That there will be work, ships to build, French ships for French workers, for French families. Nothing, and I repeat nothing, will be made for my government, either civilian or military, beyond the international borders of France. That's my slogan, that's my belief, those are the words written on my heart. Those are the words that will carry me to victory."

"*Vive la France,*" grunted Pierre. "Hopefully not in a hearse."

"Ignore him, Raul," said Foche. "What's your view?"

"I'm afraid I'm instinctively with Pierre," said the former British colonel. "That you should not go. But I understand that is not an option. So we'd better fight the war we're in rather than the one we'd like to be in. And the first thing we ought to ensure is you have the absolute maximum security in terms of numbers. By that I mean government troops, and every police officer they can draft in . . . "

Pierre pushed back his chair and stood up. "I'm calling Homeland Security right now. If I have to, I'll speak to the president. But we're not going to come up shorthanded in Saint-Nazaire."

He left the room again, and Henri Foche continued to question his new chief of security. "No more clues about this Morrison, I suppose."

"Not really. I have had another word with our Central Africa chief, a former British army major, very reliable, and he had a slim lead via Alabama in the American South. But it was only a vague contact, no number, and he was not dealing with a principal. It turned out to be just a blind alley."

"We've had quite a few of those today," said Foche. "Do we have an overall strategy?"

"It's a very simple and safe one. I will have seven of my men, plus myself, watching every relevant inch of that shipyard, every window and doorway, every potential hiding place, every rooftop, every gantry, every half-finished hull. If he's there, we'll stop him. Each one of my guys will be assigned a specific area to check, recheck, and check again. And remember, sir, every last one of them is as ruthless a killer as he is."

Henri Foche nodded. He missed Marcel, but this man from Marseille was making an excellent attempt to replace him.

"One more question, sir. Should one of my men locate him, his orders will be shoot to kill. If we do take someone out, do you anticipate any trouble with the French police? Because there may be no time to do anything else."

"No trouble whatsoever. You will earn their undying gratitude."

"And—I have to ask this—what if there should be a mistake? An innocent person is injured in the general melee? Does that represent trouble with the police?"

"Only if they would all like a massive pay cut when I become president," replied Foche with a wry grin.

Even the slightly fraught Raul had to smile at this naked use of overwhelming power.

"And finally, sir, I must ask about money. I am already incurring heavy expenses, flying the guys in. When do I see the first million?"

"How about Wednesday morning? Right here in Rennes. Before we leave for the shipyards in Brest."

Raul tried not even to think about the possibility of death tomorrow afternoon. He replied, "Perfect, sir. That will suit me very well."

At this point Pierre Savary returned to finish his dinner and his wine. "It's settled, Henri," he said. "The president has ordered a thousand security forces into the Saint-Nazaire region tomorrow morning. I have told them there will be a briefing from myself and Raul at 2:00 P.M. I'm assuming you will arrive at 4:45."

"Correct," replied the politician.

———— •◆• ————

By 8:30 P.M. Mack had been walking the streets for ninety minutes. He had located the big main gates and the tall steel framework that proclaimed right across the top in letters of cast iron: *SAINT-NAZAIRE*

MARITIME. There was a poster outside announcing the speech of Monsieur Henri Foche late the following afternoon. But it warned: *Restricted Entry—Shipyard Staff Only.*

Mack read it on the run, not wishing either to stop or to be noticed in any way by the gate men. He had established his bearings, and was about to establish his base. But first he went into a delicatessen and purchased a baguette, a salami, sliced cheese, and a pack of butter, plus two bottles of Perrier in the lighter plastic containers.

About three hundred yards along the street from the main shipyard entrance there was a bright, inexpensive restaurant, and at nine o'clock Mack set himself up at a window table, placed the toolbox under the chair, and ordered his dinner.

It was impossible to look more unobtrusive. He was plain in his shipyard overalls and boots, like everyone else. He gave the appearance of a mild-mannered, quietly spoken, fair-haired man, wearing rimless spectacles to read the afternoon newspaper. He could easily have been an electrical engineer, or even a sonar or radar specialist. But not a laborer. Definitely not a laborer.

There was, so far as he could see, no mention of the two men murdered in Val André. But there was a story speculating on the level of security being put into place for the visit of Henri Foche to Saint-Nazaire the following day. Readers were warned to expect roadblocks and delays throughout the afternoon.

Accepting the proprietor's advice, Mack ordered a fillet of sole, off the bone, with french fries and spinach. He ate slowly, impressed with that special touch the French manage to give their cooking, from the highest level down to . . . well . . . this, a workmen's café, outside a shipyard. It was delicious, as was almost every other morsel he had tasted since he'd arrived with such a thunderous, if accidental, impact fourteen hours ago. *The bastards were going to kill me,* he pondered. *And Tommy wouldn't have liked that.*

Up 'til now, there'd been no time to work out how the French were on to him with such alacrity. He understood the coast guard was only reacting to an SOS from their British counterparts, that someone had made off with the *Eagle.*

Those two characters carrying loaded revolvers in Val André were not in the police or the coast guard, but they were expecting me, they knew my name, and their task was to get rid of me. Well, who the hell were they? Either the French police or the coast guard had tipped someone off, because I should have faced just instant arrest, not a couple of dodgy hit men ready to gun me down.

Mack pondered the problem. And he came up with only one answer. Someone must have tipped off Henri Foche that a highly dangerous character was coming in from England, with orders to assassinate him. There was no other explanation.

The two guys I took out must have been paid by Foche. And the only man in all the world who could possibly have alerted him to the danger was that scheming little prick Raul. It must have been him. No one else knew, except Harry. Raul tells Foche there's a threat; the coast guard tells Foche, here he comes. Simple, right?

Mack was secretly rather pleased with his powers of deduction. He sat in the window of the dockside café, wondering what the hell he would face, if he made it into the shipyard tonight.

Outside there were intermittent groups of workers leaving the yard and walking along the street, almost all of them dressed like him. Some even carried toolboxes like his, but few, he guessed, had the interior lined with black velvet.

Mack believed this yard was probably as big as Bath Iron Works, and he felt certain there would be a major shift change taking place at ten or ten thirty. He ordered coffee, a double espresso with sugar, and sat quietly sipping.

At ten minutes before ten he pulled out his toolbox and attempted to fit his assorted food from the deli into the lower section with the Draeger. But it was hopeless. The butter could just about sit on top of the bullets, but the baguette was longer than the rifle barrel and the salami was too thick to slip alongside the stock.

He settled for the big brown bag he had been given at the deli, but put one of the bottles of Perrier in a pocket of his overalls, thus reducing the size of his package. But now he could see workers heading toward the shipyard rather than away from it, and noted several of them carried both toolbox and food for the night shift. There would be nothing unusual about him. He stood up from the table, paid his bill, and stepped outside, ready to join the next large group heading in for the long night ahead.

The street was quite busy now, ten times busier than it had been all evening. This was a shift change, no doubt. Workmen were leaving the yard as others came streaming in, and initially Mack joined those who were leaving, watching for a sizable group coming the other way. The men he walked with were cheerful and speaking to each other, and Mack knew it was only a matter of time before someone spoke to him. He kept his head down, lingered at the back of the group, then dropped his package. He bent down to retrieve it, but when he straightened up he was facing the other way. Quickly, he drifted into a pack of maybe a dozen workers, all walking resolutely toward the big shipyard gates. This crowd was more silent, and they were not together, just guys going to work, to the same place, tonight, like every night.

He noticed that of the twelve, five were carrying metal toolboxes, two of them like his. Seven had plastic lunch boxes, four of them paper bags from a deli or supermarket. He placed himself in the rear center of the group, with seven men in front of him, the others surrounding him. One of the leading group was talking, but no one else.

As they approached the gate, Mack suddenly noticed a police cruiser, blue lights flashing, parked just inside. Two policemen were talking to a uniformed security man.

They reached the gates and veered left toward the small guardhouse. Two more armed security men were on duty. One of Mack's group called, "Ça va, Louis!"—and the guard responded, "Bonsoir, Gérard." They were not checking the men on the night shift, the regular, familiar workforce, but Mack guessed they would have instantly apprehended a stranger wearing "civilian" clothes, and demanded to know his business.

The group kept walking, straight into the yard, tightening up to avoid others whose shift was finished and were now headed home. Ahead of them was a vast concourse, surrounded by tall buildings, and the men began to separate, heading in different directions, the electricians, the shipwrights, the marine engineers, the laborers.

It was dark but well lit, and Mack could make out the electronics area, the machine shops, and the obvious administration block. Looking right ahead down to the water he could see three enormous drydocks, sprawling along the edge of the deep tidal basin where ships were launched. The outline of an oceangoing freighter was plain on the jetty. Brand new, Mack guessed, about ten thousand tons.

The drydocks were as big as aircraft hangars, like gigantic shoe boxes, with the end closest to the water open to the elements. The trouble with ships is they have to float, and the only way to get them in and out of such docks is to flood them down, bring the ship in, and then pump out the water. The floors of the docks were thus twenty feet lower than sea level.

High up on each structure was a line of windows fifteen feet in depth. Mack could see two of the three were brightly lit, signifying work in progress. The third was dark, one of only two structures in this central part of the complex that showed no lights.

About twenty yards beyond the main gate, Mack could see the stage, the same one he had seen in the newspaper picture. It was like an open-air theater, the main speaker's platform about four feet off the ground. Above the lectern he could now see the same banner they had slung across the street in Val André. *HENRI FOCHE—POUR LA BRETAGNE, POUR LA FRANCE.*

Directly ahead, in front of the stage, was the other unlit building, a tall structure that looked like either a warehouse or workshops. Mack counted ten stories. There were double doors on the front, and high above some kind of gantry that housed an obvious lifting device. Directly below it, on two of the highest floors, there were wide doors with a platform, designed for dispatching and receiving heavy loads. In Mack's view this almost certainly made it a warehouse.

The concourse was still very busy, but it was approaching ten thirty, and Mack guessed he had about five more minutes to recce the place. After that everyone would have left for the workshops, drydocks, and ships' interiors.

Still in the general melee of the shift change, he walked to the front of the podium, and then, trying to look casual, he paced out the distance to the front wall of the warehouse. He made it 121 yards. And now he turned, walked along the front of the wall, and turned right into a dark throughway to the rear of the building. The blacktop ended at a low two-foot wall, beyond which was an eight-foot drop to the water. On two sides of this man-made square harbor, ships were moored, but at this, the far end, there was nothing, just the back wall of the warehouse. He estimated it was around 300 yards across the harbor waters to the end of the seawall, on which was a flashing red light, marking the entrance to incoming vessels. Mack muttered the old seaman's mantra—*Red, Right, Return*—meaning, keep the red buoys on your starboard side incoming. The route out of the harbor was thus to the right-hand side of the red light, not the left.

There was no one around in this part of the yard, at least no one Mack could see. Way out beyond the red light, he could see a ship steaming up the estuary, but it was too dark to see whether it was a freighter, tanker, ferry, or yacht.

Mack slipped along the side wall of the warehouse until he reached a single door that looked like some kind of a fire escape. Gingerly, he twisted the handle and slightly to his surprise it opened. The reason for this apparent lack of security was simple: (a) the warehouse was in full view of the guardhouse, 140 yards away; (b) various foremen may have wanted something from it urgently during the long night shift; and (c) the heavy-duty, cumbersome stuff in here was not the kind of gear anyone in their right mind would want to steal and then attempt to walk past the gate men. As a matter of fact, the big double front doors of the warehouse were not locked either.

Mack softly shut the door behind him, pulled out his flashlight, and inspected the area. He found himself in some kind of a stairwell, with stone steps leading upward. In front of him was a steel door, with a large handle that looked like a spare part from a submarine. Mack quietly opened it, and cast a beam of light around the huge room in which he now stood. All around were shelves containing marked boxes, stacked high, ships' components. Mack slipped back into the stairwell and clicked the door shut behind him.

Still holding the toolbox and food parcel, he climbed the stairs to the second floor, where there was another steel door, same type of ship's handle. Painted on the steel were the words, *SAM FITTINGS AND COMPONENTS: 0800–1600.*

Mack had no desire to linger in the surface-to-air missile department, so he kept going up, climbing the stone stairs, checking the notices painted on each door: electronics, sonars, radar, Exocet launchers. Finally, on the sixth floor, he found something more promising. The notice was stuck over the previous lettering. It read: *Freight Assigned. No Cargo.* At which point Lt. Cdr. Mackenzie Bedford pushed open the door and, using his flashlight, surveyed a totally empty room, surrounded by high shelves containing absolutely nothing. He closed the door behind him and rammed the handle into the locked position. Out through the front window he had a clear view of the podium. It was three minutes before eleven.

———— • ◆ • ————

Back in Brittany's capital city of Rennes there was a frenzy of journalistic activity. News of the two men murdered on the seafront at Val André was out, despite the efforts of the police to keep the lid on it for the moment. The story broke early in the evening, as it was bound to, with the entire population of Val André speaking of practically nothing else: the legions of police, the cruisers, the flashing blue lights, the ambulances, the helicopter on the beach, the gunshots, the broken windows. *Zut alors! C'est formidable!*

The local stringer for *Le Monde* in Rennes was Étienne Brix, and he'd made his routine afternoon call to the police department at around five thirty. He'd been doing this for more than three years, and he had a few friends among the officers. One of them, a young sergeant of around the same age, late twenties, tipped him off. No details, no clues, just, "Why don't you check what was going on up at Val André today? Can't tell you anything else."

Étienne checked. What was going on? Everything in the goddamned world was going on. He called the local pharmacy, announced himself as the representative of *Le Monde,* and for his trouble received a chapter-and-verse, blow-by-blow account of what appeared to be a double murder. The pharmacist had been right there on the beach when the bodies were removed, and he was proud to recount his firsthand experiences. He knew about the kids and the gunshots, and he knew about the sheer volume of the police presence. He also knew that Monsieur Laporte of the local garage was involved. He'd seen police cars there twice that afternoon.

Étienne, like any good reporter, went straight for the ambulance staff, requesting that the Saint-Malo Station inform him of any deaths that had occurred that day. Such information, all over the Western world, is public. You can't hide death, not when paid public servants, like ambulance paramedics, are involved.

Ten minutes later, Étienne had the names and addresses of the deceased Marcel and Raymond tucked into his notebook. Both were residents of Rennes. He also wanted to know the causes of death, but the ambulance staff did not know, and would only confirm there was damage to Marcel's eyes and that Raymond appeared to have a broken arm.

Étienne jumped into his car and just before six thirty came flying into the Rennes Police Department with a heavy set of demands. No, he did not wish to speak to the station sergeant. He was the official representative of the biggest newspaper in France, and he wanted to speak to a senior detective inspector. Pronto.

The station sergeant was worried, but he asked Étienne the nature of his inquiry before he would consent to call the senior man in the entire building.

Étienne replied, "I am inquiring about the murders of two men in Val André this morning. I have their names and addresses, and they are both from Rennes. But I sense a deliberate attempt at a cover-up by this police department, and, as you know, murder in this country is a public matter. Unless you want *Le Monde* on your case, in a very big way, you'd better get someone out here fast."

The station sergeant did not like being spoken to in that manner, but he knew trouble when he heard it. Without a word he went to the office of Detective Inspector Varonne and explained the drama currently being acted out in the front office.

Varonne was not pleased. "I was taken off this case before it started," he said. "I understand Detective Inspector Paul Ravel in Saint-Malo is in charge. Let him deal with it."

"Sir," said the station sergeant, "I cannot advise that. We have been told to keep the lid on this for as long as possible. But now it's off, and we should do no more in the way of concealing anything. It's up to you, sir, but I strongly advise you do see Étienne. He's a decent chap, but right now he thinks he's been given the runaround."

"Which of course he has," said Varonne. "Show him in."

One minute later the reporter and the detective faced each other across the desk. "Monsieur Varonne," said Étienne, "this morning two murders were committed in Brittany, and I believe the police are deliberately withholding this information. I am here to ask you why."

"Look, Étienne, we've known each other a while now, and as far as I know, neither of us has done the other one bit of harm."

"I agree."

"So, before we continue, I would like to get the ground rules straight. This is not my case, but I will tell you what I know, if the entire conversation is to be on the record. If, however, you want my help, my advice, and my guidance, there are certain matters that cannot be attributed. And certain matters that you must keep to yourself, for the moment. You may find the first course of action the easiest."

"No, Monsieur Varonne. I would appreciate your guidance, and I will accept some of what you say is off the record."

"*D'accord.* I will not allow a tape recorder, but you may take accurate notes. However, when I say put down that pen, you will put it down, and then just listen."

"I agree. Before we start I already have the names and addresses of the two deceased, Marcel and Raymond. I would like to ask if the police have any idea who perpetrated the crime."

"Yes, we do. Late last night the coast guard received a signal from the British that a fishing boat out of Brixham was on the run in the Channel driven by a large black-bearded foreigner who had apparently thrown the crew overboard."

"All of them!"

"There were only two. Anyway, the coast guard chased this fishing boat, a sixty-five-foot dragger named *Eagle*, inshore, and put out an alert that it was plainly going to land in Val André. However, in the morning mist they lost the *Eagle*, but the man did come ashore sometime after 6:00 A.M. At 9:00 A.M. the bodies of the two men were found on the beach. And at 11:00 A.M. the proprietor of the local garage confirmed he had sold a vehicle for cash to a big man with long black hair and a black beard, the precise description of the hijacker we got from the Brits."

"Was there any identification on the car registration documents?"

"Yes. He was, or seemed to be, Gunther Marc Roche, a Swiss national with a Swiss driver's license, of 18 rue de Basle, Geneva. All those details turned out to be false. But the French police have launched a nation-wide search for the car he purchased from Laporte. So far it has not been located."

"So, basically, we have a murder hunt for a foreign national who murdered a couple of guys at this vacation town on the ocean?"

"Not quite. And now you may put down your pen. Because what I am going to tell you is only a tip-off. You must establish the facts from another source."

Étienne put down his pen and sat back.

"The two men who were murdered," said the detective inspector, "were the private bodyguards of Monsieur Henri Foche."

The reporter's eyebrows shot skyward. "Non!" he said, an electric bolt of excitement lancing through his entire body.

"Oui!" said the detective. "Both men worked for him full-time and had done so for several years. The late Marcel was a true confidant of our Gaullist leader."

Monsieur Varonne paused and looked down at his desk. Then he looked up and said, "But, Étienne, there is something else. A few days ago we were given a tip-off there was a threat against Monsieur Foche's life, and it may emanate from England. The coincidence of this renegade ship-stealing maniac from the UK, landing in Val André, and being met by Foche's guards is too much."

Étienne weighed the difference between a huge front-page story, maybe the biggest he had ever written, and the alternative of a story on page 7, a minor murder and a modest headline. "Are you forbidding me to use it?" he asked.

Varonne replied, "Absolutely not. But I have tipped you the truth, and you must find a way to establish it from another source. My advice would be to try Detective Inspector Paul Ravel in Saint-Malo, and then Henri Foche himself."

"I'm still not sure why you are so jumpy about it," said Étienne. "The murders are public. Their employment details surely cannot be kept secret for long. I can't see the fuss."

"And that is essentially why I sit in this chair and you have to run around writing silly stories," said Varonne. "Now pay attention. We have a killer on the loose somewhere in France. He has committed two murders today, and may commit more. But his target may be the next president of France, and we do not wish to make it any easier for him than it already is."

"How do you mean?"

"First, we do not wish to alert him that we are on his trail. We don't want him to know we are aware he's after Foche. We want him to be confident. That way he'll make a mistake. But things cannot be kept under wraps. And when you found out something was going on, then you had to be told the truth."

Étienne stood up and thanked the inspector. But before he went he asked one last question. "Sir, what was the cause of death?"

"I was told he broke both their necks. But so far as I am concerned, that is unconfirmed. Try the police mortuary up the road. The pathologist is in there now."

"Thank you, Monsieur Varonne. Thank you very much."

By eight Étienne had spoken to Paul Ravel, who was not prepared to tell a lie, however badly the police wanted the matter kept under wraps. And while he did not offer much, he did confirm the facts. Étienne then called Henri Foche at home, and the politician also confirmed that Marcel and Raymond did indeed work for him and had for several years. Yes, he did understand there had been a threat to his life. But no, he had not detailed his men to go to Val André. However, his men always worked very closely with the police department, and he imagined there had been some cooperation when the hijacker's landing place was established.

Henri Foche had no intention of upsetting *Le Monde*, and Étienne rang off happy that he had parted on good terms with the next president of France. He now had sufficient information to write a very polished front-page splash for his newspaper. He called the night editor at eight thirty, and filed immediately. His story read:

Millionaire Henri Foche, the Gaullist front-runner for the presidency of France, was in shock last night after learning that his two personal bodyguards and close friends had been savagely murdered on a Brittany beach early yesterday morning.

The dead men are Marcel Joffre and Raymond Dunant, both in their early thirties and residents of Brittany's capital city, Rennes. Police believe death was caused in both cases by an expert in unarmed combat who broke their necks. Marcel also had been blinded in both eyes, and Raymond's right arm was snapped in half at the elbow.

At the time of death the men were armed with heavy-duty service revolvers, though neither gun had been fired. Detective Inspector Paul Ravel of the Saint-Malo Police Department assumed command of the case this morning, following a visit to the scene of the crime by the chief of the Brittany force, Pierre Savary, himself a close friend of Monsieur Foche.

The bodies were discovered by two young boys who were attracted by Raymond's handgun, which was lying on the sand. One of them fired it and blew out a neighbor's bedroom window. "We were lucky he didn't kill someone," observed Detective Inspector Ravel.

At first police suspected a terrorist involvement, since Monsieur Foche is a director of an international arms manufacturer in the field of guided missiles. He is known to have Middle Eastern business connections. But by lunchtime no Islamic extremist organization had claimed credit for the murders.

As the afternoon wore on, a tale of much deeper intrigue became apparent. In the past two weeks, an elaborate plot by a foreign power to assassinate Monsieur Foche has been bubbling below the surface. Police and private bodyguards have been placed on high alert to deal with it.

All signs pointed to the threat emanating from Great Britain, though it was not thought the British were in any way involved. Someone, however, intended to launch an attempt on his life, and the source, police say, came from London.

Nothing definite emerged until last night when the British put out an SOS for a stolen fishing trawler, from which the crew had been hurled overboard. The description of the man who perpetrated this crime fitted that of the suspect in the double slaying at Val André beach. Tall, Caucasian, powerful, black curly hair, thick black beard. He is believed to be of Swiss origin. The trawler is still missing.

Étienne did as he was instructed and left out all references to the car and the police manhunt in progress. But essentially he was out in front with the story, with the press pack on both sides of the English Channel trying to catch up. *Le Monde* led their first edition with the scoop.

All day a stratospheric level of gossip was winging its way across France from the residents of Val André. By nine that night even the notoriously sluggish newsrooms of the television stations were on the case. The state-owned France 2 led their 10:00 P.M. bulletin with "The Mysterious Events on Val André Beach." As a general rule, when television news broadcasts use the word "mysterious," it means they have only the remotest idea what they are talking about, and no one is very anxious to help them out.

A growling *Le Monde*, in search of the truth, might strike fear into the heart of the steeliest French policeman, whereas television news has an ephemeral quality that can be fobbed off—*I'm sorry, there is a government inquiry pending on that. We can say nothing at this time. . . .*

Nonetheless, France 2 somehow got a few facts into gear and offered the public an interview with the lady in Val André whose bedroom window had been shattered by the gun-wielding young Vincent Dupres, aged eleven. The lady confirmed there were two men lying on the beach. In her opinion they were dead, but she had no idea how or why.

Detective Inspector Paul Ravel told the television reporters almost nothing except that there were circumstances that laid themselves open to the gravest suspicions. Yes, a helicopter from Rennes Police Department had flown up to Val André. No, he could not reveal the names of the dead men until next of kin had been informed. Yes, the police were hunting for the killer, but had not yet located him.

When the first editions of *Le Monde* came up in a few hours, the France 2 news editor threatened to fire about seven people.

Thus, the cat peeped out of the bag at around 10:15, but it did not leap out, red in tooth and claw, until the small hours. And of course the small hours in France are not the small hours in the USA.

It was only 8:30 P.M. when the newsroom of Fox Television in New York picked up the developing story in France—and the part that grabbed them was the revelation that someone was planning to assassinate the Gaullist leader, Henri Foche, who was certain to become the next president of France. That was terrific. And it got better. The double murder of Foche's personal bodyguards on the beach at Val André. The black-bearded killer, on the run, after hijacking the fishing boat. The near certainty that this was the man who was coming after Foche. Is that a massive story or what?

Oh la la! Holy shit! BREAKING NEWS! BREAKING NEWS! The Fox foreign editor would gladly have kissed far-away Étienne Brix, whose byline adorned the *Le Monde* lead.

CNN, the rival twenty-four-hour American news station, was too busy criticizing the Republican president for everything he had ever done to find time for the big story in Europe. They caught on just before 10:00 P.M., by which time Fox was up and charging.

They had a top-class foreign editor, an ex–Fleet Street newsman in London, brought on board by the laser-eyed Aussie media tycoon

Rupert Murdoch and his henchmen. His name was Norman Dixon, and he knew how to update a hot story like a mongoose knows how to nail a swaying cobra.

"The only new angle we'll get at this time of night in Paris is the security," he snapped. "The new heightened security on Foche. It has to be immense. Get Eddie in Paris and tell him to get me something. Anything—just a line to say the entire French security forces went on high alert in the small hours of the morning."

"But Norman," offered a girl reporter who looked like she'd just jumped off the front page of *Vogue,* "they'll all be asleep."

"ASLEEP!" yelled the fabled Dixon. "With some black-bearded psychopath on the loose, trying to put a bullet straight between the eyes of the next president of France? And if they are asleep, wake 'em up. Just get Eddie on the case."

Thirty minutes later, Fox News staffer Eddie Laxton came through from his apartment in Montmartre after speaking to a wide-awake duty officer at the Prefecture de Police, an officer he knew by sight.

"Yes, of course there has been a substantial security increase. And it will continue until this killer is apprehended."

"Will it come into operation today?"

"Of course. Monsieur Foche is speaking in Saint-Nazaire today, and there will be an extra thousand men on duty all through the town and shipyards."

"A thousand! Christ! Who made that decision?"

"Who the hell knows, Eddie? But it came from high up. It was a political decision, not the police."

"Could it have been the president himself?"

"Shouldn't be surprised. Anyway, it's done. There are guys swarming to Saint-Nazaire from all over the country."

"Armed?"

"Damned right they're armed."

The opening sentence from the Fox newscaster on the 10:00 P.M. bulletin was: *The president of France stepped in last night and ordered a massive security cordon around the Gaullist leader Henri Foche, whose two bodyguards were savagely murdered on a beach in northern France this morning.* The rest was pretty well rock-solid Étienne Brix, to whom the network gave full credit for the world exclusive in France's most important newspaper. Norman Dixon wanted to give him a job.

Almost four hundred miles to the northeast of the Fox newsroom, Jane Remson almost jumped out of her chair. Harry was on the phone, and she rushed out into the hall and urgently advised him to come and watch the newscast.

Harry wound up his call, but by the time he reached the study, the newscaster was winding it up with political background on Henri Foche. He ended the story by saying, "The question is, can Foche survive until the election with this dangerous assassin on the loose?" The anchor was instantly on the wrong end of a growled reprimand from Norman Dixon, who told him, "Never end a newscast with a question. You're not here to ask questions. You're here to answer them. Just give them the news."

As reprimands go that was mild. A lot milder than the one Jane Remson was about to issue to her husband.

"What's going on?" asked Harry, as he came into the study.

"Going on! Oh, nothing much, except your personal assassin is currently being hunted by the entire security forces of France, having just murdered Henri Foche's two bodyguards."

"Is Foche still alive?" asked Harry.

"Yes, thank God."

"Have they caught the murderer? Or named him?"

"No, they haven't done either."

"Then it's not that bad, right?"

"Harry, I respect our pact that the subject is never to be mentioned. And for a few weeks I have pretended it wasn't happening. But we both know it is happening. And now half the world knows it's happening. So there's not much point in the pretense anymore, is there?"

Harry Remson did not reply. He walked across the room and poured himself a drink. And then he turned to face his wife. "Jane," he said, "you've got me on the hop right now, because you saw the broadcast and I didn't. Can you just tell me what was said?"

"Oh, that's easy. Someone in England stole a big fishing boat and crossed the English Channel into France. It seems the coast guard was waiting for him, plus two of Henri Foche's bodyguards. They were both found dead on the beach, and there is now a nationwide manhunt for the killer, who police suspect may be after Foche himself."

"Jesus Christ," said Harry. "Any clues about the killer?"

"Yes. He's apparently a big guy, well over six feet tall, with long, curly black hair and a black beard. They think he's Swiss."

"Sounds just like Mack Bedford, right?"

"Well, we can only assume he's hired someone else to carry out the deed itself. But it does not in any way lessen the obvious danger to ourselves. And the dreadful position you have put us in."

"Jane, I can assure you, Foche has a lot more enemies than just us. Some people believe he owns the factory that makes that banned missile, the Diamondhead, the one that keeps burning our boys to death in Iraq."

"I don't care how many enemies he has. Nothing alters the fact that you have somehow taken out a contract on the next president of France, and it's just a matter of time before the assassin is caught. They're on to him before he's started."

"Are they?"

"Of course they are. There's a thousand men in the shipyards in Saint-Nazaire, looking for him. Foche is apparently speaking there tomorrow."

"But they haven't caught him yet?"

"Not yet. But no one can evade that many armed security guards in a controlled space. The odds against him are a thousand to one. And when they catch him, it will all come out—Mack's involvement, your involvement, and in the end mine. We'll all be in court within a month, charged with either murder, conspiracy to commit murder, or maybe just conspiracy. None of it is very appealing, and all of it is utterly, stupidly unnecessary . . . jeopardizing our entire lives."

Harry stared at his beautiful, angry wife. "If the hit man, whoever he is, gets Foche before the guards get him, Remsons Shipbuilding is back in business. I spoke to Senator Rossow today, and he's been in contact with Foche's rival, Jules Barnier. Not only did Rossow assure me the order for the French frigates would continue to come here, but Barnier himself is considering buying a small holiday cottage with a dock somewhere on the Maine coast. He's a big sailor, and he's bored with the Med."

"Not as bored as we'll be in some prison cell," said Jane.

———•◆•———

Mack Bedford surveyed his new world headquarters. At the front of the room there were two windows that looked directly out onto the shipyard concourse. On the rear wall directly opposite there were two more dust-covered windows that looked out directly over the harbor. The other two walls were lined with wide floor-to-ceiling wooden shelves, with inch-wide gaps between the struts like decking.

The room was probably 12 feet high, and behind the top two shelves on the door wall there was a high window, smaller than the others. The first thing Mack did was to see which windows opened and which ones he might have to force. All four of the lower sash windows were stiff with dust and neglect. But they all gave way before Mack's upward onslaught, and they all opened. He closed them all slowly, attracting no attention from the dark shipyard below. And there was one thing he knew—this was a perfect spot to strike at Henri Foche, but it was almost certain the room would be "swept" by the security forces sometime in the coming hours. If that happened, he would at first try to hide among the shelves, or even retreat farther up the building, maybe even to the roof. But if push came to shove, he may need to go into combat. And that would change the rules, because it would almost certainly mean he would need to evacuate and regroup.

Mack walked back to the front window and stared down at the podium. One hundred and twenty-one yards from the base of the building. And now he was six floors above that point, and the rooms were 12 feet high. Five times 12, plus 3 feet for the window ledge. That was 63 feet, 21 yards.

"The square on the hypotenuse is equal to the sum of the squares on the other two sides," he muttered. "Okay Pythag, old buddy, let's hit it."

He squared 121 and came up with 14,641. Then he squared 21 and came up with 441. He added them together for 15,082, and hit the square route button, which revealed a number a fraction short of 123 yards—the precise distance from the window ledge to the lectern.

The telescopic sight on the rifle was set for his last shot of some 600 yards, straight at the red lights high on the Brixham crane. This required adjustment, and he preferred to do it now, at night, overlooking the podium, rather than in broad daylight.

He pulled on his driver's gloves and opened the metal toolbox. He removed each precious part of the rifle and smoothly screwed them together. Then he opened the window very softly about two feet and stared across the concourse. Mack stood back from the window for the adjustment, and gazed through the telescopic sight, which was, as he knew it would be, slightly blurred. Quietly, in that darkened warehouse room, deep in the Saint-Nazaire shipyard, he turned the small black precision-engineered wheel that brought the podium into focus.

Finally, he held the rifle more firmly and, for the final adjustment, aimed it directly at the microphone. The chromium stem that held it glinted in one of the concourse yard lights. There was hardly a sound as Mack brought it into acutely sharp focus. No sound at all, except for three infinitesimal clicks on the wheel, as Mack Bedford softly signed Henri Foche's death warrant.

CHAPTER *12*

Shortly after midnight Mack clicked the lock on the door. Thus far he had made sure the sixth floor was open like all the rest, but now he wanted to sleep a while, and the lock would buy him time if anyone tried to come in. He folded away the rifle in case he had to move real fast, and took the toolbox with him as he climbed up to the top shelf and tried, unsuccessfully, to get comfortable on the decking.

In the end he went down and collected his food package and re-arranged the produce, broke the baguette in half, placed the salami strategically against the Perrier bottle, and created without question the worst pillow in the entire history of sleeping.

But he had not closed his eyes for forty-eight hours, not since the hotel in Brixham. Mack could have slept, if necessary, on a carousel. It took him about twelve seconds to crash into a deep slumber, high up there on the warehouse shelves, his head propped gently on the Genoa salami.

Unsurprisingly, his dreams were vivid, but the one that crowded into his subconscious every night of his life was not discouraged by the rock-hard shelves. And again Mack watched helplessly as the Diamondhead missile ripped into his tanks, and once more he saw Billy-Ray and Charlie burning alive. The screams echoed though his mind, and he heard again the roar of that blue chemical flame from hell, and he could not get to his guys, and he awakened with sweat and tears streaming down his face. He was literally gasping for breath. But before he assembled his scattered thoughts, he once more saw, stark before him, the face, which to him at least, represented pure evil. The face of Henri Foche.

He dismantled his pillow and opened the Perrier. He drank almost half the bottle in big gulps. And then he rearranged the package and lay down, flat on his back, and tried to relax, thinking only of Tommy and Anne. This time his dreams were sweeter, and he had them both in his arms, saving them, protecting them, as he was sworn to do by the creed of the SEALs—*to fight for those who cannot fight for themselves.*

He was awakened at around four when there was noise from a lower floor. He vaulted down from the shelves and moved, light-footed, to the window. The guardhouse was undisturbed, and below him the noise was not growing any louder. Finally, he heard the front door of the warehouse slam, and he could see three men transporting two large packages on steel carts, heading back to Drydock 2, the one with all the lights.

Mack reclimbed the shelves, but was unable to sleep again, and he spent the next two hours before the rising sun contemplating the immediate future . . . *If I should die today, what will happen to Tommy and Anne? There should be enough money, with my pensions and Harry's second million. But no one will ever know who I am, and I will be buried here in some French prison yard. An unknown murderer.* The idea made him shudder, as it would make any U.S. Navy SEAL shudder. One of their proudest traditions is that no SEAL has ever been left behind on the battlefield, dead or alive. The prospect is anathema to SPECWARCOM, an unspoken dread among the fighting men of the Special Forces: *that I will somehow be left behind, with no headstone back home in the USA, nowhere for my family and friends to remember me, to think of me, to know what I tried to do for my country.*

Mack, however, understood how thoroughly he had covered his tracks, how no one in the whole of France had the slightest idea who he was. And if Foche's guards, or the police, should gun him down, right here in this shipyard, as they surely would, given half a chance, who would ever come to claim him? No one. Because no one knew except for Harry, and he'd never come, not if he had any sense. Which would leave him, Lt. Cdr. Mackenzie Bedford, United States Navy, murderer, buried in the yard of some foreign prison. Because no one would come. Except perhaps, down the years, one person. Tommy Bedford. Yes, somehow Tommy would find him, and he would come. Tommy would bring him home.

Still, he thought, *the bastards haven't got me yet.* And once more he tried to sleep, but he dozed only intermittently, right through the six o'clock shift change that he never even noticed, as hundreds of men changed places in the buildings around the yard. Mack was finally awake when, at quarter of seven, the spotlight of the sun streamed rose-pink out of the east, straight into his rear window, the one above the harbor.

Mack climbed down and used the empty Perrier bottle the only way it could now be used. He shoved it out of sight, under the shelves on the far side of the room. Then he glanced outside and made himself some French breakfast, slicing the salami with his fishing knife and eating it with a slice of cheese on buttered baguette. He had to admit, it was probably the best pillow he had ever tasted. With no radio, no television, no phone, not even the newspaper, Mack felt strangely desolate. For a start he had no idea what had happened to the Red Sox, and of course there was Tommy and Anne. How had things progressed in the Nyon Clinic? Had the operation been completed? Was it a success? How was Tommy? Would he live?

The questions rattled through his mind, and he knew if he allowed them to continue they would probably drive him nuts, cloud his judgment. So he shut them out, concentrated on his task today, the one that would, in a sense, set him free, set his family free, set Harry free, set the whole goddamned town free.

Once more he focused his mind, and he stared out at the podium, knowing there was an eight-hour wait before the action. Well, he hoped it would be that long. But as he stared out at the main gate, he sensed that things might move more swiftly than he wished.

Shortly before nine a black limousine pulled up at the guardhouse. The driver spoke briefly, and the car was waved through and parked on the far side of the podium. Three men climbed out, two of them smartly dressed—suits, jackets, and ties. The other was wearing black trainers, casual pants, and a black windbreaker. This third man carried a submachine gun, and looked as if he might know how to use it. Mack did not recognize the arrival of Henri Foche's new head of security, Raul Declerc.

Neither did he realize the second man out of the limo was Brittany's chief of police, Pierre Savary. The third man was Detective Inspector Paul Ravel, the policeman who had grilled and prized the truth out of Monsieur Laporte. Savary had considered it politic to invite Paul to the shipyard, since he was the detective in charge of the hunt for the killer of the two men on the beach of Val André. The shipyard at Saint-Nazaire was the most likely place for him to appear.

Mack watched the three men walk slowly down to the waterside, staring up at the drydock, wandering down toward the jetties, deep in conversation. He had a clear suspicion they were talking about him. But he was cocooned in this warehouse room, out of touch with the rest of the world. He wished he could somehow flick on a car radio, just to hear what was going on. But he had no such luxury.

If he had possessed a radio and tuned to any channel in the entire free world, any channel in Great Britain, even the local FM in Maine, he would have heard the following. Or something very like it:

A nationwide manhunt is taking place in France, according to the front page of the most important French newspaper, Le Monde. *Following the murder of his two personal bodyguards, police fear for the life of Monsieur Henri Foche, who is favored to become the next French president.*

At this moment the search is intensifying around the city of Saint-Nazaire, where Monsieur Foche is to give a major political speech on behalf of the Gaullist Party later this afternoon. On the orders of the French president, an extra one thousand armed security guards have been drafted in.

Officials now believe the killer may be part of an international cartel, possibly linked to al-Qaeda, which plans to murder Monsieur Foche, in response to the arrest of four Muslim extremists in Algiers last month.

French police believe they will catch the man, who is believed to be a Swiss national. They say he is tall with a black beard and may answer to the name Gunther.

But Mack did not have a radio. And he knew less than almost anyone in the world about the powerful dragnet that now surrounded him.

Down on the jetties, Paul Ravel had drifted off to conduct his own thoughtful investigation of the area. Raul was laying out his initial strategy for the shipyard. "Pierre," he said, "there's not the slightest use in us deploying highly trained men into the buildings that surround the concourse. It's too early, and we probably won't find anything anyway. However, the time scale is important. We could deem a building clean between now and noon, and by 4:30 an assassin could be inside, ready to strike at Henri. Therefore, we should not conduct any full-scale search of the closest buildings until the last minute. We don't want them clean now. We want them clean at 4:45 this afternoon."

"I agree on that," said Pierre. "And we'll have buses coming in very soon. Do you have a view about mass deployments as soon as the guys arrive?"

"I think we should take a half-mile radius from the center of the concourse," said Raul. "And start working out on the perimeter. Heavy-handed searching, lots of guys, lots of yelling. That way, if we either disturb or discover our man, he's got two choices, either to run for it, away from the datum, or to move in closer. If he runs, well, we at least saved Henri's life. If he closes in, gets nearer, we'll have a hell of a chance of catching him by sheer weight of numbers."

"You've done this a few times before, my friend," said Pierre.

"A couple. Both times with Middle Eastern royalty. But this should be easier, because we are operating on a very concise time frame. And Henri's not just wandering around the shipyard waiting to get shot."

"So you think a mass deployment to the outer areas as soon as the guys start to arrive?"

"Absolutely," said Raul. "And then I'll use my guys as sentries. Two on the main doors of each building that faces right onto the concourse.

The police should concentrate on the area around the podium as soon as they start. I mean, get under it, sweep it for explosives, climb all over the fucking thing. Then check the outside walls. I already noticed a man out in the street could climb that wall and pump a bullet straight into the back of Henri's head."

"It's already a 'no parking' area. You want it 'no walking' as well."

"*Absolument!*" replied Raul, ever anxious to establish his French credentials, especially to a policeman of any nationality. "And while you're at it, Pierre, make it 'no driving' as well. We don't want some kind of a ram raid to break out . . . you know, machine guns from the roof of a van."

"Consider it done," replied Pierre. "I'll have the entire street cordoned off." He removed his cell phone from a jacket pocket and murmured instructions into it.

"Christ, I'm glad you're here, Raul," he said. "And remember one thing—this is serious for you, but my whole career, my whole life, is on the line. If we find and eliminate this bastard, the credit's all yours. You were the first to hear of the plot, you acted quickly in the interest of the French Republic, you told Foche, and when there was trouble, you flew in and took over Henri's personal security. You'll be a hero. But if this bastard shoots Henri, they'll blame me."

"In my opinion," said Raul, "we want to make bloody sure he doesn't shoot us as well."

The French police chief nodded, and just then the first four buses pulled in, each one carrying fifty armed, uniformed, trained security troops—half-military, half-policemen, but experts in their field. They disembarked in good order, then formed ten lines of twenty men, and stood to attention.

Pierre spoke briefly to the four commanders, told them of the intended half-mile radius from the concourse center, and instructed them to move out to the perimeters and begin a tough, noisy search. "Lots of shouting and yelling," he ordered. "We want to unnerve this bastard if he's in here. You have the full police description of the man, I believe?"

"Yessir. Big guy, tall, black curly hair, and a black beard. Description corroborated by the British police, French coast guard, Brittany police, and garage witness in the town of Val André. Suspect answers to the name Gunther."

"I wouldn't put your life savings on that last one," advised Pierre. "It was almost certainly a false name."

"But he is Swiss, sir?"

"Maybe," replied Pierre. "Start the deployment. Anyone you find with a firearm, you may shoot on sight."

"Yessir."

Thirty minutes later, in a minibus direct from the airport, Raul's five ex–French Foreign Legion combat troops arrived in company with the two former SAS veterans, both from South Wales, both ex-paras, midthirties. They were deployed in three groups, with one man detailed to comb the area around the podium, a kind of frontline storm trooper, to back up the French police if things got really rough. It was Raul's opinion that if someone was trying to shoot Henri Foche, there was a 50 percent chance they would get as close in as possible. A suicide assassin was not out of the question, particularly if al-Qaeda was connected.

At two the eight-hour shift changed again. The men who had begun work at six began to stream out of the yard. Mack was having his lunch at the time, and there was not a huge variation in the menu, just a slight adjustment in placing the excellent cheese slices right on the buttered baguette and then adding the salami, which he again sliced with his fishing knife. On reflection he slightly preferred this to the direct hit of salami on baguette that he had engineered for his breakfast. He leaned on the wall beside the window, chewing thoughtfully and watching the long lines beginning to form at the main gate.

There were two police cruisers parked at the entrance, and the incoming workers were being shepherded through a line of six guards, all of whom were checking the IDs of the men who built the ships. No one could remember being asked for ID at Saint-Nazaire Maritime, not in living memory.

Mack, who was of course still out of contact with the world, could not make up his mind whether they were on to him, aware of his possible presence in the shipyard, or whether this was mere routine, the usual procedure for a major political speech.

Monsieur Foche would not be the first politician to address this particular workforce. The only difference was that for years, the other speeches had been decidedly left-wing, urging the workers to rise up against the establishment that exploited them.

Mack decided it was obvious the police knew of both his existence and his intent. Which did not unduly worry him, because he had always intended to leave a very definite, but false, trail to set them in search of a killer who did not exist. A big bearded killer named Gunther. If, however, the police had somehow found the unmarked Peugeot, they must by now have guessed he was either in the shipyard or, at least, trying to get in.

Again he watched the workers clearing the security system, and wondered how long it would be before the police conducted their inevitable search of this warehouse, and whether he could hide, and whether the guards would just take a cursory look around the empty sixth-floor storage area in which he now resided. He considered the possibility of discovery by one, two, or even three guards as *"a kinda pain in the ass,"* but not terminal.

By two thirty ten busloads of security guards were in the shipyard. The other ten were deployed around the city, especially along the wharves beyond Saint-Nazaire Maritime, both east and west. They hunted in packs of four, rampaging through boatyards, marine stores, parking lots, shops, and private residences, asking questions, probing like Nazi SS men in Belgium, seeking out the bearded killer.

In the shipyard, the dragnet tightened by the hour as squads of guards, directed by Pierre and Raul, closed in on the concourse, clearing out buildings and leaving small platoons of guards in each one. Mack watched them from on high, passing the time counting the active security operators in their bright-yellow jackets, the afternoon sun glinting off their rifles.

————— • ◆ • —————

Shortly after two thirty the accompanying police convoy that would travel to Saint-Nazaire with Henri Foche was assembled outside the elegant townhouse in the most expensive part of Rennes. There were four armed officers positioned in the tree-lined front driveway, one on the front door, and one inside the hallway. Four of them would ride shotgun on police motorbikes that were parked on the street, blue lights flashing. The street was temporarily cordoned off. The Foche Mercedes-Benz was flanked front and rear by police cruisers, each of which contained four armed officers, including the driver. They waited with engines running, blue lights flashing. To the casual bystander it looked like a psychedelic nightclub had escaped into the daylight.

Henri Foche and his wife were finishing their coffee, and Claudette had asked him for the umpteenth time to "call off this crazy trip to this stupid shipyard where a madman is waiting to shoot you, and probably me."

"No one is going to murder me in Brittany," he scowled. "These shipyard people are counting on me. Nothing is going to prevent me from addressing them this afternoon. For them! And for France."

Claudette rolled her eyes heavenward. "I just have no idea why you want to do this—deliberately walking into danger, and taking me with you."

"First of all," he replied, "the danger is minimal. Half the security forces in France are swarming through Saint-Nazaire. And in Raul Declerc I have one of the best professional killers in the world. And he works with the French police. I made sure of that. He's with Pierre in the shipyard right now."

"Even Pierre wanted to call it off."

"Claudette, my policies must be heard by the workers, the people who look to me. They want to know their jobs are safe, and that I will protect those jobs. We will build France, with our own hands. *Pour la France! Toujours pour la France!*"

"Well, since you are obviously planning to get us both killed today, I ought to tell you that little actress you're seeing in Paris telephoned about two hours ago. I know it was her, even though she put down the phone. Why don't you send her a condom with *Viva la France!* inscribed on it?"

"Shut up about that. I'm not even seeing her. And stop changing the damn subject. This is a big day for me. I must be faithful to the wishes of the voters."

"Wow! Faithful! Coming from you, Henri Foche, alley cat. *Pour la Bretagne! Pour la France!*"

"Claudette, for the wife of the next French president, you have a low mind."

"And for the next French president, you have a low life. And one day, it will catch up with you."

Foche just stared at her, incredulous that she could not comprehend his true greatness. He shook his head, at a loss for words at the astronomical level of her dumbness.

Just then the guard at the door called, "Monsieur Foche, the police think we should leave now. Everyone's ready when you are."

Henri and Claudette both stood up from the table. Foche picked up his jacket, and his wife walked over to the mirror and brushed her hair. Within two minutes they were seated in the back of the Mercedes, with the final two police guards in the front, one driving. The convoy moved slowly through the streets to the southwest side of Rennes and then drove swiftly out to the fast N137 highway that leads down to Nantes and the road along the Loire to Saint-Nazaire.

Foche was not talkative. There were times when he detested his wife, whom he knew he had treated abominably. But his stature, his ability to allow her to live like a duchess, must surely have overridden that. She was, after all, a former call girl, and in Henri's mind that overrode his marriage vows.

There was a natural law in the universe, he believed, a law that ensured the order of things, and he, Henri, had married a trophy wife, beneath him in every sense. And all he wanted from her was gratitude, and plenty of it. Not insolence and smart-ass remarks. Surely that was not too much to expect?

The procession sped south. The two lead motorbikes kept their flashing lights going all the way. But the other police vehicles drove without illumination. The plan was that all lights and sirens would go on, blazing and blaring, once the outskirts of Saint-Nazaire were reached. It was an integral part of an overall scheme masterminded by Pierre Savary, designed to unnerve the assassin.

Foche read his speech and occasionally made pencil marks on the pages. Claudette tried to sleep, even though, in the deepest recesses of her mind, she thought it entirely possible this might be her last day on this earth. Christ, she hated Henri. But she had an ingrained code of loyalty in her soul. And if he wanted to walk into the jaws of death, and he wanted her with him, then she would follow.

They reached the city of Nantes around four. The police officer in the front seat was on the phone to Raul Declerc, reporting speed and position. Back in the shipyard Raul ordered the final search of the buildings around the concourse to begin.

He was particularly concerned with the drydock, where there were so many workmen, all in blue overalls, all looking the same, all toiling on the hull of a new freighter. There were steelworkers, painters, plumbers, and electricians. There were men on the scaffold, dozens more inside the hull. How the hell could he tell if one of them had a hidden firearm right here in the drydock, with the intention of attacking the Gaullist leader?

It was the busy places that concerned Raul. The remote outlying places would be accurately searched, and were easy to locate. Around the main concourse vast squads of guards were beginning to congregate, and, as he had planned, Raul deployed them into the workshops and unfinished ships. Their orders were simple: search every inch of this place for a hidden gunman or firearm. Raul ordered the underside of the podium to be swept with metal detectors every twenty minutes. The street beyond the yard was out of bounds for both cars and pedestrians.

When Henri Foche walked to the podium on this simmering summer afternoon, there would be a steel curtain of forty guards surrounding him. As far as Raul and Pierre Savary could tell, Henri would be the most difficult man in the whole of France to assassinate on this particular day.

Up on the sixth floor of the warehouse, Mack Bedford began to change. All plans to bluff his way out of trouble as a workman were abandoned, just because it was too late. Foche would be arriving in a half hour. Mack stripped off his blue overalls and slung them high onto the shelves. He had nowhere to carry a flashlight, but the SEAL wet suit had a slim custom-made recess on the thigh for the combat knife.

He removed his Jeffery Simpson wig, mustache, and spectacles. Deep inside his wet suit top, there was just one waterproof pocket, and he folded the lightweight wig and slid all three items inside. Then he took down the toolbox and assembled the rifle made with such loving care by Mr. Kumar in Southall.

Into the breech he slotted all six of the chrome-colored bullets, setting one of them into the firing chamber. He slid the telescopic sight into place, and screwed the silencer onto the barrel. Then he held it in the firing position, almost caressed it, as he pulled the stock into his shoulder and stared through the sight, balancing the rifle, centering his whole body for the shot that would echo around the world.

He delved once more into the toolbox and removed the Draeger, the underwater rebreathing equipment, and he strapped it to his back rather than the correct position on his chest, where it would be a hopeless encumbrance. He pulled up his hood and fitted it snugly over his forehead.

He took out his big underwater goggles and tightened them on, fixed high on the hairline, ready to be tugged down fast as soon as he was in the water. Last time Mack did that he'd just stormed and dismantled Saddam's offshore oil rig.

Then he took out the attack board and fitted all three instruments—the clock, the compass, and the GPS—with the batteries he'd bought at the hardware store. He screwed them back into place, watertight. When he'd completed this he pushed the rifle, the toolbox, and the attack board back into the shelves behind his locked door.

But soon he would unlock it. If they searched this building, as they surely must, and found just one locked door, they would definitely blast it open and come charging in, mob-handed, as the SAS was apt to describe a full-blooded raid. If, however, the door was unlocked like all the rest, there was an excellent chance that just the regular two- or three-man search party would come in alone—unsuspecting and, he hoped, not particularly thorough. *The door gets unlocked—no ifs, ands, or buts. But not until the last moment.*

Mack walked to the window and looked down. He could see two of the three men who had emerged from the limousine seven hours previously. They were standing in the center of a great throng of guards, probably waiting for orders. When Raul's cell phone rang at 4:30, Mack saw him answer it. Foche was within seven miles of the shipyard.

Immediately, Raul ordered the search of the big empty warehouse that faced the podium. He'd ordered it last because it was the emptiest, most obvious, and easiest place to clean right out. There were ten floors. Raul ordered fifteen men into the building, three armed guards to each floor, moving up. The two Foreign Legion men were to close right in on the front door, ensuring no one went in or came out while the search was being conducted.

Mack could see the sudden surge of the guards, and he turned away and climbed the shelves once more to the smaller window, set high above the little side throughway that led to the wall above the water. This window had a different catch, and he quietly pushed it open and peered outside, looking down to the single door on the side of the building, through which he had entered the previous night.

The guards were beginning to arrive in formation and move into the warehouse. Mack pulled the window shut and climbed down, listening. Far below he heard the general commotion as the security parties separated and began to search each floor. There were footsteps on the stone stairway, and the shouts of the men echoed in the cavernous stairwell.

Mack pulled his driving gloves on and opened wide one window on the front side and one on the back. He unlocked the door. Then he flattened himself behind it, tight against the hinges. Three or four minutes went by before the men from the ground floor leapfrogged the others and ran up to the sixth-floor landing.

Outside, Raul's cell phone rang again to announce that Henri Foche and Claudette were now only two miles from the main gate of the shipyard.

That was when Mack Bedford's door was pushed open, tentatively, and a machine gun barrel was pushed forward into the room. Mack could not see it, because the door was wide and pushed back almost to the wall. If he had not been standing there, it would have been flat against the wall. As it was, the door was flat against his chest.

The three armed guards walked into the room, and swiveled into a three-pronged attack formation, each man facing a different way, their backs toward each other. The room was by no means bright, but it was perfectly light, and each one of them scanned the shelves, the room, and its corners.

One of them called out in French, "There's no one in here. Room's empty." None of them spotted the toolbox and the assembled rifle because they were pushed back into the corner shielded by the door.

"Okay, guys," said their leader. "All clear on floor six." Outside a sentry called down to the team, "No problem floor six. It's empty."

The first two guards made for the doorway, but the third man suddenly spotted the blue overalls slung up on the high shelves. "Is that anything?" he asked.

"Well, it's not a person," said another. "You want me to go up and check it out?"

"Go ahead," said his colleague.

The man walked over to the shelves, put down his rifle, and started to climb, which was when he saw Mack Bedford jammed behind the door.

He let out one hell of a shout, which was only cut short when Mack's iron hand clamped over his windpipe and dragged him bodily off the lower shelf. He then delivered one of the most brutal attacks in the entire SEAL repertoire, a crushing bone-shattering bang in the middle of the forehead, delivered with the butt of his knife handle, and then a pile driver of an uppercut, delivered with the butt of the open hand, which rammed the nose bone deep into the man's brain.

This took five seconds, and the door swung back. The other two men had heard the strangulated yell, and came charging back into the middle of the room. Mack Bedford by now had his hands on the barrel of the dead man's rifle, and he took the first of the other two with a baseball swing that obliterated the skull behind the right ear, smashed the nerve center, and killed him instantly. The third man swung around, on the attack, his rifle leveled as he tried to draw a bead on Mack Bedford. He almost succeeded, but Mack had his left hand on the barrel and turned it away, swiveling the third guard to the right, just about at arm's length, just about far enough to slit the man's throat almost in half with a slashing pinpoint-accurate swipe with the fish knife from the hardware store. No civilian can kill quite like that. This was combat, close combat, designed by SPECWARCOM to eliminate an enemy.

Mack reached the door. The landing was empty, the sentry having made his call and progressed to floor seven. Quietly, Mack closed the door. Only seventeen seconds had passed since the first intruder had stepped into the room, and now he clicked the lock shut. Even as he did so he heard the wail of the police sirens as Henri Foche's motorcade came speeding along the main street that led to the shipyard's entrance.

So far the three dead guards had not been missed. Everyone had heard the all-clear call from the sixth floor sentry, and everyone was busy with the rest of the warehouse search. For the moment Mack was safe behind the heavy-duty door.

He placed the toolbox and the attack board at the base of the rear wall. Then he picked up Prenjit Kumar's sniper rifle, the precision Austrian SSG-69, and moved to the edge of the open front window. Right inside the main entrance he could now see clearly the police outriders talking to two of the men who had arrived by limousine.

The convoy was waved through, and the police car moved forward just far enough for Foche and Claudette to disembark right at the foot of the steps that led up to the podium. Right now he was not surrounded, as he would be six seconds from now. Raul stood on his left quarter, just behind. Pierre was marshaling the police to form their cordon at the back of the stage.

Mack was on his knees, the rifle rock-steady on the window ledge. Everyone was looking at Foche and his strikingly beautiful wife. And now Mack had him in the crosshairs of the telescopic sight. A clear, unimpeded, uninterrupted shot. It was never going to be better than this. For a second Mack's heart ceased to beat, and then he squeezed the trigger.

The high-velocity bullet ripped out of the finely turned, shortened barrel, and it hit Henri Foche with fantastic force slightly left of center, almost in the middle of his forehead. Deep inside his brain, the bullet exploded, blasting a hole that blew blood and tissue out of the back of his head, through a gaping hole five inches across.

Mack snapped the bolt of the rifle back hard, and fired another. The bullet hit Henri Foche as he fell backward. It smacked into him on the left-hand side of his chest, straight through the scarlet hand-kerchief, and blew his heart asunder. The Gaullist leader never knew what had hit him.

"I guess that one was for you, Charlie," gritted Mack Bedford. "From the goddamned Euphrates River to right here in Saint-Nazaire, that one was for you."

And then he moved as fast as any human being had ever moved, dismantling the rifle, fitting it back into the toolbox, ramming down the lid. He then turned his Draeger around, fastening it tight to his chest. He stuck to his belief that an unlocked door does not attract, and he flipped back the lock, still working on the theory that if one or two men tried it and it opened, they would not sound an alarm. If it was tightly locked, a hefty steel door like this might attract thirty gun-toting guards with det-cord or even dynamite.

Meanwhile, down on the concourse, there was nothing short of total pandemonium. Only those closest to Henri Foche understood he had been hit by an assassin's bullet and was now dead. Pierre Savary was among those. Raul Declerc thought he had other problems, and Clau-dette was cradling her dead husband in her arms, loyal to the bitter end.

Savary called the ambulance personally, and now the crowds began to surge around the shocking scene that had evolved at the foot of the podium steps. The body of Henri Foche was slumped backward close to the car. It was crimson with blood, and Claudette was spattered, kneeling down, holding his head, saying over and over, "Why did we come here? Will someone just tell me why we had to come here?"

Raul Declerc was staring up at the warehouse, scanning the front of the building. It took him a full minute to spot the wide-open window on the sixth floor, but 99 percent of the crowd still had no idea what had happened. Raul knew he still had men in that building, and he began dodging through the still-growing throng. It was only 4:45 when he began heading to the side door of the warehouse. Plainly, the guards at the front door had heard nothing because no one had moved, and these were trained guys.

Raul, in his former life as Reggie Fortescue, had never served in Special Forces, but he had seen combat with the Scots Guards in Iraq, and he was more highly trained than any civilian to deal with trouble. Especially if he had a submachine gun in his hand.

He entered the stairwell and began to climb, floor by floor, conscious that the guard detail he had sent to search the building was all on the higher four floors. He reached the sixth and was nearly certain this was the correct level for the open window. Nearly certain, but not quite.

Raul pulled the handle, pushed the door, and stepped into the room. At first he did not see the black-clad Mack pressed against the wall next to the rear window. Instinctively, he headed directly to the open front window and glanced out. Quickly, he turned and saw Mack, and instantly leveled his machine gun at the big frogman's heart.

"Freeze!" he snapped.

Mack Bedford answered calmly, in his natural voice, "Okay, buddy, you got me. No problem. I'm not armed."

The thoughts in Raul Declerc's mind raced. He had the assassin, right here, all on his own. If he marched him down at gunpoint, no one could deny him a very large payment for professional services. He had not stopped the killing, but he would have done what no one else could do and captured the culprit. That had to be worth big money.

He gazed across the wide room at Mack Bedford, and there was something about that voice, something in the steady timber, something about that North American accent. And something suddenly clicked in his brain.

"Morrison?" he said quietly.

"No, not me," replied Mack, "I'm not Morrison. Morrison's right over there." Mack raised his arm and pointed to the far wall on his left, and then shouted suddenly, unexpectedly—*"KILL HIM, BILLY, RIGHT NOW!"*

No SEAL in the entire history of SPECWARCOM would have fallen for that. At the very least, any one of them would have shot Mack Bedford dead before turning to deal with "Billy." But Raul Declerc was not a SEAL, and he was startled, frightened, and he turned quickly, unsure which of these two desperadoes to shoot first, the unarmed one in front of his eyes or Billy, who obviously had a gun.

The split second of Raul's hesitation earned Mack just that: a split second. It was by no means decisive, but it was crucial. Mack dived right, straight to the floor, rolled, and came up low and hard. The arc that Raul's gun needed to travel, to re-aim away from the far wall, was much wider now. That was the split second.

Mack's right fist slammed into Raul's left kidney like a jackhammer. It landed with such force he dropped the gun. Mack swooped to pick it up, and Raul, who was no pushover, landed a mighty kick to the side of his head. The ex-SEAL commander took it, but still came up with the gun, which he swung at Raul's head, a fearsome blow, slightly off-center. The force was, however, enough to fell the former Scots Guards colonel, who landed flat on his back.

This was the most dangerous opponent Mack had faced thus far. Mack knew it must be Raul. The commander of the Forces of Justice from Marseille was the only person on earth who knew the name Morrison. Raul not only knew for certain that Mack had just killed Foche but also knew about the plan, the money. Worst of all, he was the only person in France who knew precisely what Mack looked like, and what he sounded like.

Of all the security guards in all the warehouses in all the world, Raul Declerc had to go. Raul was still conscious, and Mack leaned down and with his left hand grabbed him by the yellow flak jacket right near the throat, and with his right hand grabbed the crotch of Raul's pants.

Mack lifted, stepped back, and with astounding strength he swung the prostrate Raul back, lunged forward, and then launched him clean through the open window like a yellow torpedo. Raul never even touched the sides. He was definitely still conscious because Mack heard him scream all the way down to the concourse, where he landed with a dull, life-ending thud.

There were now more footsteps on the stairs, coming down and coming up, voices shouting and yelling. Mack locked the door, buying more seconds. Then he grabbed the toolbox, tucked his attack board under his arm, and climbed through the rear window.

He stared down at the water. It was a drop of sixty-three feet, high, damned high, but not as high as the oil rig in the Gulf. And he'd jumped from that. For the first time, Mack was scared. He straightened right up on the window ledge and summoned his courage. He could not go back. He had to jump or die. When the door gave way, they'd shoot him down.

He must have stalled for five seconds, and then there was an enormous blast right behind him. The steel door cannoned off its hinges, shot right across the room. There was smoke everywhere, and the smell of cordite. Someone bellowed, *"Right here, guys, he's in here!"*

A machine gun opened fire, a random volley in the smoke. Mack took a deep breath, pulled down his mask, and jumped, dropping through the air, ramrod straight like an Olympic diver, except he was spearing down feet first, toes pointed in his French work boots, the toolbox under one arm, the slender attack board under the other. When he hit the water, the toolbox made the only splash, and Mack was still rigid, as he knifed deep, leaving barely a ripple on the surface.

On the low wall adjacent to the warehouse a guard saw only a blur, but he could see the little whirlpool made by Mack and his toolbox on the surface of the harbor water. He pointed to the spot and blew three loud blasts on his whistle. And the guards came running.

Thirty feet down, close to the floor of the tidal basin, Mack was shaken, but hugely helped by the supreme SEAL protective wet suit, which had taken the sting right out of the entry. He opened the toolbox and let the water flood in. He dropped it and watched it descend. Then he put the Draeger line into his mouth, turned on the valve, and breathed normally, despite a heartbeat of about seven thousand revs per minute.

He tugged off his work boots and unclipped his big flippers, pulling one onto each foot. In the gloom of the deep water he could still see his painted BUDs numbers, Class 242, right on the instep. Which was, more or less, when the bullets began to fly.

A line of guards now in formation at the low wall, under the personal orders of Pierre Savary, opened fire at the surface of the water. Someone was shouting, *"I thought I saw him! Right there, sir. Something went into the water. I'm sure it was a person."*

They pumped round after round into the harbor, and the bullets zinged deep, leaving sharp, straight, white lines in the water. But they were losing velocity all the way. By the time they reached Mack Bedford's area he could have caught them with one hand.

Savary ordered his men to fan out along the harbor walls, right to the entrance that led to the mighty Loire River, and to keep firing no matter what. The problem was, the guards were strangers to great waters. They were men who were essentially out of their element. And they were up against an underwater machine named Mack Bedford.

He kicked to the floor of the harbor and found the toolbox, which he clipped shut and shoved down into the silt and sand. There was little tidal movement down here in the enclosed waters, and he left it, a slightly exposed metallic object, unlikely to be disturbed by men searching for his body.

Then he held out his attack board and kicked around to face the south, checking the board and swerving until the compass aimed him southwest, out toward the harbor entrance. With the bullets still flying, but oblivious to the shouts and commands of the security forces above, Mack stayed deep and kicked, slow and steady, directly to this inner gateway to the great river.

Any long swim conducted by the SEALs requires colossal discipline. For starters there can be no gasping, forcing, rushing, or panicking. That way the Draeger will run out of gas in about half the time it was meant to last. Mack's Mk-V model had a cylinder that held thirteen cubic feet of oxygen at two thousand pounds of pressure per square inch. On land it weighed a hefty thirty-five pounds, but it was weightless in the water.

The trick was to breath normally, nothing erratic, no stress or adrenaline. That way this particular design provides recycled, breathable air for almost four hours. Mack did not think he would need it for that long. The Loire estuary was two miles directly across, and in the big BUDs swimming pool at Coronado that would have taken approximately forty minutes with flippers. A trained Olympic swimmer can knock off fifteen hundred meters in under fifteen minutes. But the second mile would take a lot longer.

And this huge tidal flow, swirling out of the heartland of central France, had about as much to do with a swimming pool as a popgun to a guided missile. Mack's diagonal course to the far bank, on the far side of the Saint-Nazaire Bridge, would be one-three-five, southeast, and the distance possibly two and a half miles, maybe more. The true distance would depend on the outward pull of the tide that would be doing its level best to drag Mack into the Atlantic.

The ballpark numbers for a long-distance swim in tidal waters by a U.S. Navy SEAL were approximately ten powerful double kicks per minute, each one taking the swimmer ten feet, or one hundred feet per minute, fifty minutes for a mile. But those distances could vary. As every seaman knows, it's possible to run an engine at five knots and remain dead still over the ocean floor while the tide rages past.

Mack had no reason to think it would be that bad at the mouth of the Loire, but all big rivers have variable degrees of "pull," especially on the ebb, as the Loire now was. In fact, low tide would be around six thirty, which meant the last part of Mack's swim would be in slack water, which would be one heck of a respite.

For the rest of the way, he would use the time-honored SEAL rhythm—*BIG DOUBLE KICK, BAM! BAM!* . . . one . . . two . . . three . . . four—*BIG DOUBLE KICK* . . . one . . . two . . . three . . . four—kick and glide . . . kick and glide . . . and hope to hell he wasn't standing still.

The bullets continued to rain down on the surface of the water. Guards were shouting and shooting. First they saw something, then they didn't. Pierre Savary had been informed about the death of Raul Declerc. And it seemed so bizarre, less than one day after the three of

them had dined together at the Foche residence, making their elaborate plans, plans that now lay shattered on the blacktop of Saint-
Nazaire Maritime.

Detective Inspector Paul Ravel had arrived from out of the blue at
Pierre Savary's side. "Things are changing fast," the chief told the man
he had promoted on the beach only thirty-six hours previously.

"Not so much for me," replied Ravel. "I came here in search of one
murderer who had just killed two civilians at Val André. Right now I'm
still looking for the guy, except he's now killed at least five more men. The
only real difference is, I've got a much better idea where he is—either
in the water, down there somewhere, or hiding along the wharves."

Pierre Savary looked up at him sharply. "What d'you mean, five
more—surely only two?"

"Nossir. We have three guards brutally murdered on the sixth floor
of the building, shocking wounds, two caved-in skulls, one slit throat."

"Jesus Christ. How d'you know?"

"I just saw them. Lying on the floor in the room where he fired
from, before he jumped."

"How do you know he jumped?"

"There's no other way down. Not unless he was one of the security
guards and just walked out with his mates."

"I'll tell you what, Paul, that was one helluva jump. But he won't get
far, and you still think he's definitely in the harbor, right?"

"Not definitely, sir. He was. But he might have gotten out. Could be
just about anywhere now."

"What's your best guess, Paul?"

"I don't think he's still in the water, sir. I think he just used it for
a soft landing. But the coast guard boats are going out right now,
with radar. And if he's there he's finished. But this cat tends to stay
one jump in front of the pack. I'm betting he's out, on dry land, getting changed, ready to run, or maybe get picked up by whoever hired
him."

"D'you think he'll kill again?"

"That all depends, sir. Depends if anyone gets in his way."

Savary decided this was a waterfront situation, and he summoned the Saint-Nazaire police, the officer commanding the national security forces, and the coast guard captain conducting the seaward operations. He advised everyone to concentrate on the land on the north shore, the docks, jetties, and hulls. "This guy is trying to get out of the water on this side of the river," he said. "That's where we're going to catch him. That's where he is."

More than one thousand trained men began to make their way to the outer edges of the yard, waiting and preparing for the black-bearded Gunther Marc Roche to emerge from the deep.

Mack was essentially missing all the strife. He never heard the two ambulances come racing into the shipyard, sirens wailing. And he never heard the audible gasp of the crowd, as Monsieur Henri Foche was lifted on a stretcher into the rear doors, with a white sheet covering his body and face. Many of those who could not get close still thought he had merely been taken ill.

When Claudette made her way out from behind the limousine, her entire outfit, yellow Chanel, was covered in blood. Women screamed. And the shipyard's Klaxon fire alarm blared out their ship's emergency call—*BAHAA . . . BAHAA . . . BAHAA!*

With three separate forces in full operation—the local police, the national guard, and the coast guard—there was the inevitable uproar, dissent, and too many chiefs. Bodies were being carried out of the warehouse, someone had spotted the killer, someone else swore to God he was still in the harbor.

One commander ordered his men to the roof of the warehouse for the better vantage point; Savary insisted every gun in the shipyard head for the harbor entrance, through which any swimmer must pass, if he hadn't already. The coast guard was unused to homicide and demanded formal orders from the police to launch every patrol boat in the area, and for the cutters in the near range of the Atlantic to head up the estuary.

Pierre, in his soul, believed the assassin was still in the water, even if he might be trying to get out. He told the coast guard commander,

"Get every small boat into the harbor, or just beyond, as fast as possible. Then keep combing the north shore. He's got to land somewhere. He's not a fucking fish, right?"

"No, sir. He's not a fish. And we'll keep the security radar sweeping the surface at all times. Helicopters launch in fifteen minutes. We got three. North shore and harbor, sir?"

"I think so. But tell me, Commander, could he get to the other side?"

"If he'd had a fast boat waiting, he could, I suppose. But he didn't. We were sweeping the surface within three minutes of Monsieur Foche's death. We have permanent radar projected out there. The navy has always insisted."

"I actually meant could anyone swim across?"

"Swim! Oh, no, not swim. I don't think anyone could do that, not without a safety boat running alongside. People have drowned out there, or been pulled out to sea by the tide."

Pierre Savary stared across the broad waters of the estuary, all the way to the distant shore. "Well," he said, "how about the greatest swimmer on earth? An Olympic champion, with a safety boat, no tide? How long would it take him?"

"Well, it's all of two miles in a dead straight line. Hard to imagine anyone crossing right here, where it's so wide, in an hour. I guess it would take an hour and a half . . . I don't know . . . maybe a little more. Swimmers get slower as they go, right? Not faster. If you ask me that swim could not be done without a couple of large scuba tanks and an electric motor."

"I suppose so. And that means he's got to be still here, either in the harbor or along the jetties."

"If he's in the harbor, sir, he's dead. Because he's been in there for at least twelve minutes. If you ask me, we're already looking for a body."

Mack, swimming toward the outer harbor wall, was unhurried, still thirty feet below the surface, conserving his oxygen on a journey that basically had not even started. With no wide, flailing, or driving arms to disturb the water around him, he moved as smoothly as a long black eel. His arms were pole-straight out in front, gripping the attack board, his Draeger released no bubbles, his gunmetal-gray underwater goggles made no glint in the water, and the turbo charge of the SEAL flippers made no swirl, no ripple, like the flicking tail of a cruising tiger shark.

The numbers on the attack board read: *Time 1658. Compass two-two-five. GPS 47.17 North 2.12 West.* At almost five Mack knew the sun would be sinking in the west, and he crossed the channel, under the gunfire, still deep, seeking the western wall of the harbor, where the shadows would be greatest. When the looming concrete darkness appeared immediately to his right, he came four degrees left, and moved forward, almost touching the wall, kicking along under the eyes but out of the sight line of the guards.

Above him the bright-white streaks of the gunfire were intense as he reached the exit. He guessed the sky had clouded over, because he could just discern the flashing red light up and to his left. The water looked cleaner now, bigger, clearer, and he made his turn, a full 86 degrees left—in his old SEAL mode, *come eight-six red to course one-three-five.*

Ahead of him was the longest, hardest swim he'd ever attempted. People can die in currents like this, just get swept away, out to sea, never to be seen again. Mack knew the danger. He'd been preparing himself mentally for a long swim for the biggest part of three weeks, somehow to get away from the datum, somewhere, probably across a shipyard estuary.

He'd been living it, reliving it. He would never have attempted it without his attack board, that supreme handheld electronic navigator that had saved the lives of a thousand SEALs. The board would show him the way, make sure he stayed on the right course, correct him, guide him, warn him when he was losing the battle.

And deep beneath the tidal sweep of the Loire, he caught the bright black-silver flash of an Atlantic turbot cruising the estuary. And it reminded him of Tommy; Tommy the fisherman, Tommy the catcher. Always Tommy. And it galvanized him for the swim, just the thought of his little boy. . . . *I'm coming home, kid. Trust me, I'm coming home.*

He kicked hard, out toward the south bank of the river, making his diagonal line to the towering southern edifice of the Saint-Nazaire Bridge. He counted as he kicked, clocking off the minutes, knowing that every three he knocked off another hundred yards.

The GPS confirmed that in the first twenty minutes he had moved almost a half mile offshore, and thus far he had not been edged off course by the ebbing tide. Like all rivers, the central tidal stream of the Loire is less defined on the ebb than it is on the flow, and Mack was aware that life was going to be a lot tougher sometime in the next fifteen minutes.

He calculated he was a tad ahead of schedule, but so far there was only a very faint pain in his upper thighs, same spot it always hurt on a long swim. He'd even felt that on those hard-driving laps in Harry's country club pool. He'd felt it as he drove through the water to Saddam's oil rig. Jesus Christ, he'd felt it that night. But he'd fought it then, and he could fight it now, no matter how hard the journey. *I'm coming home, Tommy.*

Mack was kicking along at his cruising depth of twenty feet, listening for the approach of engine propellers. Not many ships draw twenty feet—in fact, most of them draw well under ten—but he did not much want to be sliced in half by the gigantic blades behind a soft-running oil tanker.

At this depth almost all surface sound was deadened, but props running shallow in the water make a serious din, and he'd already heard two or three way back behind him, going fast. The coast guard helicopters were aloft now, one hovering over the harbor and two flying low, clattering over the inshore surface, close to the jetties.

And with every passing three minutes, their quarry powered another hundred yards farther away, kicking and gliding, ramming the water with those huge flippers—

BAM! BAM! . . . one . . . two . . . three . . . four.

The north shore search was intense. Eleven hundred men, three helos, six patrol boats, radar, sonar in the harbor, machine guns raking the surface. Only rarely in the history of modern crime has so much hardware and brainpower been leveled at one man, in so short a time, and in such a limited area.

Pierre was growing more anxious by the minute. This had been going on for nearly an hour. And every coast guard commander, every security officer, even Paul Ravel, believed there was only one certainty—Gunther, whatever the hell's his name, could not possibly be alive and out in the middle of the river. The chances were he'd either drowned, failed to survive the death-defying drop to the water, or been shot in the harbor. How could the Swiss assassin possibly be alive against such an onslaught?

Yet Pierre was not so sure. This Gunther character had evaded every police officer in France on his way to Saint-Nazaire. He'd penetrated the steel cordon that surrounded Henri Foche. And as far as Pierre could tell, no one had ever seen him and lived to tell the tale, except for old Laporte at the Val André garage.

All right. So he's not in the middle of the river. I accept that. But he's still got to be somewhere. And I won't believe he's dead 'til I see his body.

Those were the thoughts of Chief Savary, who'd never even had a moment to mourn his lost friend, Henri, and who also, as a result of *"this fucking fiasco,"* might have to resign from the police department.

He punched numbers into his cell phone and asked the coast guard to call in another helicopter, one with the latest dipping sonar that he knew they had, somewhere.

"Sir, that's stationed at Cherbourg, 180 miles away. It would take an hour minimum to get it here. That would be two hours after the suspect jumped, probably far too late, wouldn't you say?"

"I suppose I would," said Pierre, adding, ungraciously, *"Merde!"*

Back under the water, Mack's clock on the attack board read 1805. He'd been swimming for more than an hour, and the pain was beginning to kick in. The lactic acid coursing through his system was getting worse by the minute. Mack ached. He ached like hell. He ached in an agonizing way, most often experienced by only two other breeds of elite sportsmen, international rowers and cross-country skiers. And Mack wasn't even a sportsman, except when he had a fishing rod in his grip.

All he could do was to repeat in his mind the timeless creed of the SEAL under intense physical pressure—*I've sucked it up before, and I can suck it up again.*

Worse yet, his attack board was giving him bad news. The line of latitude, 47.17, was not important; the two-mile crossing would tick down to 47.15 as he headed south to the far shore. And the tide would not drag him backward. It would drag him sideways, to the west. Thus, the second set of numbers, depicting the lines of longitude, were the most significant. That 2.120 West would click to 2.119 as he swam, then 2.118, then 2.117. And he was storing the numbers in his mind. Right now he was coming to the halfway point north-south. But the 2.117 had flicked back to 2.118. The tide was pulling him off course, out into the Atlantic. By the time he reached 47.16 North, he might be at 2.119 West, almost as far from the span as when he started.

He was tired, and the twinge of concern he felt deep in his stomach was just a few degrees short of mild panic. He couldn't fight everything, not this monstrous eight-hundred-mile-long French river that could drown him without mercy.

He knew what to do. He needed to change course, to face the oncoming tidal surge head-on, to reduce his body area, to lead into the current with the slim top of his shiny rubberized head, rendering him a black arrow, not a six-foot-three log, going sideways.

Mack swerved east, swimming zero-nine-zero on the attack board compass. He felt faster, as if the water was sliding past him more smoothly. That was just an instinct, and a hopeful one at that. But he kept kicking and counting, and sure enough the GPS numbers flicked forward to 2.117, as he powered on at right angles to the bridge, striving to get under it, to make it upstream.

The judgment call, which he knew he must make, was how far east should he swim? How quickly would that tide sweep him west, maybe even back to the wrong side of the bridge again? Mack now ached from head to foot. Every kick was painful. But if he stopped he would die. If he came to the surface he might be arrested, or even shot.

With the setting sun behind him, he would have no early warning of the bridge, no long shadow into which he could swim and gauge his line of approach. The bridge was at once his objective, his friendly landmark, and his nemesis. For all he knew there were dipping sonar systems up there on the span, aimed down into the water to trap him.

With the sun in the wrong place, he might be under the bridge before he knew it. And he might first have to come to a depth of only ten feet a few minutes from now. But when he saw the span, he would go as deep as he dared, as far from human and electronic eyes as he could manage, as deep as the river if he could.

The numbers flicked again—2.116 West. Beautiful. If he could just keep going, he'd make it. He'd make it for Tommy and Anne. And he double kicked again, hard—*BAM! BAM! . . . one . . . two . . . three . . . four.* The bridge must be close, and at 1829 on the attack board clock he angled up, until he was just seven or eight feet from the surface. Somewhere to the south he could hear the steady beat of a relatively small engine, maybe a tug or even a fishing trawler—he was an expert on those.

And there was the bridge. He could see it through the goggles, maybe a hundred yards ahead. He was just beyond the middle of the river, since the latitude still showed 47.16 North. He went deep, kicking down, until the water grew very gloomy, and up ahead there was only darkness.

Back on shore, Pierre Savary was just about at the end of his tether. The search was still roaring ahead with boats, helicopters, and people, all doing their level best. They had located everything that could ever be located along the north shore. They'd questioned local fishermen, grilled freighter skippers, started to dredge the harbor for Gunther's body. Low-swooping helicopters, thundering ten feet above the surface, had terrified the turbot.

Pierre had more or less had enough of what must now be a dead-end operation. "Paul," he said to his equally worried assistant, "we have to check the south shore. We need to switch this operation right across the river."

"But we know it's impossible for him to be over there," replied Ravel. "The coast guard say it's out of the question. He couldn't have gotten there. He could not have survived."

"Quite frankly, kid, I don't give a shit what they say, not at this stage. We're going to hit the opposite shore with the big battalions. Cars, boats, choppers, and people."

Pierre Savary was one of those educated Frenchmen who looked as if he had just stepped out of the front row of a rugby scrum. He could scarcely help that, but his face looked as if he was scowling even when he was chuckling. He had a permanent five o'clock shadow, and there was a tough aura about him that he knew and cultivated. But the scowl he wore this afternoon was genuine. He didn't know why this was such a complete screwup, but it was, and Pierre was angry.

"Paul," he growled, "I'm going to catch this fucker. If it's the last thing I ever do, I'm going to catch him."

CHAPTER *13*

At 1830, the tide turned. The flow of water out of the river into the ocean petered out and died. The twice-daily miracle of the planet Earth was in progress, and out beyond Pointe de Saint-Gildas, the Atlantic's turbulent, cresting swells prepared for their onward drive up the Loire estuary.

As ever, it took the long rollers a half hour to brace themselves, to get organized, and to begin the big push into the river. During this time, a tired Mack Bedford gained the first respite of his swim. The water went slack, running neither one way nor the other. For the next twenty minutes the center of the Loire, up there under the road bridge, would resemble the BUDs swimming pool back at Coronado. But it would be for only twenty minutes. Mack knew that as well as the river gods themselves. And with all of his remaining strength he kicked under the bridge, and then came a full ninety degrees right, heading south, straight across the now placid, good-natured stream, toward the far bank.

He was more than a quarter of a mile south of the center line of the river, which left him with around 1,250 yards to swim. If he was ever going to gain time, this was the moment. He drew on every last vestige of his strength; he kicked and counted, kicked and glided, kicked until he thought he must surely give up and drown. But as that BUDs instructor once said, *There ain't no quit in you, kid.* And Mack kept going, uncertain whether his next kick, that big double *BAM! BAM!*

would be his last. The lactic acid pounded through his body, and his muscles throbbed. His thighs felt as if they were made of stone, tight, aching, but still driving on, through the pain barrier.

Mack remembered his "bible," that book about the 1983 America's Cup when the Australians fought a bloodcurdling tacking duel against the Americans on the last leg of the last race. The big winch grinders called it the "red zone," the state where everything hurts so badly a man almost loses consciousness, but somehow keeps going. He remembered the calls of the big Aussie winch men, hammering away in the "engine room" of the boat, shouting, dedicating each murderous tack to some beloved member of the team, trying somehow to personalize the agony, to make it count more—*"THIS ONE'S FOR YOU, JOHN!" "AND NOW ONE FOR HUGHIE!"* Holding Denis Conner's big red boat at bay—closing their eyes and driving the winches with massive arms that felt like jelly. The shouts of the tactician, the screams of the sheets flying off the reels. The sheer bloody pain of the contest.

A long time ago, Mack had lived it through the words of the legendary Aussie helmsman John Bertrand. Now, for the first time in his life, he felt it, the experience of total, all-encompassing pain. Finally, he knew. And he too began to dedicate, not the tacks, but the minutes. He did not need an entire crew to give him a choice. He understood too well how to personalize the agony, and he pounded into the shallows of the river, with the same words in his mind that he would have for all of his days. Anne and Tommy. Just Anne and Tommy.

He felt the jolt of the attack board as it hit the river bottom. The clock said 1850, and he had to get the hell out of the water. He stuck his head into fresh air for the first time in almost two hours. He spat out his Draeger line, and breathed deeply. But he was too exhausted to stand, and for a few moments, he lay wallowing in the water, feeling the strength ebb back into his body, as the tiredness evaporated, the way it surely must in the iron constitution of a man who has just achieved the impossible. The swim, that is. Not the assassination.

Mack looked around him. This part of the riverbank, a couple of miles from Saint Brevins, was deserted. Vacationers, looking for a beach, go the other way on the south side of the river, down toward the Atlantic

Coast. If ever there was a time to make a run for it, it was now, and Mack dragged himself upright and stumbled, unsteadily, onto the bank.

Even as he did so, he heard the wail of two police sirens, speeding across the Saint-Nazaire Bridge. He glanced back, and he could see the blue lights coming toward the south end of the roadway. If anyone saw him, he was dead. Mack ripped off his flippers and goggles, held on to the attack board, and ran for his life, up the bank, over the grass, across the road, and into the woods. Whereupon he collapsed into the foliage, not having even the remotest idea where his base camp was located.

Now there was another sound splitting the evening summer air, the distinctive clatter of two helicopters, flying low across the river, their rotors making that familiar *BOM-BOM-BOM* on the wind.

In an instant Lieutenant Commander Bedford understood the search had switched sides, and they were now combing this southern bank, despite its hopelessness, despite the pure impossibility of a man swimming across the estuary of the Loire. The police might be desperate, and they might be disheartened, and they might think this was all a waste of time. But that would not stop them from finding him if he was not damned careful.

He wriggled forward back toward the road, and then kept going right to the edge of the woods, "walking" on his elbows like the sniper he was. The coast seemed clear, and, still lying face-down, he scanned the road up to the right, looking for the bus stop, which was about two hundred yards farther along.

Mack stood up and headed back into the woods and then turned to his left and jogged back through the trees to the little camp he had left in the twilight last night. It was a hundred yards in from the road, on a direct line with the bus stop. And it was intact, the two bushy strands still jammed into the ground, which had not been disturbed.

Swiftly, he took the attack board and smashed it against a tree trunk. He hurled the wrecked GPS as far into the woods as possible, obliterated the compass on the tree, and ground it into the soil. The polystyrene he scattered as he walked, and he carried the clock with him.

Mack dived under the overhanging branches of his camp and pulled out the stems he had cut. With his knife he scraped off the top layer of earth, scrabbled around for the handles of his leather bag, and heaved. It came out easily, and Mack shook off the dirt. He set it aside and then stripped off his wet suit top and retrieved his Jeffery Simpson wig, mustache, and spectacles, which were all bone dry.

He pulled off his rubberized trousers and folded them neatly. Then he placed the wet suit, goggles, and Draeger flat in the hole, complete with the flashlight and calculator. Finally, he took the fishing knife and cut away the numbers on his flippers before placing the three items on top of the wet suit. He covered them with dirt until they were completely obscured, a foot below the surface. Then he covered the earth with stones and leaves and bent three branches into position. He jammed in the two fronds he had cut and surveyed his work. In his opinion it would be years before anyone found this little woodland cache, if ever. And so what if they did? Nothing was traceable. Everything was brand new, save for the Taiwan-made wet suit, unmarked flippers and goggles.

It was two minutes after seven o'clock. He pulled out his clothes and dressed—dark slacks, clean white T-shirt, sport jacket, socks, and loafers. He slipped the Jeffery Simpson passport into his inside pocket and stuffed a wad of euros in there with it. He fitted on his wig, mustache, and spectacles and placed the clock in his bag.

Then he moved a hundred yards along the woods and made his exit, onto the river road. He walked casually to the bus stop, where a young girl of around eighteen was already waiting. It was 7:08, and the scene on the river was chaotic. A helicopter was running up and down the shore at a low level, east of the bridge, right in front of them. Another was searching the bank downstream, on the far side of the span. Two coast guard launches were on their way across the river from the north shore. The evening sky had clouded over, and the two boats had bright search-lights on the water. There were four police cars in the middle of the bridge, blue lights flashing, officers aiming radar guns hopefully over the surface, guns normally used to trap speeding motorists. There was an-other cluster of police cruisers at this end of the bridge, and Mack could see three red lights, probably signifying crash barriers, barring traffic from crossing before a search of their vehicles was conducted.

None of that mattered to Mack. What did worry him was the police car coming dead ahead along the river road, moving slowly, watchful and deliberate. When it reached the bus stop, it pulled up right along-side, and the driver jumped out and opened the door to allow the passenger in the near-side rear seat to exit. Detective Inspector Paul Ravel stepped out. Chief Pierre Savary stayed where he was.

"Good evening, *mademoiselle, monsieur,*" said Paul. "This is just a routine check—but have either of you seen anyone along here who looks as if he might have just swum across the river?"

Mack raised his eyebrows, in the time-honored way of the truly astonished. The girl giggled and said, "Swum across the river! I didn't think anyone had ever done that."

"Sir," said Mack, "could you tell me what is going on over there?"

Detective Inspector Ravel replied, "There has been an attempt on the life of Monsieur Henri Foche. We are searching the area."

"Wow!" said the girl. "My father was going to vote for him. Is he okay?"

"We have not yet been informed. But I would like to see identification."

The girl produced a couple of credit cards, and Mack pulled out his passport, handed it over, and inquired, "Al-Qaeda again?"

"No one's said so yet. But we wouldn't be surprised."

Ravel looked at the passport carefully and then said, "American, eh?"

"Yes, Officer."

"How long have you been in France?"

"Two weeks."

Ravel flicked through the pages and said, "There's no immigration stamp. How did you come in?"

"Cross-Channel ferry to Calais. They just looked at my passport through the car window."

"Do you have a return ticket?"

"No, Officer. I'm going on down to Rome with friends. Then I'm flying home via Dublin."

"Do you have that return air ticket?"

"I have the e-ticket document."

"May I see it?"

Mack groped in one of the side pockets of his leather bag, produced it, and handed it to Paul Ravel.

After a very quick glance, he handed it back to Mack and said, "Thank you, Mr. Simpson. I'm sorry to bother you. But if either one of you sees anyone who looks as if he might have been in the river, don't approach him, but please do let us know, won't you?" He handed them each a card containing a succession of police numbers.

"Sure will," replied Mack. "Hope you catch him. From what I read, Henri Foche is a very capable man."

Paul Ravel reboarded the cruiser.

"Any good?" asked Savary.

"Well, he was the right height, and his passport was not stamped when he came into the country. But there were a few gaps."

"Such as?"

"As you know, at the busy times of the day, hundreds of people come through French ferry ports without having their passports stamped. Especially Calais, where he came in. The rest were just minor discrepancies, like his entire appearance, name, address, nationality, and the fact that he was dry. That's quite unusual for someone who just jumped from a seventy-five-foot building into the harbor, and somehow swam across the Loire fully dressed. There was no other way he could have reached this side of the river."

"Hmmmm," replied Savary expansively. "Was he French?"

"No. American. American passport and address somewhere in Massachusetts. Showed me his return ticket."

"I suppose it was only about a billion-to-one shot that he was our man."

"Don't be so hard on yourself, sir. There are only sixty million people in France. Half of them are women, and half of the rest are babies or elderly. So it must have been fifteen million to one."

"I feel better already," said Pierre.

The cruiser accelerated farther along the road and stopped alongside two more pedestrians. As it did so, the bus to Nantes came into sight, rumbling along from the bridge. There were just two elderly ladies on board.

The girl and Mack both climbed aboard, and the doors shut. Mack chose the corner seat on the empty back row bench. As he sat down he glanced ahead and noticed the police cruiser was making a U-turn and heading back to the bridge.

Pierre Savary had finally accepted there was no point in searching on this side of the river. Not only had they found nothing, seen nothing, but everyone to whom they had spoken looked at them as if they were stark-raving mad at the mere thought of some maniac jumping in the Loire and swimming all the way across.

Paul Ravel knew how badly his boss had taken it—the assassination against all the odds, his friend Henri gunned down right before his eyes, new security chief Raul Declerc hurled out of a window to his death, and then the total disappearance of the perpetrator.

Just twenty-four hours previously everything had seemed so controlled. They had the killer's name, address, and description, confirmed and corroborated by several sources. They even had his passport number, driver's license. The shipyard had contained sufficient security guards to defend the beaches of Normandy in 1944. And they *knew* the assassin was in Saint-Nazaire. His car had been found in a public parking garage on Place des Martyrs. And now he was well and truly missing, vanished from the face of the earth. Paul Ravel's logic told him the man was dead, probably drowned, and his body would wash up somewhere along the coast in the next five or six days.

Pierre Savary's logic also told him told him the man must have drowned in the powerful currents of the estuary, and he might well never be seen or heard from again. Yet a sense of failure settled on him. That was inexplicable, except that Pierre was damned sure the assassin was somehow still alive. And he could not be seen to give up. "We'd better keep the police cordon around the town," he said. "Stop and question every driver. And intensify the search of the shipyard. Because that's the most likely place he'll be. He can't still be in the water."

"Sir, we've searched that place high and low."

"I know we have," replied Pierre. "But this character is on the move. Just think. He could have been hiding out along the wharves, staying in the water for maybe an hour, then crept out and found somewhere to wait it out. He may have had an accomplice. But somewhere, some-place, if he's alive, he must have come out of the fucking river."

———— • ◆ • ————

At 7:15 P.M. the head of the Administration Department walked out onto the steps of the Central Hospital of Saint-Nazaire and announced to the waiting journalists that Monsieur Henri Foche was dead. He had died of two gunshot wounds, to the head and chest. Surgeons had worked for some time to revive him, but the official hospital report would state he was dead on arrival. "There was never any realistic pos-sibility he could be saved," said the spokesman. "But everyone in our emergency room wanted to try."

He was accompanied on the hospital steps by Claudette Foche, who was still wearing her blood-spattered clothes. The sight of her was a chilling, inevitable reminder of that November day in Dallas, Texas, in 1963, when the devastated Jacqueline Kennedy stepped, blood-spattered, onto the aircraft bearing the body of JFK, her slain husband.

The spokesman had no intention of conducting a press conference, and after the formal announcement, with a barrage of questions being shouted at him from all angles, he led Madame Foche back inside the building.

Among the pack of reporters at the base of the main steps to the hospital was Étienne Brix, Le Monde's newly promoted bureau chief for Brittany. He had driven down from Rennes on pure instinct, shar-ing a car with a three-man television crew from France 3, a station al-ways on its toes for regional news.

Étienne, the man who had first cracked the story of the Val André killer and his relentless pursuit of Henri Foche, knew more about the background to the killing than any of his journalistic cohorts. Most of them knew only what he had written in this morning's edition of his newspaper. None of them knew about the missing car or the police manhunt that had gone so severely wrong.

When the scribes began to write their hastily assembled stories for the news media all over France, Étienne would again be way out in front, because he alone, thanks to the distant Inspector Varonne back in Rennes, understood the catastrophic failure of the security forces. And right now there were no further restrictions on what he could and could not use.

He called the news editor in Paris instantly and alerted everyone to the story. The wire agencies would probably be on the case, but he would file personally in one hour. He needed to make three more calls. Étienne's epic, which landed on the news desk of *Le Monde*, bylined by Étienne Brix, read:

Henri Foche, the front-running leader of the Gaullist Party and almost certainly the next president of France, was gunned down by an assassin's bullet in a Saint-Nazaire shipyard late yesterday afternoon.

Monsieur Foche was pronounced dead on arrival at the city's Central Hospital. He had been shot twice, in the head and chest. His wife, Claudette, who had accompanied him on the journey from their home in Rennes, was in the operating room while surgeons fought to revive him. Bravely, she stood on the steps outside the hospital as the announcement was formally made that her husband was dead.

In truth, Henri Foche never had a chance. The first bullet took him in the central area of the forehead, and police say it was a deadly high-velocity projectile that blew his head asunder. The second one did the same to his heart. Henri Foche was almost certainly dead before he hit the ground.

Police have long believed there was an assassin stalking the Gaullist leader, much as the Los Angeles Police Department did during the final hours of Bobby Kennedy's life in 1968.

Two days ago both of Foche's personal bodyguards, Marcel Joffre and Raymond Dunant, were murdered on the beach at Val André in North Brittany. Police believed then that their killer was really after Foche himself. And I can now reveal that for the past twenty-four hours there has been a massive nationwide police dragnet spread across France.

Desperately they searched for the killer, watching the hours tick away to the fateful moment when the Gaullist firebrand would take his place on the podium in the shipyard to give what many anticipated would be one of his greatest speeches. They had the assassin's description: big, black hair, black-bearded. They had his name and address: Gunther Marc Roche, of

18 rue de Basle, Geneva, Switzerland. They had his passport number. They had his Swiss driver's license number. They had the license-plate number of the car he purchased to make his getaway from Val André. They even found the car, in a public parking garage in Saint-Nazaire.

According to Fox News in the United States, the president of France himself ordered an extra thousand security men into Saint-Nazaire to protect Henri Foche. The entire town swarmed with armed police and national guards.

But the authorities had other information—French military experts, called in to assist in the original investigation, were certain the man who broke the necks of both bodyguards had served as a member of the Special Forces somewhere, either in the French Foreign Legion, Great Britain's SAS, or the U.S. Navy's SEAL teams.

The killings bore the hallmarks of a man trained in the most brutal forms of unarmed combat, not to mention the accompanying skills such men have as snipers. With his assassination mission accomplished, the man apparently made a death-defying leap from the high floor of the warehouse into the Loire River. Again, authorities consider this was likely to be the action of a trained Special Forces combatant.

And so it proved. Henri Foche was shot down in what turned out to be a welter of blood. Three security guards were found dead in the empty sixth-floor warehouse room from which Roche fired the shot that killed the king of the Gaullists. Two of them had crushing, murderous wounds to their skulls; the third had had his throat cut.

Sometime in the moments after they were killed, Monsieur Foche's new head of security, Raul Declerc of Marseille, was hurled out of the same window, presumably by the same man. He died instantly after the sixty-three-foot fall, in full view of the hundreds of shipyard workers who were on the main concourse to hear Henri Foche's speech.

The remainder of the story was essentially background, though Étienne Brix would spend much of this night interviewing local people and the police.

He ended his front-page lead for *Le Monde* with these words:

Last night police were warning that the big bearded killer from Geneva was still at large. He should not under any circumstances be approached by members of the public.

Le Monde's splash headline was:

HENRI FOCHE SLAIN BY ASSASSIN'S BULLETS
POLICE CORDON FAILS TO PROTECT GAULLIST
LEADER FROM "PREDICTABLE" MURDER

The wire agencies, operating under terrific pressure at 7:20 in the evening, flashed:

Saint-Nazaire, Brittany. Wednesday. Henri Foche assassinated, 4:45 P.M. in Saint-Nazaire Maritime shipyard. Shot twice, head and chest. Gaullist leader dead on arrival at Central Hospital. Wife Claudette by his side until the end. Assassin still at large.

By 7:30 P.M. every media newsroom in the world was onto the story. Fox News in New York was quickly into its stride, leaving CNN standing, with most of its staff still trying to find another dozen reasons to criticize the Republican president.

Fox interrupted everything for the news flash. Norman Dixon was yelling instructions, Laxton was on the line from Paris with one of the fastest stories ever written, wrapping up details from every which way with uncanny accuracy and perception.

Things were happening so fast that Dixon pulled "the talent," removing the girl who looked like the cover of *Vogue* from the front line of the action. Instead, he installed in front of the camera a very sharp young former sportswriter from London named John Morgan to address the nation.

"We need someone who can hang in there," growled Norman. "They gotta read fast, adapt, adjust, edit, and add stuff, without a break. Sports guys know how to do that—get in there, Morgan, and let's go."

Fox was first by a mile. It was 1:30 P.M. on the East Coast of the United States, just about at the conclusion of the lunchtime bulletin. *BREAKING NEWS!* flashed on the screen, and John Morgan came on to announce the murder of the next president of France.

Eddie Laxton's story was packed with detail, mostly gathered and rewritten from Étienne's galaxy of innuendo, using his time-honored Fleet Street knack of putting 2 and 2 together and getting about 390. But Eddie knew what he was doing, and while he was not quite up to speed with on-the-spot Étienne Brix, he was not that far behind, and he was gaining.

The hub of the investigation now swung automatically to the Prefecture de Police in Paris, and by 7:38 Eddie Laxton was in there, talking to officers, chatting to old contacts, and firing back the minutiae on what was now an open cell phone line, direct to Norman Dixon's assistant in New York.

Of all the reporters in the entire world working on this story, trying to make sense of arched, defensive police statements, Eddie was the first one to conclude, "These bastards haven't the first clue who the assassin is. They don't know his name, his address, or his nationality. They don't know who hired him, or why. I'm not even sure about that black-beard bullshit, either."

He told the reporter in New York to put him directly on the line to Norman Dixon, to whom he spelled out his doubts. Norman never hesitated. He wrote down on a sheet of copy paper, "French police yesterday admitted they had no idea as to the identity of the assassin. They suspected a completely false trail, and they'd heard nothing from al-Qaeda. Worse yet, the man who had killed Henri Foche had vanished."

The subeditor passing the copy over to John Morgan risked a note of caution. "What if the gendarmes deny this?" he asked.

"Don't worry about that damned rubbish," replied Norman. "They'll only deny it if they have answers. And Eddie says they have none. Hand it to John."

———— • ◆ • ————

Jane Remson was out on the terrace reading a magazine and waiting for Harry to come and join her for lunch. Awaiting him was his favorite combination of food in all the world—a smoked salmon sandwich, with just a light sprinkle of lemon on brown bread and butter, accompanied by a glass of chilled white wine.

There were, however, several provisos for this modest-seeming lunch for the emperor of Remsons Shipbuilding. For starters, the wine had to be French, and it had to be white burgundy, and it had to be from the legendary vineyards of Montrachet on the Côte de Beaune, and it had to be Puligny from the supreme Olivier Leflaive Frères estates. The salmon was even more esoteric. First, it had to be Scottish. It had to be wild, and it had to have been caught in a Scottish river. But the Scottish river had to be the Tay, and the fish had to have been residing in one of the glorious, lonely reaches southeast of Loch Tay, in Kinross.

Harry's father had taken him there to fish one summer when he was fifteen years old, and the spell the river cast on the future shipyard boss was lifelong. He had never forgotten killing his first salmon, the largest fish that can be taken on a fly in freshwater—the thrill of outwitting the fish on his double-handed twelve-foot-long Scottish fly rod, judging the speed and drift, and all the life-or-death guile brought to bear in this silent, occult art. This was Izaac Walton's *King among Gamefish*. Harry had never forgotten his father's story of the wild salmon's long and mysterious journey from the depths of the Atlantic, back to the waters of the place where it had been spawned, in the Tay River. And he had never forgotten the taste of the sandwiches packed up in the small hotel where he and his father had stayed.

Harry had been back to fish the Tay several times, but one ritual he never missed. Every year he ordered from a small Scottish smoker, not four miles from the hotel where he had first stayed, twelve full sides of wild salmon from the Tay, one for every month of the year. Today Jane had asked the butler to slice one of the precious fish for Harry's lunch.

And now the Remsons boss was on his way through the house. The problem was that he spotted the sandwiches at precisely the same moment John Morgan announced on Fox that Monsieur Henri Foche had been assassinated. Harry shouted involuntarily, "Jesus Christ!"

Jane came rushing in and saw him staring at the television screen, transfixed by the account of the death of the Gaullist, the public announcement of the only serious wish for which he had prayed in living memory.

Harry did not speak. Just listened to the trail of havoc that had plainly dogged the soft footsteps of Lt. Cdr. Mack Bedford in France. Neither he nor Jane uttered one word until the opening part of the newscast was complete.

Each of them stood there in their own private space—Harry thanking Christ no one knew who the hell had rubbed out the Gaullist, and glorying in Eddie Laxton's assessment that there was a pretty good chance they never would. Jane was personally thunderstruck. She had overheard the conversation. She knew as well as anyone that her husband had taken out a contract on this Henri Foche in order to save the shipyard, that a huge sum of money was involved, that Mack Bedford was involved. That whatever foul deeds had taken place in France, they had almost certainly emanated from her little town of Dartford, Maine, courtesy of her own husband.

Jane spoke first. "Harry," she said, "I think you owe me an explanation, a reasonable account of just how deeply we are both involved in this."

Harry smiled at her, his normally cheerful face reflecting his personal joy and gratitude. "I think I once told you never to broach the subject again. Henri Foche had many enemies, especially in the military. And while I cannot pretend I am sorry he has died, neither can I shed any light on how it happened." He walked out onto the terrace, followed by his wife. "Let's just treat this day as if it were any other," he said. "The only difference may be that I have an extra glass of that delicious white burgundy with my sandwich."

———— •◆• ————

The assassin was still asleep, right there in the back seat of the bus, his left arm resting on the leather bag. They had reached the outskirts of Brittany's former capital city of Nantes, and the bus was much busier than it had been when Mack first boarded.

He awakened at the first stop inside the city limits when several people left and even more boarded. He checked his watch and saw the time was five minutes past eight, which left him twenty-five minutes to catch the last train running from the South Station in Nantes to the city of Bordeaux.

Mack left the bus at the Gare Central Station and walked the remaining half mile to the trains. In a deserted shop doorway he removed his wig, mustache, and spectacles and slipped them into his bag before purchasing a one-way first-class ticket down to the great capital of France's most illustrious vineyards. It was the first time he had looked like Mack Bedford since he left the United States almost two weeks previously. Unless you count the view that Loire turbot had of him earlier today.

His general policy was to leave no continuity behind him. Just as Gunther Marc Roche had vanished totally three miles beyond Laporte's garage, so Jeffery Simpson vanished totally before Mack stepped onto the train for the four-hour, 240-mile journey to Bordeaux.

The train was not busy, and he slept most of the way, secure in the knowledge that no one was looking for him. No one in France even knew he existed. No one knew his name. And there sure as hell was no record of him entering the country. He awakened when the train stopped at La Rochelle, the old Atlantic seaport that dates back to the fourteenth century. It was dark now, almost ten thirty, and Mack was asleep again before the train pulled out of the station.

The conductor awakened him by calling out, "Bordeaux—cinq minutes. Gare de Saint Jean—cinq minutes."

Mack grabbed his bag and hoped to high heaven there was a hotel still open near the train station. He disembarked and was pleasantly surprised at the warmth of the night. There was a porter still on duty, and he cheerfully told Mack he should go to the Hotel California, which was a very short distance away.

The Bordeaux railroad station is not in the most ritzy part of the city, and there was a slightly rowdy gang of unpleasant-looking youths loitering on the street. Mack had to walk past them, and as he did so one of them made a feeble attempt to trip him, and another couple shouted something that sounded threatening.

Mack ignored it and kept walking. Generally speaking, he considered he'd killed quite a sufficient number of people for one day. And that particular section of French youth would never know that this was indeed their luckiest of nights. All of them still had their eyesight, no one's arm had been snapped in half, their noses were still in place, not having been rammed into their brains, and no one's throat had been cut.

The hotel was still open, and the peace-loving Mack Bedford walked to the front desk, where the receptionist was listening to the radio. He heard only a short part of the newscast before she turned it down. . . . *The Northwest of France has been brought almost to a standstill following the assassination of Henri Foche. Every major highway north of the Loire has been blockaded by the police. Ferry ports are closed and are not expected to reopen in the morning. All airports are experiencing . . .*

"*Bonsoir, monsieur,*" said the girl.

"I'm just glad you're still open," replied Mack, speaking in an American accent.

The receptionist was bilingual. "We always wait for that late train from La Rochelle. One single room with a bath?"

"Perfect."

"May I see your passport, *monsieur?*"

Mack handed it over and watched her copy down the number. She glanced up at him, checked the photograph, and said, "Merci, Monsieur O'Grady."

Mack said he'd pay cash in advance since he was leaving early and would not be using the phone.

"No problem," said the girl. "That will be two hundred euros."

Mack gave her four 50-euro bills, and she handed over the key to Room 306. She automatically turned up the radio, and the subject had not varied. Shaking his head, Mack said, "Terrible thing, that murder, eh? Have they caught him yet?"

"*Oh, non, monsieur.* There is nothing else on this channel, and I've been listening the whole evening. Some people are saying he is a big Swiss man with a black beard. A couple of people say they saw him in the shipyard. But a policeman was speaking just before you came in—

he said they have been able to confirm nothing. They have no idea who he is, or where he is."

Mack fought back a grin of pure delight. He nodded gravely, saying, "A bad business, a very bad business." And he walked over to the elevator, assuaging his conscience with one thought—what did Marcel, Raymond, Raul, and the three dead guards have in common? Every one of them had been trying to kill him, would have killed him. "Self-defense, Your Honor," he murmured.

He did not even consider Henri Foche. That had been a military mission, nothing personal, just the elimination of an enemy, an illegal combatant, who had effectively opened fire and killed members of the U.S. armed forces serving in Iraq.

That night he slept the sleep of the just. But he awakened early and flicked on the television, tuning to the satellite channel, BBC World, out of London. The first words he heard were, "It's been a long night, but we will be staying with the main story throughout the day." Then the anchor started again with the same lead item Mack had heard on the receptionist's radio the previous night, about Northwest France being paralyzed while the police combed town, country, seaport, and highway for the mystery assassin who had cut down Henri Foche at the age of forty-eight.

There had been no update for eight hours. Mack Bedford was delighted. Norman Dixon would have fired someone. All Mack could do was to thank his lucky stars that nothing had happened. He fell only slightly short of actively congratulating himself when the newscaster mentioned that police had appealed publicly for any information leading to the arrest of the alleged Gunther Marc Roche, the bearded Swiss boat thief, who remained their number-one suspect.

Throughout the night they had been inundated with phone calls and e-mails from members of the public who had definitely seen the man, from Paris to Cherbourg, on to Saint-Nazaire and all stations in between. They'd seen him driving, walking, running, robbing, hiding, kidnapping, and fighting, in places as diverse as seedy late-night bars to the crypt of a cathedral, from the main street of Rennes to a pole-dancing club in Paris.

"No wonder I'm still tired," said Mack to the empty room. He switched off the television and opened the door to his room. There on the corridor carpet was today's *Le Monde*, Étienne's headline blazed across the width of the front page: HENRI FOCHE SLAIN BY ASSASSIN'S BULLETS.

"That was a hell of a rifle," he muttered. "Pity I had to leave it at the bottom of the goddamned harbor."

He shaved and dressed, and decided to find some breakfast at the airport, which the hotel guidebook told him was out at Merignac, seven miles west of the city, thirty euros away.

He handed back his key, checked there was no further money owing on his bill, and asked the doorman to call him a taxi. It arrived almost immediately, and Patrick Sean O'Grady of Herbert Park Road, Dublin, climbed aboard.

The city was busy in the morning rush hour, and it took a half hour. Life was not much quicker at the ticket desk, either. They did run a direct flight to Dublin but not until noon, which was neatly in time for Mack to miss the only two daytime flights Aer Lingus ran from Ireland to Boston.

Not having any choice, he purchased a first-class ticket in cash from Bordeaux to Dublin. He showed the girl his passport, and she replied, "Thank you, Mr. O'Grady. Enjoy the flight."

Then he wandered off to the restaurant and ordered an omelet with toast and coffee, his first hot meal since the night before last, the grilled fish in the workmen's café near the shipyard.

On the arrivals board he had noticed an aircraft was in from London at 10:00 A.M., and he wondered if it had brought the morning newspapers to France. For some reason there were no English publications in the rack at the airport store, but there was a copy of *USA Today*, the entire front page of which was dedicated to the assassination of Henri Foche. In a black box in the center of the page was a short list of French airports in the Northwest where long delays could be expected while police searched for the killer—Rennes, Saint-Malo, Quimper, Lorient, Caen, Cherbourg, Nantes, Saint-Nazaire, Tours, Le Mans, Rouen, and Paris.

Inside the newspaper, on page 4, crushed by the events at Saint-Nazaire, was a story on which most U.S. publications would normally have splashed—

SIX MORE U.S. SPECIAL FORCES
BURNED ALIVE BY DIAMONDHEAD MISSILE
UNITED STATES DEMANDS ANSWERS FROM FRENCH GOVERNMENT

Mack Bedford was horrified. The attack from some lunatic group of insurgents had been launched from the wreckage of an apartment block in the northern suburbs of Baghdad. Of the six men who died, four of them had been SEALs, guys he almost certainly knew. SEAL Team 10, Coronado.

The missile had blasted out of a downstairs window, crashed straight through the fuselage of the tank, and incinerated all the occupants. If that thing hit, no one had a chance, and its heat-seeking guidance system was so powerful, the bastard never missed. At least that was how it seemed to Mack.

There was a statement from the United Nations Security Council expressing its "intense displeasure," deploring the use of the missile, and issuing formal reprimands to both the Islamic Republic of Iran and to all Shiite Muslim militia leaders in the Middle East.

"As if anyone gives a shit," murmured Mack. "There's only one effective way to deal with these fucking savages, and that's well documented in the navy's record of my court-martial."

The fury of the U.S. military was barely contained in a statement from General Thomas, the U.S. C-in-C on the ground in Iraq, who was quoted as declaring, "This illegal killing has gone far enough. It is beyond our understanding why no one, and I repeat no one, seems capable of tracing this missile to its source, the factory that makes it, and stopping the production.

"We're getting reports that six of them have just been fired at U.S. forces in Afghanistan, fortunately on armored personnel carriers that turned out to be empty. We have Intel on possible Diamondhead stockpiles in Iran, and it is the opinion of both myself and my senior commanders that we should take them out with an air strike and the hell with the consequences."

The final words of the American C-in-C were the words of a very angry soldier. "Everyone knows the damned things are made in France. Checking the explosive and chemical is nothing less than elementary. The Diamondhead is as French as the Eiffel Tower, and it's time someone was forced to admit it. France is, I believe, a founding member of the UN Security Council."

"Hey," breathed Mack, "they finally managed to make old Ben Thomas good and mad. And that means the president will pay attention. They were at West Point together."

It was still another hour before the flight to Dublin was due to be called, and Mack whiled away the time in deep thought. Inevitably, he found it impossible to cast aside the vivid image of the burning tanks on the bank of the Euphrates. But another more urgent issue was muscling its way into his mind—how and when to contact Anne and Tommy.

He had vowed to himself that he would never use Harry's magic astronaut cell phone unless it was a matter of his own life and death. There would be no footprint left, anywhere in France, to prove Mackenzie Bedford had ever left the shores of the United States. He knew the phone was as secure as modern aerospace science could make it. But he also knew there is no such thing as 100 percent security for anything, anywhere, anytime. Jesus, you could put the most highly trained group of U.S. combat troops, armed to the teeth, in a battlefield tank that the record says is impregnable, and a bunch of crazed, illiterate tribesmen, guys dressed in fucking sheets, somehow find a way to wipe everyone out.

The superphone was still the superphone, but would Mack risk leaving even the most fleeting set of footprints right here in France at this stage of the game? Answer: no, he would not. He would call immediately after he arrived in Boston, not before. So he just sat in the restaurant, sipping a second cup of coffee and fighting back the obdurate truth that he had no idea whether his little boy was alive or dead.

But he couldn't be dead; the greatest surgeon in the world wouldn't let him be dead. No, Tommy was alive—he had to be alive. They'd go fishing together very soon. *Hang in there, kid. I'm nearly there.*

———◆•———

Senator Rossow was in his office in the Capitol when the telephone rang from Paris. "Monsieur Jules Barnier on the phone," called his assistant.

The senator picked up the phone, and said in his naturally rather sophisticated manner, "Good morning, Jules. Do I have the pleasure of speaking to the next president of France?"

The full impact of murder, assassination, shock, and sorrow had not hit Washington, D.C., as it had France, essentially because citizens of the USA are inclined to think France is just another country full of goddamned uncooperative foreigners.

Jules Barnier was startled at Stanford Rossow's somewhat flippant attitude to a crime that had stunned his nation. But the two men had been friends for many years, and the ex–Lazards Bank chief understood that many powerful Americans lack just a little savoir faire in certain matters, particularly of the heart.

Jules Barnier and Henri Foche had a long association. They were not close buddies, but they dined together occasionally, and while Jules lacked the driving ambition that would take Henri to the very pinnacle of French power, the brutal manner of his death had caused the Parisian banker considerable sadness.

"Ah, Stanford," he said. "Ever the pragmatist."

"Well, I'm correct, aren't I? You will now be the Gaullist candidate in place of the departed Henri, and there should be nothing to stand in your way. My friend, you have a clear run to the Elysée Palace, where I very much look forward to a lot of high-class hospitality."

Jules Barnier, grief stricken or not, was unable to avoid laughing. "I really called to let you know I have just resigned from the bank. Obviously, it would have been quite incompatible with my projected political career. It was all very agreeable, and the board members were generous to me."

"I should think they would be," replied Rossow. "You've made them all a lot of money. You'll miss it, you know, that cut-and-thrust of the world economy."

"I expect so, but I'll probably have enough cut-and-thrust of my own if they make me president of France."

"There's no doubt, is there?"

"Well, not really. The Gaullists are plainly going to sweep to victory. Every opinion poll has us miles ahead. And I am now the candidate."

"A few months from now, you will be all-powerful, hiring and firing cabinet ministers on a daily basis. Frenchmen will quake in their boots at the mention of your name."

"Frenchmen of my class don't wear boots. They wear highly polished Gucci shoes. And no one quakes when they wear those."

Senator Rossow chuckled. "Do you still want me to keep a weather eye for a cottage here in Maine?"

"Very much so. France is even more inclined than America to close down for the summer. I have always loved that Maine coast, and I can't think of anything nicer. In any event, waterfront real estate on your coastline is an excellent investment."

"Always the banker, Jules, always the banker."

"Not at all. But the dollar's weak against the euro, trading this morning at 1.54. For me, that cottage is a buy."

Both men laughed. "Well, it would be great fun to have you here for a few weeks each year. You'd bring the boat?"

"Certainly. I might even keep it there."

"Just so you remember, Maine has a very short summer. End of August, we're all done. It's likely to snow in October, and it doesn't get real warm until the middle of June at best."

"That will suit me very well. I look forward to it, all those beautiful islands, with the pine trees coming right down to the shore, the deep water, and the *homard! Formidable*."

"Oh, Jules, there was one thing I wanted to mention. Will you carry out Foche's intention to cut right back on the purchase of foreign hardware for the military?"

"I will not. Because it goes against every principle I have about international trade. There's nothing sillier, in this day and age, than any form of isolationism. I believe in expansionism, and to tell the truth I thought some of Henri's ideas were very old-fashioned. I expect you are talking about that little shipyard you have mentioned before."

"Well, I was about to talk about Remsons," replied the U.S. senator. "And I have explained how important it is to them—that frigate order from the French Navy. And it's pretty damned important to me. As you know, I don't have a huge majority in this state."

"Stanford, my friend, the frigate order stays in place, for a lot of reasons. I value my connections in the USA, and when I'm president, I'll value them even more. And I like the . . . er . . . cross-pollination between our defense industries, that we buy and sell from you and vice versa. Warships and missiles. I want to increase that, not shut it down.

"Stanford, I'll tell the navy to order three of them, keep Mr. Remson busy for ten years, and then you can be carried shoulder-high through the town as the great savior of the shipyard!"

"I like that, Jules. I like the way you're thinking."

"Listen, Stanford, I have to go. But don't worry about that frigate anymore. You can consider it done. And tell your Mr. Remson I'm coming down for a visit, to see my new ship, just as soon as you find my new house."

"'Bye, Jules, and *bonne chance.*"

———•◆•———

The Air France passenger jet took off into a light southeast wind, banked hard right, and flew up the left bank of the muddy Gironde River estuary, high above the greatest wine-producing châteaus in the world. They passed over the little port of Pauillac, which is surrounded by the fabled appellations of the Haut-Medoc, Margaux, and Saint Julien. There are eighteen *crus classes* around Pauillac, including the world-famous Rothschilds' Lafite, and Mouton, and Château Latour.

Mack Bedford was oblivious to the splendor below. He was staring out to the west, out to the Atlantic, and he could feel the aircraft inching its way toward the ocean. In a few moments, he would be clear of the French coast, and somehow safe from the ten thousand police and security forces currently searching for him.

On reflection he considered his masterstroke was in moving so quickly, so far to the south of Saint-Nazaire. It was obvious now that the police had written off entirely the possibility of anyone making the south bank of the Loire. Every broadcast, every newspaper stressed that the search was concentrated in the northern part of the country. Especially the Northwest.

As a strategy, that was 100 percent wrong. Henri Foche's assassin had headed due south immediately after his mission was accomplished, and that decision had allowed him to make an almost serene getaway. Aside from the policeman at the bus stop, nobody had challenged him, because no one was looking in his part of the country.

And now he was on his way out, beyond the reach of the goddamned gendarmes, back to Ireland and then home, leaving no trace. It was thus a relaxed flight, past the great hook of the northwest coast of Brittany, up the Irish Sea, and into Dublin at 2:00 P.M. sharp.

Mack just held up his Irish passport, the one bearing the name and identification of Patrick O'Grady, and the immigration officer waved him through. He walked across the airport to the escalators and traveled up to the second floor. He had the document for his first-class open return ticket, and now he changed for the last time, slipping into the men's room and fixing his Jeffery Simpson wig, mustache, and spectacles. This rendered him precisely the same person who had entered Ireland almost two weeks previously.

He walked to the Aer Lingus ticket desk, and asked if there was space on the evening flight to Boston. He was told it was half empty, and five minutes later he had a boarding pass and a seat in the front row of the aircraft, which would depart at 7:30 P.M. local time, arriving in Boston a little before 10:00 P.M.

Mack showed his passport. The emerald green–clad Irish ticket assistant handed it back with a smile. "Have a nice flight, Mr. Simpson."

Which essentially left Lieutenant Commander Bedford with four hours to kill. But Dublin was a big airport with outstanding shops, and Mack still had a pile of euros in his leather bag. So he passed through security and then went shopping, taking care to purchase nothing that would betray even to Anne that he had been in Ireland.

He bought her a bracelet of green tourmaline stones with a gold-chain pendant to match, which knocked a serious hole in five thousand euros. Never in his life had Mack Bedford done anything that extravagant, and he quite liked the feeling. So he hopped into a breathtakingly expensive ladies' store and bought his wife a dark green silk Christian Dior shirt that he would later inform her had cost more than the Buick.

He strolled along to the café in Terminal B and unloaded the jeweler's boxes into the trash. He put the bracelet and pendant into his jacket pocket, and then removed from the shirt the Dublin wrapping, dumped that into the trash with the boxes, and folded the shirt neatly into his bag.

Assailed by doubts that he had "somehow turned his wife into a fucking leprechaun, with all that green," Mack ordered a plate of Irish sausages and scrambled eggs and settled in the corner to read the *Irish Times*.

And once more the enormity of his actions was brought home to him.

The front page offered nothing except varying accounts of the death of Henri Foche. Inside there were two full-page broadsheet photograph displays of the Gaullist politician and his wife, their home in Rennes, and the shipyard on the Loire estuary.

He finished his "lunch" and went to the Aer Lingus first-class lounge and attempted to watch television, which someone had tuned to Fox. The twenty-four-hour American news channel was concentrating on nothing else, but constantly updated its coverage with accounts of the police search switching to different areas where the giant Swiss murderer had been sighted.

But thanks to the hard-driving Norman Dixon, Fox also had a scoop. They screened an interview with the two fishermen from Brixham, the ones who had been thrown overboard, Fred Carter and his first mate, Tom.

Fred was still outraged. "It was just piracy," he said. "This bloody great hoodlum dragged me out of the wheelhouse and flung me overboard. Christ! Was he ever strong! I'd just hit the water when Tom came over the side as well, landed about twenty yards from me."

And did he just leave you to drown?

"Well, not really. He backed the boat up and threw lifebelts over to us. They landed real close, like he may have been a seaman himself."

Were you scared?

"I was a bit. Because we both had sea boots on, and they can fill with water and take you under. But we kicked 'em off and started swimming."

Was it dark?

"Yes. But we could still see the lights on the shore. I'd say we were two miles out."

Would you recognize the attacker again?

"I'd recognize him anywhere. He had a big black beard, and he spoke with a foreign accent. Supposed to be from Switzerland, they say."

Any idea why he stole your boat?

"Stole it and lost it! The *Eagle*'s never been seen since."

You were fully insured?

"Oh, yes, all fishing boats are well insured. We get pretty good rates because we don't often lose a trawler. I've claimed for the night's catch as well."

Did they pay?

"Not yet. They say, how can they pay out for a cargo of fish we never caught? I told 'em we would have caught. There were haddock out there, thousands of 'em. And they owe us the bloody money. That's what I pay the premiums for."

The interviewer smiled, and asked one last question: *Do you think they'll catch the pirate?*

"I'd be surprised if they didn't. He was as big as a bloody house and as hairy as a bear. They can't hardly miss him. He looks like King Kong."

Mack was unable to stop chuckling, taking cover behind the *Irish Times*.

They called his flight at 6:45, and he slept almost the entire way across the Atlantic. He was still exhausted from his long swim across the river, the swim that had undoubtedly earned him his freedom and completely baffled one of the top police forces in Europe.

The aircraft was already over Massachusetts Bay, a few miles to the east of Boston's Logan International Airport, when the flight attendant finally awakened him and asked him to fasten his seat belt.

Because of his front seat he was one of the first to disembark, and he made straight for the glass booths where the immigration officers scrupulously inspect every visitor's passport, photograph them, check their visas and fingerprints. This was Mack's last hurdle, Jeffery Simpson's exquisitely forged document.

But American passports are not nearly so scrutinized. The officer opened the passport, checked the photograph against the bearer, noted it had first been issued in Rhode Island years ago, and said, "Welcome home, Jeffery."

Mack walked through and went downstairs to the baggage area. Only then did he realize it was a quarter past four in the morning in Switzerland. And anyway he could not possibly go home to coastal Maine right now, so he walked outside and picked up the bus to the Hilton, which stands less than a half mile from the terminal.

He checked in with impeccable honesty, Lt. Cdr. Mackenzie Bedford, U.S. Navy. It was the first time he had told the truth to a hotel receptionist in living memory. He ordered an alarm call for 4:00 A.M., when he would call the Nyon Clinic.

The hotel bar was quite busy, and he asked for a Scotch and soda, the way he drank them with Harry. The television was on above the bar, and he was astounded to see the French police had made an arrest in connection with the murder of Monsieur Henri Foche. The man was a Swiss national from Lausanne who had been picked up in Saint-Malo, where he had been enjoying a brief holiday with his wife and two children on board a chartered yacht. His name was Gunther, and he was six-foot-four and bearded.

However, his lawyer claimed he was a coach to the Swiss national soccer team, had never fired a gun in his life, had never even heard of

Saint-Nazaire, and had been having coffee with his family on the Saint-Malo waterfront at the time of the assassination. He added that on Gunther's behalf, he would be suing the French police for an undisclosed amount of money, for wrongful arrest, loss of reputation, mental anguish, and God knows what else. Meanwhile, Gunther was very much in the slammer, awaiting a court hearing. Brittany's chief of police, Pierre Savary, said he was hopeful they had the right man.

"Stupid prick," muttered Mack uncharitably.

That night he slept only fitfully, mostly because he was worrying about Tommy. And when he was awakened by the hotel alarm call, he dialed the number of the clinic with considerable trepidation. He identified himself and was swiftly put through to the office of Carl Spitzbergen, and then to the great surgeon himself.

"Well, Lieutenant Commander, that's a very fine boy you have there."

"Thank you, sir," said Mack. "I am really calling to find out if he's okay."

"He's as okay as I can make him," said Carl Spitzbergen. "And I have to say that's about as okay as he can be. He's tough and strong, and he came through an eight-hour operation as well as any young boy could."

"I believe it was a complete bone marrow transplant?"

"Exactly, and I conduct these operations only rarely, because they are life-threatening. But it worked for Tommy. I cannot promise anything, but everything went fine, and if I had to give a professional opinion I would say we have reversed the condition. Tommy can look forward to a long life."

"Can I speak to him?"

"Well, you could if he was here. But he recovered so fast, only twelve days, I sent him home. He and Anne left Geneva on the morning flight yesterday."

"You mean he's back home in the States?" asked Mack.

"I sincerely hope so," replied the surgeon.

———— •◆• ————

There was no possibility of further sleep, and Mack dressed, paid his bill, and took a cab to the bus station, booking a ticket on the first bus to Brunswick, Maine, which left at around seven.

He sat almost in a daze of happiness, reading the *Boston Globe*. Foche had been bumped off the front page, but an inside story revealed that the Swiss national who had been arrested in Saint-Malo had been released without charge late last night, owing to insufficient evidence.

It was a little after ten when the bus pulled into Brunswick, and Mack was the only passenger disembarking. He stood at the bus stop, waiting for the local one to come along to take him home, and it arrived ten minutes late.

It was a strange feeling returning to Maine after all that had happened. Absence had seemed to heighten the natural glory of the landscape, and Mack stared appreciatively at the long waters of the Kennebec River, flowing down to Dartford, past the coves and the bays, and below the tireless screeches of the gulls and arctic terns.

When the bus eventually pulled up at the stop at the top of his road, he climbed down and set off, wondering what the hell he was going to tell Anne—where had he been, why hadn't he called, and why did he want her to look like a leprechaun?

But today, nothing mattered. He marched down the middle of the lonely road, carrying his leather bag. Up ahead he could see the estuary of the Kennebec, and soon he would see the house where Anne and Tommy would probably go into shock when he walked in, straight out of the wide blue yonder. Except that he had punctuated their entire married life with sudden comings and goings. There had been so many times when he could not call, could not tell her what he was doing, where he was going, or when he was coming back.

All SEAL missions were highly classified black operations. Each mission "went dark" days before they left: no phone calls in or out of base; no contact with the outside world. Anne knew that, accepted it as the wife of a Special Ops naval commander. Anne might never ask him what he had done or where he had been. She never had before.

He reached the house and walked across the broad front yard, striding over the grass, and onto the covered porch. And that was where Anne spotted him, through the window. She ran out of the house and into his arms, and he dropped his bag and held her so closely she thought she might suffocate.

She could feel the beat of his mighty heart, and she whispered to him in the softest, most seductive tone she could manage, "Welcome home, my darling, and shhh. Tommy's asleep. He won't wake up for another couple of hours. Aren't we lucky?"

———•◆•———

Dawn. Five Days Later
Persian Gulf

One by one they came screaming off the flight deck of USS *Colin Powell*—twelve F/A 18C Hornets, the delta-winged angels of death, built by McDonnell Douglas, and generally regarded as the most lethal fighter bombers in the skies. At the controls were the men of the fabled Florida-based VMFA 323 squadron, the Death Rattlers, men who referred to their aircraft as *Snake 200* or *Snake 101.* This crowd represented Top Gun to the tenth power.

The deck of the gigantic Nimitz Class carrier was still vibrating from the sonic shock waves from the Hornets' engines, the thunderous sound of the launch of the last one, hurled skyward by *Bow Cat Three.*

The carrier glowered in the early morning light, fifteen miles off the Iraqi port of Basra, way down south of the Shatt-al-Arab. High above, the Hornets moved into their attack formation. Lt. Cdr. Buzzy Farrant led them at more than six hundred knots, straight up over the flat, watery land to the left of the disputed seaway.

They came in low over the ancient territories of the Marsh Arabs. The deafening roar of this full-blown U.S. air assault would have shaken the waterside homes to their foundations, if they'd had any. Trees swayed, the earth shook, as they ripped through the skies, heading north. They reached the Tigris and changed course, coming hard right, straight for the Iranian border. Four of the Hornets peeled off and made for the port of Korfamshah. Four more kept going, following the GPS numbers, until they were almost in Iranian airspace.

Buzzy Farrant fired two Sidewinder missiles AIM9L straight at the stone bunker where the Diamondheads were stored. The bright-blue chemical explosion he left in his wake dwarfed the sunrise. They pressed on the attack, bombs and missiles, blasting a huge warehouse in the oil-refining city of Ahvaz, and then switched their attack to the airfield, where they smashed to smithereens a giant Ilyushin 11-76 military freighter.

They hit the railroad, wiped out a freight train, destroyed the jetties of Korfamshah, and put two oceangoing freighters onto the bottom of the harbor. Both ships, underwater, still burned with a dazzling bright-blue chemical flame. As did everything else in the path of the American bombardment.

The Intel had been top class, and the pristine accuracy of the attack frightened the Iranian military badly, frightened them as Gadhafi had been frightened when President Reagan explained to Tripoli precisely how displeased he was with them in 1986.

The Americans wanted their ruthless destruction of Iran's Diamondheads kept secret, but the government in Tehran put out a halfhearted statement to the effect that it deplored yet another example of reckless American aggression. Which well and truly let the cat out of the bag.

Time magazine, which is famously well connected in these regions, worked on the story for two weeks before coming up with "The Death Knell for the Diamondhead." The account was masterful, detailing the dawn raid on every known storage area for the missile, especially on the huge shipment down in Korfamshah, preparing to weigh anchor for Afghanistan. It ended the story with a less well-documented, but obviously accurate, account of the reaction in France:

The assassination of Monsieur Henri Foche, believed to be the majority shareholder in Montpellier Munitions, appeared to take the pressure off the French government, which, for the first time, admitted the missile was French.

Acting with United Nations military personnel, the government of France has closed down the arms factory, set deep in the Forest of Orléans. Sources claim that at least two of the senior directors left the building in handcuffs. The entire complex has been dismantled, and eyewitnesses believe much of the ordnance has been removed by the French military.

The vexed question of the illegal missile, which caused so much sorrow in the U.S. armed forces, has thus been finally solved. But it would never have been solved had Henri Foche become president of France. And it took his untimely and brutal death to make amends for the Diamondhead, and to end its reign of terror in the Middle East.

Lt. Cdr. Mackenzie Bedford read the article with a wry grin, and an acute observation right out of the SEALs' playbook. . . . *Sonofabitch had it coming, right?*

EPILOGUE: THREE MONTHS LATER

There was an October chill in the air now. And an October chill in Maine is not the same as an October chill in Washington. Nonetheless, the World Series had not yet been played, and Mack and Tommy, both in warm jackets, were still practicing, on the beach, throwing and catching the dying embers of the summer game.

They stood wider apart now, wider than they had been all year on the lawn outside the house. In fact, it was close to the full sixty feet between mound and plate.

Mack threw pretty hard, steadily to Tommy's left, and the little boy kept snagging the baseball, pulling it out of the air, and throwing it back at his father, high, low, left, and right. And Mack kept catching.

He wanted to test the boy, but he didn't want to see him fail with a wide ball, not after all he had gone through. He remembered that bad afternoon back in July when Tommy had overbalanced on an easy one and then not wanted to play again.

And he really remembered the words of the doctor who told Anne that loss of balance was one of the symptoms of ALD. But he could not help noticing that Tommy's quick feet and fast glove were getting better every time they played.

Tommy threw a high one, up over Mack's right shoulder. He twisted suddenly and caught it, and almost as a reflex whipped the ball back, sending it hard and low to the boy's right. Tommy brought his left arm over in an arc, swooping low, taking the ball but rolling onto the sand, right over.

Mack started toward him, but Tommy was up in a flash, on his feet, hurling the baseball back to his father. Mack was so astounded that he just stood there as the ball shot by his left ear.

"Thought you'd get me, right, Daddy?" yelled Tommy. "And look where the ball is—quick, it's going in the stupid water."

Mack took off, pounding toward the ocean's edge, splashing through the little wavelets as they rolled up over the hard sand. Coronado all over again. He could never get it out of his mind. And he looked back at his little boy, and he heard again the far-lost voices of the SEAL instructors who had once taught him.

My Trident is a symbol of my honor. It embodies the trust of those I am sworn to protect. I seek no recognition for my actions. I voluntarily place the welfare and security of others before my own.

The memories stopped him in his tracks. The sand, the sea, the cold evening breeze in his face. The voices. It all reminded him of what was gone. And what could never come back. What had been said. And what would never be said.

And he heard again his own voice now, distinct but distant, firm and certain, the words he had uttered so long ago, back on the grinder in Coronado, the creed of the Brotherhood.

For all of my days I will be a United States Navy SEAL.